Praise for *Eli's Promise*

"National Jewish Book Award winner Ron Balson returns triumphantly with *Eli's Promise,* a captivating saga of the Holocaust and its aftermath spanning decades and continents. Readers will not be able to put this book down but will turn the pages compulsively with heart in throat, eager to learn the fate of the Rosen family. Balson's meticulous historical detail, vivid prose, and unforgettable characters further solidify his place among the most esteemed writers of historical fiction today."

—Pam Jenoff, *New York Times* bestselling author of *The Lost Girls of Paris*

"A powerful, superbly crafted tale . . . equal parts heartbreaking and life affirming, with themes that are as relevant today as ever."

—Jane Healey, bestselling author of *The Beantown Girls*

"Readers will surely enjoy this well-researched historical novel, brimming with characters who represent both the good and the evil aspects of war and politics. Well-suited for book clubs, *Eli's Promise* is bound to incite lively discussion since many of the issues raised are still very current; immigration, political corruption, war crimes, and justice."

—Jewish Book Council

"Ronald Balson skillfully weaves the novel's plot over twenty years while maintaining an engaging pace with a series of seamless flashbacks. Furthermore, he integrates the complexities and the scope of the systematic dehumanization of Jews before, during, and after World War II."

—Melissa Warren, Historical Novel Society

"Superb . . . *Eli's Promise* is a moving and suspenseful work of authoritative historical fiction. It is profoundly informative, entirely compelling, and highly recommended."

—Jack Kramer, Bookreporter

"Balson pulls no punches. . . . His story is a five-star version of a period of history that proved a horror for those living in it."

—Stacy Alesi, BookBitch

"Balson juggles between his three stories effectively, writing with great emotion but without overt melodrama, always aware of the tragic ways in which history repeats itself."

—Bill Ott, *Booklist*

ALSO BY RONALD H. BALSON

The Girl from Berlin

The Trust

Karolina's Twins

Saving Sophie

Once We Were Brothers

Eli's Promise

Ronald H. Balson

ST. MARTIN'S
GRIFFIN
NEW YORK

Published in the United States by St. Martin's Griffin, an imprint of St. Martin's Publishing Group

www.stmartins.com

Designed by Meryl Sussman Levavi

The Library of Congress has cataloged the hardcover edition as follows:

Names: Balson, Ronald H., author.
Title: Eli's promise / Ronald H. Balson.
Description: First edition. | New York : St. Martin's Press, 2020.
Identifiers: LCCN 2020016412 | ISBN 9781250271464 (hardcover) | ISBN 9781250271471 (ebook)
Subjects: LCSH: Holocaust survivors—Fiction. | World War, 1939–1945—Fiction. | Poland—History—Occupation, 1939–1945—Fiction. | Jewish fiction. | GSAFD: Historical fiction.
Classification: LCC PS3602.A628 E45 2020 | DDC 813/.6—dc23
LC record available at https://lccn.loc.gov/2020016412

ISBN 978-1-250-80537-9 (trade paperback)

Our books may be purchased in bulk for promotional, educational, or business use. Please contact your local bookseller or the Macmillan Corporate and Premium Sales Department at 1-800-221-7945, extension 5442, or by email at MacmillanSpecialMarkets@macmillan.com.

First St. Martin's Griffin Edition: 2021

10 9 8 7 6 5 4 3 2 1

For Monica.
Promises kept.

He who does not oppose evil commands it to be done.

—LEONARDO DA VINCI

PART I

CHAPTER ONE

In the waning weeks of the Second World War, as the German defenses retreated into ever-shrinking circles around Berlin, the Nazi concentration camps sitting in the outer reaches, once heavily fortified, lay pregnable in the path of the Allies' advance. The German high command knew that liberation of those camps was imminent, but they steadfastly refused to release their grip on the Jewish prisoners. They intended to finish implementing their Final Solution of the Jewish Question. In pursuance thereof, Reichsführer Heinrich Himmler ordered the SS to transfer the Jews from the outlying camps to locations inside Germany.

Just before abandoning each of those camps, the SS guards corralled as many prisoners as they could and marched them deep into Germany in what came to be known as the Nazi death marches. Already weakened by disease and malnutrition, tens of thousands of men, women and children were forced to walk long distances in the throes of winter to other camps within Germany's interior. Buchenwald was the largest of those camps.

On the eighth day of April 1945, at approximately the noon hour, a frantic message went out from the underground resistance in the camp. It was sent by Morse code and repeated several times in English, German and Russian.

"To the Allies. To the army of General Patton. This is the Buchenwald concentration camp. SOS. We request help. They want to evacuate us. The SS wants to destroy us."

The response came quickly. "KZ Bu. Hold out. Rushing to your aid. Staff of Third Army."

The Sixth Armored Division, proudly known as the Super Sixth, was the first division of Patton's Third to reach Buchenwald. The soldiers entered the vast complex through the main gate and were shocked to find inmates but no guards. They quickly discovered that a contingent of SS had marched some prisoners north. Other guards had fled and were scattering through the woods like rats from a foundering ship. In their wake, thousands of inmates had been abandoned and left alone to fend for themselves with no food and very little water. Some had found clothing. Some had not. Some were too weak to do much more than lean against a wall, sit on the ground or lie on the wooden slabs that served as beds. Some were merely apparitions. Ghosts and skeletons.

The bewildered GIs, their helmet straps hanging loosely, their field jackets partially unzipped, their trousers bloused above their leather boots, had come upon a vision of human deprivation that would haunt each of them for the rest of their lives. These were not weak men. They were battle-hardened soldiers. They had landed on the Normandy beaches, secured a bridgehead across the Seine, cut across France for seven hundred miles and reached the German border on December 6. They were a tough, confident bunch. But they were not prepared for what they saw.

CHAPTER TWO

BUCHENWALD, GERMANY
APRIL 11, 1945

Corporal Reilly swallowed hard and softly uttered, "Jesus, Captain, these fellows . . ." He stopped. He couldn't find the words to finish.

The soldiers of the Fourth Platoon had entered a long wooden building, formerly designed for eighty horses but later configured to hold 1,200 prisoners on five levels of wooden shelves they called bunks. No heat, no water, no toilets. Inmates, too weak to rise, lay on their wooden slabs watching the GIs. They strained to lift their heads. They smiled and nodded. Many expressed their gratitude in languages the GIs didn't understand.

The men of the Fourth Platoon were seasoned soldiers. They fought and defeated the German offensive at the Battle of the Bulge. They were Patton's boys. They won the decisive battles in the European theater. Just ask them, they'd tell you. But standing in the rancid air of the Buchenwald barracks, amidst the dead and dying, a soldier's knees could weaken. Many couldn't hold their lunch.

"All right, men," the captain barked, "let's get these people out of here. Williams: the ones that can walk, lead them to the train. The ones that can't, the rest of you get them onto the stretchers and out to the hospital trucks. Pronto!" To his adjutant, he said quietly, "Take the strongest ones first. Some of these poor fellows are more dead than alive. They won't make it."

One man, little more than bones held in place by a thin wrapping of skin, lay with two others on a third-level bunk. He reached out and grabbed a fistful of Reilly's jacket. "Whoa, fella," Reilly said. "Take it easy. We're going to help you, I promise. We're gonna get you out of here."

The man shook his head and uttered words Reilly didn't understand. "Don't worry, buddy," Reilly said, patting the man's bony hand, still tightly clenched on his coat. "We'll get to you real quick, I promise."

Mustering all of his strength, the inmate shouted, "Nein, nein," followed by a long string of incomprehensible phrases. Tears ran from the man's sunken eyes, and his body shook in desperation. "Captain," Reilly said, "this fella's trying to tell me something pretty important, but I don't know what the hell he's saying. I think he's talkin' Kraut."

The captain motioned to a tall soldier at the other end of the building. "Steiner, what's this man saying?"

Corporal Steiner walked over and listened to the inmate's pleas. He nodded. "I don't think he's speaking German, Captain. It could be Yiddish. They're similar. I think he's saying his name is Eli. He's saying we have to find Izaak. That's his son. He says Izaak is in the children's building. He says there's a thousand children in that building."

"A thousand children? Holy shit, where are these children? Which one of these buildings?"

"He says Block Eight."

The captain stood in the doorway and looked out over the huge complex. "Hell if I know which one's Block Eight. Can he show us?"

"I don't think he can get up."

The captain nodded his head and started to walk away when Eli spoke again. Steiner translated. "He says he can take us there, Captain. He just needs a little help."

The captain sighed. "I don't know how much help we can give him. He's barely alive."

"Izaak, Izaak," the man cried. "Meyn zun."

Reilly looked at Eli, at the desperation on his face, and said, "Captain, I can lift him. He's okay. He needs to find his son. I'll take him. I'll carry him if I have to. He can lead us to Izaak and the rest of the children."

Eli grasped the meaning and smiled. Reilly lifted him down off the bunk, conscious that the man weighed less than a field pack. He helped him to his feet. With his arm around Eli's back and under his shoulder, he started to slowly lead him out but stopped abruptly. "Jesus, he's got no shoes on. He's got rags wrapped around his feet. Anybody see any shoes?"

Eli looked at his feet and waved it off. "Nein, nein, nein." He pointed sharply to the door. "Izaak," he said. "Der kinder." The captain nodded. "All right, Reilly, take him out. Find those kids." The corporal unzipped his coat, placed it over Eli's shoulders and walked him out the door.

Other soldiers of the Super Sixth were converging at Block 8 and were starting to attend to the children. All sizes, all ages. Some as young as six. Some of the children were being gathered into groups for transport out. Eli's eyes scanned the hundreds of children. His fear was palpable. What were the chances he'd find his son? There were so many. Suddenly, his whole body stiffened. "Izaak, Izaak!" he screamed, and stumbled forward. A boy, no more than ten or eleven, came running. "Papa! Papa!" Eli dropped to his knees as the boy ran into his arms. Reilly watched the two hug each other, and the hardened soldier broke into tears.

"Come on, Eli, Izaak," Reilly said, bending down. "We gotta get you out of this cold, muddy prison camp and let some doctors fix you up."

Reilly waved for a stretcher, and two corpsmen were quick to respond. One of them patted Izaak on the head and said, "You go with the other kids, little guy. We'll take care of your pops." But Izaak wouldn't leave his father.

Reilly placed his hand on the corpsman's shoulder. "Martin, how many of these kids still have a parent? This boy needs to stay with his father. Let's make an exception this time."

Martin pulled Reilly aside and whispered, "His father's in bad shape. He's probably not going to make it. A lot of them aren't."

"All the more reason to let his son stay with him," Reilly answered.

The corpsman shrugged and placed Eli on the stretcher. Eli looked up at Reilly and in little more than a hoarse whisper, through cracked lips, he said, "A dank, a sheynem dank." The two corpsmen carried Eli with little Izaak in tow toward a line of white canvas-covered trucks bearing Swiss license plates with Red Cross stenciled on the transom. Reilly smiled and rejoined his squad.

CHAPTER THREE

⁓

On the seventh day of May, 1945, at 2:41 Central European Time, Generaloberst Alfred Jodl sat on a wooden chair in a redbrick schoolhouse and signed his name to a two-page document. He paused for a moment, lifted his eyes and passed the document across the table to General Walter "Beetle" Smith, General Eisenhower's chief of staff. The paper, entitled Act of Military Surrender, recited, "We the undersigned, acting with authority of the German High Command, hereby surrender unconditionally to the Supreme Commander, Allied Expeditionary Force and to the Soviet High Command, all forces on land, sea and in the air who are at this date under German control." Beneath the signature line, he simply scribbled *"Jodl."*

In Europe, the war had ended. Inmates of the concentration camps, like those liberated from Buchenwald, found themselves free from their prisons but adrift in unfamiliar and disparate locales. The Allies, in anticipation of this day, had formed an organization entitled United Nations Relief and Rehabilitation Agency (UNRRA) to provide housing, food, clothing, medicine and basic necessities to the war's displaced survivors. It was primarily an American undertaking. It called for camps and housing areas to be established in Germany, Italy and Austria.

The great majority of the Jews who were liberated from Nazi prisons and concentration camps sought the protection of the United States Army and gravitated to the displaced persons camps established in the American Zone. Föhrenwald, meaning Pine Forest, set in the wooded foothills of Bavaria, was one of the largest American camps.

FÖHRENWALD DISPLACED PERSONS CAMP

AMERICAN ZONE

JUNE 1946

The door of the small wooden house on Florida Street swung open, and a twelve-year-old boy with a mop of brown hair burst into the room. Thin as a stick but full of energy, he yelled, "Papa, guess what?"

Eli smiled. "What is it, Izaak?"

"Mr. Abrams came to school today to teach us about writing and stuff, and after class he asked if Josh and I could help him deliver his newspapers tomorrow afternoon."

"The camp newspaper? You mean the *Bamidbar*?"

"Yes, the *Bamidbar*. We're hoping he pays us with chocolate like he did last time."

Eli laughed and patted him on the head. "Chocolate. My businessman. You can go with Mr. Abrams, but don't eat all the chocolate at once and come home as soon as you're finished. Homework, you know?"

Izaak sighed. "I know, I know."

"How do you like your new teacher?"

"She's okay, I guess. She says she's from Eretz Israel. She speaks Hebrew and Yiddish. And English, of course. The lessons are hard."

"Well, you understand Yiddish, don't you?"

"Sure, but not much English or Hebrew. Those languages are strange to me, but Mrs. Klein says I'm doing well. The English letters are a lot like the Polish letters, so I can write them. I can even draw some of the Hebrew letters. Better than a lot of kids. Some of the kids in my class can't read or write anything. They've never been to school. Especially the ones who were hiding."

Eli proudly hugged his son. He had been through so much and was rebounding so well. "Okay, deliver Mr. Abrams's newspapers and come right home. I'll leave a sandwich for you. I have a camp committee meeting tomorrow night, so I'll be home late."

"But you'll tuck me in when you get home, no matter what time it is, right?"

"Absolutely. Always do."

※

The Föhrenwald camp committee convened in the assembly hall on Roosevelt Place. On the agenda this evening was the troubling housing shortage. Meetings were attended by the camp's administrators, an UNRRA representative and several interested residents. There was always an opportunity for people to raise grievances and it was often a spicy affair. On this night, though the news was generally disturbing, a certain revelation would rock Eli to his core.

Camp Director Bernard Schwartz, a burly man from eastern Poland, gaveled the meeting to order. "All right, settle down, everyone. We have serious matters to discuss tonight. Let's get right to the housing issue. Harry?"

A tall thin man with tufts of white hair rose with a sheaf of papers in his hand. He rattled the papers for all to see. "We are now up to 5,600 residents, and even with the additional structures we've converted from commercial space, we're 2,000 over our capacity. All of you know this little village was originally built to house workers for I. G. Farben's factory, and they had 2,500 residents. Some of our families are now sleeping five in a room, double-decker beds. We desperately need to construct more housing."

The UNRRA delegate shook his head. "I'm sorry, Harry, but expansion is not in our plans. Föhrenwald is meant to be a temporary solution to house survivors until they find their permanent home."

Harry stood his ground. "Tell the U.S., Canada and Britain to issue visas, Martin, and there wouldn't be a single person left at Föhrenwald. In the interim, we need building supplies and materials. We can't have our people sleeping on top of each other; we need to expand our housing. I know that Eli Rosen has the experience to manage new construction projects, but UNRRA has to supply the materials."

The delegate answered solemnly. "I'll take the matter up with my superiors, but I know what they're going to say; it's not in the UNRRA budget to build cities in Germany. And they will tell me that the camp population is increasing far beyond expectations. They'll tell me the birth rate is out of control."

"Oh, come on, Martin."

"He has a point," said a voice in the back. "At the hospital we are delivering six to nine babies a month. There are two hundred women currently pregnant in this camp. Our population is increasing rapidly. We must make accommodation for them."

"It's inevitable," Bernard said. "Our people have been liberated and they want nothing more than to rebuild normal lives. They're finding partners, relationships, marriages—all those aspects of humanity which were denied to them in the camps. And normal lives mean children. We should all appreciate that children are essential to reconstructing our personal and collective identities. I agree with Harry. We need to build more housing."

Martin shook his head. "Look, I'm just the UNRRA rep. I don't set budgets or the policies. I'll go and beg for it, but I'm telling you the sad truth: there's no current funding for residential expansion. The solution is to get everyone out of the camp and to their final destinations."

Harry scoffed. "You can't emigrate without a visa, Martin. Tell Truman to issue more visas."

On the side of the room a stocky man with a barrel chest, a square jaw and tousled black hair leaned against a wall. He breathed heavily through his nose, and when he spoke it was in a deep gravelly voice. "I want to say something," he growled. People turned their heads. "I hear rumors, Bernard. Bad rumors. Someone is out there selling visas."

"Selling?"

"On the black market."

"Seriously, Daniel? Visas to what country? Real or counterfeit?"

"From what I hear, they're genuine visas to the United States. For money or jewelry, this man will deliver a genuine U.S. visa. Pay him what he wants, and you can jump the immigration line."

Muffled comments skittered through the room.

"Who is this man?" Bernard demanded.

Daniel shook his head. "I don't know him personally. They say he's tall, has short black hair and he's a slick dresser. He goes by the name of Max."

Eli's jaw dropped. The color drained from his face. "Impossible! He's dead."

Daniel shook his head. "The guy I'm talking about is definitely not dead. Frau Helstein knows him. She's the one who told me."

"Well, that might explain it," Bernard said. "She's a gossiper and she's always spreading one crazy rumor or another. It's probably nonsense."

"I don't think it's nonsense, Bernard," said another man. "I heard the same thing. From Shmuel. For the right price, and it's pretty steep, you can get a U.S. visa. He'll even supply the sponsor for you."

Daniel uttered a gravelly huff. "It's all true, Bernard, and it's not good. Cheaters spawn resentment. Anger. People waiting in line don't want to be passed up by a cheat. It could undermine the stability of our community."

Eli felt his blood boil. "What else did Frau Helstein tell you about this man named Max?"

Daniel slowly shook his head. "She said he's arrogant. He has powerful connections in America, and you do business on his terms or not at all. Why do you say it's impossible, or that the man's dead? Do you know this Max?"

Eli pursed his lips and nodded. "Maybe. I knew such a man in Lublin— tall, black hair, fancy clothes, arrogant. And his name was Maximilian. But there was no way he survived."

"Who are you talking about?"

"Maximilian Poleski, as crooked as any thief that ever roamed the earth. An unprincipled profiteer. Soon after Lublin was occupied, he cozied up to the Nazis and curried their favor. He was quick to supply them with a bottle of the finest brandy or to pick up the check at a trendy café or to supply some SS commandant with an innocent young girl. He'd bide his time, lie in wait like a predator, waiting for desperate people to come to him. If you needed food, he could get it. You needed housing, you needed to be transferred from ghetto A to ghetto B, you needed a place to hide, you needed an exemption ID card, Maximilian was only too happy to oblige. For a price. He was open for business—the merchant of war."

"He could do all that during the occupation?" Bernard asked.

"Oh, yeah. He had his own office in Nazi headquarters. But in the end he double-crossed the wrong people. I was sure that they killed him."

"Did you see the Nazis kill him?"

"No. But he was as good as dead when I last saw him."

"Then maybe he's not dead," Daniel said. "Or maybe this Max is not your Maximilian after all."

Eli felt his muscles tense. "If Maximilian lives, he and I have unfinished business. He will answer to me for what he did to my family, and he will tell me what I need to know. If Maximilian roams the earth again, I will have my day of reckoning. That is my sacred promise!"

Bernard slowly stroked his beard. "This is all very distressing. We've dealt with black market butchers and black market cigarettes, but the illegal sale of an official U.S. visa? That's a new one on me. Let me know if you find out anything more about this man."

After the meeting was adjourned, and as people were filing out, Dr. Weisman pulled Bernard, Eli and Daniel aside. "Please treat what I'm about to say confidentially. I don't want to raise an alarm, but two more people have come down with symptoms."

Eli and Daniel were puzzled. "What symptoms?"

Bernard understood. He had an uneasy expression. "Are you sure?"

The doctor nodded. "We've put them under quarantine, but we're fairly certain."

"What's he talking about?" Eli said.

The doctor sighed. "Tuberculosis."

Daniel's expression froze. "The White Plague."

"Is there a cure?" Eli said. "Do we have medicines for that?"

The doctor shook his head. "Not in Föhrenwald, not in Europe. There are trials of a new medicine at the Mayo Clinic in America, but the drug is still experimental and not available. We treat the disease with sulfonamides, rest and fluids. Some recover on their own, but not many. I'm proposing that we post bulletins warning residents of a flu-like virus and advising them all to wash carefully, avoid someone coughing or wheezing and report that person to the camp hospital immediately."

Bernard spoke soberly. "For the time being and until we're sure, let's keep the word 'tuberculosis' to ourselves. News like this could cause a panic."

As Eli walked home, his thoughts returned to Lublin, to Maximilian Poleski. And to that first day of September 1939, when the world caught fire.

CHAPTER FOUR

❧

LUBLIN

LUBLIN, POLAND
SEPTEMBER 1, 1939

In the predawn hours of September 1, 1939, the German battleship *Schleswig-Holstein* moved silently southward through the Baltic Sea toward the free city of Danzig. At 4:45 a.m. Central European Time, its massive guns commenced firing on the tiny Polish fort of Westerplatte, ushering in what would become the Second World War. Contemporaneously, sixty-two German divisions supported by 1,300 Luftwaffe aircraft crossed the western Polish border. A million German troops invaded Poland from Prussia in the north and Slovakia in the south. The first bombing raids hit Warsaw at 6:00 a.m. The Polish Air Force, caught totally by surprise, was vanquished on the ground within hours.

In Lublin, Poland, not far from the Grodzka Gate, a hand-painted sign over the entrance to a brickyard read ROSEN & SONS BUILDING AND CON-STRUCTION MATERIALS. The sun was warm, the sky was clear, and it was forecasted to stay that way all day. No one predicted storm clouds rising in the west. Eli was hard at work in the yard filling an order. Although there had been a lot of noise on the radio—threats, assurances, and still more threats from Adolf Hitler—there was no reason for Eli to think this day would be anything out of the ordinary, which was why he was so startled when Jakob Rosen rushed out of the office, yelling "Eli, Eli, we're at war!"

Eli set a load of bricks onto a pallet, turned and wiped his brow. He stood six-two and was strong, tan and fit. His ribbed tank top carried the dust and sweat of the morning's work. "What are you talking about?" he said as his father approached.

"Germany. Hitler. They have declared a war on Poland. I heard it on the radio. Tanks and planes have crossed our borders! They're shelling Danzig."

"Papa," Eli said. "Calm down. Look up at the sky, what do you see?"

"Nothing, but . . ."

"Exactly. Hitler wants the free city of Danzig. It's no secret. He's said so for months. He whines that Germans in East Prussia are cut off from the mother country. So he'll occupy Danzig and then he'll tell Britain and France that he doesn't want anything more and there'll be a truce until the next time."

"No, son, you're wrong. This is not Czechoslovakia; this is not Austria. He's not just marching in; he's bombing Poland from the sky. According to the radio, there are hordes of troops and tanks crossing our western border."

"Then I will keep an ear to my radio and listen for what comes next. But right now I have a load of bricks and cement that is due at our construction site near the Gate."

❧

The sun was setting when Eli arrived home. Though his day had been physically demanding, and though he was troubled by the political news, it always lifted his spirits to walk into his home, watch his young son bound into his arms and see his sweet wife, Esther, her apron around her waist, come out of the kitchen with a smile and a small piece of whatever she was creating for dinner. As he walked over to embrace her, she held up a finger, kissed him on the cheek and said, "Maybe you should shower before you give me one of your famous Eli bear hugs. You have half a brickyard on your shirt." He chuckled and started for the bathroom but turned around and said, "Essie, did you hear the news?"

"About the Germans?" she said. "It was all anyone could talk about at the clinic. What do you suppose that means for us in Lublin? Will the war come here? Should we be worried?"

He shrugged. "I know my father is. He was upset when he heard it on the radio. But I think it's just a political maneuver to annex the Polish corridor, similar to what was done with the German population in the Sudeten mountains. Hitler will go into Danzig, full guns blasting, the world will give him the Polish corridor and then there'll be peace. Just like Austria and Czechoslovakia."

Esther wrinkled her forehead. "Eli, those countries are now occupied by German troops. They're hardly at peace."

Eli shook his head. "He'll occupy Danzig. That's all he wants. What would he do with Poland?"

"Does he need a million troops and tanks just to capture the corridor? The radio reported that German troops were crossing from the north into the corridor, but also from the south through Silesia and Slovakia. Does he need to drop bombs on Poland? It sounds like a lot more than politics to me."

"Nah. I doubt it. Hitler is full of bluster. He's heavy-handed in everything he does. He'll get his way, he always does, and then he'll quit. Anyway, there's nothing the Rosen family can do about it. We might as well have dinner."

She smiled. "Beef and noodles."

Esther's smile was gone when Eli emerged from the shower. She was putting on her nurse's uniform. "The Germans are bombing Warsaw," she said in a frightened tone. "I heard it on Warsaw radio. There are planes over Lodz. Those cities are nowhere near the Polish corridor. The radio reports that the Polish army is moving to defend the west and calls have gone out to Britain and France for military assistance. I'm going to the hospital. The director has asked us all to come in. We're making triage plans in case the war comes to Lublin."

"Essie, you can't leave. You have to stay with Izaak tonight. Louis called to tell me that there's an emergency meeting at the Chachmei tonight. All of the town leaders will be there. I have to go."

"Then you have to take Izaak with you."

"Esther, he's six years old."

Esther placed her hands on her hips. "I can't take him to the hospital, and we can't leave him here alone. So, Papa, *you* have to take your son."

❧

Izaak and Eli walked hand in hand to the five-story, sand-colored stone structure that anchored the Jewish quarter. Covering an entire city block, the Yeshiva Chachmei of Lublin, the most important center for Torah study in the world, held the largest collection of biblical writings anywhere on earth. A half-moon crown formed an apex over the eight-columned en-tranceway. Gold Hebrew letters were scrolled over the doorway. A line of men had already begun to file into the building when Eli and Izaak arrived.

"Why is it called the Chachmei, Papa?"

Eli loved Izaak's inquisitive nature. "It is the name for the yeshiva. Ye-shiva Cachmei. School of the Wise Men."

"Will I go to this yeshiva someday?"

"Maybe. You have to be at least fourteen years old, and what's even more important, you have to memorize four hundred pages of Talmud. Only the best students from all around the world are accepted. The teach-ers are very choosy."

"Did you go there, Papa?"

Eli laughed. "No, son. Your papa was not a very good bible student."

"But you're a real good builder, right?"

Eli hugged his son. "That's right—you know it! Rosen and Sons built this yeshiva. Your grandpa laid the cornerstone fifteen years ago, in 1924. It took six years to build, and when it was finished in 1930, they presented Grandpa with an award. They named the entry hall after him. Now it is the most important building in Lublin, and that is why we are all meeting here tonight."

Aaron Horowitz tapped the podium and began the discussion. "We have gathered here tonight under the darkest of clouds. The Nazis have invaded our country. We know what happened to our Jewish brothers and sisters when they occupied Vienna and Prague. If they come to Lublin, we should expect no less."

"Aaron, they haven't occupied Poland," said a man dismissively. "They sent troops and bombs, but it may only be a show of force to secure Danzig and the corridor."

"That's foolish," shouted a man from the back. "They're bombing War-saw, Lodz and Poznan. I heard it on the radio. There are panzer tanks roll-ing in only two hundred kilometers away from us. They could be in Warsaw in a week. Lublin as well."

There were several grunts of approval.

"Rabbi, what should we do?"

The rabbi held up a finger. "The roads east and north are still open. I wouldn't think it cowardice or unwise to take your families and go. Lithu-ania, Latvia, Ukraine. Find a place in a community far away."

"What about the Russian army? They are Hitler's allies."

"This is true, and we believe the Soviets have designs on Eastern Poland, but as far as I know, the roads to the Baltic countries are still open. For those who choose to stay here in Lublin, our ancestral home, we must make plans. We must hold regular meetings here in the Chachmei. This building will stand as our center for information. We don't know what the future holds for Lublin, and maybe, God willing, the Nazis will never come this far, but we must plan for the worst."

CHAPTER FIVE

LUBLIN, POLAND
SEPTEMBER 8, 1939
ONE WEEK AFTER THE NAZI INVASION

By the sixth day of September, two Wehrmacht army divisions had joined forces at Lodz and cut Poland in two. Two days later, panzer divisions had compressed the Polish army into five isolated areas around Pomerania, Poznan, Lodz, Krakow and Carpathia. On the seventh day of September, German planes strafed and decimated Warsaw. On the eighth day of September, the war came to Lublin. The city was unprepared.

"Eli, don't go to work today," Esther said, getting out of bed. "Stay home. I'm afraid for us. I'm afraid for Izaak. Warsaw radio has gone off the air. The Germans are marching through Poland, and I think it won't be long before they reach Lublin. Last week Britain and France declared war on Germany. That didn't stop Hitler or even slow him down. What if the bombs start falling here? Eli, we should listen to the rabbi and leave Lublin. Leave Poland. Now. Today."

"The rabbi didn't advise everyone to leave. He only mentioned it as an option. He is staying here along with all the leaders of our community. That includes me, Essie. I'm a councilman, and I don't think I should run away from my people. I have to stay and protect our town."

"The Polish army can't protect our town. How can the rabbi and a few Jews?"

"I didn't mean we would pick up rifles. But we have forty thousand Jews in our community. Our council needs to speak for our people and assure them during times of trouble."

"The Nazis wage a hate campaign against *our people*. You have heard the tales about what they did to us in Vienna. How they torture and abuse us in Germany. The rabbi's right. We can expect no less in Poland. I think we should leave."

"And go where, Essie? Where do you want to go? East? Do you trust the Soviets? They're no friends of the Jews. Things will be just as bad in Ukraine as they will be here."

"Then maybe we should move into the Polish countryside. Get a cottage on a farm or in a wooded area where the enemy won't bother with us. Some small village that's too little to occupy. Think about it, Eli."

Eli sighed. "All right, I will. We'll talk about it when I come home tonight. Right now, I have to go to the brickyard. We still have a business to run and we're working on a huge project. I'll try to come home early. I promise."

The sounds came first. Frightening sounds that caused Eli's bones to resonate like a tuning fork. Whirring and buzzing and thundering sounds off to the west that shook the ground as though they were earthquake tremors. Eli stood with a sledgehammer in his hand and looked across the yard. Dark clouds were rising on the western horizon, unmistakable bursts of bomb smoke, at first far away but drawing ever closer. Buzz bombers circled in the western sky like swarms of dragonflies. He dropped his tool, dashed into the office and yelled, "Everyone go home. Go to your families. Lublin is under attack!"

By afternoon, German Stukas, single-engine dive-bombers with a hideous whining growl, dove out of the sky above Lublin's main street, Krakowskie Przedmieście. The city's main Catholic cathedral and several apartment buildings were destroyed or badly damaged. Like giant wasps, the Stukas dove and soared, dove and soared, stinging their victims and returning for more.

Eli reached his home, burst through the door, and screamed for Esther. If she heard him, and if she answered, Eli couldn't tell, as the deafening noise caused his ears to ring. He finally found Esther and Izaak huddled in the cellar next to the coal furnace.

"Essie, you were right all along. I should have listened. We should have fled the city."

"We cannot focus on what we should have done," she said, "but on what we must do now."

There was panic in Eli's voice. "I don't have answers, Essie. I don't know what to do now." He wrapped his arms around his wife and son and pulled them close. "Whatever comes, we'll face it together. That's the only answer I have."

"When the bombing stops, I'm going to try to get to the hospital," she said.

"How will we know when the bombing stops?" Izaak said.

"The earth will stop shaking."

Ten days later, Nazi tanks and trucks rolled into badly damaged Lublin, followed by hundreds of goose-stepping soldiers. Five hundred Jews who lived on Lublin's main street, Krakowskie Przedmieście, were given ten minutes to grab whatever belongings they could carry and move into the poorest quarter of Jewish Lublin. Krakowskie Przedmieście was renamed Reichsstrasse, and it quickly became the Nazis' main thoroughfare. The famed Litewski Square was renamed Adolph Hitler Platz.

CHAPTER SIX

✦

LUBLIN, POLAND
SEPTEMBER 25, 1939
ONE WEEK AFTER THE NAZI OCCUPATION OF LUBLIN
"Please take Izaak with you again today," Esther said. "We don't know when or if the schools will reopen. The synagogues are still shuttered. We are treating hundreds of people at the clinic. More come in every day. Some of the Polish soldiers who fought in the Lublin suburbs escaped capture but suffered wounds. I treated four of them yesterday. They tell a horrible story. They were overwhelmed."

"I'll take Izzie," Eli said. "He doesn't mind. He'll sit in the office and draw or read his books. We're very busy now, overloaded with contracts for repairs. Some of the Catholic churches suffered structural damage in the bombing, and they are hiring us to do the work."

Esther put on her coat. "Stay away from the Nazis. Yesterday, I saw them grabbing men at random, pulling them into the street, and ordering them to clean up bomb rubble. Some were elderly and disabled, but it made no difference. They were forced to pick up heavy pieces of concrete and bricks with their bare hands while the German soldiers stood by watching and laughing. Anyone who hesitated was beaten. Eli, they are treating us so cruelly."

"My father told me that there's been general looting of Jewish stores. German soldiers walked into Birnbaum's jewelry store and cleaned him out. I heard that Clare Hersch objected when they tore through her millinery shop, and they swatted her down with a rifle stock."

"She came to the clinic yesterday," Esther said. "I treated her bruises. I think that the council should know that the stores are being looted and should file a protest to whatever German is in charge. I also think you should tell the council that there are many displaced families that cannot find apartments in the Jewish quarter. They're forced to find shelter in archways and beneath overhangs. The council should compile a list of available apartments. Tell them that when you go to the Chachmei tonight."

Eli smiled. "You should join the council."

☙

The brickyard was busy when Eli and Izaak arrived. Because of the heavy demand, Jakob had hired extra help. "They bomb our city, destroy half the buildings in town and we are left to repair them," Jakob said. "I've had to put on six extra men. At any other time, we'd be happy to have the business, but to tell the truth, many of our customers can't pay very much. It's a hell of a time to go into the charity business, Eli, but I don't know what else we can do."

At the noon hour, the rabbi rushed into the brickyard office, sweaty and out of breath. "They took our yeshiva," he said in a shaky voice. "Nazi soldiers, no better than Huns, barbarians in fancy uniforms. They marched in and ordered everybody out of the building. I protested, I said you cannot do this, but they laughed at me, Jakob. Two *mamzers* picked me up, carried me out of the Cachmei and threw me onto the grass. They said, 'It's not your building anymore, priest. It is *Juden verboten*.' It's off-limits to anyone but authorized German staff. I tried to tell him that the Cachmei is a holy place, our school, our library. It holds priceless books and papers, famous throughout the world."

"What did he say?"

The rabbi shrugged. "Nothing. He turned a deaf ear to me. He just ordered everyone out and said it was no longer our building. I begged him please to be careful with the books and papers, that they are precious and irreplaceable. Some of them are hundreds of years old. I told him we would organize a group to come and pack up the library."

"What was his answer?"

"Nothing. He didn't respond. I was invisible."

☙

Jakob closed the brickyard at sundown, and Eli and Izaak headed for home. As they turned the corner, they heard shouts and screams coming from the direction of the Chachmei. People rushed past Eli yelling, "Save the yeshiva." Eli picked up Izaak, put him under his arm and ran in step with the crowd. As he neared the building, he stopped dead in his tracks. A line of helmeted soldiers standing shoulder to shoulder barred their approach. Behind the line, soldiers were carrying books and papers out of the yeshiva and throwing them into a pile on the street.

"Our scrolls, our history," the crowd yelled, but they were blocked by the soldiers. When the pile reached a height of five feet, gasoline was poured, a torch was thrown and the flames of the bonfire rose to the sky. People wailed. "The fires of hell," they cried. Eli grabbed Izaak and put his hands over the youngster's eyes, trying to hide from them a vision that could haunt him for the rest of his life. He held his son tightly against his chest and turned for home.

The bonfire continued for hours, and the cries could be heard throughout central Lublin. The Nazi command ordered a German military band to stand in front of the yeshiva and play marching music to drown out the cries. Ultimately, German soldiers carried the Torah scrolls out of the yeshiva and tossed them onto the flames. Several of the Lubliners tried to rush up and save the holy scrolls, but they were swatted away like houseflies.

The interior of the Yeshiva Chachmei was ripped apart that night and stripped clean of its religious significance. The next morning it was designated the headquarters of the German Order Police.

CHAPTER SEVEN

LUBLIN, POLAND
OCTOBER 25, 1939
WEEK 5 OF THE NAZI OCCUPATION

"Eli," Jakob called. "Can you come to the office?"

Clipboard in hand, pencil behind his ear, Eli walked from the brickyard into the small office.

"Yes, Papa."

"The rabbi was here again. He said that the Germans have demanded a contribution of three hundred thousand zloty from the Jewish community of Lublin."

"Contribution? For what?"

"According to the rabbi, it is to reimburse the Germans for keeping their army in Lublin."

"That's insane."

"Go complain to Hitler. I'm sure he'll be attentive."

"What does that mean for us?"

"The rabbi wants twenty thousand from the brickyard. He says we're still busy, we're doing business and we can pay."

"He has some chutzpah! Half the repairs we're doing are at our cost. We're not making money off the occupation."

"It doesn't matter; we have to contribute. There is other news. I learned that the Nazis will conduct a census in the next two days. They will require all Jews to register with the Nazi command."

"For what purpose?"

"Because they are conquerors and we are the conquered."

"How do you know this will happen?"

"Maximilian. He was here earlier today, and he told me."

"Maximilian Poleski? How does he know anything at all? He's nothing but a salesman who brokers our supplies to the Catholic side of the city, for which, by the way, we pay him a damn nice commission. Why would he know anything about the Nazis' plans?"

Jakob raised his eyebrows. "He knows. You know how he sidles up to influential people, how he walks around town in his fancy suit and straw hat. Now he's managed to worm his way into favor with some of the Nazis. He says the Nazis are paying him to identify and register Jews."

"He's denouncing Jewish families to the Germans? That snake! Six years ago, he came to you with his fancy hat in his hand begging for a job. You gave him the church accounts. Now he turns on us? He's pointing out Jewish families for the Nazis to arrest?"

"Not to arrest, just to identify. They want to know who is Jewish and who is not. He hasn't turned on us, but he is definitely working for the Nazis. He came in today to give me a warning. He says all Jews must voluntarily register."

"Register for what?"

"Maximilian does not know. Or he is not saying. But if people don't register, they will be punished."

"He's a rat, Papa. Sever all ties with him. Louis can take over his accounts."

"I've thought about that, but I've decided not to make a change. Maximilian is still managing the Catholic Church accounts and making us money in a very difficult time. Your brother does not have contacts in the Catholic community. Besides, Louis is more of a teacher than a salesman. Let's leave him to his duties at the yeshiva."

"What yeshiva? The yeshiva is gone. It's a Nazi police station and a jail."

"Louis has been studying with the elders in the synagogue basement since it reopened. It's a makeshift yeshiva. He has also been appointed to the *Judenrat*. The Nazis have demanded that a Jewish council be established to speak for our people."

"The *Judenrat*? We already have a Jewish council."

"Now it is the *Judenrat*. Since Henryk Bekker was president of our community council, he was appointed president of the *Judenrat*. Louis is one of several named to the committee. At least in that regard you should be proud. He is well thought of in our community. Therefore, Louis is too busy to take over any sales accounts. We still need Maximilian to handle the church accounts, and we are overloaded with their business."

"But Papa, how can we associate with a man who makes his bed with the Nazis? Today he's identifying Jews. What's he doing tomorrow? He's no better than they are. The Nazis are confiscating Jewish homes and businesses all over the city. They're rounding up Jews and shipping them off to who knows where?"

Jakob raised his index finger. "That is exactly the reason we should continue to employ Maximilian. We don't know where, but he might. He's found a way to ingratiate himself with the vermin. Through Maximilian, we have eyes and ears inside the German administration."

"What else did the great Maximilian tell you?"

"Well, it's no secret that the Nazis are seizing Jewish businesses. He told me that the Nazis are paying him to identify which businesses to take, but he promises that he will protect us and our brickyard."

"He's full of shit."

The older man put a gentle hand on Eli's shoulder. "We are at war, son, and we must keep our heads. We have families to protect. Although we have known Maximilian when he was nothing but a well-dressed street scrounger, he has now cultivated a relationship with the Nazis. Yet he professes to have loyalty to us. When he came by today, he told me that he would protect the brickyard from seizure and safeguard our family."

"Do you believe him?"

"I believe he will *try* as long as it suits his ambition and is financially advantageous to him. He makes good money as our sales agent."

"And you trust him?"

"Of course not, but he sees opportunities to work his rackets and he is privy to information that others are not. Last week, a trainload of Jewish families from Bohemia and Moravia arrived here in Lublin. Maximilian told me that Jews from other provinces are being sent here as well. He has learned that the Nazis intend to build a huge reservation designed to hold five hundred thousand Jews."

"Five hundred thousand! There are only forty thousand Jews in Lublin. Where is this reservation supposed to be?"

"Nisko."

Eli's face turned red. "That's a swamp, Papa."

Jakob nodded. "True. Maximilian told me that it is designed to hold only the Jews brought in from other towns, not the Lublin Jews. He thinks the Nazis will register us and leave Lublin families alone to live in the Jewish Quarter."

"I don't believe him, Papa. They're confiscating homes and businesses in our neighborhood. The Bornsteins were given one week to vacate their home. Why would they leave the Rosens alone?"

"Because Maximilian will intercede on our behalf."

"At what price?"

"On that, we shall see."

❧

"The Cohens were forced to give up their house today," Esther said as she stirred her stew on the stove. Eli could see that Esther's nerves were on edge. Her movements were tense, her muscles taut.

"Where did they go?" Eli said, snitching a warm piece of challah.

"Leah told me that they rented a small unit in the quarter. Most of the families who have lost their homes are trying to find apartments there. Even storefronts are being rented. It's becoming a teeming, unhealthy mess. The Nazis gave the Cohens three hours to gather their belongings. Three hours, Eli! Leah called me at the clinic. She was frantic. 'What can I possibly gather in three hours?' she cried. I rushed over to help her. That poor girl. She had so many lovely things, but we could only collect essentials—clothing, shoes, bedding, pots and pans, Mikal's books, a few dishes. We wrapped them in sheets and blankets to wheel them in a cart like a peddler. All of her beautiful things, Eli—you know what a lovely home she made—she had to leave them all behind for some filthy Nazi. She was heartbroken. Why, Eli? Have they no respect for anyone? Would they like someone to do the same thing to their mothers?"

"As my father said, it's because we are the conquered."

"Are we next? When will they come in here and give us three hours?" Esther began to weep. "When will they take our home from us? All my precious things, my mother's things. Everything I've put together to make a lovely home for you and Izzie." She wiped away her tears with the back of her sleeve.

"There is no acceptable answer, Essie, but you speak only of possessions. They are things. They are not you, and they are not me, and they are not Izzie. As precious as they are, they are objects. Maximilian says he is protecting us from Nazi seizures. Whether he is or not, what's important is that we hold on to each other. We'll always have each other. You, me and Izzie. If we have to move into some little apartment, we'll move, and we'll do it together and make the best of it. Sooner or later this storm will pass, and we'll establish a new normal. The three of us. You have to have faith."

Esther nodded. She wrapped her arms around Eli and held him tightly. "I'm trying, and I do have faith. I don't have confidence where Maximilian is concerned, but at least we are still living in our home and you still have your business. And you're right, this may be temporary. No matter how severe the storm, you will always be my sunny day."

"That's my girl. Our love can weather any storm. Never forget it."

She kissed him and folded into his embrace. "You and I are forever," she whispered.

CHAPTER EIGHT

❧

Maximilian, sporting a new wool overcoat, homburg hat and polished wing tips, strutted into the brickyard with a uniformed SS officer and three armed SS guards.

"Allow me to introduce SS Brigadeführer Odilo Globočnik," he said. "Brigadeführer Globočnik has been appointed the governor of the Lublin District."

An acerbic man with a long oval face and close-cropped hair, Globočnik gave an ever-so-slight nod. He proceeded to stroll around the brickyard with his hands clasped behind his back, mentally inventorying the variety of materials and the manner of operation, after which he and Maximilian returned to the office, where Eli and his father stood waiting.

Maximilian briskly approached with a broad smile. "Eli, Jakob, I bring you good news. Because of . . ."

Before he could finish his sentence, Globočnik stepped forward, moved Maximilian aside as though he were a waif, and said, "So this is the primary source of Lublin's construction and building supplies?" He spoke without emotion in an imperious tone.

"Yes, it is, Herr Brigadeführer," Maximilian said deferentially.

Globočnik looked pleased. "Hmm. I see your point, Maximilian. This business will be useful in several of our projects, and we shall take it immediately. We may begin by transporting construction materials to Lindenstrasse. That will shortly become Lublin's center for mandatory workshops, and it must be operational as soon as possible."

"Understood, Brigadeführer, and I am most anxious to help," Maximilian said with a series of obsequious nods.

"Excellent. We'll appropriate this business, but how do you propose we manage it? No one on my staff has experience in managing a brickyard and construction company. I suppose I could bring in someone from Berlin, but that would take time."

"May I humbly offer a suggestion, Brigadeführer? Appoint me as the operator of the brickyard."

"You, Maximilian? Are you fully confident of your management ability? I will not tolerate a failure."

"Oh, of course I am, Herr Brigadeführer, or I would not suggest it. I have worked at this business for six years, and I am intimately familiar with its operation. My sales are the highest in the company. No one knows the inside operation of a construction business better than I do. I would be proud to operate this business." He quickly added, "For the benefit of the Reich, of course."

With a flick of his hand, Globočnik gestured to Eli and his father. "What about the former owners? Do you have any use for them?"

"Most respectfully, I think they could be useful. The Rosen family has operated this business for many years, and they have done so more or less efficiently. I propose that we keep them on as employees. They will be even more efficient under my leadership."

Globočnik seemed skeptical and raised his chin. "They are Jews. We can expect no loyalty. You will have to be watchful."

"I can assure you that I will tolerate no laziness or inattention," Maximilian said confidently. "Work will be done diligently and promptly under my supervision. Allow me to start filling orders for the project at Lindenstrasse at once."

Globočnik nodded. "Very well. I am depending on you, Maximilian. Do not disappoint me." The SS general slapped a crop against his leg and walked out the door.

Maximilian winked at Eli and Jakob and said, "You see, I told you that I would protect you."

"Oh, we feel great," Eli scoffed. "You just stole our business. What the hell is Lindenstrasse?"

"Oh, that's the new name for Lipowa Street. The Nazis are clearing the old athletic fields and they're going to build a labor camp there."

"What sort of labor camp?"

"Well, they don't tell me everything, Eli, but I've seen some plans. There will be several workshops and barracks for laborers. The workshops will produce products needed by the German army."

"And where are they going to get the laborers for their workshops?"

"They don't share every detail, but it doesn't take much imagination to know that the only workers in this area are Lubliners. So I guess they will recruit workers from the city."

"Recruit?"

Maximilian shrugged. "Poor choice of words. You know what I mean." Then he turned and scampered after Globočnik.

"Over my dead body," Eli said. "I will never work a minute for that scoundrel."

The day's exchange hung heavily on Jakob's shoulders. For all of his adult life, he had run his business honestly and ethically, as had his father before him. Now it was Nazi-controlled and an instrument for building labor camps. He sighed. "Maximilian has no integrity, Eli, but our options are limited. For the time being, we will continue to operate the business as before. We will pray for better days."

"Are we supposed to follow Maximilian's orders? I cannot do that."

"I doubt he'll ever come around, except to drop off material requisitions or to collect his commissions."

Eli's jaw was set. "Papa, it's time to get out. I mean leave Lublin. I've been talking to Esther, and we think things will only get worse. She wants to find a cottage somewhere in the countryside. Before they give us three hours to get out of our house, we think we should pack up and move out of Lublin altogether."

"Where shall we go, Eli? A cottage in the country? How will we eat? How do we survive? And if we rely on provisions from some other occupied Polish city, how is that an improvement over what we have now? All of Poland is under occupation."

"What if we all moved north to Lithuania or Latvia? The Kaplans moved to Lithuania."

"The Kaplans have family in Kaunas. What is waiting for us in Lithuania,

and what do we do when we get there? Do we have jobs, a business? How
do we survive in Kaunas?"

"I will find work. There's a large Jewish community in Kaunas."

"Have you considered how you will make this journey to Kaunas, Eli?
Certainly not on the roads. The Russian army crossed the Polish border a
month ago and they are Germany's ally. If you go north or east, you will
run into them. No, son, as distasteful as it seems, it's best if we carry on as
before. As of right now, it is functionally still our brickyard. Maximilian
cannot possibly run this business on his own. He needs us or he will fail,
and you heard the ruthless Globočnik: failure is not an option. That is our
leverage. We will use Maximilian as necessary to survive until things settle
down."

CHAPTER NINE

"Here," Maximilian said as he handed a paper bag to Eli. "I have something for you."

"What is this?" Eli said.

"Armbands," Maximilian said flippantly. "I saved you a trip to city hall. There's quite a line there now. In the bag are white armbands, one for each member of your family. Each band has a blue Jewish star, which has to be visible at all times. Whenever you go out, you must wear them."

"For what reason?"

"The Nazis don't give reasons; they give orders. If they catch you without the band, they'll punish you. What's the big deal, anyway? Wear the band; don't cause any trouble. By the way, the Germans are charging Jews two zloty apiece for these armbands. I paid the bill for you when I picked them up. You're welcome."

"Who came up with this idea? Was it your buddy Globočnik?"

"Oh no, this order comes directly from Governor-General Hans Frank. He decreed that all Jews in Poland must wear the Star of David and all Jewish businesses must permanently display the star on the window."

"For what purpose?"

Maximilian smirked. "I think you can figure it out. But be thankful that there will be no Star of David hanging over this brickyard, because it's not a Jewish-owned business anymore, is it? Never underestimate the advantage of associating with Maximilian Poleski. You know, my mother always told me that we have royal blood. From the first Polish dynasty, no less. That's why she named me Maximilian."

"Oh, please."

"Seriously. General Globočnik was impressed when I told him I had royal blood."

Eli scoffed. "Let me bow deeply before you, your lordship. Then get the hell out of my brickyard."

"*My* brickyard. We'll need to change the Rosen and Sons sign. Repaint it 'M. Poleski—Building and Construction Materials.'"

"Is that all? Can I get back to work?"

"Don't be like that. I'm protecting your family. You still have jobs while many do not. In case you haven't noticed, the SS is rounding up Jews, especially craftsmen and those with building skills, and sending them to Lipowa Street and other labor sites. You didn't get rounded up, did you? Nobody in your family was dispatched to a work camp. You can thank me for that. Jewish houses in the nicer part of town are being confiscated and given over to SS officers. You, your father and your brother still have your homes. You could show a little gratitude."

Eli did not hide his disdain. "Okay, Maximilian, I'm very, very grateful. Is that it?"

"Well, no it's not. I have a couple more agenda items. Housekeeping items, they say. I need an office here at the brickyard. Louis doesn't need his office; he's rarely here. I'll take that one."

"Why on earth would you need an office? You don't do any work."

"How would it look if the owner of the brickyard didn't even have an office? We must keep up appearances. And I want an office where I can conduct some of my private business."

"What private business do you have, Maximilian?"

He smiled and wagged his finger back and forth. "Ah, that's why they call it private. One more thing: I need to take possession of the financial books and records. Have them sent to my office at the city hall."

"You have an office inside SS headquarters?"

Maximilian raised his eyebrows. "Yes, I do. I'm pretty important around here, in case you hadn't noticed, and lucky for you that I am."

"Why do you need our books and records? You have nothing to do with running our business."

Maximilian smirked. "*My* business, Eli. *My* books and records. Don't forget, it's *my* company now. Be thankful that the Nazi command didn't just give it over to some Berliner. You'd be out on your ass. I assured Herr Brigadeführer that I would personally keep an eye on the finances. He thinks we're paying out too much in salaries."

Eli's face was turning red. He popped a finger on Maximilian's chest. "You're not touching my salary, my father's salary or my brother's salary, understood? Some of my foremen have been with us for years. You don't reduce their salaries either. Understood?"

Maximilian took a step back. He spread his hands and smiled. "I don't think there's much I can do about that. With regard to the employees' salaries, Globočnik knows he can get workers anytime for free. He'd just grab them off the street. As to *your* salaries, if General Globočnik wants to cut them, I'll have to obey. I think you'd be smart to watch what you spend, because my sense is that he *will* cut you. He doesn't like Jews making money in his city."

"His city?"

"That's what he says."

"Well, there's something you should consider, Mr. Fancy Brickyard Owner. If I don't get paid, I don't work. Are you going to run this brickyard by yourself? How will Herr Globočnik like that?"

"Don't overvalue yourself, Eli. You're not the only person in Poland who knows how to run a brickyard. I'll get you what I can, but it won't be that much."

❧

It was evening when Eli entered his home and laid the armbands on the table. "What are these?" Esther said angrily, as though she already knew the answer.

"Armbands. We are now required to wear them whenever we leave the house."

"Why not just paint a target on our backs?" she said. "Then the Nazis won't have any difficulty knowing which persons to kick or trip or push aside."

"Esther . . ."

"Don't Esther me. Have you seen what they do if you don't move out of their way on the sidewalk, or if you dare to look directly at them, as though your eyes will tarnish them? They'll push you over or beat you. Even women!" With the back of her hand, she brushed the armbands off the table and onto the floor. "I don't want their bands of hate on my dining room table."

"It doesn't matter, Essie. It's a law and they'll punish you if you don't comply."

"I told you before, Eli, first they will mark us to separate us from society, then they will collect us and then they will eliminate us."

Eli reached for her and wrapped her up in his arms. "Essie, does it make sense to tear your hair out? It's only an armband."

She looked up into his eyes and said softly, "Oh, my husband, I'm afraid you don't see. It's an armband today. Tomorrow it's a yoke."

CHAPTER TEN

❧

Jakob Rosen called his son in from the brickyard. "Eli, there's a delegation from a Catholic church in our office, and they're demanding to talk to ownership directly. I don't know anything about their account and Maximilian isn't around. I'd like you to come in and help me."

Three people were waiting when Eli entered the office. The spokesperson was a woman in a long brown coat with a tan scarf and a soft wool bowler. "I am Lucya Sikorska," the woman said. "I am the lay business manager of the Church of Saint Peter the Apostle." She gestured to her right, to a petite woman with a black-and-white cowl and a cloth coat over her habit. "May I introduce Sister Maria." Then, pointing to an elderly man in a floor-length cassock, she said, "And this is Father Jaworski."

Eli wiped his hands on a towel. "Please forgive my appearance," he said. "I was out working in the brickyard. We're short of help these days. How can we assist you?"

"As I'm sure you know, our church was badly damaged in the September bombings. The entire southwest corner was destroyed. Our roof suffered major damage. We have been waiting for our repairs. I think we've been more than patient, Mr. Rosen."

Eli looked puzzled. "One moment, please." He pulled the project book off the shelf and thumbed through. "I'm sorry, Mrs. Sikorska, I don't see a work order."

Her lips tightened, and she quickly glanced at her companions. She pulled a paper out of her purse and slapped it on the table. "This is a receipt for the down payment given to Mr. Poleski, your account executive."

Eli sighed and picked up the paper. "Received of Saint Peter the Apostle, the sum of 12,500 zloty as a deposit for wall and roof repairs. Detailed estimate to follow." It was signed "Maximilian Poleski, account manager for Rosen & Sons Construction Company."

"I am very sorry, Mrs. Sikorska. The deposit and the work order do not appear to have been recorded."

"What does that mean?"

"It means I don't have a record of repairs to be made to your church. Or a 12,500 zloty deposit. Did Maximilian ever come back to the church after you gave him the deposit?"

She shook her head. "We haven't seen him since October."

The priest stepped forward. "Mr. Rosen, we are not a wealthy parish. That deposit was given to your agent in good faith after we pooled all our resources. We can't even hold a mass at Saint Peter in its present condition because it's not safe. How can you allow your account manager to take our money and . . ."

Eli held up his hand. "Whoa, wait a minute please, Father. I haven't *allowed* anyone to take your money. I didn't even know about it until you came in. But Mr. Poleski was working for us at the time, and we will honor the deposit. He wasn't exactly a manager, but he was an authorized salesman, and we will assume full responsibility. When can I come out to examine the condition of the church?"

"I am there at all hours," Father Jaworski said.

"I thought it wasn't safe," Eli said.

The priest shrugged. He had a beneficent smile. "It is my church and I must tend to my flock."

Eli reached over to shake his hand. "I will be there tomorrow morning."

The group left and Eli turned to his father. "Wait till I get my hands on Maximilian."

The wind was blowing hard from the northwest, bringing arctic snow and freezing temperatures into Lublin. It whistled down the streets, across the walkways and through the broken walls of the Church of Saint Peter the Apostle. Lucya Sikorska and Father Jaworski stood in the vestibule in their winter coats to greet Eli and his construction foreman just before the noon hour. Just as she had described, the southwest corner of the building had suffered significant structural damage. The brick and masonry had been blasted loose. Plywood boards, placed over a wide cavity in the fractured wall, were all that separated the church's interior from the harsh winter elements.

"It's pretty bad, isn't it?" Lucya said. In the cold interior of the church, her breath immediately condensed into a misty fog.

Eli jotted notes onto a pad, looked up and said, "I'm afraid so, Mrs. Sikorska."

"Lucya, please."

"Would you like to see the damage to the roof?" Father Jaworski asked.

Eli pointed to a grouping of buckets on the floor in the western transept. "Is that the only area?"

"We think so. It's the only spot where we've observed snow and water coming in."

"Do you mind if my construction foreman takes a walk around your church and makes some notes?"

"Please," Father Jaworski said, extending his arm.

"Our church has been here almost two hundred years," Lucya said. "It's a solidly built church, but the bombs fell close by. We also lost some precious relics in the air raids." She pointed to a ceramic statue of the Blessed Virgin lying on the floor. "She's a beauty, over a hundred years old." She sighed. "She fell from her platform and cracked across her midsection. You can see there are plaster chips lying all about. We're trying to enlist the services of an experienced sculptor to put her back together. The statue of our patron saint was also damaged, but we think he's beyond repair."

Eli walked into a small chapel where the damaged statue lay on its side. "This is indeed a beautiful work of art," he said.

Lucya smiled. "We feel the same way. The parishioners who regularly come to offer their prayers to her and seek her guidance miss her the most."

"Have you found a sculptor to perform the repairs?"

She shook her head. "None that we could afford."

Eli nodded. "I know one."

The construction foreman returned to the room with a grim expression. "Eli, this western wall is in trouble. Load-bearing masonry has been destroyed. We would have to scaffold it from the outside and replace substantially all the brickwork in the southwest corner. Four men, six brick loads, plaster, wooden struts, four to six weeks, depending on the weather. You're talking twenty-five thousand to thirty thousand zloty."

Eli saw the color drain out of Lucya's face. "Tomasz," Eli said, "can we finish it in time for Christmas?"

The foreman threw up his hands. "That's three and a half weeks, Eli. It's impossible."

"These are good people, Tomasz. I want their church open for Christmas. Can we get enough of the work done to make it safe and keep the weather out? Take the crew off the Strodza Crossing."

"But, Mr. Rosen," Lucya protested, "we cannot afford the repairs. It would be months, maybe years, before we . . ."

Eli waved his hand from side to side and interrupted. "We'll work it out. Don't worry. Let's get it done, Tomasz."

Later that afternoon, Maximilian appeared at the brickyard. "I'm here to pick up the financial books and records," he said. "Globočnik's orders, you know."

"Guess where I was this morning, Maximilian?

He shrugged. "How on earth would I know?"

"I was at the Church of Saint Peter the Apostle."

Maximilian emitted a nervous laugh. "Ugh. That place is really busted up, isn't it? I don't know if they could ever get it right. Probably a waste of time to bother. They'd be better off tearing it down and building a brand new one. More modern and nicer."

"Is that why you took a twelve thousand five hundred zloty deposit?"

"They told you that? Really? You believe them?"

Eli nodded and showed him the receipt.

"Oh, now I remember. I was going to turn the order in, but everything went crazy in October and I got appointed to my prestigious position at Nazi headquarters and that took up all my time and the whole thing about this crappy little church slipped my mind."

"I see. So now, Maximilian, you may consider this a reminder. Rosen and Sons is going to repair the crappy little church. Turn over the deposit."

Maximilian hung his head. "I can't. It's gone."

"You spent their money?"

"I've had a lot of expenses with the German hierarchy. They expect stuff. You have to grease a palm every now and again."

"You have to make good on that deposit, Maximilian. Go get the money and bring it in."

"I can't do it. There's no way I can raise that kind of money. Listen, give me a break. I'm your ambassador with the SS. I'm watching out for your family. You're still here doing business while others are getting sent away. You still have your houses. No one bothers your wife when other women are being snatched off the street. Let's call it a prepayment for my protective services. You don't want me to be your enemy; you want me to secure your future, and I can do it, I swear. It's a nasty climate out there, I don't have to tell you."

"Get out."

CHAPTER ELEVEN

LUBLIN, POLAND

DECEMBER 1939

WEEK 12 OF THE NAZI OCCUPATION

Construction noise—the music of hammers, saws and tradesmen shouting to each other—greeted Eli as he entered the church. Sounds like progress, he thought. Christmas is coming.

"Lucya, I'd like to introduce my brother, Louis Rosen. I brought him over to look at the broken statue."

Her lower lip protruded sorrowfully. "She used to be so beautiful, the grandest figure in the church. But now she breaks my heart."

Eli nodded in concurrence. "Louis knows art and I'd like him to take a look, if that's all right."

"Sure."

Lucya stood to the side and watched them. Louis and Eli were a study in contrasts, like black-and-white keys on a piano. Where Eli was stocky and powerful, Louis's body was thin and smooth. Eli's face was ruddy, a working man's face. Louis, in his black suit and wide-brimmed hat, had a gentle, pasty white complexion beneath his bushy beard. Eli was rough and to the point. Louis was contemplative and patient. The Rosen brothers—contrasts to be sure, but put them together and they produced sweet music on the same keyboard.

Louis bent over the broken sculpture and softly ran his index finger over the severed edges. He gently lifted the fragments, deliberating how and if they could be reassembled. Finally, he looked up and nodded. "I can do the restoration. It will take time, but this lovely work can and should be restored. This is a priceless piece."

"I'm afraid we have no funds for repairs at the present time," Lucya said. "We've spent all of our money on the church reconstruction."

"So I understand," Louis said. "When may I begin?"

"But I said . . ."

Louis smiled and gently waved her off. "Please, allow me the privilege of working on this precious piece of religious art. Let's preserve it. Especially now, at a time when religion is under assault."

Brushing away a tear, Lucya said, "May God bless you for your generosity. I don't know what to say, Mr. Rosen."

"Just say 'You may begin right away.' We don't want to lose any of these broken pieces. I am eager to start."

"Our church doors are always open. You may begin whenever you like."

❦

Later that afternoon, when Eli returned home, Esther met him at the door. "We have a houseguest," she said quietly. "My sister is here."

"From Warsaw?"

Esther nodded, held her finger to her lips and whispered, "She's in pretty bad shape."

Eli walked into the living room where Klara was seated on the couch. Her hair was disarranged, and her clothes were soiled and frayed. Eli knew Klara to be a stylish dresser; he had never seen her in such a state. She held a handkerchief bunched up in her fist. Eli sat next to her and put his arm around her shoulders. "Klara, did you come alone?" he asked.

She nodded.

"Are Milosz and Bonita all right?"

She shook her head.

"I'm so sorry."

"Thank you," she whispered.

"Warsaw is one hundred and seventy kilometers away," Eli said. "How did you get here?"

Klara began to cry and her body trembled. "I'm sorry," was all she could say.

Esther gently took her hand and led her from the room, "Come, Klara, let's get you into a hot bath."

After dinner, after Izaak had been put to bed, Esther, Eli and Klara sat in the kitchen and found time to talk. "Things are so much worse in Warsaw," Klara said. "There are random shootings. Cruel attacks. I swear, the Nazis do it for sport. It is their amusement. And they snatch people off the street, and no one knows where they're taken."

Eli raised his eyebrows. "That sounds worse than here."

Esther said, "No, Eli, it's not worse. You're in the brickyard all day. You don't know. I see what happens on the street. I hear what other women tell me at the clinic. It's the ORPO, the German Order Police. They go into homes, into cellars, looking for Jews to send to labor sites. They boast that they're on a 'Jew hunt.'"

"Maximilian told me that the SS is gathering workers for the labor sites, like the one they're building on Lipowa Street," Eli said.

"Gathering?" Esther scoffed. "Maximilian called it *gathering*? Like the Portuguese slave hunters *gathered* Africans in the seventeenth century? That kind of *gathering*?"

Eli sheepishly looked at his wife. "I'm afraid so." Shifting his attention, he said, "What happened to Milosz and Bonita, Klara?"

She swallowed hard. "A week ago, Bonnie went missing. She didn't come home from her job at the pharmacy where she worked after school. They said she never showed up at work. I was hysterical. We knew the Nazis were grabbing young girls off the street, and Bonnie is fifteen. Milosz and I went looking. The baker told us that he saw her talking to two young uniformed soldiers as she was walking to the pharmacy. The baker recognized one as Helmut Grausburt, a man who frequents his bakery. He said he saw them walk away. Milosz ran off to find them."

Klara's shoulders trembled from her sobs. "Milosz didn't come home that night. Or the next. I went out in the morning. I asked around. I went to the baker. Someone must have seen something, heard something, but no one would say. Later that day, a Warsaw councilman told me that Milosz was dead. Somehow, deep inside I already knew. They shot him, Essie, and left him for dead in the street. In the gutter, Essie, where the horses piss. I said goodbye to him at the undertaker, my poor Milosz, shot so many times."

"I'm so sorry, Klara."

"I kept asking people about Bonnie. Everyone told me the same thing—she was probably taken. The message was conveyed to me so unemotionally, so matter of fact, like I was asking about the weather. *Probably taken.* That's how things have devolved in Warsaw. They've all become numb." She reached over, grabbed Esther's arms and squeezed. "What am I supposed to do, Essie?"

Eli brought a glass of water. "You're safe here," he said. "Maybe Bonnie has been assigned to a work camp and she's unharmed. You never know."

"People are fleeing Warsaw. They're running away, and everyone is so scared. I waited three more days and then I decided to come here. I said to myself, Essie would know what to do. I was able to take the bus part of the way, but German soldiers got on in Kurow, laughing and joking, and I panicked. It shook me to my bones, I swear. I jumped off the bus and walked the rest of the way."

Esther hugged her tightly and let her cry onto her chest. "I'm so sorry for you, Klara. I'm glad you came to me, and you're welcome to stay with us as long as you like, but things are not very good in Lublin either."

"Are there shootings in the middle of the street? Do the Nazis shoot at a *tzadik*'s foot just to watch him dance? Do they grab him by the beard and spin him around?"

"Not that I've seen."

"The Nazis froze our bank accounts and took our money. They closed our synagogues, saying that Jews were dirty and would spread epidemics. They made us wear armbands and put signs on the Jewish stores, the ones that they hadn't already closed or vandalized. Now they have issued food stamps on cards, but there's hardly any food for us to buy. There were over three hundred thousand Jews in Warsaw before the war started. Over a hundred thousand fled, the smart ones. Then the Nazis brought in train-loads of a hundred thousand more. They arrive and there's no place for them to live. No food to eat. The rumor is that the Nazis are going to build a ghetto in the Jewish quarter and imprison all the Jews. That's why they're collecting them from other towns."

Esther looked at Eli. "I told you."

"I don't know what to do," Klara said, and she squeezed her sister's arms. "And I don't know where my little Bonita is."

"The Germans are building work camps and the Nazi command is demanding workers. Thousands of them," Eli said. "Many Lubliners have been compelled to work in camps like Belzec and Majdan. The Germans are building a wall on the eastern front along the Russian border. They are also setting up sewing camps, and maybe that's where they've taken Bonita."

"Everywhere I looked in Warsaw, things were in chaos," Klara said, "but it's different here. For you and Esther in Lublin—it looks like nothing's changed."

Esther shook her head. "No, Klara, things have definitely changed. They change every day. We are a subjugated people. We don't know what tomorrow will bring. Maybe the Nazis haven't decided what to do with Lublin yet. But they will. We live in fear of that. Be assured, life has changed for us, too."

"You're still in your house. You still have your business. You have food on the table. Nobody in your family was *probably taken*."

"Thanks to Maximilian," Esther said. "According to Eli, he's protecting us."

"So far," Eli said. "So far, that's true."

✺

The house was quiet. Klara was asleep in the guest bedroom. Eli, his head on his pillow, his arm around Esther, stared at the ceiling. Was he was making the right decisions? Was he a fool to place any trust in a man as loathsome and spineless as Maximilian? What were his alternatives?

Esther lifted her head. "Are you awake?"

"I am."

"My sister will never return to Warsaw, you know. She's here permanently."

"I know."

"God only knows where Bonita is. People who are sent away never come back. Are we next, Eli? Can we afford to sit here and wait? It's our responsibility to protect Izaak."

"I think about that every day, but right now I don't see a solution, one that would justify the risk of fleeing into the countryside, maybe directly into a battlefield. Our home, our business, our daily lives are still intact. Oppressed to be sure, but manageable. Maybe that's how we survive. We lived through the Great War. Millions of soldiers were killed, but Lublin survived. It was never necessary to leave."

"I'm sorry, my husband, but that is so naïve. You cannot compare the two wars. First of all, we were children twenty years ago. What do you really know? We have little memory of that war. My uncle was a soldier in the Austro-Hungarian army, and he came back injured. Secondly, there was no Hitler, no madman, no war against the Jews. Look at Lublin today, only four months into the war. It was never like this."

"I understand, but whether it's Maximilian or whether the Nazis have achieved their purpose in occupying our city and have now stopped inflicting new punitive measures, Lublin seems to be in a relatively static position."

"Achieved their purpose? Are you wearing your armband, Eli? Do you walk down the street and avert your eyes? Have you seen the Jews being marched to the train stations by armed soldiers? Is it happening every day? Are we so simpleminded that we would put our faith in a worm like Maximilian? No, Eli, it is more than just the occupation of Lublin. It is their war against the Jews. Ask yourself, why are they doing this? What sense does it make for Germany to single out Polish Jews? We have no army. We have no weapons. We pose no threat."

"Because they want slave labor."

"It's more than that, Eli. Far more. It's a hatred. In Germany they have been resentful of successful Jews for years. Now the Nazi leaders have whipped their followers into a state of hatefulness that they carry everywhere they go. They make vile cartoons of us in their magazines. They write lies about us in their newspapers. They despise us. They won't be satisfied with slave labor."

"What do you mean?"

"I think they mean to kill us."

"Esther . . ."

"You said it yourself. They planned a reservation with five hundred thousand Jews. Klara said a hundred thousand have been brought into Warsaw and that they were building a ghetto to imprison them. Women and children, too. Do they collect children for slave labor? It doesn't sound to me like they are building a labor force. If that was their intention, they would take healthy Catholics and Protestants as well."

"Esther, they're not eliminating the Jews in Lublin. In fact, they're bringing in more and more Jews every day. The Lublin Jewish community is larger than ever. I am still working at the brickyard every day. We're still billing our customers. We're still living as before."

"Not as before. There are areas of our city that are *Juden verboten*. They took your business away from you. You work for Maximilian now. The Nazis are taking away businesses all over the city. They are forcing people out of their homes and into the poorest Jewish neighborhoods. Now they force us to wear armbands. There's only one reason for that. They will identify us, they will collect us and concentrate us and then they will eliminate us."

"Esther, Esther, I think you are getting carried away. What would it gain them? What possible purpose is served?"

"Maybe to have a banner to march beneath. Maybe it unifies them."

"They're at war! What could be more unifying than that? They're unified against their enemies—Britain, France, Poland."

"All I know is what I see. They look at us as though we are vermin, and people exterminate vermin. Even Maximilian has assumed a superior mantle. He patronizes us. You think he will protect us? Bah. The King of Denunciation. If push comes to shove, he will turn his back on us and denounce our family as well."

"What would you have me do, Esther?"

"I defer to you, Eli. I always have. But I would encourage you to think about moving. We have a child and he must grow up in a land where he is loved, not despised."

Eli nodded. "I can't argue with that. It won't be easy. We'll have to go on foot, but we will do it. I will make plans. When the winter ends and the snow melts, we will go. I promise."

"Then we will wait until the snow melts. Together we will find a safe place for our son. What about your father and Louis?"

"My father will never leave his brickyard, and he's not strong enough to make the journey. I will talk to Louis, but I'm certain he will decline. He is deeply involved with the *Judenrat*. He believes that Lublin needs him to weather the occupation."

"If it can be weathered."

Eli rolled over, wrapped his arms around his wife and pulled her close to him. He inhaled the sweet scent of her hair. He bathed in the warm softness of her body. He lifted her chin and kissed her lips. "How did I get such a wise and beautiful woman to marry me?"

"Because I had my eyes on you, Eli Rosen, and I willed it to be so."

CHAPTER TWELVE

◦~

LUBLIN, POLAND
APRIL 1940
MONTH 7 OF THE NAZI OCCUPATION
It was nippy for an April Sunday, and Izaak needed a jacket when he and Eli left the house. A smattering of daffodils and tulips had poked their heads out of Esther's flower garden. Patches of green were replacing the winter browns. Spring had finally arrived, and Eli was making mental preparations to take the family out of Lublin and flee into the southern foothills. The snow had melted and it was time to go.

Over the winter, life had settled into a fragile and precarious routine in occupied Lublin. No new edicts had come down in several weeks, but the cruelty of the oppressors continued unabated. Random arrests and disappearances occurred almost daily. As Klara would say, they were "probably taken."

Jewish families from other Polish towns were arriving by the trainload. Many were sent on to other locations, but a substantial portion was always left behind to fend for themselves in the overcrowded Jewish quarter. The *Judenrat* struggled to find them housing and a way to coalesce, but accommodations were scarce. The Jewish economy had all but ground to a halt.

With Eli's massive hand wrapped around little Izaak's hand, they walked across town to the Church of Saint Peter the Apostle. A few days earlier, Lucya had come to the brickyard to extend an invitation to Eli and his father to attend the grand unveiling of the newly restored statue of the

Blessed Virgin and the ceremony honoring Louis. Jakob had awkwardly declined, offering an excuse that there was too much work to be done at the brickyard.

"He still has one foot in the old days when Jews and Catholics did not attend one another's religious celebrations," Eli whispered to Lucya. "I don't think he's ever been in a church. But I'll be pleased to attend the unveiling and support my brother's work. I'll bring my son, Izaak. My wife would also come, but she works at the clinic on Sundays."

A large crowd had gathered at the entrance to the Renaissance-styled church. Izaak, more shy than frightened, huddled close to his father. Lucya came out to welcome them, took Izaak by the hand and led them both into the church. Cookies, pazckis and Polish gingerbread were set on the refreshment table in the vestibule with tea and juice. Lucya winked and stuffed a handful of cookies into a napkin for Izaak.

In the corner of the sanctuary, just to the right of the pulpit, the statue of the Blessed Virgin stood covered with a large white drop cloth. Louis, in his black suit and fur-trimmed black hat, stood proudly beside Father Jaworski. Right on cue, the bells began to chime, and the parishioners took their seats. Izaak and Eli were led to seats reserved for them in the front pew.

Father Jaworski climbed the steps to the pulpit. After a few short welcoming prayers, he directed his attention to the covered statue. "She was commissioned by our church in 1787," he said in a pleasing baritone. "It has been said by many that she radiates the spirit of the Blessed Virgin. She has welcomed pilgrims and worshippers for over one hundred fifty years. I cannot begin to count the number of brides who have knelt before her and presented their bouquets, seeking her blessings on their wedding day. Sadly, as all of us know, our lovely statue was badly injured when the Germans dropped their bombs last September. We held little hope for her recovery. Not only was it artistically challenging, but the cost of the restoration far exceeded our budget. Yet through the generosity of Rosen and Sons Construction Company, and through the tireless efforts of Louis Rosen, our Blessed Virgin has been fully repaired and restored to her original beauty."

Father Jaworski stepped down and took his place beside the covered statue. He reached for Louis's hand and raised it high. "This is Louis Rosen, a talented artist to whom we owe our gratitude. He is not a member of our parish. He is not even a Catholic. He owes us nothing, yet he has worked for months, many times late into the night. And, may God bless him, he has done it all out of charity and generosity and for the love of art. He did not charge us a single zloty. He is a godsend for our parish." Applause echoed off the ancient walls.

Father Jaworski puffed up his chest and said, "And now it is the time we have all waited for." He nodded to Louis, who reached up, untied the ropes and pulled down the drop cloth. For a moment the church was silent but for gasps of awe. Then, slowly at first, and mounting in intensity, the church filled with a thunderous applause. The Virgin Mary stood high in all her radiance. There was not a sign of damage. No cracks, no chips. Even the colors were blended true to the original. A line quickly formed to appreciate the work.

"It is a miracle," Lucya said.

Louis blushed and shook his head. "No, just some cement and glue and paint and time."

Lucya extended her arm. "I want you to look around, at our parishioners, at the smiles on their faces. True, she's only a statue, only a representation, but she touches the depths of their faith. You have not only restored a work of art, you have spurred a heightened sense of spirituality at a time when many question their faith. They believe, as do I, that God sent you to us in a time of need. Both you and Eli."

She bent down to talk to Izaak. "You can be very proud of your father and your uncle. They are a blessing." Izaak smiled and hid his face behind his father. She spoke quietly to Eli. "We have made a connection here. A bridge. Let's keep it open. Please come and visit from time to time. I will do the same. Times are perilous. Keep me in mind."

❧

Eli and Izaak left the church and went straight to the clinic. It was the end of Esther's shift and they intended to walk home with her. Izaak couldn't wait to tell her all about his uncle and his new friends at the Catholic church. He had a bounce in his step.

"She's not here," a nurse said. "Esther didn't come in today. I hope she's feeling all right."

Eli was shocked. "Not here? I thought she was working today. Maybe I misunderstood her schedule." Eli turned to leave but paused. "She seemed fine this morning. Are you sure she's not in the back with some patient?"

"I think I would know, Eli. She's not here."

Eli was confounded. He didn't like surprises or sudden changes in plans. Especially these days. He felt uneasy. "Okay. It must be my mistake," he said, but he didn't believe it. Something was wrong. He took Izaak by the hand and walked directly home.

"Mama," Izaak yelled when he burst into the house. "Mama, I went to a church. Uncle Louis was the star. He fixed their statue. They all clapped for him. Mama? Mama?" There was no answer. "Mama?" he yelled again. Nothing but silence.

"Esther? Klara?" Eli called. No response.

Eli quickly searched the house. It was almost evening. If Esther wasn't at work, she would have been at home. She would have been starting something for dinner. "Esther? Klara?"

Izaak pointed to Esther's coat hanging in the closet. "She doesn't have her coat, Papa. She'll get cold."

Eli's mind raced through all the possible reasons why Esther and Klara were not where they should have been. He went outside and walked around the house to see if she was in the garden. Spring flowers were blooming, and she might be picking a few for the dinner table. Esther loved fresh flowers. Maybe she had run to the store at the last minute for a missing ingredient. But Izaak was right: she didn't take her coat. And where was Klara?

Eli stood on the walk in the front of his house, his mind in a whirl, when the elderly man who lived across the street called out, "Eli, they're gone."

A jolt ran through Eli. "What happened?"

"They were here earlier," he said. "The Jew Hunters. They took her and every woman on this street. I saw them pull your wife out of the house, and also the smaller woman, and they put them into a truck."

Eli picked up Izaak, put him under his arm and ran all the way to the brickyard. "Papa," he yelled as he entered the office. "Papa, they grabbed Esther and Klara. They came while we were at the church and took every woman on our street. I'm going off to find her. Watch Izaak."

"Stop, Eli. You're not thinking clearly. Who grabbed her?"

"My neighbor said it was the Jew Hunters."

"That would mean it was the ORPO, the German Order Police. I have heard they are rounding up people to take to work camps."

"I have to go find her."

"Where would you go, Eli? Even if you knew the location, what would you do? Would you fight the police?"

Tears welled up in Eli's eyes. His nerves were on fire. "I have to do something. They've taken my wife."

"I think we both know the answer: it's Maximilian. If he doesn't know where she is today, he can find out tomorrow. As much as I hate to say it, we need Maximilian to keep his promise."

"You're right, I'll go straight to city hall. He has an office there."

Jakob shook his head. "No, son, it's a Sunday, and evening is approaching. He won't be there. Besides, I doubt you'd get close to Globočnik's city hall."

"Then what are you saying? Do nothing?"

"Don't we know Maximilian's home address?"

Izaak was holding tightly to Eli's trousers. Eli stooped down and gently said, "Izzie, I'm going to find Mama. I want you to stay here with Grandpa." Izaak's lips were quivering, and his eyes were full of tears. "I don't want to stay," he said. "I want to find Mama, too."

Eli hugged him tightly. "I know you do, but I need for you to stay with Grandpa for a little while."

Maximilian lived in a large house that had been confiscated from its Jewish owners three months previous. Eli knew that Maximilian lived there with his new girlfriend, a seventeen-year-old brunette. The circumstances of that union were unclear, but many feared that she wasn't there because she was fond of Maximilian. Eli took the delivery truck and drove straight to the house. He rapped on the door, yelling "Maximilian, open up. It's Eli."

The door swung partially open, and Maximilian stood in the doorway in his shorts and stocking feet. He was clearly annoyed. "What in the world are you doing here, Eli?"

"Esther. They took Esther and Klara this afternoon. The Jew Hunters."

"Hmm," Maximilian mumbled and nodded his understanding. "That could be. I heard they would be working in your part of town. They're rounding up laborers for the workshops they built at Lindenstrasse." He gestured off to the south. "You know, Lipowa Street. We've opened sewing shops making clothing for the army. They need women."

"*We've* opened?"

"You know what I mean. The bosses at headquarters have opened them. Not me personally."

"You knew they were going to sweep my neighborhood and you didn't tell me?"

"I didn't know they would take Esther. They're supposed to leave her alone."

"Well, then, put on your shoes. We're going to get her."

Maximilian glanced back where a young woman stood in a semi-transparent nightgown. He shook his head. "Not tonight. I'll look into it tomorrow."

"You son of a bitch," Eli said through clenched teeth. "I swear I'll strangle you right here on this doorstep."

Maximilian was amused. "Really, then who would rescue your sweet Esther? Face it, Eli. You need me. I said I'll check into it tomorrow. There's nothing I can do tonight. The people I know won't be in until tomorrow morning."

"You don't understand. Esther is a sweet, gentle woman. These Nazis are animals. They abuse women like Esther and her sister."

"They have her sister, too?"

Eli nodded. "Klara."

Maximilian raised his eyebrows and whistled softly. "That makes the assignment doubly difficult. Getting one person out is hard enough, but two? I can tell you right now it'll take some money. I might have to grease the wheels, if you know what I mean."

"You bastard. You saw it coming and let it happen. You were supposed to protect us."

"That is a decidedly unfair accusation, Eli, but I'll overlook it, given your current hysteria. I knew nothing of Esther's selection. I have always sought to protect the Rosens. Do you still live in your home? Do you go to work every day? Give me some credit. Get some money together and meet me at the brickyard first thing tomorrow morning. I can't guarantee anything—you know the way those Nazis are—but I'll see what I can do."

CHAPTER THIRTEEN

LUBLIN, POLAND

APRIL 1940

Tomorrow morning could not come soon enough. The wait seemed interminable. Whatever patience Eli possessed had long since abandoned him. Every muscle in his body was tied in a knot. He paced back and forth, a hyena trapped in a cage. He checked the wall clock every few minutes, urging the hands to move more quickly. He was disturbed that little Izaak had borne witness to his father's panic; there was an observable chink in the armor. How would his son process his father's vulnerability? As it was, Izaak was too frightened to be left alone in his bed and he fell asleep on the couch.

Eli opened the icebox for a glass of water only to see the Sunday dinner that Esther had planned to cook. He walked into the dark living room and sat in the overstuffed chair, remembering the day that Esther was so excited to find it at the little store.

"Everything I do has you written on it, Essie," he said aloud. "You're a part of every breath I take, every dream I ever had." He clenched his fists. "Esther, sweetheart, hang on. I'm coming for you. I promise."

At 5:00 a.m. he could wait no longer, and he left for the brickyard. He put Izaak in the office and pulled up a folding chair to wait outside the doorway. Maximilian didn't arrive until ten o'clock. He casually strolled up wearing an expensive, fur-trimmed Chesterfield topcoat, new shoes and a felt hat, tipped slightly to the right. Sartorial elegance. A portrait of confidence. It only served to magnify Eli's anger.

"Do you have what I need?" Maximilian said with an air of aloofness.

"Here's a thousand zloty," Eli said, handing Maximilian an envelope.

Maximilian shrugged. "Hmm. I hope it's enough. A thousand Polish zloty doesn't go very far these days. Stay here. As soon as I know something, I'll come back."

~

Maximilian returned two hours later. "I was right, of course. She was taken to Lindenstrasse, to a sewing facility. I believe the workers there are sewing military uniforms."

"Well, where is she?"

He scoffed. "Did you hear what I said? At Lindenstrasse. Sewing."

"You were supposed to get her out and bring her here," Eli said. "I gave you a thousand zloty. Where is she?"

"Sewing, Eli, and you can put away that Rosen arrogance. It won't do you any good. I am your only hope. I'll go at four o'clock, when her shift is over. I can't walk into a working factory in the middle of the day and pull a worker off her shift."

"This is my wife, damn it. She doesn't have a *shift*."

"She does now. Four o'clock, Eli. I'll bring her to you."

"Four o'clock, and you'll do what's necessary to see that she's finished sewing at Lipowa."

"I'm afraid it's not that easy. These women have been assigned to positions at a workshop and the assignment is permanent, not temporary, not hourly. Every day, seven days a week. Their names are written on a permanent labor record and Globočnik reviews it. The Lipowa camp has a commandant and he also reviews it. It's written in stone, Eli."

"I don't want her there."

"Would you rather she be sent to Burggraben? That's where they're sending a lot of the recruited workers."

"Recruited?"

Maximilian snickered. "Sort of, in a way."

Eli's right arm shot out, grabbed Maximilian by the lapels of his fur-trimmed Chesterfield overcoat, lifted him off the ground and shoved him back into the wall. "You son of a bitch, don't you dare make light of this. Don't you dare give me a smirk. This is my wife! You promised to protect us. We gave you our business and twelve thousand five hundred worth of *prepayment* to be our protector, remember? This morning I gave you an extra thousand zloty."

"Hey! Get your hands off me. Put me down. I'm trying to help you."

Eli held him for a moment in a tense grip, exhaled and let him down. "I want my wife at home. Do you understand?"

Maximilian brushed off his coat as though Eli's hands had been full of dust. "I don't appreciate your attitude, Eli. Not one bit. I did a real favor for you today. Esther's going to come home tonight and every night after her shift. Do you know what that means? She has home privileges. Almost all of the other women are confined to the Lipowa barracks. They have to eat the commissary food there. One meal a day. They don't get to come home at the end of the day to a fancy house and a big nutritious meal. To their husbands and their sons. They may never come home."

"I don't want Esther sewing clothes for Nazis. You have to get her out of that job. She works at the clinic. She's a nurse."

Maximilian gave a quick shake of his head. "Well, now she's a seamstress. The Jewish clinic means nothing to Globočnik. He doesn't care if it's open or shut; it caters to Jews. At this time, sewing is the best thing that can happen for Esther. Just yesterday, General Globočnik ordered that ten thousand Jews be immediately deported from Lublin to shops in other towns because he said that too many Jews live too close to his headquarters in his city."

"His city? Jews in his city? If you're talking to me, you can stop talking like a Nazi. We're not some species called 'Jews'—we're *people,* citizens of Lublin, just like you, no better, no worse, mothers and fathers and children. Don't you dare depersonalize Jewish people in my presence."

"Well, it's a descriptive term. Especially in 1940."

Eli moved forward. His words came through clenched teeth. "Did you hear me?"

Maximilian backed up. "Okay, they're people, citizens of Lublin, does that make a difference? These citizens are going to be sent to work camps far away. Some of these women are going to be working underground in munitions factories. I've managed to keep Esther in Lublin, where she can go home at night. You should be kissing me on the lips for that."

"Where do I go to pick up Esther and Klara at four o'clock?"

"I'm not positive about Klara yet. I'm having trouble getting her released. I may need to drop another thousand on her supervisor. How important is she to you; after all, she's just a sister-in-law?"

Eli's nostrils flared, and before he could respond, Maximilian said, "Okay, okay, I get it. She's important. Hey, don't blame me for the question. Sisters-in-law aren't *always* so important." He forced a chuckle. "But I'll get her home privileges, too. It'll just take another thousand."

Eli went into the office, withdrew another thousand zloty from the safe and handed the roll to Maximilian. "Where do I go at four o'clock?"

"Let me bring them to you. You won't get near Lipowa without getting arrested. I'll bring them home to you at four o'clock. You can trust me."

ᳱ

At four thirty, a small German staff car pulled up in front of Eli's residence. Maximilian opened the back door to let Esther and Klara out. They were both attired in uniforms—formless gray cotton shifts. Esther ran to Eli, who wrapped her in his arms. He started to ask, "Essie, how . . ." She put her finger on his lips and tipped her head toward Klara. "We're all right. Maximilian drove us home. We'll talk later." Eli glanced at Klara, visibly distraught, her mouth open, her eyes wide, her hair in tangles; the image of an institutionalized patient in a state of shock. Eli put his arms around both of them, and repeated, "It's all right. We're all home now." Maximilian smiled at Eli, waved, tipped his hat and drove off.

No words were exchanged for the first hour. The women bathed and changed their clothes. Esther busied herself making dinner. Klara sat motionless on the couch. Finally, Esther said, "Where's Izaak?"

"He's with my father."

"We'll have to make arrangements for his care during the day. Klara and I need to be back at the shop before seven. Our hours are seven to four every day. We were warned not to be late."

"Maximilian is going to try to get you released from that job."

"Maximilian? What can he do? He saw us walking home and he drove us the rest of the way."

"Well, for starters, he managed to get you home privileges. You don't have to live in the barracks like the other women."

Esther had a puzzled expression. "Home privileges? Eli, the women who live in Lublin all go home at night. The only ones who are forced to live in the barracks are prisoners and Jewish women who have arrived from other towns."

"I gave the bastard two thousand zloty . . ."

Suddenly, Klara moaned, a long mournful tone that came from deep inside, and she stared at the ceiling with vacant eyes. "My arm," she cried, "you're twisting my arm. You're hurting me."

Esther and Eli rushed over to her. "It's okay, Klara, I'm here with you now," Esther said. "No one is hurting your arm." She turned to Eli. "The ORPO yanked her up into the truck by her arm. They were rough with us."

"I'm not going back there!" Klara announced. "I'm not working for the Nazis. They killed my Milosz. They abducted my Bonnie. They're rapists, they're sadists and murderers!" Then she broke into sobs.

"Klara, it's just a job," Esther said gently. "It's just sewing. A simple job. If that's all that happens, we can survive it. Sooner or later this war will end. Wars always do. Maybe the British and the French will prevail on the battlefield, or force a truce. We just need to survive until then."

Klara's body shook in Esther's arms. "I can't do it. I can't take orders from demons. They are the devil's envoys. They scream all day. They push us to work harder and faster. They throw garments at us. How do we survive that?"

"Because we have to."

CHAPTER FOURTEEN

"Esther and Klara left for Lipowa again this morning," Eli said, standing in the brickyard office with his father and Louis. "It's slave labor—nothing more, nothing less. Their guards could just as well be Egyptian overseers with whips. Esther tells me that the conditions are intolerable. The shop is dirty, the air is full of dust and cloth particles and the guards who supervise them are cruel."

"Esther is a strong woman."

"That she is, and she is better able to adjust than Klara, at least in the short term. Klara has exhausted whatever emotional stability she possessed. She cries all the time. Just last night at dinner, she started sobbing and bolted from the table. I don't know how to explain this all to Izaak."

"He's not blind, Eli," Jakob said. "He sees what's going on. He tells me about it when you bring him here in the morning. We talk. He's a smart boy."

"More people are arriving every day, and many are being sent to Lipowa," Louis said. "Carpenters, ironworkers, woodworkers. They want men to work in the tannery. The *Judenrat* is employing every available resource to absorb these new workers into our community. People are rounded up in the outlying villages as though they were wild horses. They arrive here with nothing but the shirts on their backs. Some of them are sent into the Lipowa camp, and they're not allowed to leave. The rest are left to find housing and provisions in our community. The *Judenrat* is overwhelmed. Right now, we're collecting clothing and shoes for them. We're doing everything we can."

"Everything you can?" Maximilian said, with a mocking laugh as he walked into the office. "Oh, the generous and hardworking *Judenrat*. Tell us what happened to the group last month, Louis, the ones your fancy *Judenrat* turned away from *your community*."

Eli looked quizzically at his brother.

"It's true," Louis said solemnly. "Thirteen hundred arrived in Lublin in February. They were Jewish prisoners of war brought in by train from another camp. The Nazi command told us, 'Here, take them in and provide for them. They're your responsibility.' Our chairman called an emergency meeting. It was a heated night, a lot of hollering. Finally, the *Judenrat* decided to make a stand, to show a modicum of resistance, a trace of courage, and force the Nazis to provide for the new arrivals. Otherwise, we felt they would flood our city with thousands of homeless people and we would be overwhelmed. We issued an official statement to the Nazis: 'We can't take them in. Our resources are spent. We have no room, you brought them here, it's your responsibility, you provide for them.'"

"Good God, Louis."

Louis closed his eyes. "Our collective judgment was poor. It was a bad mistake. The Nazis turned right around and marched them north, on foot, all the way to Biała Podlaska, a hundred and twenty kilometers away. There were over a thousand prisoners, and they were forced to follow Nazi guards on horseback. It was snowing. Freezing. The horses walked quickly. People stumbled, they lagged behind, and if they fell in the snow, they were shot. Only two hundred made it to Biała Podlaska. There's no shifting the blame here, Eli. It was all on us. The *Judenrat*'s decision condemned those people. We'll never do that again, no matter how crowded it gets. Now we gather clothing and shoes, and we take care of new arrivals the best we can."

Maximilian stepped forward. "You said you wanted to see me, Eli."

"I want you to get Esther and Klara out of the sewing factory."

"Of course you do."

"Workers come and go. Esther tells me that there was substantial absenteeism this week. Two of the girls were missing from their desks in Esther's section, and Klara said three were missing in her section. If the requirements are so lax, why can't we get Esther and Klara off the list altogether?

You can do it, Maximilian. You have the connections. Just erase them from the list."

Maximilian shook his head. "General Globočnik has issued a standing order to the Lipowa camp commandant, Sturmbannführer Hermann Dolp. If a worker misses work or does not come in on time, she is to be considered a scofflaw, and Dolp is directed to punish that worker. Severely. If she fails to arrive, he is to send the Jew Hunters out to find her and to arrest the members of her family as well. They are all to be punished. Globočnik has given Commandant Dolp authority to hang them all in the yard as an example to the others. I've seen the order. It's harsh, but effective."

"Well, despite that order, there were at least five girls missing yesterday. Why can't Esther and Klara be considered missing and written off the list?"

"Esther was misinformed. Those five women were not missing. They did not skip work. Did you hear of the incident on Reichsstrasse?"

Eli shook his head. "What is Reichsstrasse?"

"Before the Germans changed the name, it was the Krakowskie Przedmieście, where the fine restaurants and cafés are located. I'm sure you've eaten there many times ..."

"We don't go there anymore, Maximilian. It's off-limits. *Juden verboten*."

"Hmm. That's true. You wouldn't want to be there, anyway. It's filled with SS and Gestapo now. The street has become a Nazi night spot. Lublin's Moulin Rouge." He snickered. "Anyway, Brigadeführer Globočnik and his staff were dining at Café Chopin three nights ago. It's a lovely, quaint little café on the Reichsstrasse that Germans have become very fond of. It serves fine French ..."

"I'm familiar with the café, Maximilian. What happened?"

"Globočnik ordered soup, lentil I believe. When the server brought the soup, one of the general's staff put his hand out. 'Halt,' he said. 'I smell monkshood.'"

"Monkshood?"

"It is a poisonous plant. Very deadly. Quick-acting. The Germans have been using it to coat bullets and to poison water supplies. Globočnik's lieutenant thought he detected the scent of monkshood when the soup was placed on the table. Globočnik became incensed and demanded that the entire restaurant staff be brought to his table. He challenged the chef to sit and consume the bowl of soup. The chef was terrified, which only served to confirm Globočnik's suspicions. His lieutenant forced the chef into a chair and placed a bowl of soup before him. The chef ate the soup with no ill effects, but Globočnik wasn't satisfied. 'Bring another,' he commanded. With the entire kitchen staff standing at attention behind the chef, the poor man, shaking like a leaf, was forced to consume five bowls of soup until he retched all over the floor, whereupon Globočnik said 'Aha!' and had them all taken into custody for questioning."

"What happened to them?"

"Some died during questioning."

"How many died during questioning?"

"All of them, I'm afraid."

"What does that have to do with the five missing women?"

"Globočnik was still suspicious of a plot. He decided to question the families as well."

"And the five women?"

Maximilian hung his head. "They died during questioning."

Eli shut his eyes. "Then I pray for the souls of those victims and I pray for the success of the resistance. I'd like nothing more than to see Globočnik's head on a spike."

"I would watch my tongue if I were you."

"I want you to arrange for the release of Esther and Klara. Not absent, not missing. Their names are to be erased from the employment list. You're an important guy, Maximilian. You can do it."

Maximilian smiled. "Well, I do have some influence; you're right about that. Sturmbannführer Dolp has become a close friend of mine. He's a jolly fellow in the tavern, quite different from his demeanor at the Lipowa camp, where he's a maniac. He whips workers that look at him the wrong way."

"How do you know him?"

"We share a few cognacs now and then. You know, in the cafés on Reichsstrasse."

"So you go out drinking with Commandant Dolp?"

"Oh yes, and can he drink. Hoo boy."

"Everyone needs money, Maximilian, even sturmbannführers. What will it take? I want my wife and her sister out of his shops."

"That's a tall order, Eli. If not handled delicately, yours truly might find himself in a work camp. Or subject to questioning. It would require all my social skills to accomplish such a feat. But . . . if we have a few drinks . . . and he's feeling no pain . . ."

"How much, Maximilian?"

"Hmm." He made twisting movements with his lips and clicking noises with his tongue as he considered the question. "To get them released . . . it would have to be at least ten thousand."

"Come in tomorrow; I'll give you the money. You better not disappoint me."

❧

Eli pulled Esther aside after dinner. "How is Klara tonight?"

"Not well; she's in her room again. After work, she goes straight in and closes the door, only to come out for dinner, and she doesn't eat much of that. I tell her that our lives are different now, that she has to get used to it, that she has to adjust. She asks me how well the Israelites adjusted to Pharaoh's slave masters? Did they get used to being whipped?"

"Fair question."

"She's walking a thin line, Eli. I'm worried. It won't take much to push her over the edge. This afternoon, she asked her guard for permission to go to the bathroom. We are allowed one break per nine-hour shift. The bathroom is a public facility outside in the yard, and it's cold. Her request was rejected because her section had a bathroom break in the morning. She told her guard that she didn't have to go in the morning, but now she did. He wouldn't let her. He laughed at her. He told her to plan her day better, to make sure she goes whenever her section gets the privilege. Can you imagine having to justify your need to urinate to some Nazi heathen? She ended up wetting herself, Eli. It was so humiliating for her."

"Can you help her at all during the day? Do you see her at break?"

"No. We're in different sections. Different buildings."

"I'm working on something, Essie. Maximilian believes he may be able to get you released. He says he's close to the commandant."

"Sturmbannführer Dolp? The man's cruelty is beyond description. He's not about to release anyone."

"Maximilian says he has influence, that they drink together."

"Maximilian's full of crap. You know that. Don't fall into his trap. He took money from you before."

"I gave him money to get you home privileges. You do come home every night."

"Not because of Maximilian."

"Maximilian thinks he might be able to get you removed from the list."

"You're throwing your money away."

"Money means nothing if you're not here with me. I would give him all my money if it would ensure your safety."

Esther raised up on her tiptoes to give Eli a hug and a kiss. "You know, I love you. More than anything."

"I love you ten times more."

"If you can do it, we have to get Klara out as well."

"I know. I told Maximilian."

"Although it pains me to say so, I will pray for Maximilian's success. My sister will not last much longer."

"Should we let Klara know? It might lift her spirits. Maybe she'll see a light at the end of the tunnel, and it'll give her some strength."

"And what if he fails? What if Maximilian proves himself to be a fraud again? I don't think Klara could handle the disappointment. I'll tell her that you're working with Maximilian and we have hope, but it's only a possibility."

"That's wise. It may not happen right away, in any case. Maximilian told me that Dolp had left the camp and wasn't expected to return for a couple of weeks."

Esther shook her head. "Maybe we should move up the time for our escape. I have no faith in Maximilian. Today we come home, but what about tomorrow? Things get worse by the day. Winter has ended; the snows have melted. That was our target date. Let's go now."

Eli did not respond immediately.

"What?"

"Maximilian told us that Globočnik issued a firm order to Commandant Dolp. If a woman does not come to work, the Jew Hunters are to search for her, arrest her and her entire family. The penalty is death by hanging. If we leave, they will search for us. We'd put Izzie at risk, and we will have also condemned my father and Louis's entire family."

"Then we are doomed either way."

CHAPTER FIFTEEN

❦

Though it was forbidden, Eli kept a shortwave radio hidden in the cellar. Late at night, he would scan the airwaves. He listened to reports of Nazi bombers over England and Soviet massacres in Ukraine. He learned of Germany's invasion of France on May 10 and Brussels on May 17. He learned that the Soviet Union had occupied the Baltic countries and installed puppet governments in Lithuania, Latvia and Estonia.

Esther walked downstairs and handed a cup of coffee to Eli. She stood behind him and placed her hand gently on his shoulder. "What do you hear tonight, my husband?"

"Nazi tanks are rolling down the Champs-Élysées. All Europe is a giant battlefield yet again. The dead lie everywhere." He shook his head. "Peace in Central Europe is an intermittent condition, merely a pause before the next war."

"What is the rest of the world saying, Eli? The other eighty percent of the globe? Do they not condemn Hitler? What do you hear?"

He shook his head again. "Outside of Europe, it doesn't seem like the rest of the world is paying attention. I hear music playing in the American ballrooms. Brazilian restaurants are opening, and Argentine politicians are arguing about tax reform."

"Do they say nothing about Poland, about Jews being snatched off the streets to be sent to far-off labor camps? Do they broadcast news of Nazis hunting down Jews like the seventeenth-century slave hunters? Are those stories not on the airwaves?"

"Sometimes they are, and from time to time I hear sympathetic speeches, but to the people who live in distant countries, Poland may as well be on the moon. Their lives are far away and unaffected."

"What has become of Maximilian since you gave him ten thousand zloty? That was several weeks ago. At the shop, there is much talk. German demands for slave labor are high, and the Lipowa shops are now working around the clock making clothing and other supplies for the army. Extraordinary pressure is being applied to the seamstresses."

Eli stood and embraced his wife. "I know, and I'm so sorry for you and Klara. It breaks my heart. I feel so helpless. I wish there was something I could do."

"It isn't so much for me, Eli. I am worried about my sister. She's trying her best to hold it together, but every day she slips a little further. She has a faraway look in her eyes. She keeps asking about Maximilian. I told her you were working with him. She asks why is it taking so long?"

"She's right. It has been too long. Ever since I gave him the money, Maximilian's been scarce. He needs to account. I'll go see him in the morning."

⁓

Maximilian had taken to leading the gentleman's life, partying deep into the predawn hours, and Eli knew it was a safe bet he would be at home at ten in the morning, sleeping one off. Eli parked the company truck at the curb and banged on the door. Once again, Maximilian opened it, partially dressed, and once again there was a young girl standing in the background in her lingerie. This girl seemed younger than the one before.

Eli stared at the young girl. "That's Sophie Schlossberg," Eli said. "She's fifteen years old. What the hell is she doing here?"

"Well, I could tell you that it's none of your business," Maximilian said, with his arms crossed on his chest, "but her mother asked me if I could provide for her safety. She's living here for the time being."

"Living here with you? She's a young girl and she's in nightclothes, Maximilian. For God's sake."

Sophie hung her head and turned the other way.

"She's not in a labor camp, is she? What do you want this morning, Eli?"

"You know what I want. My wife and her sister are still working at that shithole. Why? I paid you to get them released."

Maximilian spread his hands in a gesture of helplessness. "And I gave Commandant Dolp the money three weeks ago, but wouldn't our luck have it? Dolp was reassigned. The new shop commandant is Horst Riedel. Your wife should have told you. Riedel has taken over and he is under watchful eyes. There is great demand from Berlin for increased production at Lipowa. Hitler's army is now eight million men. They need clothing and arms to fight the war, and shops like Lipowa are required to put out as much product as is humanly possible. Tardiness and absenteeism are capital offenses. The Jew Hunters are dispatched to bring in missing workers. Sadly, hangings have become all too frequent in the Lipowa courtyard. Nobody dares to be late. Entire families have been executed. No worker is to be released for any reason. Commandant Riedel's orders. He's the new boss. What can I do?"

"Listen, I don't give a damn who the new boss is. Dolp has my ten thousand and I want my wife released."

"Dolp isn't running the show anymore, Eli. He's not even in Lublin anymore. Personally, I think Dolp will return and replace Riedel, but I'm not sure when. No one seems to know."

"Did you give Dolp my ten thousand or did you keep it?"

"Oh, I gave it to him, of course. Why is it always your first impulse to accuse me?"

"Then Dolp has to make it right or return the money."

Maximilian chuckled. "Are you serious? Hermann Dolp return money? That's laughable. These people are not like you and me, Eli. They're Nazis— they run the world and they know it. Dolp is not about to return money. Truth be told, he probably drank it all. Should he return and replace Riedel, I can appeal to him to honor his bargain and release your wife. But I wouldn't count on it."

"Stop with the stories and the excuses. I want my wife and her sister out of Lipowa now! I paid you ten thousand to get that done. I personally don't give a damn who the commandant is. If you can't do it with Dolp or Riedel, find some other way. As far as I'm concerned, it's your responsibility and you're on the hook."

Maximilian leaned forward and talked softly, as if some passerby might overhear. "Let's get our facts straight. You asked me to bribe a Nazi official to get your wife and your sister-in-law out of a work detail that almost every other able-bodied woman in Lublin is required to do. And because of my long-standing relationship with you and your father, and due to my unique abilities to ingratiate myself with the Nazi command and influence Commandant Dolp, I accepted the assignment. Not without considerable risk to me. The commandant's transfer was entirely unexpected and out of my control. I do not have the same relationship with Commandant Riedel. If you're lucky, I may cultivate one in the future. But I don't have it yet."

"What about my ten thousand zloty?"

"I think you have to face reality, Eli. The money's gone."

Eli's face turned bloodred. He grabbed Maximilian by the shoulders and pulled him outside. "I gave you that money to get something done. As you just said, you *accepted* the assignment. Now get it done. If it takes more money, then *you* go find it and fund it."

Maximilian lifted Eli's hands from his shoulders. "Remember this: I am your buffer—the only thing that stands between your family and the Nazis. You're still in your house, your wife comes home at night, your sister-in-law comes home at night and your brother's wife, Sylvia, comes home at night. No one in your family has been sent out of town to a distant labor camp. Your father, your brother—they still have jobs that pay a salary. The rest of Lublin is starving."

"My sister-in-law won't last. She's in the grip of a mental breakdown. If I tell her that she's never going to be released, she'll fall apart. What about getting her a medical leave of absence?"

"Will the hospital admit her? If she's in the hospital, then it could be viewed as an excused absence. Otherwise, there's nothing I can do."

"There's no chance that any Lublin hospital will admit Klara," Esther whispered softly in the kitchen. "Their beds are filled with patients who are near death. They have dysentery, they're malnourished, they suffer from typhus, vitamin deficiencies and a myriad of bacterial diseases. They suffer from war injuries. They have broken bones. There are children who sleep on the street and suffer from rodent bites. There is simply no room in any hospital for patients who suffer mental breakdowns."

"Then she's going to have to go to work every day," Eli said. "You'll have to talk to her and keep an eye on her. Let's try to stay positive and tell her that I'm still working with Maximilian."

"I can't keep an eye on her. She's in another building in a different section, but we walk to and from work, and I'll keep encouraging her. If she loses hope, there's no telling what she'll do. We can't let her lose hope."

One month later, in the swelter of a record-breaking July heat wave, when the internal temperature of the sewing factory soared to 110 degrees and the air was too thick to breathe, Klara lost hope. She was sitting at her station when she suddenly stopped, slumped down in her chair and stared forward in a catatonic state. Her coworker leaned over and asked if she was all right. She didn't answer. She urged Klara to pick up her garment and sew. She didn't move. The uniformed section guard caught sight of Klara's inactivity, hurried over and screamed at her. He shook her listless body so hard that her head flopped back and forth like a rag doll. Still, she would not respond. He lifted her out of her seat and dragged her into the courtyard, where she crumpled to the ground in a heap. He drew his leg back and kicked her as hard as he could with his steel-toed boot, breaking her ribs. She didn't cry. A shot rang out and they carried her body away.

Esther heard the shot. Everyone in the shop heard the shot, and it shook the women in the same manner that a sudden crack of lightning would. A single shot. Someone was killed. Keep on working.

Esther waited for Klara on the corner. It was their custom to meet every day at the end of the shift and walk home. On the way, Esther would listen to Klara. She was her sounding board. It was therapy. Klara would vent and it made her feel better. Esther would ultimately steer the conversation to other, more mundane topics. What should they make for dinner?

The women on the day shift were filing out of the shops and leaving the area and Esther waited. When Klara didn't appear, Esther feared the worst. A slender woman, much younger than Esther, approached. "Are you Klara's friend, the one she walks with?"

Esther nodded. Tears formed in her eyes. She didn't need to hear the rest. "I'm so sorry," the woman said. "Klara just gave up. So many of us feel the same way; we don't want to keep on going in this devil's furnace. We want to give up, too, but we don't have the courage. Klara just couldn't do it anymore. I shook her. I begged her." The woman hung her head. "I'm so sorry."

❧

Eli saw Esther walking alone and he knew. He rushed to her and wrapped her in his arms. "She's gone, Eli. My poor sister couldn't take it anymore, and now her suffering is done. Maybe it's for the best."

Eli looked for words, he stumbled through an "I'm sorry," but Esther stopped him. "There's nothing to say," she said. "I want her buried in the Jewish cemetery. Tell Maximilian to recover her body and bring it to the mortuary. I'll speak to the rabbi."

Eli anticipated that nothing would come of Maximilian's efforts to recover Klara's body, and he was right. The Nazis had no concern for Klara or her remains, and Maximilian reported that they disposed of her as they saw fit. He had obtained a two-hour excused absence from Commandant Riedel for Esther to attend a memorial service. That was the best that he could do.

CHAPTER SIXTEEN

❦

FÖHRENWALD

FÖHRENWALD DISPLACED PERSONS (DP) CAMP
AMERICAN ZONE
JULY 1946

Since the camp committee meeting the previous month, there had been no further mention of the black marketeer who called himself Max. Camp residents had been urged to report any information to Bernard Schwartz, director elect, but no one had come forward, and Bernard was forced to consider that the rumor of visas for sale was nothing more than a fairy tale.

Bernard knocked on Eli's door in the late afternoon. "I have two favors to ask of you, Eli. First, I need someone to ride with Daniel and me through the camp tonight. The butchers are at it again. We've learned that there will be a secret shipment of meat tonight. They'll be cutting it up and selling it tomorrow."

"Who are *they*?"

"Well, we're not sure this time. That's why we ride at four a.m. If the lights come on in a basement room, we'll know it's them and we'll bring in the camp police."

Eli nodded. "I'll go, but I have to tell you, selling meat to hungry residents does not seem like a capital offense to me. What is so wrong with butchering meat for people who can afford it? I assume the cows are lawfully purchased from area farmers. They're not poaching, are they?"

Schwartz shook his head. "No. They buy the cows from Bavarian ranchers.

Then they butcher them here in the camp in secret. All strictly kosher. Under a rabbi's supervision."

"Which rabbi?"

"We don't know yet. But, Eli, it is wrong and it's unfair. Most of our residents arrived at Camp Föhrenwald with nothing. Some were barely alive. You, of all people, would know that. When you and Izaak arrived a year ago, you were but a shadow of the man you are today. Föhrenwald relies on UNRRA to supply food and provisions. In fact, just today we received word that twenty-nine UNRRA ships left New York bound for European DP camps loaded with American food. When our share arrives, it will be distributed fairly. It's important that no one receives more than anyone else: three ounces of meat or fish per person per day, that's it. So you can understand when meat is sold in the dark of night for money or other property, it not only violates camp rules, it undermines our sense of community."

Eli nodded. "Okay, I understand. May I ask you something about last month's meeting?"

Bernard raised his eyebrows. "Pretty stormy, wasn't it?"

"Without a doubt," Eli said, "but . . ."

"The meetings get like that sometimes. There's a constant stress level in Camp Föhrenwald. People are frustrated. They want to know when they will be liberated from yet another camp, free to start their new lives. You can't blame them."

"No, I don't blame them, but at the meeting there was discussion about a man selling visas on the black market. Have we heard anything more specific about the operation, or the man who calls himself Max?"

"No. Daniel told me that you might know the man."

"Well, I might, and that's why I asked. I knew a man in Lublin who matched the description, but I was certain that he died in 1943."

"How were you certain?"

Eli shrugged. "I saw him being led away. He was a fixer, but he double-crossed the wrong people."

"A fixer?"

Eli nodded. "The lowest of his kind. Soon after the occupation, he made his contacts with Nazi officials. He was a rat. He scurried around our community snooping for the SS, denouncing Jews, ferreting out resisters, stocking the Nazi labor camps. Then he turned around and sold favors to the people. For a price, he could get you food when your rations were gone, keep you in your house when your neighbors were losing theirs or get you an ID exempting you from deportation."

"How did you know him?"

Eli scoffed. "My father gave him a job when he didn't have a coin in his pocket. We taught him to sell, and he was able to live a comfortable life. He became a dandy—the finest clothes, polished shoes, officious airs. He was totally unprincipled, a despicable person. During the occupation, we knew what he was, but when your back is up against the wall, and he is your only hope . . . well, you do what you have to do. Ultimately, he betrayed us all. If the person selling black market visas is indeed Maximilian, I will have my reckoning and I will get my answers. And that's a promise."

"We'll keep our eyes open, Eli. Whether it's your Max or not, we're going to put a stop to illegal sales. If you see him in the camp, let us know. And please don't take direct action. If this man is truly selling authentic U.S. visas, someone in America is supplying them. We need to know his source. We can't allow our emigration process to be corrupted. We owe it to our residents."

"What was the other favor you needed from me, Bernard?"

"Back in Lublin, you were in the construction trade, no?"

Eli nodded. "My family owned the brickyard. Rosen and Sons Building and Construction Materials. We were also concrete masons and carpenters. My father's company built a large portion of Lublin."

"Good," Bernard said. "I have need of your services and supervision. We are going to convert a storage building into an infirmary suitable for a sanitarium. There are now twenty-two people diagnosed with tuberculosis and under quarantine. We're facing an epidemic."

"Lord have mercy. Once they're under quarantine, how do we treat these people?"

"As Dr. Weisman said, we have no medicinal cure for tuberculosis. We treat the disease with rest, fluids and traditional remedies. In civilian areas, there are large sanitariums and some recover. Sadly, many do not. But we want to make our patients comfortable and separate them from the rest of the community. That's why we need you."

"I'll do whatever I can."

Bernard smiled, patted Eli on the back and walked away. Eli lingered in the doorway, gazing down the block at the building that would become a sanitarium. *A tuberculosis epidemic in a DP camp. Will our misfortunes never cease?*

CHAPTER SEVENTEEN

In a scarred and field-battered U.S. Army jeep, Bernard, Daniel and Eli motored slowly through the streets of Föhrenwald at 4:00 a.m. A light rain fell and played a staccato rhythm on the jeep's canvas top. The air was sweet and humid, rich with the scent of mountain pines. With the headlights off, Bernard drove carefully.

"What will you do if you see a basement light?" Eli asked.

Bernard held up a black walkie-talkie. "I'll contact the camp police. We'll arrest the butchers and bring them up before the Honor Court."

"Even the rabbi?"

"Especially the rabbi."

"And the meat?"

"We'll put it in the commissary and distribute it fairly. If this is Zygmund Stern's operation, it will be the third time we've caught him. Each time, he has vowed not to repeat his crimes, but he's not trustworthy. If he is the offender, I intend to bring him up for expulsion."

"I know Zygmund," Eli said. "His son is on Izaak's football team. He's really not a bad fellow."

"One does not cancel out the other," Daniel said in his deep gravelly voice. "He runs a black-market butcher shop to line his pockets. He does not butcher meat for benefit of our camp. He does not give to those in need. I hear the meat will be sold first to camp residents who can afford his price, and the leftovers sold to Germans who live in Wolfratshausen. The rations we receive from UNRRA are small. There are many who would benefit from larger portions of fish or meat. Myself for one."

After a few minutes, three figures came skulking around the side of a house and entered a warehouse building. "That's it," Bernard uttered, and radioed the police. "I wish we didn't have to do this. If it was cigarettes or an occasional bottle of vodka, I wouldn't give a damn. I'd look the other way. But hundreds of kilos of beef when people are hungry? That's criminal. Blatant profiteering. War always brings out the profiteers."

Eli heard shouting, the warehouse door opened and four men were led out by six camp policemen. "Rabbi Bernstein," Bernard said, with a look of disgust. "I wonder what they paid him to certify the beef. Let's go find out."

Eli, Daniel and Bernard walked up to the group. Zygmund, a large, barrel-chested man in a stained white apron, scowled and bitterly said, "Why don't you leave me alone? I am a butcher. I have a right to engage in my profession. What right do you have to stop me from cutting beef to feed my family?"

"I have the rights granted to me by our camp's constitution, by the UNRRA and the U.S. Army," Bernard said. "And who are we kidding? Are you going to feed your family two hundred kilos of beef, Zygmund? We have been through this with you on two other occasions. Now it ends. You and your associates will be brought before the Court of Honor. In your case, I will recommend expulsion. There will be no black-market meat at Camp Föhrenwald. Period."

Then Bernard turned his attention to the rabbi, who hung his head. "And you, Rabbi Bernstein. I would have expected much better. You're aiding a criminal."

"The meat is being butchered for Jewish families. It should be certified kosher," he said.

"And no doubt you donated your rabbinic services for the good of the camp?"

"I have nothing more to say."

Zygmund spat on the road. "Bah! I'm cutting meat. Does that make me a criminal? Is eating meat a crime?" He looked around. "Then we are all criminals. What about the bastard who's selling visas? That's far more serious. Why don't you arrest him?"

"I would in a split second. Can you identify him?"

Zygmund's eyes opened wide, and he rubbed the gray stubble on his jowl. A wide smile showed a mouth full of broad teeth. He glanced at his captors. "Perhaps I can. Does the director now wish to strike a bargain with the butcher?"

Bernard narrowed his eyes. "Hmm. What does the butcher have to offer?"

"Information. Cooperation. An exercise of good citizenship for which the butcher expects reciprocation."

"You are a scoundrel, Zygmund, not by any means a good citizen, but if you have useful information about the man who calls himself Max and you're willing to cooperate, we can talk."

Zygmund raised a pointed finger. "I have only met him once, but I can easily pick him out of a crowd. He came through the camp a couple of months ago, said his name was Max. He wanted twelve thousand Swiss francs or the equivalent in gold or jewelry for two visas, one for me and one for my wife. Six thousand per visa. Of course, I did not have the money, but I told him I could raise it. He patted me on the back and said that I would soon be on a ship to America. He said he would come back."

"When?"

"He said soon."

"Can you describe this Max?"

Zygmund puffed his ruddy cheeks and nodded. "Tall. Skinny. He had black hair, well combed. Pointy nose like a weasel. Dressed to the nines, fancy clothes."

Eli's muscles tightened and he swore under his breath. "That's him," he said to Bernard. "Maximilian Poleski. It's a perfect description. I want to be there when he returns."

"Let me off the butchering charge, Bernard," Zygmund said, "and I'll notify you as soon as he walks into camp."

Eli glared at him. "How do we know you won't take the visas and run?"

Zygmund scoffed. "And how would I pay him? Where would I get twelve thousand francs? Why do you think I was butchering meat? I was going to raise the money."

Bernard nodded. "Okay, this is what we're going to do. You're going to contact Max and tell him you have the money and you want your visas. Tell him you want to meet him and exchange the money for the visas as soon as possible."

Zygmund exhaled. "It's not easy to contact him. He gave me a mailing address in Munich. I will send a letter. Now what about the beef I'm cutting? It'll spoil."

"You're right. Finish butchering the meat and deliver it to the camp kitchen. No black market, no sales to any individual."

"Bernard, please," Zygmund said. "Have some compassion. We pooled our money and paid for that cow. Can't we get reimbursed? It's not fair."

"You're breaking my heart," Bernard said. "The committee will thank you publicly for your generous contribution. Good night."

The rain had stopped, and the skies had cleared. In an hour it would be dawn. Bernard and Eli walked back to the jeep.

"Do you really think all the meat will make it to the commissary?" Eli said.

Bernard smiled. "Not a chance. I suppose most of it will, but certainly not all. They'll sell some outside the camp to recoup their losses, but I think we've succeeded in putting a halt to Zygmund's black-market activities. So this is the same Maximilian that you knew from Lublin, is that right, Eli?"

Eli pursed his lips and gave a couple of quick nods. "I would never have believed it, but the description is accurate—skinny, pointy nose, black hair, fancy clothes. The fact that he could now be running loose in Europe is a testament to his resilience. He should be in the ground with a cross above his head or sitting on trial at Nuremberg."

"He's a Nazi?"

"A collaborator. He grew up on the streets of Lublin. When the Nazis came to town, he worked for them, he was paid by them, he spied for them and he did their dirty work. So as far as I'm concerned, he's as much a war criminal as the Nazis they are prosecuting. He preyed upon the Jews of Lublin, made a fortune scamming them and then betrayed them when it suited him. Sometimes he was the difference between life or death."

"He had that kind of influence?"

"He had connections, and he dangled those connections in the face of those who were desperate. He took their money or whatever they could give him, and he sold them hope. He delivered on those promises when it was convenient for him, and he apologized with a shrug when it was not. He would betray without hesitation to remain in good standing with the Nazis. I was certain he didn't survive the war, that he played fast and loose once too often. The last time I saw him, he was being led away."

"Where was this?"

"Lodz, Poland. If it is him, and if he comes around Föhrenwald, do not try to stop me, Bernard. I have unfinished business with him. He's mine before anyone else gets to him."

"I understand and I won't stand in your way, but I would ask that you be mindful of the value of interrogating Max, or Maximilian, or whatever his name is. We need to put a stop to black-market visas. Someone in the U.S., most likely a government official, is his source. We need to expose the American supplier, or he will only find another Max."

✤

Back at the house, as was his habit, Eli walked into the bedroom where Izaak was fast asleep. He bent to give him a kiss on the forehead. Izaak opened his eyes.

"Oh, I'm sorry I woke you," Eli said, taking a seat on the edge of his bed.

"I'm not sleeping so good tonight," Izaak said, and propped himself up on an elbow. "Tomorrow is Mama's birthday, and I just keep thinking about her." Tears filled his eyes.

Eli wrapped him up tight, holding him close to his chest and rubbing his hair. "I miss her too, Izzie."

"Do you suppose that she's all right? Somewhere? That maybe someday she'll find us here in Föhrenwald?"

Eli's lips quivered. "Sure. I mean, you and I survived, didn't we? There were thousands and thousands of German detention camps, and they were all liberated within the past year. Mama could be anywhere in Europe. We have to keep our hopes up."

"How would she know we're here in Föhrenwald?"

"The U.S. maintains lists of people in the American DP camps."

"Did you look at the lists? Is Mama on the list?"

"Izzie, I have asked. I am told she's not on the lists, but our names are."

"So then if she checks the lists, she'll know where we are?"

"Exactly."

"Where did the Germans take her?"

When Izaak steered the conversation in this direction, as he so often did, Eli was beset with a painful dilemma: how to juggle hope with reality. "With the other mothers, sweetheart. She went with the other mothers. I don't know exactly where they took them."

"Sometimes I think I hear her. Sometimes when the wind blows, I can hear her voice calling me."

Eli's throat tightened, and he strained to get the words out. "I can, too, Izzie. Almost every day. And when we hear her voice, we know she's near." He kissed him on the top of his head. "It's time to get back to sleep. There's a football game this afternoon."

"I know, and we don't have our best goalkeeper."

"Heschel? Is he hurt?"

"No, he moved. His family went to America."

Eli looked surprised. "They've only been here a couple of months, isn't that right?"

Izaak nodded. "They got lucky. They got visas to go to America."

Eli stood. "Pretty lucky—that's for sure. Now let's get some sleep."

"When will we get our visas, Papa?"

"Someday soon, I hope. We've made application and our names are on the list."

"Shouldn't we wait for Mama? If we went to America without her, how would she ever find us?"

Eli stood, blinked a few tears and kissed his son again. "So many questions, my boy. We will pray, we will keep our hopes high and we will trust that we'll all be together again." He started to walk when Izaak grabbed his arm. "Papa, explain something to me."

"What is it, Izzie?"

"America's a big country, right?"

"Oh, yes."

"Bigger than Poland?"

"Much bigger."

"And I've seen the movies, Papa. They have mountains and deserts and large open spaces where cowboys ride their horses."

Eli chuckled. "Oh, that's true. Where is this going?"

"I would think that America has plenty of room for people like us that want to move there."

"Well, you make a good point, my son, but it's not about the room."

"Then what is it? Why can't we move there? Why do we have to stay in a camp? Why won't they give everyone in Camp Föhrenwald a visa? I know America likes us, because we're living in an American camp. They made it for us. They bring in food and clothes. They're taking care of us.

So why make it so hard to move to America, where we could take care of ourselves?"

Eli looked at his son. The decade's great enigma, so formidable yet so simple that a child's logic cuts right through it. *What can I say to him? How can I explain immigration quotas to my twelve-year-old boy? How do I even broach the subjects of nationalism, distrust and prejudice?* He patted him on the head. "I wish I had the answer, Izaak, but it's late. Good night."

Eli sat with a cup of tea and stared out the window. The soft orange glow of dawn was rising over the Bavarian hills. "What am I supposed to say to him, Esther? He has questions that I'm not able to answer. I know you would tell me that we must move on with our lives. You were always that direct, always that practical. But Izaak and I are treading water here at Föhrenwald. How do we move on? He's a terrific kid who deserves more, and I'm not sure I can deliver.

"He asks about you, Esther, and I let him believe. I want to believe as well, but all this time and we haven't heard a word. People say that the toughest postwar dilemma is reuniting families. We are a broken people, and the pieces are scattered all over Europe. I don't want to lose hope, but I have to be realistic. Every day that passes brings more doubt. After what Izzie's been through these past four years, and as far as he's come, the progress he's made, how do I dare introduce a doubt and shatter his hope? He laughs, he plays with the other children, he believes in the future. And in Izaak's future, we are all reunited. What would it do to his psyche if he lost hope? Sooner or later, everyone has to face the truth. More people died than we can count.

"Talk to me, Esther. Am I a good father or am I a failure? I always looked to you. You were the wise one, the complete parent. I would stand to the side and watch you so effortlessly and lovingly guide our son in the right direction. How would you answer Izzie? I'm lost without you, sweetheart. Tell me."

Eli watched the sun rise, silhouetting the pines. "Visas!" he said aloud. "How did the Blitsteins get visas so quickly and we did not? We've been at Föhrenwald for almost a year. The Blitsteins just arrived in the spring. Did they enlist the services of Maximilian? Did he sell them a way out?"

CHAPTER EIGHTEEN

⌒

FÖHRENWALD DP CAMP
AMERICAN ZONE
AUGUST 1946

In the warmth of a mid-August morning, several workers stood waiting at the curb outside the storage building on Föhrenwald's Kentucky Street. Over the previous several days they had gutted the building and stripped it of its interior walls. It now stood as a two-story shell. A light-duty truck pulled up to the curb and the workers began to unload sheets of gypsum drywall and two-by-fours and carry them into the building. Eli, in his role as construction superintendent, had organized the men to transform the facility into a building suitable for a TB sanitarium.

At a recent committee meeting, it was reported that another eighteen residents had exhibited symptoms of tuberculosis and were now in quarantine. The meeting was tense. Many had come seeking answers. What could they do to prevent their families, and especially their children, from contracting the disease in such a tightly packed community? They felt trapped.

Dr. Weisman tried his best to calm their fears while remaining truthful. Reminding them that TB is spread by close contact with infected persons, he said, "We face a problem in that some people don't know they're infected. Inhaling TB bacteria into the lungs provides an environment for the bacteria to multiply, and the disease develops rapidly. Sometimes, our body's defenses, our immune systems, will fight off the infection, and the person will not contract the illness, but let's face it, many of our people come here with weakened immune systems."

"How do we avoid breathing the air?" an angry mother asked. "There are six thousand people jammed into eight square blocks. My family's healthy. Why can't the healthy ones move to a different camp?"

Dr. Weisman sadly shook his head. "I'm sure you can understand that other camps don't want an infectious disease transmitted into their area. Some of us may think that we're healthy, but we may be carriers. We may have what they call latent TB."

"What about medicines?" a man asked. "Are we getting the best treatments here?"

Dr. Weisman took a folded letter out of his pocket. "I sent this message to USFET, the U.S. Forces European Theater, asking for medical supplies, and I marked it urgent. I said, 'Our confinement is a principal factor of physical disease and mental fatigue. We have nowhere to go and are at the mercy of UNRRA and U.S. Command in the American Zone. We need help.' I sent that two days ago, and I am waiting for a reply."

As many of the residents knew, Weisman's plea was practically a restatement of the report sent to President Truman the previous summer by Earl G. Harrison, U.S. Commissioner of Immigration and Naturalization. Truman had dispatched Harrison to the American Zone to evaluate and report how the needs of displaced persons were being met. Among his findings, Harrison reported, "There is a marked and serious lack of medical supplies."

Harrison urged the president to immediately issue immigration certificates to resettle the Jewish displaced persons. He wrote, "The civilized world owes it to this handful of survivors to provide them with a home where they can again settle down and begin to live as human beings." In an oft-quoted conclusion, Harrison stated, "We appear to be treating the Jews as the Nazis treated them, except we do not exterminate them."

Newspapers reported that Truman was shocked with Harrison's report, and in response he issued the "Truman Directive," instructing Immigration and Naturalization to give preference to displaced persons. However, as of 1946 the quotas remained in place, and in the year following the directive, fewer than ten thousand U.S. visas were issued, despite the requests of 250,000 displaced Jews. Britain still held tight to its prewar Palestine quota. Thus, with the number of tuberculosis cases approaching an epidemic, there was little the Föhrenwald community could do other than try to avoid exposure or hope for effective medical assistance.

Eli found himself conflicted, torn between his obligations as a leader to remain in the Föhrenwald community and his responsibilities as a parent to find a way out before Izaak became ill.

CHAPTER NINETEEN

FÖHRENWALD DP CAMP
AMERICAN ZONE
AUGUST 1946

Bernard asked Eli to join him at the camp administration office. He had received new information about Max and the black-market visas. Two residents were already seated when Eli arrived. Bernard made the introduction. "I believe you know Chaim and David." Eli nodded. "I'll let Chaim begin."

Chaim was a gaunt man, and when he spoke, he had a habit of rubbing his clean-shaven chin as though he had a beard. "Recently there was a bulletin circulated in the camp. It described a man named Max and warned us not to transact business with him, but by the time I read the bulletin, it was too late."

"You paid money to Max to get you a visa?" Eli asked.

"Not money. I had some jewelry: a ring, a sapphire pin, my wife's wedding ring. I managed to keep those items through the war by sewing them into the lining of my jacket. I offered the stones to Max."

"And in exchange, he promised to get visas for you and your wife?" Eli asked.

Chaim lowered his head. "Just me. There's only me. My Mildred didn't make it. I have a cousin in Philadelphia. That's all the family I have left."

"I'm sorry," Eli said.

A tear rolled down Chaim's cheek. "Mildred was murdered in December 1941 outside Riga. I didn't protect her; I wasn't even there at the time.

I had been sent to a labor camp, a quarry in Latvia. While I was gone, the people in the Riga ghetto, all of them, they were taken to the Rumbula forest . . . and they were . . ."

"We know, Chaim," Bernard said softly. "We know what happened in Rumbula."

"In a pit, Bernard. In an open pit, for God's sake. Fifteen thousand Jews in one day! My sons and my daughter . . ." Chaim's lips were pressed and he strained not to cry. He covered his eyes, and there was silence in the room. Then Chaim sniffed and raised his head. "I'm hanging on by a thread here, Bernard," he said, struggling to catch his breath. His voice broke. "I don't know how much longer I can hold out. I thought if I could only get to Philadelphia, maybe . . ."

"It's okay, Chaim," Bernard said. "We understand. We all understand. Take your time. Tell us about Max."

"I had a friend in the Feldafing DP Camp. His name is Mort. We correspond. He told me about this man who had contacts in America. Real high up. A man who could procure a visa for the right price. I knew it was illegal, Bernard, and I knew it was wrong, but I'm desperate. I have to get out of Europe, Bernard. I can't live in a camp anymore."

"And you believed this man could get you out of Europe?"

"Oh, it's true. He can. Mort is now living in New York. He sent me a postcard. I told Mort that I was interested, that I could pay. He said he would arrange a meeting with Max."

"Where and when did the meeting take place?"

"Last May, outside the camp, in Wolfratshausen. I waited in a coffee shop. He walked in, and I knew in a minute it was him. He was dressed very classy—a long coat with a satin collar. He said his name was Max, but I already knew that. He quoted six thousand Swiss francs. I told him I had stones worth twice that. I showed him the stones; he examined the diamond and the sapphire, made a sour face and shook his head. He said, 'Chaim, they're not worth six thousand francs, but as a favor to Mort, I'll take them and get you your visa.'

"I cried, Bernard. I broke down right then and there and cried like a little boy. I asked him when I'd get it. He said it might take a few weeks. Now it's been three months, and I haven't seen or heard from him."

"Can you describe him?" Eli said.

"Fairly tall. Thin. Glasses. Short black hair. He wasn't an American, I can tell you that. He spoke German, but with a Polish accent. I know I was foolish to give him the stones, but Mort is living in New York. Somehow this guy has the right connections."

"Don't punish yourself, Chaim. Bastards like Max prey on vulnerable people in desperate times. All he needed to do was complete a single transaction, and people would line up to give him their money."

"That's true. I did."

Bernard turned his attention to the other man. "And you, David, is the story the same?"

"Pretty much, except that I met Max here at Föhrenwald. It was Frau Helstein who told me about him. I was out for my morning walk with Shmuel and she joined up with us. Naturally, we were complaining about how long it takes to get immigration certificates, and she said, 'I know a man who can cut through the red tape and get you a U.S. visa right away, if you're interested.' We laughed, but she was insistent. 'I know what I'm talking about,' she said. Shmuel said, 'Then why don't you have a visa? Why are you still here walking with us in a DP camp?' The question didn't faze her. 'I'm in no hurry,' she said, 'but I can arrange a meeting for you if you want.' Shmuel scoffed and walked away, but I told her I would talk to the man. She set up a meeting."

"Tell us, David," Bernard said, "what happened at the meeting?"

"It was me, Frau Helstein and Max. He said he'd get me two visas for twelve thousand Swiss francs. I said I don't have that kind of money. We talked a little longer, and he said he would do two visas for ten thousand. I didn't have that much either, but I told him I would pay him after I got a job in America. Then he put his hand on my shoulder, like I was his good friend, and he said, 'How much can you come up with as a down payment? I'll take the rest in installments once you get settled in America.' I said two thousand. He said that would be okay, he would order the visa and work out the balance with me. I gave him the two thousand and I haven't seen him since." David hung his head. "Don't I feel like a schmuck."

Bernard stood. "Thank you both for coming in to talk to us. Don't lose hope. Your names are still on the official immigration list here at Föhrenwald. God willing, all of us will soon get a visa."

When they had left, Bernard turned to Eli. "We need to pay Frau Helstein a visit."

"Yes, we do. I have to pick up Izaak at football practice, but I can meet you there at seven."

"That will be fine. How is young Izaak doing?"

"He's too smart for me, Bernard."

Bernard laughed. "They grow up fast, don't they? I think they're smarter than we were at that age. Of course, they've seen things that children should never, ever see. They ask hard questions."

"That they do. The other night he asked why the U.S. doesn't bring us into the States and let us earn a living instead of housing and feeding us in displaced persons camps? You can't fault his logic. How do I answer that?"

"You could tell him the truth. You could tell him that the U.S. changed its immigration policy in 1924, restricting visas for Central and Eastern Europe while increasing them for Britain and Northern Europe. You know what that was all about. Flat out prejudice. Romania, with a million Jews, was given a quota of 377 at the same time that Britain's quota was raised to 65,000."

"I'm not going to tell my son that it's hard to get visas because of prejudice in the U.S."

"Not just the U.S., Eli. Canada needs farmworkers and industrial workers, everybody knows that, but Mackenzie King's government doesn't want to admit Jewish refugees. The head of Canadian immigration stated, 'None is too many.' But you're right, you can't tell your kid that the world is prejudiced against him. He's had enough of that here in Europe."

❧

Eli watched Izaak run toward the sideline. He ran with abandon, with all the boundless energy of a healthy twelve-year-old. A smile spread from ear to ear. His shorts and shin guards evidenced an afternoon of mixing it up on the dirt and grass of the football field.

"How did it go today?"

"Good. We have a game Sunday with the team from the American army base. It will be tough because they have a fifteen-year-old. Josh is our oldest player, and he won't be fourteen until next May. Do you know that the Americans call it soccer, not football?"

"I've heard that. I'm sure you'll do fine Sunday."

"I hope so. We were missing three players at practice today."

"How come? Did they also leave Föhrenwald?"

Izaak shook his head. "Nah, they were sick. They had a cold or something."

"Izzie, do you remember what I told you about kids that are coughing?"

"I know, I know. Stay away, wash my hands. I don't want to catch their germs."

"That's right, and if someone has a really bad cough, you should tell me about it."

"Why? You're not a doctor, Papa."

"That's true, but I would pass the information on to Dr. Weisman and make sure that the sick person gets medical help."

CHAPTER TWENTY

⚜

FÖHRENWALD DP CAMP
AMERICAN ZONE
AUGUST 1946

Olga Helstein was startled when she answered the doorbell to find Bernard and Eli standing there. "Oh, hello, Director, what brings you by tonight? What can I do for the committee?"

"Are you busy, Olga?"

"I, uh, I was just listening to the radio." She pointed to her bookcase. "The Kraft Music Hour."

"Could you spare us a few minutes, please," he said, walking straight past her without waiting for an answer. Olga backtracked a few steps and nervously gestured toward her kitchen table. "Of course, Director. We can all sit right here. May I offer you each a cup of tea?"

"Thank you, Olga. Very kind of you. I think you know Eli Rosen?"

"Not really."

"Well, Eli is helping me with a very serious problem, and we thought maybe you could help as well."

Bernard watched as Olga moved about her kitchen. It was obvious she could feel their stares. Their eyes were locked on her. She became more and more unsettled as she went through the motions of setting a pot of tea on the stove. Her facial muscles twitched. When she brought the teacups to the table, they rattled in her hands.

"Is there something you want to tell us, Olga?"

She hesitated for a moment and then replaced her forced smile with narrowed eyes and curled lips. She set her hands on her hips and raised her voice. "Oh, no you don't! I survived Treblinka; do you know that? I survived! They did not break me! You do not come into my house like the Gestapo and accuse me! Not now, not ever. Get out!"

Bernard spoke calmly. "We haven't accused you, Olga. We want your help."

"What help? Don't take me for a fool, Bernard. I know why you're here."

Eli pushed his cup aside and leaned forward. "Do you know what kind of man you are doing business with, Olga? Maximilian Poleski is a liar, a thief and a Nazi collaborator. He was responsible for helping the Nazis commit terrible atrocities in Lublin. He's a war criminal. And I hold him responsible for what happened to my family."

Olga took a breath. "I'm sorry for whatever happened to your family, and I don't know how or if Max is to blame. I don't know the name Maximilian Poleski or if he's the same person. To me, Max is a businessman with connections in the United States. He knows how to pull strings, how to cut through red tape. He can get a visa while the rest of you sit here in this lousy camp rotting like fruit on the vine. You should applaud a man like Max who can get people out."

"For six thousand Swiss francs?"

She shrugged and answered smugly, "He provides a service. He has costs. If you want a visa badly enough, you'll pay. No one's forcing anybody to do anything."

"He's not going through lawful immigration channels," Bernard said. "He's selling visas to the highest bidder. What he's doing is illegal, and you are helping him. We're here to put a stop to this scheme and see to it that criminal activities are punished."

Olga scoffed in denial. "I don't think what he's doing is illegal. Max told me he was working with people in Washington. How could that be illegal?"

Bernard lifted his eyebrows. "Olga, you know damn well it's illegal. The U.S. doesn't sell visas. How much was he paying you?"

"None of your business!"

Bernard stood, looked at Eli and said, "Okay, we're done here. Olga, you're finished at Föhrenwald."

"What do you mean 'finished'?"

"I mean goodbye. Pack up; you're leaving."

"Where am I supposed to go?"

"Why don't you buy a visa?"

"Very funny."

Bernard leaned forward. "Where's Max?"

She smirked. "Are you and the mighty camp police going to arrest him? Good luck."

"As soon as we catch up with him, I assure you he will be arrested. And you as well, Olga. You have both committed crimes."

"This is a U.S. DP camp. The camp committee doesn't own it." Her sly smile widened. "Your camp police aren't even real. And your Honor Court has no authority, Bernard."

"It isn't the camp committee that will be prosecuting you and Max. The United States Army has plenary jurisdiction over Camp Föhrenwald. Judgment of the military courts is swift and final."

Olga's smile disappeared. Then her eyes widened as though an idea came to her. "But the army didn't come here tonight, did they? *You* came here."

"That's right, Olga."

She looked at Eli and then at Bernard. She understood there was a play for her. "You could have sent the military police, but you two chose to come here alone because you want my help, am I right?"

"That's the first thing we said when we walked in the door. Now you're getting smart. How much did Max pay you?"

She tipped her head from side to side. "If I brought him a customer, I was supposed to get twenty-five percent."

"How many of our residents did you bring to Max?"

"Six."

"Does that include Chaim Warshawski and David Fromen?"

She nodded.

"How many paid money or property to Max and didn't get their visa yet?"

"Three. Max says he's waiting for the visas to come from Washington. He's sure they'll come. He just doesn't know when."

"Who is his contact in Washington?"

She shrugged. "I don't know. He would never tell me. Maybe he figured I'd go into business for myself and cut him out of the profits." She smiled broadly. She had teeth missing.

"When is he scheduled to return to Camp Föhrenwald?"

"Not until there's a reason. Either he'll bring the visas for Chaim, David and Sylvia or he'll come for a new customer." She paused. "You want me to get him here, don't you? You want me to get him here so you can arrest him."

Bernard sat down and folded his hands on the table. "That is exactly what I want you to do. I want you to reach out to Max and tell him that you have two new customers for him. Tell him they have the money."

"He'll want to know who they are."

"Tell him it's Joel and Leah Weisman."

"The doctor?"

Bernard nodded. "And his wife."

"I'll write to him. I have an address in Munich where he gets his mail, but there's no guarantee he'll come."

"How many other camps is he working?"

"I'm not sure. I know Landsberg and Feldafing. I'm sure there are others, but I don't know which ones."

Bernard stood. He pointed his finger and spoke emphatically. "Olga, you write to Max. Tell him Dr. Weisman and his wife want visas. Tell him they're desperate. Set an appointment as soon as you can. But be careful, Olga. If you betray us, if you tip him off, I'll turn you straight over to the U.S. Army."

"And if I help you, then this whole thing goes away?"

Bernard nodded. "We'll tell them about your cooperation. You might have to come up with some restitution."

Olga looked confused. "What restitution?"

"The money you took as a commission, Olga. The twenty-five percent."

She laughed. "Oh, yeah, I'm wealthy. I got a total of fifty francs! Max still *owes* me my cut."

Bernard opened the door. "I want to know as soon as you hear from him."

❧

Once outside, Eli said, "Does Joel know that you just offered him up as bait in a sting?"

Bernard smiled. "Not yet, but he won't mind."

CHAPTER TWENTY-ONE

FÖHRENWALD DP CAMP
AMERICAN ZONE
SEPTEMBER 1946
Four weeks later, Frau Helstein told Bernard she had received a communication from Max. She wanted to know what to do next. Bernard told her they would meet her at the assembly hall at eight o'clock, and together they would make a plan.

Eli, Bernard and Daniel sat in the empty assembly hall playing cards, passing time and waiting for Frau Helstein when a young woman entered, walked up to the table and asked for Bernard. "I am Bernard," he said. "How can I help you?"

"Camp Föhrenwald is having David Klyber, the Yiddish poet, next Sunday."

"That's right. He is giving a reading of his poems here in the hall. Do you know him?"

She shook her head, and as she did, her long blond hair danced from side to side. Eli tried not to stare, but the smooth lines and light complexion of her face reminded him of Esther. He quickly dismissed the thought. Only Esther should remind him of Esther. The woman was very thin, but that was not unusual, especially for those who had newly arrived.

"My name is Adinah," she said. "I sing."

"Where are you from, Adinah?"

"Zamość."

"Are you a professional singer?"

Again, a slight shake of her head. "I wanted to be. Before. Now, I just sing."

"Are you asking us to put you on the program next Sunday? It's not a musical."

"Poetry is music."

She seemed so quiet, so shy, and when she moved, her movements were delicate and gentle. Eli thought her stage presence might not be strong enough to carry off a performance before a packed assembly hall.

"May I sing for you?" she said softly.

Again, the men looked at each other and shrugged. Bernard said, "Sure, if you like, you can sing for us, but we are not on the entertainment committee. We're not running the program."

For the first time, a slight smile came to her lips. "You are the camp director. You are running the camp. I will sing now, if you will permit me."

Bernard returned the smile. "Please."

Adinah closed her eyes, perhaps to imagine herself at another time or place, took a deep breath and began the lovely Yiddish song, "Oyfn Pripetchik." Her voice was pure and strong, and her artistry superb. The traditional melody flowed from her lips and carried throughout the hall. Eli and Bernard looked at each other in astonishment, as if to say, *this voice cannot possibly be coming from this demure woman.* And when she sang the fourth verse, Eli, his vision blurred by tears, could not stop from quietly singing along.

She finished and smiled. Daniel said, "That was lovely, but I am not from Poland and I do not know the song. What is it?"

Adinah shrugged. "Just a song."

"No, it's more important than that," Eli said. "It is a song known by every Jewish child growing up in Poland. And in the camps, if you heard someone humming or whistling the melody, it was an instant connection. A piece of our lives the Nazis could not take away. 'Oyfn Pripetchik.' 'On the Hearth.' It's about a rabbi teaching young children the letters of the alphabet. It's warm and it's sweet, but the fourth verse is prophetic and poignant. It goes, 'When you grow older, children, you will understand how many tears lie in these letters and how much sorrow.'"

"You are a marvelous singer, Adinah," Bernard said. "Do you know other Yiddish songs as well?"

She nodded. "Many."

"Do you know 'Tumbalalaika'?"

"Of course."

"Will you sing it for me?"

Once again, she sang, but this time her tone, her delivery, was more upbeat and playful. Adinah captured and held their attention with the traditional song about a young man and his riddles for the young lady he is courting. What can burn and never end? What can yearn and cry without tears? And the young lady answers, "narisher bokher." "Foolish boy . . . love can burn and never end. A heart can yearn and cry without tears."

"Adinah," Bernard said, rising from his seat, "you have quite a gift. I will make sure that you are on the program and that your performance will be properly promoted to the camp residents. Our folks should have the pleasure of listening to you as we have tonight. Do you have an accompanist?"

She gently shook her head.

"Would you like one? Myron Levy is an excellent pianist."

A slight hunch of her shoulders. "Okay."

Eli smiled. "I am looking forward to it, Adinah. I'm going to bring my son Izaak. Bernard, make sure I get a seat right up front. By the way, Adinah, back in Zamość, did you happen to know the Solomon family? Abraham and Leah Solomon?"

She nodded. They had a daughter Beka. She was my age."

"And a son named Ben?"

She nodded again and quietly said, "There's no one left in Zamość."

"I understand," Eli said. "I will see you at the program."

She smiled and walked from the room as silently as a house cat.

Frau Helstein entered the hall shortly thereafter and looked around, as though there might be hidden eyes spying on her. "What news do you have for us, Olga?" Bernard said, pulling out a chair for her.

"Max took the bait. He's excited that there are new customers, or should I say new pigeons. He is going first to Landsberg, and then he will come here."

"When?"

"Soon. He didn't give me a specific date. He told me to personally verify that each customer has the money before he comes. He doesn't want to waste his time like he did with David."

"Waste his time? David gave him two thousand francs."

"And he didn't get a visa yet, did he?"

"The bastard."

"Max also told me to be careful who I talk to. He thinks the U.S. Army might be on to him. He says they would bust up his operation. He has to protect his sources in America."

"Where are you supposed to meet him, Olga?"

"He said he'd let me know." She stood to leave. "I also asked him about my commission. Where's my money? He still owes me a lot. He said I'd get it out of the new money. Ha! The guy would cheat his own mother."

After she left, Eli said, "Are her commissions going to be a problem, Bernard? I don't trust her. What's to stop her from meeting Maximilian, taking a payoff, getting a visa and then skipping out on us?"

"No doubt, that's a strong enticement. We'll have to keep our eyes on her."

On the way back to the house, Eli stopped in the administration office to talk to Lawrence Davidovich. "Are there any updated residential lists?" Eli asked.

Lawrence shook his head. "Not today, Eli. The new lists won't come out for two more weeks. But don't lose faith. Esther could be anywhere. There are 416 camps in the U.S. zone, 272 in the British zone and 21 more in Italy. There's more than a million displaced persons, but people do reconnect every day."

Eli hung his head. "Thanks, Lawrence."

"Whenever a new list comes in, I always check it for Esther. You have my word."

"Thanks, I appreciate it."

"You never know, Eli. Someone might show up who's seen her or knows where she is. Stranger things have happened."

Eli nodded and left the office, thinking, *There's one person who will have the information. A man I thought was long dead.*

CHAPTER TWENTY-TWO

FÖHRENWALD DP CAMP
AMERICAN ZONE
OCTOBER 1946

The opportunity to apprehend Max was at hand. Bernard requested that Daniel and Eli meet him at the assembly hall at 5:00 p.m. He had also summoned Olga Helstein, Chaim Warshawski, David Fromen and Zygmund Stern, the individuals who had contact with Max and his black-market visa scheme. Bernard addressed the group as a whole. "Olga has received word that Max will be coming to Föhrenwald. We're going to work together, and we're going to catch him and stop his schemes once and for all. Olga, tell them what you know."

"I contacted Max through his address in Munich. I told him that Chaim and David were waiting for their visas and that Zygmund had raised the money. I also told him that two other residents were interested in talking to him and they had money as well."

"Exactly," Bernard said. "Those were my instructions. What was his response?"

"Well, he praised me for being such a good agent, and he promised that he would pay me my share. Hmph. Then he told me he would be coming next week and he'd send me the details. I don't know if he plans on coming to the camp or if he wants to meet somewhere else."

"What about the visas?"

"He said he had David's and Chaim's visas in his possession. He was going to bring them."

"That's great. When we learn the location, I'll need all of you to be there. When the money and visas change hands, the military police will grab him, and we'll have more than enough evidence to convict him. If we put enough pressure on him, if he sees that he's going to prison, he'll give up his contact in America."

Chaim stepped forward and cleared his throat. "Bernard, I want to say something. Olga said that Max has the visas in his possession. And let's be frank, an American visa represents liberation. Freedom. A new start. Before we destroy a person's chance of getting out of the camp and going to America, are we absolutely certain that the visas are illegal? I mean, what if it's not a crime to get visas for a person and charge him a processing fee, you know, for services rendered? Back in Warsaw, if you wanted to get a license, you always had to pay someone. There was always money passed around, often under the table. That was an accepted way of doing business, part of the transaction."

"Chaim," Bernard said sternly, "these are not liquor licenses. They're not bakery licenses. These are United States visas that can only be issued by the Immigration and Naturalization Department of the United States through an authorized consulate. They are not sold by individual salesmen. The consulates keep careful records and they have quotas. Right now, there are three hundred thousand people in American Zone DP camps, and do you know what the immigration quota is? It's set at a mere *six thousand a year*. There's a waiting list a mile long, Chaim. If there are only six thousand visas and you buy one of them, you have deprived the person who was next in line. Don't you see that? Visas are not for sale, and Max is a criminal."

Chaim's eyes were red. His voice quavered. "But he already has the visa in his possession, and it has *my* name, *Chaim Warshawski,* on it. It's already been issued. To me! I don't know what's so wrong if I take it and go to my family in Philadelphia. Bernard, I'm begging you. I've got to get out of here. I can't stay in a damn camp anymore. I've been in a camp since 1941. I'm losing my mind." His voice caught in his throat. "Please, please, I'm begging you. Let me take the visa and go. You can arrest Max for trying to sell the other visas. You'll still have plenty of evidence, and you will have stopped him from future violations. Bernard, I can't go on living in a camp."

"I'm sorry, Chaim. We can't permit it." Then to the group he said, "When we find out the day, time and place, we'll contact all of you. The military police will be there, and it will be over quickly."

⋙

Two hours later, Eli called out, "Izzie, get your coat. It's time to go."

"Papa, I don't want to go to a stupid poetry reading. Let me stay home. I'll do my homework."

"I thought you already did your homework."

"I'll check it over for mistakes. You can never be too careful."

Eli smiled. "Izzie, you're going to like this program. It's not just poetry; there is a singer, a lovely woman named Adinah who sings like a bird. Beautiful music. And she knows 'Oyfn Pripetchik.'"

Izaak's face lit up. "I like that song! I learned it in Lublin. I used to sing it with Mama."

"I know, and wait until you hear Adinah. She's a wonderful singer. And she knows lots of other Yiddish songs. You'll have a good time."

Eli and Izaak found seats next to Bernard in the first row, right in front of the stage. News of the program had spread throughout the camp, and the assembly hall filled up quickly. There was a palpable buzz, an air of anticipation, and it wasn't to hear poetry. Word had spread that a professional singer, maybe even Isa Kremer herself, was appearing in Camp Föhrenwald!

The poetry reading was first on the program, and unfortunately for Mr. Klyber, the audience was a bit restless. They were waiting for an evening of Yiddish music, as advertised. Finally, it was time. Myron Levy took a seat at the piano, and Adinah quietly walked onto the stage. All eyes were on this shy and modest woman. What a surprise when her perfect voice filled the hall with the familiar melodies.

She began with "Her Nor Du Sheyn Meydele." "Just Listen, You Pretty Girl." Almost all of the residents knew the words, and they sang along quietly. It was a touch of home in a place that would never be a home. It harkened back to a stolen youth, a lost love, a quiet village. It beckoned the heart to revisit a way of life before the cataclysm in a way that only music could.

Izaak was mesmerized, totally immersed in the melodies he hadn't heard in years. During her performance, Adinah locked eyes with Izaak and smiled. Now he was enamored by more than the music. Throughout the performance, Izaak felt that Adinah was singing directly to him. He leaned over and said, "Papa, don't you think she looks a lot like Mama?"

Eli nodded. "Yes, I do. I thought the same thing when I first met her."

She closed with "Bay Mir Bistu Sheyn"—"To Me, You Are Beautiful"—an internationally successful Yiddish song written in New York and immensely popular in Germany before Joseph Goebbels realized it was written by a Jew and banned the song. The applause was long and loud, and Bernard made Adinah promise to perform again in a few weeks.

As the crowd was filing out, Adinah stepped down off the stage and sat down next to Izaak. "I saw you singing with me on some of the songs," she said. "Did you know all the words?"

Izaak bit his bottom lip. "I knew some of them."

"You knew the words to 'Oyfn Pripetchik.'"

"That one I know pretty well. I used to sing it with my mother."

"Me too. My mother taught it to me. What is your name?"

Izaak looked to his dad, then back to Adinah. "Izaak Rosen."

"How old are you, Izaak?"

"Twelve."

"If your father permits, would you join me on the stage next time for 'Oyfn Pripetchik'? We'll sing a duet. I think it would be fun."

Izaak blushed and looked to Eli for approval. "Could I, Papa?"

"I don't see how you could turn that down, Izzie."

It was later than usual when Eli put Izaak to bed. "Let's get some sleep," he said, tucking the covers under him. "You've got school tomorrow and a big football practice."

"There's no practice tomorrow. Not enough players."

"No? How come? Did more players get sick?"

"No. Their moms won't let them play. They're afraid they're going to *get* sick."

"Well, that's a shame. I hope this strain of illness goes away soon."

Eli turned off the lights and started to leave the room when Izaak said, "Papa, did you like Adinah?"

"Yes, of course I did."

"She's nice. She smiles like Mama. Could we ask her to come over for dinner someday?"

"I don't know much about her, Izzie. She may have her own children to attend to."

"Then they could come, too. Please."

"We'll see. Good night, Izzie."

CHAPTER TWENTY-THREE

FÖHRENWALD DP CAMP
AMERICAN ZONE
NOVEMBER 1946

When the last of the dinner dishes had been washed and put away, Eli said, "I have to go to a meeting for a little while tonight. Do you have homework to do?"

Izaak nodded and made a face. "English class. It's impossible. I don't know how American kids ever learn this language."

Eli chuckled and said, "They might think Polish is hard."

"No, Papa, English is harder, because they make rules and then they break the rules. You memorize one thing and then you find out it doesn't work. Like the letter *c*. It can sound like a *k* in *cookie,* or it can sound like an *s* in *center*. How are you supposed to know? If you put the *t* and the *h* together, it can sound like *tooth,* where teacher says you put your tongue between your teeth. Or it can make a buzzing sound like a bee in *that*. Or an *s* can sound like a snake in *soon,* or it can be a *z* in *because*. And plurals? Forget it. They tell you that the rule is to add an *s* to the end of a word and then other times the whole word changes, like *person* and *people*. Who made up that stupid language?"

Eli smiled. "You can't get by with Yiddish on the streets of America. We all have to learn the language if we're going to live in America. You'll surely need English if you want to play football with the other boys?"

"Soccer, Papa. That's what they call it in America. Soccer. Do you think we'll ever get there?"

"Absolutely. Do you know what the Yiddish expression is for America? *Die Goldene Medina.* The Golden Land, where all your dreams come true. We'll get there, Izzie. And that's a promise."

"I hope so," Izaak said, "and I hope that Mama gets there with us." He turned his head and coughed.

Immediately, Eli said, "Are you all right? How long have you been coughing?"

"I'm fine. I think I have something in my throat. It's nothing."

"Do you have a sore throat?"

Izaak shook his head. "I'm not sick, Papa. I didn't catch anything. I feel fine. I just had something in my throat."

"Well, let's keep an eye on it, okay? If you keep coughing, I want to know. It's starting to snow outside. That wind's whistling down from the Alps. You can already see the snowcapped mountains over Garmisch. I want you bundled up when you go out tomorrow."

"I will, I will."

"And tell me if you get a sore throat or you cough anymore tonight."

"I know. I will. Go to your meeting."

Bernard and Daniel were waiting when Eli arrived at the assembly hall. "Olga received a message from Max," Bernard said. "He's bringing the visas. He wants Chaim and David to personally accept their visas, he wants Zygmund to bring his fee and he also wants to meet Dr. Weisman and make a deal for two more visas. There will be two U.S. MPs standing by and watching the transactions."

Eli's heart started to thump. "When and where is this meeting going to take place?"

"I have instructed Olga to set the meeting at her house. It's right in the center of the camp."

"I have to be there, too, Bernard," Eli said. "I have unfinished business with Maximilian."

"I don't like it," Bernard responded with a shake of his head. "If he is the same man you know from Lublin and if he sees you, he'll call the whole thing off."

"I'll stay out of sight until after the exchange, but when the MPs grab him, I want time alone with him."

"Eli, I know you have some ancient vendetta going on here, but the prime objective is to catch Max and his U.S. contact and to stop the black-market visas."

"Vendetta?" Eli said angrily. "You bet your ass I have a vendetta! But that's not the main reason I need to confront him."

Bernard was confused. "Then what is it?"

"It's about Esther. Maximilian knows what happened to her. He vowed to protect her. I *paid* him to protect her! If I have any hope of learning what happened to my wife or of finding her if she's still alive, that bastard will have the information, and I have made a solemn vow to get it out of him."

The door swung open, and Olga walked into the assembly room. "Max says he wants the meeting at the café in Wolfratshausen and he won't come into Föhrenwald. He's skittish. He thinks it's too dangerous for him."

"Olga," Bernard said, "when we spoke . . ."

"I did what you told me to, Bernard. I told Max that it's too hard for everyone to get out of the camp and get transportation into Wolfratshausen, but he said he's not coming into Föhrenwald. He's going to do it his way or not at all. If they don't like it, they don't get a visa."

"When does he want to meet?"

"Next Thursday night. Nine p.m."

"He's bluffing," Daniel said. "He won't cancel; he wants the money. It's much easier to arrest him here in the camp. The military police don't have jurisdiction in Wolfratshausen."

"Yes, they do," Bernard said. "It's in the American occupation zone. I don't want to take the chance of losing out on this opportunity. Olga, confirm the meeting at the café for next Thursday at nine. I will arrange for the MPs to locate themselves in and around the café. I will also talk to Chaim, David and Zygmund and arrange for their transportation. We will all meet here at Olga's at eight p.m. Daniel and Eli will ride with me."

☙

A silver Volkswagen and an army jeep sat outside Olga Helstein's residence with their motors idling on Thursday night. Bernard and Eli stood on the sidewalk waiting for the participants to take their places.

"I see David and Zygmund," Eli said. "Where are the rest?"

"Olga's inside the house. Daniel is bringing Dr. Weisman and should be along at any time. I don't know about Chaim. I stopped by his house, and he wasn't at home. I hope he hasn't backed out of the meeting."

"He's not essential, is he? If Maximilian brings the visas, the others can make the exchange. That should be sufficient evidence."

"It would, but I'm concerned about Chaim. At our meeting he was so desperate, so distraught."

Joel Weisman and Daniel approached. "Are we all here?"

Bernard shook his head. "All but Chaim. I don't think he's coming."

"I understand," Dr. Weisman said. "It's too emotional for him to see a visa with his name on it and know that he can't have it."

"The visa shouldn't have his name on it," Bernard said. "It's there because he paid a criminal to put it there. I feel bad for Chaim, but I feel bad for a lot of people who are stuck in this camp. You can't buy your way out."

They waited fifteen more minutes. Bernard checked his watch and said, "Chaim is obviously not coming; we need to leave."

As they drove through the night toward Wolfratshausen, Bernard glanced at Eli, who was nervously opening and clenching his fists. "Do you really think he has information about Esther?"

Eli nodded. "Oh, yeah. He would know."

The group rolled into Wolfratshausen and stopped a block from the café. Olga, David, Zygmund and Dr. Weisman walked into the restaurant. Two plainclothes MPs were already sitting at the bar. Daniel pulled his collar up, hung an unlit cigarette from his lips and took a position at the corner. Bernard and Eli remained in the jeep, out of sight.

At 9:30 Zygmund stepped outside to smoke a cigarette. He and Daniel strolled over to the jeep. "Max hasn't come in yet," Zygmund said. "How long do you want us to wait?"

"We wait a while longer," Daniel said. "He could have been delayed. From what I hear, he's a moneygrubbing thief. He'll be here. Let's wait."

At 10:30 they called it a night. Max was a no-show.

"It was Chaim," Bernard said. "There's not a doubt in my mind. Chaim tipped him off in exchange for his visa, and he's on his way to America. And I doubt we'll ever see Max at Föhrenwald again."

Eli slammed his hand on the back of the seat. "Damn! I really thought, after all this time, I'd get closer to finding Esther. Bernard, if Max is still in Germany, we've got to catch him."

"Olga said he was just in Landsberg or Feldafing, and if so then he's still in the Munich area. Unfortunately, I have no connection with the administrators of either of those camps. I'm going to have to contact OMGUS."

"Who?"

"Office of the Military Government. General Lucius D. Clay is the acting American military governor and chief administrator of occupied Germany. I met him at his office in Berlin. I'm sure he'll be happy to shut down a black-market visa operation. If anyone can throw a dragnet over Max, it's General Clay. I will try to arrange something in the next few weeks."

"I'll tell you something, Bernard. I'm going to catch up to Maximilian Poleski if I have to follow him to the ends of the earth. You have my solemn promise."

CHAPTER TWENTY-FOUR

❦

FÖHRENWALD DP CAMP
AMERICAN ZONE
DECEMBER 1946

Bulletins posted throughout the camp promoted next Sunday's winter social. Come one, come all. Volunteers were sought for decorating the hall. Experienced and inexperienced cooks were earnestly invited to bake festival cookies and cakes in the camp kitchen. The posters also announced that Adinah Szapiro would be performing her vocal artistry on stage.

Earlier in the week, Eli had received a message from Bernard. Regretfully, he would not be in attendance at the winter social. He asked that Eli stand in for him and convey his best wishes to all. Such a note was totally out of character for Bernard, and Eli feared that something was wrong. Bernard would never duck a responsibility, especially one so pleasurable. Eli decided to pay him a visit. Bernard lived in the easternmost section of the camp in a small four-unit structure at the corner of Illinois and Michigan Streets.

A light snow had fallen and covered the walkway and stoop in front of Bernard's residence, which Eli noticed had not been cleared away. He knocked on the door, waited and knocked again. He was about to leave when the door opened a crack. "I'm sorry, Eli, I'm not up to visitors today. I'm a little under the weather."

"Oh, I'm sorry to hear that. I received your note, and of course I will be happy to sub for you Sunday night, but it's only Tuesday. Maybe you'll feel better by the weekend."

"Perhaps," he started to say, but he broke into a racking cough and couldn't finish the sentence. In a hoarse whisper he added, "You should go now."

Eli headed straight to the clinic. He didn't know whether Dr. Weisman was aware of Bernard's condition. If he was not, Eli was going to make damn sure he found out. It was obvious that Bernard needed immediate medical attention.

The clinic was crowded. People were standing in the waiting room. Babies were crying. Nurses and attendants, their faces covered with surgical masks, busily darted from station to station. "Are you ill, Eli?" the receptionist asked.

"No, no I'm not. I wonder if I could have a few minutes with Dr. Weisman. It's not about me."

She gestured to the waiting area with an outstretched arm. "We are really busy today. Dr. Weisman is in with a patient right now and others are waiting. Maybe, if it's not an emergency, you could come back tomorrow, but I have to say, it seems like every day just gets busier than the one before."

"Can I wait? Does Joel take a lunch?"

The receptionist smiled. "Never."

Eli sighed. "What time does he go home?"

Again, a smile, this time with a touch of sadness. She pointed to a room. "There's a bed in that room. Sometimes he doesn't go home at all."

Eli shrugged and turned to leave. "You might try coming by at eight tonight," the receptionist said.

On his way home, Eli stopped by Daniel's apartment. "Did you know Bernard was sick?" Eli asked.

He nodded. "I was with him on Shabbat. He did not look good. He asked me if I could handle some of his duties this week. I told him that he should ask you instead. You're better with crowds. It's easier for you to talk to them. I haven't seen Bernard in three days."

"I was at his home today. He's really sick, Daniel. I'm going to track down Joel Weisman tonight and make sure he knows. Somebody should be taking care of Bernard. He lives alone."

Eli returned to the clinic at eight and there were still a few patients waiting. He took a seat and picked up a copy of the *Bamidbar*. The receptionist walked over and handed a mask to him. "Please put this on. It helps to minimize exposure. Droplets in the air do not penetrate the mask. Better safe than sorry."

The last of the patients was seen forty minutes later, and Dr. Weisman emerged from the double doors. "Eli, are you okay?" Eli nodded and said, "Can I walk you home?"

The doctor grabbed his winter coat and they headed out the door. "I went to visit Bernard Schwartz this afternoon," Eli said. "He's sick."

"I know. He's in quarantine, Eli. You should avoid contact with him."

"He has TB?"

Dr. Weisman shrugged. "He has symptoms. We'll see if he rebounds. Either way, it's likely he's contagious. I warned him about going out in public or performing his function as camp director until we're sure. It's unhealthy for him in his weakened condition, and we certainly don't want to expose anyone else to a disease."

"He's such a strong director. I don't know anyone who could fill his shoes."

Despite the snow on Sunday afternoon, the Föhrenwald winter social began right on time with a series of games for the children. Eli welcomed the crowd to the festival and invited everyone to take part in the planned activities. "Bingo begins sharply at four. Buffet dinner at five thirty and musical performances start at seven," he announced. "Many of you were here last month when Adinah Szapiro sang Yiddish favorites. She'll perform again tonight, and everyone is invited to sing along." Eli looked down at Izaak and winked.

Camp socials were popular events, and they drew big crowds. The residents shared a common bond; they had all come through hell, unimaginable circumstances, but they were the survivors, the *Sh'erit Hapletah*! The Nazis had taken away their citizenship, their passports, their identification papers, and now that the war had ended, many were no longer welcome to return to their prewar villages. They had truly lost any sense of nationality—they were a stateless people. Despite it all, they stood tall, undefeated, optimistic about their future and determined to rebuild their lives and reconstitute their community, no matter what it took. Föhrenwald was their platform, their steppingstone.

A buzz went through the crowd as 7:00 p.m. approached and people scrambled to find a seat. The piano accompanist bowed, nodded and took his place. Finally, a spirited Adinah stepped onto the stage in a bright yellow

dress with a lively bounce to her step. No shyness, no hesitation. Was this
the same Adinah? Whatever the reason, the enthusiasm of the crowd added
to her energy. She sparkled.

She began by briskly walking back and forth across the stage, rhythmically
clapping and inciting the crowd to clap along with her. When she had the audience loudly clapping in rhythm, she began a rousing "Hava Nagila." The
audience rose to sing along, and many danced at their places. One traditional
song was followed by another. In the middle of her program, she held up her
hand and asked for silence.

"This next song," she said, "was first sung in the Vilna ghetto. It spread
to the other camps, to the labor camps, to the concentration and the death
camps. It became an anthem, our anthem. A song of defiance and survival.
All of you know the song I'm talking about. It was written by Hirsh Glick
in tribute to the Warsaw ghetto uprising. A song of triumph. I sing for you
now, 'Zog Nit Keyn Mol.' Sing along with me, please."

Everyone stood. Though tears filled their eyes, though words caught in
their throats, they stood arm in arm. Their chests were puffed in pride. The
Yiddish lyrics were poignant and powerful:

> *Never say that there is only death for you,*
> *Though leaden skies may be concealing days of blue.*
> *Because the hour we have hungered for is near,*
> *Beneath our tread the earth shall tremble: we are here!*
> *From lands so green with palms to lands all white with snow.*
> *We shall be coming with our anguish and our woe,*
> *And where a spurt of our blood fell on the earth,*
> *There our courage and our spirit have rebirth!*
> *We'll have the morning sun to set our day aglow,*
> *And all our yesterdays shall vanish with the foe,*
> *And if the time is long before the sun appears,*
> *Then let this song go like a signal through the years.*
>
> [English Translation]

When the song had finished and the proud audience had retaken their
seats, Adinah winked at Izaak. "It is time for our duet, young Mr. Rosen."
With her index finger she beckoned Izaak to the stage. He glanced at his father, and his face displayed more than just a little trepidation. Eli shrugged

and said, "Now or never, my boy." Izaak bit his bottom lip, popped out of his chair and walked up to the stage. Adinah put her arm around his shoulders and nodded to the pianist. With smiles on their faces, Adinah and Izaak sung "Oyfn Pripetchik," and when they had finished, the audience gave them a hearty round of applause. Adinah leaned over and kissed Izaak on the cheek. He blushed from ear to ear.

No social event could end without the compulsory cake and ice cream. Adinah, Eli and Izaak were enjoying their dessert when Dr. Weisman approached. "Lovely duet," he said, "I enjoyed it very much." Then, turning to Eli, he said, "May I have a moment?"

They stepped to the side and the doctor produced an envelope. "This is from Bernard," he said quietly.

"How is he?" Eli asked.

"Not well. I have cleared a place for him in our sanitarium." The news hit Eli like a punch in the stomach. He sat down hard, opened the envelope and read the letter.

My good friend Eli;

I'm afraid my time as director is finished. When or if I recover, I will not be strong enough to carry on the business of our camp in the days ahead. I am recommending that the UNRRA Administration hold elections for a new director. The camp needs a strong leader, and I know of no one better suited than you. You command the respect of our community and you have the wisdom to govern. Please consider putting your name into consideration. Daniel will help you, but he lacks the confidence and background to assume the mantle. My staff at the office has all of the records and will assist the new director in whatever capacity he needs. May God bless your efforts.

One more thing—though I am ill, our quest for Max must not abate. We must find him and put an end to his criminal activities. I have spoken with General Lucius D. Clay, Chief Administrator of Occupied Germany in Berlin. He directed me to contact Colonel Bivens at the U.S. Army Garrison in Garmisch, the chief military officer for our region. I sent a request for a meeting two weeks ago. I just received notice that he will grant us a meeting next Wednesday. I am unable to go with you, but I am supremely confident that you will do whatever is necessary to bring about the arrest and conviction of the black marketeer.

Finally, I pray for you and Esther, that you will find each other, that the two of you will be reunited and that you will live long, healthy, happy lives together with your son.

> May God bless you, my friend, now and always,
> Bernard

Eli's expression conveyed it all. Adinah and Izaak knew the letter contained sad news.

"I have to go to Garmisch on Wednesday," Eli said to Izaak. "You'll have to manage on your own for a while. I'll probably be home very late."

"I will stay with him," Adinah said.

CHAPTER TWENTY-FIVE

FÖHRENWALD DP CAMP
AMERICAN ZONE
DECEMBER 1946

There was a soft knock on Eli's door at 6:00 a.m. The sun had yet to rise, yet Adinah was standing there, a white cable-knit hat pulled over her golden hair and a smile on her face. "Am I on time?" she said softly.

Eli stepped back to let her in. "My goodness, Adinah, you didn't have to come this early. Izaak is still asleep." Then he caught himself. "I'm sorry, what I really meant to say is thank you very much for coming this morning. I know Izzie will be happy to see you. Just make yourself at home; the house is yours. Izzie goes to school at nine and to basketball practice in the gym after school. He probably won't be home until five. I may be home by then, but I'm not sure. Bernard informed the colonel I was coming today, but there is no set appointment time. Depending on the colonel's schedule, I could be home late. So if I'm not here when Izzie gets home from school . . ."

"I'll fix him something to eat. Don't worry."

"I don't want to keep you too late, Adinah. You were very kind to offer, but you have your own responsibilities and your own plans for tonight. If I'm not here, Izzie can go to bed and you can leave."

"Please do not worry about me or my plans. I have no place to be tonight. I live alone and I have no responsibilities. So take whatever time is necessary to finish your business. Believe me, I will enjoy spending time with Izaak."

Bernard had arranged for a jeep, and Eli pulled out of Föhrenwald just before the sun rose. The route to the U.S. Army garrison took him east to Munich and then south to Garmisch. It was a two-hour drive through the German countryside. The weather was clear and the roads were dry. Soon the tall peaks of the Bavarian Alps came into view. The largest mountain in Germany, Zugspitze, a ten-thousand-foot snow-capped peak, rose majestically behind the alpine village of Garmisch.

The army garrison lay on the outskirts of the village and was surrounded by a security fence. Eli stopped at the guard post, showed his U.S. DP identification card and waited while the sentry called Colonel Bivens. The young corporal put down the phone and said, "The colonel's adjutant confirms that you are on his calendar, but the colonel has not come in yet. You are welcome to wait at the commissary."

"Did the adjutant say when the colonel would be in?" Eli asked.

"No, sir." A smile crept across the sentry's lips. "Welcome to the army, sir."

Eli took a seat in the commissary and spent the next few hours reading magazines and back issues of *Stars & Stripes*. Every so often, Eli would ask the desk sergeant if he wouldn't mind checking on the colonel's availability. A call would be placed, and the answer would always be a polite, "Not yet, sir." After Eli's fourth request, the sergeant said, "Mr. Rosen, the colonel's adjutant knows you are waiting here, and he will give me a call as soon as the colonel can see you. Sorry for the inconvenience, sir."

At four thirty, Eli got the high sign from the sergeant. "I'll take you back to his office now, sir," he said.

Colonel Bivens, a decorated officer with white hair and a square jaw, was seated behind his polished desk. Over his left shoulder was a picture of General Eisenhower and to his right was a picture of President Truman. Colonel Bivens wore a crisply pressed uniform with four rows of service ribbons. He did not get up to greet Eli.

"Take a seat, Mr. Rosen," he said flatly. "What brings you down to Garmisch?"

"Thank you, sir. I live in the Föhrenwald Displaced Persons Camp. I've lived there since I was rescued from the Buchenwald concentration camp by the American forces in 1945. Like all of the Föhrenwald residents, my son and I are waiting for a visa to go to America."

The colonel had a confused expression on his face. "And you came to me to get a visa?"

"Oh, no, sir. My name is on the waiting list, like everyone else. I came here because there is a man, I believe his name is Maximilian Poleski, who is attempting to sell American visas on the black market."

A disbelieving grin appeared on the colonel's face. "United States immigration visas? He's *selling* them? Hmph. Impossible. They're issued through the immigration office in Washington and distributed through consulates. No one sells visas."

"With all due respect, sir, this man is selling visas for six thousand Swiss francs apiece. And we believe they are genuine."

The colonel sat back in his chair and his smile disappeared. "You know, when people disagree with me and they say 'with all due respect,' I wonder what the hell that means. I don't think that phrase is respectful at all. I think it's pejorative. Due respect? What does it mean, Mr. Rosen, when you say you're giving me *due respect*?"

Eli started to apologize, but Bivens cut him off. He pointed to his chest. "You see these service ribbons? They were awarded to me by the United States Army. These ribbons *demand* respect. Not some vague 'all due respect,' but *real* respect. See this one here, the red one with the blue stripe and the star? That's a Bronze Star, Mr. Rosen, awarded for meritorious service in a combat zone. Do you think that commands respect?"

"Of course, sir."

"You better believe it."

Eli paused and took a breath, wondering how to get the conversation back on point. "Well, sir, getting back to the visas, the man who calls himself Max is going from one American DP camp to another and selling these visas, and people are giving him money and property. The administration at Camp Föhrenwald wants to put a stop to it."

"Then go ahead. What do you want me to do about it?"

"We don't have the authority to arrest and prosecute the man. We need to enlist the assistance of the U.S. Army, which has plenary jurisdiction over the camps in this district. Not only do we want Max prosecuted, we want to know who is providing him with the visas."

Bivens nodded and pursed his lips. "Hmm. Well, let me tell you something about my priorities, Mr. Rosen. My job here is fivefold." For Eli's benefit, he counted the priorities on his fingers. "One, the elimination of Nazism, which is still very strong here in the Munich area; two, to seek restitution for people who have unjustly been deprived of their identifiable property;

three, to assist in rebuilding the local economy, banking, foreign exchange and currency; four, to reestablish a system of justice in these parts; and five, to provide security for German citizens and for your DP camps. So to be honest, Mr. Rosen, if some twerp is scamming the system and letting a few people skip ahead in the line, I frankly don't give a shit."

Eli stood. "Well, thank you for your time, sir. I will report the results of our conversation to General Clay."

"You'll what?"

"General Clay sent me to you."

Bivens sat up straight. "Lucius Clay directed you to talk to me?"

"That's right."

"Well, damn, why didn't you say so? What does Lucius want me to do?"

"Well, as I was saying, sir, he wants Max arrested, charged and tried for black-market visa sales."

Colonel Bivens nodded. His expression slowly changed to warm and considerate. He reached into an inlaid wooden box on his desk and took out two cigars. He offered one to Eli, but Eli politely declined. The colonel cut the end off of his cigar and lit it. "So where is this fellow, Max, now?"

"At this moment, I don't know. We think he will soon be at Camp Landsberg and maybe at Camp Feldafing. He has contacted residents there who are raising money to buy his visas."

The colonel rubbed his chin. "Do you know what he looks like? Can you ID him?"

"If he's the same man I knew in Lublin, then yes I can."

The colonel pressed a button on his intercom and said, "Send in Major Donnelly." Then he looked across his desk at Eli. "We'll catch this fellow and put an end to his monkey business; you can take that to the bank. When you talk to Lucius, you tell him George says hello and that I'm on top of this assignment, okay?"

"Yes, sir."

A few minutes later, Major Donnelly entered the office. Eli explained Max's operation. "Last month we set up a sting in Wolfratshausen," Eli said, "but unfortunately someone tipped Max off and he didn't appear. We know that he has contracted to sell visas at two other camps within the next few weeks. We'll need the U.S. Army to act quickly and take him into custody."

"We thank you for bringing this criminal enterprise to our attention, Mr. Rosen," Colonel Bivens said. "We'll take it from here. Major, I want you to contact this Helstein woman and catch this rat."

"I'd like to be present when he's arrested. I can positively identify him for you."

"That won't be necessary, Mr. Rosen. You've done enough. Helstein can ID him, can't she? We'll catch this fellow in the act, and that'll be sufficient evidence to prosecute him."

"You don't understand. I *need* to be there. I need to confront him. He has information about my wife."

Colonel Bivens and Major Donnelly glanced at each other and then back to Eli. "So this is not just about a guy trying to sell phony immigration visas, is it?" Bivens said.

"They're not phony," Eli snapped indignantly. "They're valid. I know of two Föhrenwald residents who have emigrated to New York on black-market visas. That's criminal and it should be stopped. But I also have a personal matter, a history with this man that goes back several years. He was known as a fixer in Lublin. He betrayed me and many others, and I think he knows what happened to my wife."

Bivens's expression softened. "She didn't make it out?"

"I don't know, sir. I pray that she did, but like a million other people, I'm searching for a lost relative in postwar Europe."

"What makes you think this fixer knows what happened?"

"Because"—Eli paused to swallow—"I entrusted my wife to him. He pledged to protect her." Eli lowered his gaze. "I paid him. When I was sent away, I relied on him to safeguard her. When I came back, she was gone."

"And Max?"

"I thought the Nazis killed him. Apparently, I was wrong."

Bivens stood and pointed a commanding finger at Donnelly. "Major, I want you to contact the directors of the Munich-area DP camps. Alert them to the problem and find out any information you can about this character. But be careful. Make sure we don't spook him. Then get up to Landsberg and Feldafing. Talk to their directors. Impress upon them the gravity of this scheme. Tell them that the United States Army takes it very seriously." He tipped his head at Eli. "Take Mr. Rosen with you." He extended his hand to Eli. "When you talk to General Clay, you tell him that

George Bivens is going to put a stop to this fraudulent scheme once and for all. Major, show Mr. Rosen out and make arrangements to get up to the camps posthaste!"

On the walk down the hall, Major Donnelly said to Eli, "Have you requested information about your wife from the CTB Register in Bad Arolsen?"

Eli shook his head. "No. I've heard about it, everyone has, but I really don't know much about it or how to access it. I know there's an office that collects information about survivors and I've always assumed they've been sharing it with the DP camps."

"That's your first mistake. Don't assume."

"I've been checking the logs at the Föhrenwald office. Her name is not listed."

"DP logs are unreliable. The Central Tracing Bureau has a much broader database. In January of this year, the CTB moved its offices to Bad Arolsen, which is a town located at the juncture of the U.S., British and Soviet occupation zones. CTB has collected millions of documents—anything that could be found with a name on it—Gestapo records, concentration camp registers, secret police records. I've been there. It's impressive. Typists write hundreds of letters every day, trying to put missing relatives together. If anyone can help you find out what happened to your wife, they can. When you get up there, ask for Ann Stewart. Tell her I sent you. If there's any record at all, there's a good chance Ann can find it. If I were you, I'd go up there and fill out a request as soon as you can. In person. It's good to put a face with a request."

"Bad Arolsen?"

"Yes, sir. It's about 350 miles north of Munich. Unless you can requisition a jeep, you'd have to get there by train. In the meantime, I'm going to touch base with Landsberg and Feldafing. Colonel made it clear he wants arrangements made immediately. I'll leave a message for you at the Föhrenwald administration office as soon as I can set up an appointment. I'll pick you up, and we'll ride up there together." The major stuck out his hand. "A pleasure to meet you, sir."

⁂

Snow began to fall heavily on Eli's return to Föhrenwald. The roads were snowbound, the night was dark and Eli's vision was occluded. The jeep lacked a heater, and the windshield wipers swept erratically. Eli periodically stuck his arm out of his window to brush the snow off the windshield.

Speed was kept to a minimum. By the time he arrived back at Föhrenwald, the accumulated snow depth was well over a foot and Eli was chilled to the bone.

He stood in his entryway, shook the snow off his overcoat and hung it by the front door. Adinah was in the kitchen and something smelled very good. "I made soup," she said. "I asked Izzie what he wanted, and he promptly told me chicken soup." She smiled warmly and shrugged her shoulders.

"Thank you very much; that was sweet. Where is Izzie?"

She tilted her head toward the back of the house. "He's in his room. He had a small bowl of soup at six thirty and told me he was tired. He fell asleep."

"At six thirty? That's unusual for Izzie."

Adinah nodded. "I don't think he feels well tonight. He came straight home from school. He didn't even go to basketball."

Eli grew worried. "Did he say what was bothering him?"

"No, but he looked tired and he felt warm to me. He said he had a little sore throat and he asked me not to tell you. Then he went into his room."

"Was he coughing?"

Adinah nodded. "Some."

Eli hurried into the bedroom. Izaak was sound asleep in his clothes on top of his covers. His face was flushed. Eli reached over and felt his forehead. It was hot.

All the alarms went off. "I'm going to the clinic," Eli said to Adinah, quickly grabbing his coat off the hook. "He needs medical care. I'm going to ask my friend Dr. Weisman to come here and examine him. I certainly can't take Izzie out in this storm. Would it be possible for you to stay here a little while longer while I go fetch the doctor?"

"Of course. I am here as long as you need me."

PART II

CHAPTER TWENTY-SIX

❦

ALBANY PARK

CHICAGO
ALBANY PARK NEIGHBORHOOD
MAY 1965

On the seventh day of May 1965, exactly twenty years from the date that Germany surrendered, a tall man stepped off the Montrose Avenue bus at Lawndale Street in the Albany Park section of Chicago. He was dressed as a businessman in a blue suit and white shirt. His dark black hair was graying at the temples. The weather was agreeable, and he smiled as he surveyed the area. He peered down Lawndale, a pleasant residential street gracefully shaded by a canopy of elms, and then proceeded down the sidewalk with a copy of the *Chicago Tribune* folded back to the real estate section. Brick bungalows and small apartment buildings lined the parkways. Daffodils and pansies added splashes of color. He gazed at the pleasant setting. *Urbs in horto,* wasn't that the Chicago motto? "City in a garden."

Back in 1893, wealthy bankers and industrialists purchased the 640-acre McAllister Farm, developed it into a large residential and commercial area and annexed it to the city of Chicago. Streetcar magnate DeLancey Louderbeck named the project after his boyhood home: Albany, New York. Twenty years later, Albany Park had seven thousand residents, and commercial land was valued at $52 per frontal foot. By 1940, Albany Park reported 56,692 inhabitants, and the cost per commercial frontal foot had jumped to more than $3,000.

By 1965, Albany Park was an established neighborhood and a pastel mural of diversity. Its tree-lined streets and parks had become beacons for European immigrants. They came from Poland, from Sweden, from Russia and Germany. Many were refugees. They fled the Russian pogroms, the devastation of the First World War and the ravages of the Second World War. A person waiting for a bus on the corner of Lawrence and Kimball might hear seven different languages.

When the man reached a redbrick three-flat with a FOR RENT sign hanging on the front gate, he stopped. He consulted his paper, nodded, walked up four concrete steps and pressed the door buzzer.

"I'm here to see about the apartment," he said to the woman who answered the door.

"Oh, well, I can tell you straight off, it's lovely," she said. "And it's currently vacant." She appeared to be middle-aged, a tad over five foot six, and was neatly dressed in a fitted dress, navy with small white polka dots. Her shoulder-length auburn hair had soft curls. He thought she had a pleasant face.

"My name is Ruth Gold," she said.

She looked him over as well. He was square-shouldered and handsome in his suit, and his shoes were shined, always a good sign for Ruth. He seemed well mannered. In some ways, he reminded her of Cary Grant. He must be a downtown businessman, she concluded, though she detected the hint of a European accent.

"My name is Eli," he said with a smile and a slight nod. "Eli Rosen."

She took a step back and tipped her head toward the apartment door. "The unit is right here on the first floor, a very nice one-bedroom with a full kitchen. The former tenants moved to Skokie. It's only been available for three weeks." She unlocked the apartment door and beckoned him to enter. "Rent's one hundred and sixty dollars a month, payable in advance, promptly on the first."

The apartment was spotless. The kitchen was small but certainly sufficient for Eli. Two windows overlooked a small patch of grass and bushes in the front. The floor was covered in patterned linoleum. He nodded. "I think this will do nicely, Mrs. Gold," he said.

"What is your line of work, Mr. Rosen, if I may ask?"

"I work for the government."

Ruth's eyes widened. "The government? Oh, my goodness."

Eli smiled. "Just an office desk job. Really quite unexciting."

Ruth nervously tipped her head from side to side, hesitated and then said, "I know this is kind of awkward, but I have to inform you that we have rules. This is a quiet building. There's just my eighty-two-year-old mother, my twenty-five-year-old daughter and me. I mean, you don't look the type, but we don't want any wild parties or loud music or drugs, you know?"

"I'm not the type, Mrs. Gold."

"Hmm. Okay. So do you want the apartment? I have other people that might be interested."

He took a money clip from his pocket and counted out one hundred and sixty dollars. "I'll take it," he said with a warm smile. "You can tell all those other interested people that it's been rented."

Ruth took the money and shook his hand. "Welcome to Albany Park, Mr. Rosen."

CHAPTER TWENTY-SEVEN

CHICAGO

ALBANY PARK NEIGHBORHOOD

MAY 1965

In her bedroom in the second-floor apartment, with her arms contorted up over her shoulders, twenty-five-year-old Mimi Gold struggled with the zipper and clasp of her new two-piece dress. "Mom," she called, "would you please come help me?"

"I love that dress, Mimi," Ruth Gold said as she fastened the hook and eye.

Mimi did a quick spin and her pleated dress twirled. "$49.95 at Bonwit's. How do I look?"

"Fabulous!"

"Do I look professional? I'm on assignment tonight."

"I thought you were going to Christine's engagement party."

"I am, but I'm also covering it for the *Trib*. If I'm lucky, I'll get a few columns on the society page."

"Is Nathan going with you?"

"Are you snooping, Mom?"

Ruth smiled and bit her lip. "I don't know, maybe. You seem to be seeing quite a bit of one another."

Mimi smiled and kissed her mother on the cheek. "Okay, I forgive you. Nathan is a close friend of Preston's. He'll be at the party as well. I'm sure we'll meet up, but we're not going together."

Ruth disappeared into the kitchen and returned with a cake plate covered in foil. "Mimi, before you go, would you mind taking this cake down to Mr. Rosen? He moved into the Levinsons' apartment last week."

"Does Mr. Rosen have a family? The Levinsons were pretty crowded in that little apartment."

She chuckled. "Yes, they were. I'm sure that's why they moved. Mr. Rosen is a single man. Very nice-looking."

Mimi raised her eyebrows and smiled. "Do you have your eyes on him, Mom?"

"I do not! He's quite the gentleman, but there's something about him, Mimi. I sense an air of purpose. There's a reason he's moving into this neighborhood. A man like that doesn't just wander down Lawndale and ring my doorbell. He's very polished and very professional. You have to wonder why isn't he renting an apartment on the Gold Coast or on Lake Shore Drive? Why Albany Park?"

"Maybe he likes quiet neighborhoods."

Ruth wasn't convinced. "No, there's something more. He says he works for the government."

"What branch of the government?"

Ruth shrugged. "I don't know. He looks like James Bond to me. Maybe he's a spy?"

"In Albany Park? In a one-bedroom apartment? That's his purpose, to be a spy in Albany Park?" Mimi giggled. "James Bond of Lawndale Street! Seriously, Mom?"

She shrugged again. "Okay, maybe the FBI. But I'm telling you, he's here for a reason. I have a nose for these things."

Mimi laughed, took the plate, inhaled deeply and smiled. "I have a nose for Grandma's cake. Can I have a piece?"

"No."

"How is she feeling tonight?"

"Much better," Ruth said, and nodded her head in the direction of the living room. "She's watching the news. You know she has a crush on Chet Huntley."

Grandma was sitting on the couch, straight and tall. No slouching allowed, as she would say. Her silver hair was permed, and a print robe hung loosely from her thin shoulders. Her eyes were glued to the nightly news and an interview with a NASA engineer at Cape Kennedy.

"The leak in the Gemini Four rocket has been repaired," the engineer said to David Brinkley. "Lift-off is a go for Thursday."

"He's going to walk in space, Mimi," Grandma said without looking up. "Ed White, the astronaut. Can you imagine floating outside a space capsule, hanging on with some kind of a rope?"

Mimi shook her head. "Nope. Would you do it, Grandma?"

"I should say not. I'll be up there soon enough."

Mimi leaned over and kissed her on the cheek. "Good night, Grandma."

"Are you taking that cake down to the new tenant?"

Mimi nodded. "Is this your famous babka?"

Ruth walked up and interjected. "Yes, it is, and you take it straight to Mr. Rosen. No pinching pieces off the bottom. Tell him that we welcome him to the building."

"Oh, come on, Mama. Just a small pinch, just a *biselleh*. He'll never notice."

Ruth stood firm with her hands on her hips.

"All right, I'll take him the cake, but I don't think it's fair that I don't get a piece."

❦

Eli opened his door to find a pretty young woman holding a cake plate. "Yes?"

"Mr. Rosen, I'm Mimi Gold. I live upstairs. This is a welcome gift for you. My grandma baked it, and her cakes are really good. I personally vouch for them."

"Oh, how nice." He eyed the plate, pulled back the corner of the foil and said, "Oh my, this looks like babka. Is it?"

Mimi nodded. "Yes, and this one's my very favorite. It has raspberries inside." She put her finger to her lips and whispered, "And a little whiskey. My grandma's from Lodz."

It only appeared for the tiniest of moments, but Mimi saw it. A sudden freeze in Eli's expression, an unexpected splash of ice-cold water. He quickly replaced it with a smile, as though he drew a curtain to hide a secret room. "Lodz?" he said. "Of course. I know it well. It was about three hours from Lublin, where I grew up."

He pulled off the foil, pinched a small piece of cake off the bottom between his thumb and forefinger and popped it into his mouth. "Mmm, Mmm. Just like I remember."

Mimi laughed. "Just a minute ago, my mom warned me not to pinch a piece on my way down here."

"Go ahead," he said, holding the plate out. "That's how he always did it. I promise I won't tell."

Mimi blushed and pinched a piece of cake. "Mmm. It's the best."

Eli licked his lips. "This cake is fabulous. Funny how food can bring back strong memories."

"Back in Lublin," Mimi said, "did your grandma bake babka?"

"Yes, she did, and so did my wife."

"Sometimes my grandma twists the dough into little rolls with cinnamon and chocolate like . . ."

"Rugalach," said Eli, finishing the sentence.

"Right," said Mimi. "Is that what your grandma did?"

Another momentary lapse as Eli's eyes saw something far away. He took a deep breath and said, "Mostly my wife. She was the baker."

Mimi decided not to pry any further.

"Will you share a piece of this delicious cake and a cup of coffee with me, Mimi?"

"I wish I could, but I'm off to a party. Maybe another time, Mr. Rosen. The congressman's daughter just got engaged and he's throwing a big bash for her. I'm covering it for the *Tribune*."

Eli raised his eyebrows. "Oh, you're a reporter?"

Mimi smiled. "A staff reporter. I've only been there for a year and a half. I'm trying to save up a little money and get my own place."

Eli nodded. "The *Tribune*'s a fine newspaper. Would we be talking about Congressman Zielinski? Is this his party at the VFW?"

"Yes, how did you know? Were you invited?"

Eli smiled. "Invited? No. I must have read about it somewhere. Witold 'Vittie' Zielinski, the U.S. congressman for this district, isn't that right?"

"Yes, do you know him?"

"I'm not sure. We may have met many years ago, if he's the man I'm thinking of. He's been a congressman for a long time, hasn't he?"

"Yes, almost twenty years. He's the chair of the House Armed Services Committee. Very influential in Washington, and he's the father of Christine Zielinski, who's a very good friend of mine."

Eli smiled. "Well, off with you then. If you're not too late or too tired, knock on my door on your way upstairs and we'll share a slice of babka and coffee. I'd love to hear about the congressman and his party. I understand that several dignitaries and influential people will be there as well."

"That's what I hear. Good night, Mr. Rosen."

Eli closed his door, smiled and thought, *The longest journey begins but with a single step.*

He cut a slice of babka and carried it to the coffee table. In the silence of the room, he took a bite, closed his eyes and let his mind return to the Lublin he knew before the apocalypse. The sounds, the sights, the smells— they all returned to him so easily.

Eli smiled at his memories. If they had known, right then and there, would it have made any difference? Could they have avoided the inevitable? Would he have made wiser decisions, better plans, listened to better advice, had clearer foresight? Most of all, would he have ever placed his trust in a man so vile as Maximilian Poleski? All moot questions now. His heart beat heavily, and his eyes filled with tears.

He sat in the dark with his coffee, his babka and his promise.

CHAPTER TWENTY-EIGHT

The gray cement walls of the Wilson Avenue VFW were colorfully decorated for Congressman Zielinski's party, all in harmony with the upcoming Memorial Day. Red, white and blue bunting draped from the interior cornices. American flags were posted about the perimeter and on either side of the well-worn wooden stage. A large banner, in muted shades of red, white and blue, reading CONGRATULATIONS PRESTON AND CHRISTINE, was draped above the stage, where a band was playing swing music. Some of the guests were dancing.

Mimi had a small notebook, and from time to time she would jot notes to herself: quick descriptions she planned to use in her society piece. She made a note of Mayor Daley standing off to the left of the stage talking to Alderman Becker. She jotted that a long reception line had formed, waiting for the opportunity to shake hands with Congressman Zielinski. She wrote "The Congressman stood regally in his black tuxedo." Mimi especially liked her tagline: "Royalty deigns to greet its courtiers."

She felt a gentle tap on her shoulder, and a voice from behind said, "Hey, Meems, how is Brenda Starr, ace reporter, doing tonight?"

Mimi smiled. "Brenda is doing just fine, thank you."

Nathan Stone, broad shouldered and handsome in his dark blue suit, white shirt and narrow black tie, had a drink in his hand and a smile on his face. "Doesn't the *Trib* give you a day off?"

"I volunteered. If I'm lucky, I might get a byline Sunday. Who did you come with tonight?"

He grinned. "Ah, a trick question. I came alone. knowing *you* would be here." He looked around the hall. "This is like a high school reunion, don't you think? Preston and Christine together as always, Ricky Lofton's standing over there telling jokes, Myrna's already slurring her words and the party hasn't even begun. It's a replay of the Von Steuben homecoming dance, except that the homecoming king and queen are really getting married. Where is Christine? I don't see her."

Mimi scanned the room and shrugged. "I don't see her either."

Mimi gazed at the corner, where three men were talking and punctuating their remarks with pointed fingers. She jotted a few notes. Nathan tipped his head toward the congressman. "The great Vittie Zielinski. What is it now, twelve, thirteen elections he's won? He must have more seniority than anyone in Congress."

"Pretty close," Mimi said. "The man he's whispering to is Senator Paul Douglas, and I'll wager it's about the voting rights bill. Vittie's a cosponsor."

"Who's the guy standing with him?" Nathan pointed at a thin, bald man with rimless glasses.

"That's Vittie's chief of staff, Mike Stanley," Mimi said. "He's been with Vittie a long time. Christine says her dad won't make a move without Mike. She says he always stays in the background, but he's really the brains in the congressional office."

"Preston told me he doesn't like Stanley."

"Seriously? Stanley makes all the staff decisions and runs the congressional office. Preston wouldn't have a job if weren't for Mike Stanley."

"Preston has a job because he's engaged to Vittie's daughter," Nathan said. "He's been a good friend of mine since grade school, but let's not fool ourselves. All Preston does is greet people when they come into the neighborhood office. He listens to their complaints and writes them down. He doesn't like Stanley because Stanley treats him like a coffee boy and orders him around. Don't tell him I said that."

"Okay," Mimi said, "I'm going to go find Chrissie."

Nathan headed toward the bar. Preston saw him coming and gave him a thumbs-up.

"Great party, Pres," Nathan said.

"My future father-in-law spares no expense." Turning to the bartender, he said, "A shot of Jack and a beer; one for me and one for my buddy." Preston downed the shot, took a swig of beer and pointed to a group of naval recruits in their dress whites. "Look over there, Nate. All those guys came down today from Great Lakes Naval Base. Vittie brought them in to present the colors. It gives me the chills. Those poor suckers will soon be shipping off to Nam."

Nathan shook his head. "They're not suckers, Preston. They enlisted. I give those guys a lot of credit."

"They enlisted because they knew that sooner or later they'd be drafted. Bottom line, within six months they'll be loading and unloading ships in Cam Ranh Bay. Anyway, that won't be my problem."

"What makes you so sure? It's a universal draft. So far, you've been lucky; you haven't been called up."

"They don't draft married men. Single guys have to go first."

"You're not married yet."

"I will be in November. Besides, I got an ace in the hole. I work for the most powerful man on the House Armed Services Committee. Did you ever think about that? Vittie doesn't want his son-in-law shipping off to Vietnam. He wants me home taking care of his lovely daughter." He leaned over and said, "Christine comes with fringe benefits." Then he laughed and slapped Nathan on the back.

Mimi and Christine entered the hall, and Preston put down his drink. "Here comes my one and only." He lifted Christine and twirled her around. "Where have you been all night? Everyone's been asking. You better not have been talking to Fast Nicky."

Christine put her hand on her hip and huffed. "I've been talking to Mimi! And you've been too busy talking to all your drinking buddies to pay attention to me. I want to dance."

"Me, too," Mimi said, taking Nathan's arm.

Away from Preston and Christine, Nathan said, "Do you know who Fast Nicky is?"

Mimi nodded. "Nicholas Bryant, Chrissie's boss at Bryant Shipping. He's the guy over there, the one in the checkered blazer. He's some kind of business associate of Vittie's."

"Oh, well then, Preston doesn't like him either. He thinks he's too friendly with Christine. He makes her work late a couple nights a week."

Mimi smiled. "Pres is jealous."

"True. Preston doesn't like the fact that Christine spends so much time with him. Maybe he's jealous, maybe he's just protective, but Preston is flat-out nuts about Chrissie."

"And she's nuts about him. Just look at the two of them. They melt into each other and dance as though they were one. Perfect together. They truly do love each other."

"They'd better—they're about to get married."

It was ten thirty when the band played a soft rendition of Etta James's "At Last" and the VFW's lights blinked off and on. Mimi phoned her story into the *Trib*, and Nathan offered to walk her home. He pointed to her notebook. "Did you get everything you need?"

"And then some. All the rich and famous. I wish I had a fraction of the money that was in that room tonight. Did you see Grant Thomas, chairman of the board of National Steel? Or Lloyd Davis of Northern Aeronautics?"

Nathan shrugged. "I wouldn't know either one of them. I'm surprised they all showed up at an engagement party in a neighborhood VFW."

Mimi's eyebrows raised. "They're here to pay homage to the eminent Vittie Zielinski. Each of those men represents a major military contractor. The business their companies do with the Department of Defense is in the billions."

They reached Mimi's building and stopped to say good night at the bottom of the front steps. Nathan cleared his throat. "So, um, are you busy next Saturday?"

Mimi smiled. "Nope."

"Maybe a movie? Want to see *Zorba the Greek*?"

"Sounds great."

Nathan pointed to lights coming from the first-floor window. "Does your mom have a new tenant?"

She nodded. "Mr. Rosen. My mom thinks he's a spy." Mimi giggled mischievously and bit her bottom lip. "Do you want to meet him?"

"Meems, it's almost eleven o'clock."

"I know, but he told me that if he was up, I should stop in for coffee and a piece of cake. His light's still on. Come on, I'll knock softly. You can meet James Bond. If he's asleep, we'll go away."

Eli opened the door after a couple of knocks. "I'm so glad you stopped by. Your grandmother's babka must have been calling your name, am I right?"

"I confess. It's true. This is my good friend, Nathan Stone."

Eli showed them into the living room and offered them a seat on the couch while he made a pot of coffee. Mimi gazed around the room. The furniture appeared to be newly purchased and utilitarian. Functional. Nothing fancy. Nothing that bespoke the personality of the tenant, with the exception of two framed photographs: a small, faded black-and-white picture of a woman and a child in a silver frame that sat on an end table and a black-and-white photo of an odd-shaped building that hung above the sofa table. She walked over to take a closer look. It appeared to be an office building, at least five stories tall, with columns in the front and a decorative capstone over the entranceway. There were Hebrew letters scrolled above the doorway. Standing in the front of the building was a short man in a wide-brimmed hat.

"That is my father, Jakob Rosen, at the Lublin yeshiva," Eli said as he set a coffee service on the table. "The picture was taken in 1930. My father and grandfather built that building."

"I'm sorry to say I don't know much about Lublin or the yeshiva," Mimi said. "Maybe someday I'll visit."

Eli poured three cups of coffee. "The Lublin you'd visit today would bear little resemblance to the Lublin I knew before the war. My family lived in the Jewish quarter, not too far from that building. Back then, the Jewish community was vibrant and comprised a third of the city. We had twelve synagogues and two Jewish newspapers. To me, I thought the whole world was like that. I didn't know any different. Everyone spoke Yiddish. Do you know any Yiddish, Mimi?"

"A *bissel*."

Eli chuckled. "Of course, your grandmother is from Lodz. That was a big city—over six hundred thousand people, and a third of them were Jewish as well. I traveled to Lodz many times for business. And then..." He paused as a breath caught in his chest. Another one of those times, thought Mimi. A momentary digression. And just as quickly, Eli returned to the present and said, "And then for other reasons. Anyway, that was a long time ago."

Some powerful memories must be tugging on him, thought Mimi, *and someday I'm going to find out his secret. The reporter in me knows there's a story buried here. Wouldn't that be something to write?*

Eli sliced three pieces of babka and set them out on his coffee table. Mimi broke the silence. "A few minutes ago, if I said something that made you uncomfortable, Mr. Rosen, I am sorry. I apologize."

"No, no. Please don't be sorry. You said nothing wrong. A couple of things went through my mind, that's all. You asked about Lublin, and before the war it was a wonderful place to live and work. My family had been Lubliners for generations. We always said we built the famous Grodzka Gate in the year 1357." He smiled. "I can't personally vouch for that. Anyway, after the Nazi occupation, everything that it stood for was no more. No more yeshiva, no more Grodzka Gate, no more Jewish quarter, no more Lublin Jews. Barely two hundred of our people survived."

He shook his head, turned and said, "Forgive me for running on. It's a bad habit of mine. Now I work for the federal government, and I am a brand new resident of Albany Park. Tell me, how was the congressman's party tonight?"

"Lavish," Mimi said. "It was crowded and filled with politicians and businessmen."

Nathan made a face, and Eli said, "I take it you don't agree."

"Oh, it was lavish and crowded," Nathan said, "but it was a Vittie Zielinski production, more of a political rally than an engagement party. It shouldn't have been that kind of party. It should have been a celebration of two young people who have announced they are going to get married. For me, it was cold and impersonal."

Mimi nodded. "That's true. It was all about the congressman, not the couple."

"You're writing the story for the *Tribune,* aren't you Mimi?" Eli said. "Will you be expressing that opinion? Cold and impersonal? Businesslike?" He had a glint in his eye. "After all, you're a reporter. Aren't you going to report the truth?"

Mimi scoffed. "Who are you kidding? Write those things about Vittie Zielinski? Where would I be working tomorrow?"

"Didn't you make notes of all the politicians and businessmen that attended? Deals made? Smoky backroom politics? I think it would make for spicy reading."

Mimi smiled. "I made notes and there was plenty of that going on, but my story will be printed in the society pages. My readers will be more interested in what the women were wearing and what dishes were served."

"I would love to read the *real* story," Eli said. "I'd be far more interested in which politicians and captains of industry were in attendance."

Mimi raised an eyebrow and thought, *I bet you would.*

"Will you write that story for me?" Eli said.

Mimi stood. "Well, maybe someday, Mr. Rosen."

"I'll hold you to it. Good night, Miss Gold."

CHAPTER TWENTY-NINE

CHICAGO

ALBANY PARK NEIGHBORHOOD

JUNE 1965

The doorbell rang and Mimi heard her mother call, "Nathan's here."

"About time," Mimi said. She came out of the back bedroom with a light sweater over her shoulder, kissed her mom on the cheek and took Nathan's arm. "I'll be home late tonight; we're meeting Christine and Preston at the Earl of Old Town. Chrissie said they have an important announcement to make."

"Sorry, I wasn't on time," Nathan said, opening the door for her. "Mr. Rosen was sitting on the front stoop when I arrived. He remembered me from last month, and I stopped for a minute to chat with him. He was reading the *Tribune* and the headline said that fifty thousand more GIs were being sent to Vietnam. I told him my brother had been drafted and was headed out to Fort Dix. When I said that, his expression changed. He looked concerned. Sympathetic."

"Well, obviously he's been through a war."

"I know. He wished Billy well and said he would pray for him."

"He's a nice man," Mimi said.

"I told him we were going to meet up with Preston and Christine tonight, and right away he started asking me about the engagement party and Congressman Zielinski. Did I know him very well? Had I been to his office? How did Preston like working for him? Did I know any of the other members of his staff? He sure seemed curious."

"I get the same feeling," Mimi said. "He's asked me about him as well. He wants to know who was at the party. What politicians, what businessmen, what military contractors. It's more than just a passive curiosity. I wonder if the FBI is investigating Vittie?"

Nathan laughed. "Do you still think Mr. Rosen is with the FBI?"

Mimi shrugged. "Mom does. Or maybe she thinks it's the CIA. He doesn't appear to keep regular hours or even a regular job that he goes to every day."

"And I suppose the CIA is now operating out of a one-bedroom apartment in Albany Park?"

Mimi winked. "They can be very covert, you know." She put her finger to her lips and whispered, "Shh. We better be careful what we say in the hallways."

✧

The TV above the bar at the Earl was displaying the news and a segment on Vietnam. The camera panned the military base at Danang: GIs in T-shirts, cigarettes hanging from their lips, and boxes upon boxes of supplies stacked on the ground. Many more were being unloaded from C-130s. Sandbags were piled around guard posts. In the background, fighter jets of the Eightieth Tactical Fighter Squadron were taking off, and the roar forced the reporter to pause his narrative. He had been talking about the rapid buildup of men and supplies. He pointed to the sky; "Operation Rolling Thunder," he said. "Those are F-105 Thunderchief fighters, headed north toward the DRV." Going back to his script, the reporter quoted the State Department press officer, saying, "President Johnson announced today that if requested by the South Vietnamese government, he has authorized General Westmoreland to commit American soldiers to ground combat."

Nathan's eyes were locked on the TV screen. The news clearly upset him. "Jesus, now he wants ground combat. This war is getting bigger and bigger. We were just supposed to maintain a base. Provide logistical support for the South Vietnamese. This damn war is getting way out of control and my brother is headed over there. More men, more equipment, more planes, more money—where does it all end? Ground combat forces. Shit!"

At the other end of the bar, a muscular man in a khaki T-shirt was nursing a beer. He slowly turned his head. "Have to," he said. "Ya can't just stand guard with a rifle on the edge of an airbase, fella. The VC launches rockets and mortars from the trees and bushes. You wanna maintain a base, you gotta extend the perimeter fifteen, twenty miles. You gotta go flush 'em out. So now you're talking operations that run deep into the jungles. That's what they call ground combat, buddy." He shrugged. "The VC are smart. That's the way the weak fights the strong. They pick the time and place of the battles."

Nathan retorted, "Isn't this the same LBJ who said, 'We are not about to send American boys nine or ten thousand miles away from home to do what Asian boys ought to be doing for themselves?' So why the hell aren't the South Vietnamese doing the ground combat?"

The man broke into a laugh. "Right. The mighty army of South Vietnam. You guys are a scream."

"I don't want my brother going to Danang," Nathan said to Mimi. "He's just a kid."

She put her arm around his shoulders. "Right now, Billy's just going to basic. He may never end up going overseas."

Preston gave Christine a nudge and whispered, "Aren't you glad I'm not going? Getting married sure has its advantages."

Christine glared at him. "You can be such an obnoxious jerk at times, you know that?"

"Aw, Chrissie, he didn't hear me. Besides, *I* can be a jerk? *Me?* How about the fact that you've been working till ten o'clock every night this week with Fast Nicky?"

"It's my job, Preston. He pays me overtime."

Preston's voice was getting louder. "Why is it necessary to work till ten o'clock in a lousy cartage company? What's Nicky shipping at ten o'clock?"

Christine tightened her lips and glared at Preston. "First of all, it's not a lousy cartage company. We are a big-time logistics company. Nicky sends shipments to New York, Norfolk, San Diego and Long Beach every day. And they're loaded with steel and iron and important military parts. For your information, a lot of it is top-secret Pentagon stuff. He needs me there to do the clerical work, making sure the deliveries are on time and the paperwork is done. And he has meetings with clients that go late into the night. Big important people."

Preston scoffed. "Top-secret, my ass. You know that's bullshit; you could do your clerical work when you come in in the morning. I know your father got you the job, but you could work anywhere. You're a talented girl. Tell your dad you don't want to work there anymore."

"I'm not going to embarrass my father, Pres. He asked Nicky to give me the job."

"Yeah, well, the job description failed to say you'd have to work nights until ten o'clock with a pervert who wants to get into your pants."

"Oh, give me a break. He's not making moves on me."

"Didn't he offer you a glass of wine last week?"

"I didn't take it, Pres."

Nathan held up his hands. "Hold on, folks. How did this get from Vietnam to slamming on Fast Nicky?"

Christine put her hands on her hips. "And I don't appreciate you saying that you're marrying me to stay out of the army, either."

Preston leaned over and gave Christine a hug. "Aw, you know that's not why I'm getting married. I'm getting married 'cause I love ya." Preston took a swig of beer. "You wouldn't believe how many calls I get at the office every day from guys who just got their orders. They want Vittie to get them out of the draft. 'Tell the congressman I have a sick mother, tell the congressman I have flat feet, tell the congressman I just took a new job. Please tell Congressman Zielinski I voted for him.' Every excuse known to man. I must answer twenty of those calls a day."

"So what do you tell them?" Nathan said. "Do you tell them all to get married?"

"No, I give them the pat response; Congressman Zielinski will look into it, but in the meantime, you need to comply with your orders and report on time."

"Look," Christine said, "I just want to say for the record, I'm not the only one putting in long hours. Preston hasn't been home before nine o'clock any night this week."

Preston groaned and nodded. "It's true. The whole bunch is in town this week and it creates a lot of pressure on me. Mike Stanley's in and out of the office every day, and he gets me rattled. He's got those steel eyes like a leopard, and he glares at me like I'm his dinner. You wouldn't believe the crap I have to deal with because of him. I have to write down every contact, every telephone call and file a report. 'Get their name, address and telephone number, Preston. File a detailed report, Preston. Remember, you're the face of the office, Preston.'"

"That sounds smart to me," Nathan said. "A congressman wants to keep track of his constituents. It comes in handy at election time. What's wrong with that?"

"Because I get a hundred stupid complaints a day. If someone doesn't get their garbage collected on time, they call our office. Tell the congressman I want my garbage picked up. It's not enough for me to tell the idiot to call the mayor's office or the alderman's office, that this is not a *federal* matter, but then I have to make out a report with the guy's name, address and telephone number and how the issue got resolved."

Nathan laughed.

"It's not funny; it's a waste of my time," Preston said. "Just today, some crazy old guy wanders in off the street and says, 'I want to see my congressman. I'm a veteran.' Of course, Vittie's not in and I tell him that. Then he points at Stanley's private office and says, 'I can hear people back there.'"

"Stanley has a private office?" Nathan said.

Preston nodded. "Oh, yeah. Locked up tight. Even I don't have a key. Maybe it's got something to do with security clearance, but they sure don't want me to see what's back in that office. On the other hand, Vittie's office is always open. He has this fancy rosewood desk and a big leather chair and pictures of famous dignitaries all over his walls: there he is shaking hands with Truman, shaking hands with Kennedy, or Stevenson, or LBJ. Vittie doesn't care who goes in, but not Stanley. He must have the Coca-Cola formula locked up tight in his office. It's off-limits to everyone but Vittie, Stanley and the accountant. Anyway, this random guy hears Stanley and the accountant talking in the locked office, and he assumes it's Vittie. He demands to see him. 'Don't lie to me,' he says. 'That's the congressman. I can hear him.' I say, 'That's not him; it's an accountant.'"

Nathan's forehead furrowed. "What does the accountant do in the top-secret room?"

Preston shrugged. "How the hell do I know? He comes in once a month, doesn't say a word to me, hustles into the back room, where he has a key, and he locks himself in. If he goes out for lunch, he locks the door. Sometimes Stanley will come by and the two of them will work through the afternoon behind the locked door."

"Does Vittie have some other businesses besides being a congressman?" Mimi said.

"Not that he tells me about. I know that when he's in town, there's a lot of phone calls and meetings with bigwigs, but I've been told it's not my business. I don't go into the meetings, not even to bring them coffee. We have a receptionist who answers the phones, and she brings them coffee. That's Vittie's rules. Look, he's a wealthy man and he probably needs the accountant to keep track of all his money."

"He's always been a congressman, right?" Nathan said.

"Far as I know, since the forties."

"Congressmen don't make *that* much money, do they?"

Preston smiled. "They don't let me count it, Nate. They leave that for Stanley and the accountant."

"So what happened with the old guy?"

"Okay. He starts complaining in Polish or Russian or something about his brother and his VA benefits. I can't understand half of what he is saying. Something about his brother can't get medical attention and he's a veteran of World War Two. He's got headaches and high blood pressure. Now I'm fed up and I say, 'Do I look like a doctor? Is this a doctor's office?' He gets all pissed off. I give him the address of the VA hospital in Maywood. He says he's been there and they didn't help him. He wants the congressman to make a phone call. I tell him the congressman has better things to do than make phone calls about his brother's dumb headaches."

"Whoa. What did he do?"

"Just kept screaming at me. Finally, I had to show him the door. For an old guy, he put up a hell of a struggle."

"Did Stanley find out?"

"No, thank God. He and the accountant didn't come out of the office until after the guy was gone. I mean, maybe I was a little hard on the guy, but he was the umpteenth crybaby of the day."

Christine held up her hands. "Okay, enough. As I told you, Mimi, we've got a big announcement to make tonight. Are you ready?" She lifted her glass, bit her lower lip in a big smile and said, "Pres and I are moving up the wedding date!"

"What? How come?" Mimi asked. "I thought everything was set for November."

"It was, but now it's going to be August twenty-first. It was my dad's idea. He asked that we move it up because of his congressional agenda. With the war going on, he expects a busy fall, and he prefers to have the wedding out of the way before the summer recess is over."

Mimi had a shocked expression. "I think I would die. How does Vittie think you're supposed to arrange a wedding in six weeks?"

"Oh well, he's Vittie Zielinski, you know. He can do anything. He practically took the whole thing over. The wedding will be at Saint Hyacinth, and the reception will be at the Palmer House. He's arranged for the buses. I'm supposed to call in the names and addresses of the guests to the stationery company next week so the invitations can go out. And, Meems, you wouldn't believe the invitation list. It reads like a *Forbes* magazine top fifty—the rich and famous. It'll be fabulous."

"Oh my God. What about the flowers? The dresses? The food? Is Vittie supposed to get all that arranged, too?"

Christine shrugged. "He's one of the most powerful men in the country, Meems. He makes phone calls and things happen. He promised me that everything will work out fine, and it will. All our dresses will be ready for fitting by July tenth. The florist only needs five days' notice. They took care of everything for the reception and dinner, including, and get this, Steve Lawrence and Eydie Gormé and their whole orchestra."

"Steve and Eydie, are you kidding?"

"He's a friend of my dad's."

"What about your honeymoon?"

"We'll still go in November. We have tickets to Maui; it's all prepaid."

"Well, that calls for a drink," Nathan said. The boys went to the bar for a pitcher, and Mimi said, "That's great news, Chris, but I can tell something else is on your mind. What is it?"

"There is, but don't tell Preston. It's Nicky. I lied when I said he wasn't making moves. He called me into his office this afternoon to tell me how cute I looked in my miniskirt. He was sitting there with an open bottle of bourbon and a couple of glasses. I turned down the bourbon and told him he could quit looking at my legs. He laughed."

"Creep."

"When I turned to leave, I glanced to the side, and there was a briefcase full of cash underneath his topcoat. Nicky saw me staring and said, 'Some lucky girl's gonna get me and a whole lot of money.'"

"Chris, you need to get out of there. You should give your notice. That place is nothing but trouble for you."

"I know, but I can't. My dad doesn't want me to. He got me the job, and he wants me to stay and keep my eyes open. I report to him on what shipments are going out, that sort of thing. But I'd quit if I could—Nicky's getting way too friendly, and things are getting uncomfortable for me. Two nights ago, I came home at ten thirty and Preston was fuming. He said, 'I'm going to pay Fast Nicky a visit; you work too many hours.' I begged him not to. I know Nicky's a jerk, but I get paid a lot of money."

The boys headed back with the beer, and Christine whispered, "Don't say anything."

CHAPTER THIRTY

A pure-white satin runner covered the center aisle of the Basilica of Saint Hyacinth Catholic Church, and large pink-and-white rose bouquets punctuated the ends of each row. The theological center of Chicago's Polish community was a colorful setting for the much-anticipated wedding of Congressman Zielinski's daughter to Preston Roberts. As the wedding guests filed in, Nathan, Preston and Mimi stood off to the side in the anteroom. "It won't be long now, Pres," Nathan said with a chuckle. "Your single days are over. From now on it'll be 'Yes dear, no dear, what else can I do for you, dear?'"

"Very funny, Nate." But Preston was not amused. He took deep breaths and anxiously shifted his weight from one foot to the other.

"Jesus, Preston, where did these nerves come from? This is definitely not like you. You've been dating Chrissie for six years. You know each other inside and out—sorry for the pun—and you've never been the least bit frightened by big crowds. I don't get it."

Preston shook his head. "It's not the wedding or the crowds. Something happened at the office yesterday, and I don't know what I should do about it. What makes it worse, they'll all be here tonight, and I don't want a confrontation at my wedding."

"What happened?" Mimi said. "Who'll be here?"

Preston shook his head. "Meems, I can't talk about it. Something I shouldn't have done, shouldn't have seen. I've been told not to do it, but I did it anyway, and now I know why the room is locked."

"Stanley's top-secret room?"

Preston nodded.

"What did you see?"

"I can't tell you, and you don't want to know." Preston raised his eyes to the ceiling. "Son of a bitch—it's *major shit*, Nate. I mean, maybe I'm wrong, maybe it isn't what I think it is, maybe I need another look."

"You better be careful," Nathan said. "Does anybody know you went in there?"

"I don't think so, but what if they found out? Stanley and the accountant, they've got eyes and ears everywhere. I don't think Stephanie saw me, but who knows? I don't want them to mess up my wedding day."

"Did Stephanie say something?"

Preston shook his head. "They left the room unlocked when they went out to lunch. It was too tempting, and I went snooping. Stephanie was at her desk in the front. I don't think she saw me, but what if she did?"

"So big deal," Nathan said, with a shrug. "They didn't say anything. Anyway, it's just a room of accounting papers."

"No, not just papers. There's a dozen ledger books, bank records, bills of lading, shipping forms. You know, you see things, you put two and two together and you realize you're looking at major shit. Everything in that room is tightly organized, and everything is in a certain place. Maybe when I was snooping around, I moved something and didn't put it back in the right place." He drew a deep breath through clenched teeth. "I shouldn't have been in there. But I saw shit, Nate. Major shit!"

"What the hell is major shit?"

"The stuff that could send people to jail for a long time. Let me know if you see a fat guy with greasy black hair and horn-rimmed glasses at the reception tonight."

"Who is that?"

"The accountant, and I want to stay away from him."

Mimi heard organ music and said, "We have to go. They're lining up. I'm sure everything will be all right."

"I agree," Nathan said. "Tonight, you're getting married to a fabulous girl. If anybody comes to bother you, you just tell me, and I'll take care of it. Tonight, I got your back—I'm running interference. Tonight, you're nothing but the luckiest man in the world."

Preston nodded. "Thanks, Nate. You're the best! We are the *two* luckiest guys in the world. Chrissie and Mimi—they're *both* terrific."

"Now you got it. Nothing to worry about."

⁓

Following the ceremony, a line of limousines and buses waited to shuttle the wedding party and their guests from the church on the city's northwest side to the reception at the Palmer House Hotel. As the formally attired couples stepped onto the hotel's red carpet, there was a constant pop of flashbulbs from newspaper and magazine photographers. THE CONGRESS-MAN'S DAUGHTER TIES THE KNOT.

⁓

Toasts were offered while the dessert was being served. Mimi walked to the microphone. She was nervous. "I guess it's my turn. Chrissie's been my best friend since grammar school, and I am so happy for her and Preston. I want to add my thanks to Congressman and Mrs. Zielinski for this incredible wedding." She blushed a little and said, "I have called him Uncle Vittie for the last fifteen years.

"Like this magnificent hotel, Uncle Vittie is a Chicago institution. I know it must be the reporter or the history lover in me, but when I got out of that limousine and saw everyone dressed in their fancy tuxes and long dresses, I thought I must be going to the wedding of Potter Palmer and Cissie Honoré. You know, it was almost a hundred years ago that Potter Palmer built this hotel and gave it to Cissie as a wedding present."

Vittie interjected. "Hold on now, Mimi, nobody's giving Christine any hotels." Everyone laughed. "Besides, I hope you know that right after Potter gave it to her, it burned to the ground."

Mimi laughed. "Yes, it did, Uncle Vittie. The Palmer House opened in September 1871, the most luxurious hotel in America, and six days later Mrs. O'Leary's cow kicked over the lantern, starting the Great Chicago Fire. But Potter rebuilt the hotel and opened the new Palmer House two years later. Cissie was the decorator: the classic interior, the Tiffany stained glass, the ceiling fresco—that was all Cissie's work.

"Look down at your dessert plate, the brownie with ice cream. Another

Cissie creation. In 1891, Congress awarded the World's Columbian Exposition to Chicago, and Cissie was president of the Board of Lady Managers. When the exposition opened, she instructed her chef to bake small cakes to put into her ladies' box lunches. He prepared delicious little chocolate square cakes, and he named them brownies. You're all eating Cissie's dessert." She raised a glass of champagne. "Here's to my best friends, Preston and Chrissie Roberts. May your love always be as sweet as the brownies. I love you guys." Amidst generous applause, Mimi took a bow and sat down.

"Nice job, Meems," Nathan said.

The orchestra began to play, and couples wandered out to the dance floor.

"Vittie sure went all-out for this wedding," Nathan said, "and all on short notice. It must have cost him a fortune."

Mimi leaned over and whispered, "I heard it was fifty thousand dollars, but no one needs to take up any collections for Vittie."

"Fifty thousand! Holy shit! That's enough to buy a nice house! He should have let them elope and bought them a house instead."

"Nathan, he already rented them a house."

"Where?"

"Albany Park, of course."

Five days later, on August 27, 1965, Mimi learned the real reason why Vittie wanted the wedding date moved up. The *Tribune*'s banner headline read, NEW HUSBANDS NOW ELIGIBLE FOR DRAFT. By an executive order, President Johnson eliminated the marital exemption for any man married *after* August 26, 1965. He did it without any prior public notice. His proclamation was planned in coordination with the congressional Armed Services Committees but not disclosed to the public until after it was signed. By virtue of the fact that Preston was married to Christine on August 22, he remained exempt from the military draft.

CHAPTER THIRTY-ONE

CHICAGO
ALBANY PARK NEIGHBORHOOD
SEPTEMBER 1965

Grandma loved to bake, and the Jewish holidays would find her home filled with sweet fragrances. She handed a box tied up in a blue ribbon to Mimi and said, "Would you please take this honey cake down to Mr. Rosen and wish him a sweet New Year? He's a nice man. Isn't he from Lublin or Lodz?"

"Yes, he is, Grandma. I think maybe both. On occasions, he's opened a small window into his life in Poland. A couple of times, when I mentioned Lodz, I noticed a change in his expression. Like he winced. There is pain associated with Lodz, I'd bet on it."

"I can understand that. That's why so many families I knew fled to Lithuania."

"He said he was transferred from Lublin to Lodz. He mentioned his wife, his father and his brother, but very briefly. I think he said he had a son."

"What happened to them all?"

Mimi shook her head and shrugged. "He didn't say, and I didn't pry. Maybe they didn't survive. He told me that the Nazis killed almost every Jew in Lublin. Forty thousand people."

"So sad, so horrible. Well, bring him the cake and tell him I wish him a happy and healthy New Year."

Mimi knocked on Eli's door and waited. She was just about to leave when the door opened. Mimi held out the box. "Happy New Year, Eli. *L'shana tovah*. Grandma baked this just for you, and I know you love cake. It's a honey cake for a sweet new year."

"That is so kind. Please thank her for me. And you know my weakness—I do love cake! Come in for a moment. Can I offer you a cup of coffee? A soda?"

"If you have a Coke, I would take that, thank you, but I can only stay a minute."

As Mimi waited, she noticed a Samsonite suitcase bearing a Washington Dulles baggage tag sitting in the hallway. Her attention was also drawn to the small black-and-white photo in the silver frame. It depicted a young boy in short pants and a sport jacket. Standing next to him was a woman with dark curly hair. She had her arm around the boy and was smiling proudly. "May I?" Mimi said.

Eli nodded, and Mimi gently picked up the picture. "Is this your wife?"

"Esther."

"She's beautiful, and she looks very kind and loving."

"More than you can imagine."

"Is that your son?"

He nodded. "Izaak."

"He looks young in this picture."

"He was five. It was right before the war."

Mimi smiled. "My, what a handsome boy."

Eli looked away. An uncomfortable silence followed, as though neither one knew where to take the conversation. Finally, Mimi put down the picture. "I'm sorry, Eli, I didn't mean to pry. It's Rosh Hashanah and I brought you a cake. Do you have plans to go to synagogue tonight?"

He shook his head. "I haven't connected with a synagogue in a long time, Mimi. In Lublin, synagogues were targets, places of persecution. People were killed in synagogues." He looked at Mimi with sad eyes. "I prayed and I prayed, Mimi, sometimes as hard as a man could pray, and I came to believe that no one was listening, because if He was listening, and He let it all happen, then . . . what's the point? It's beyond my understanding."

"What you and the Polish people endured, no one will ever understand, certainly not me. I'm just a twenty-five-year-old journalism grad. I never took a theology course in my life and I didn't really pay attention when my mother sent me to religious school. I was taught to believe that God is pure, good, all-knowing and all-powerful. But now I question the same paradoxes. Reason tells me that when He made the world, He could have made it any way He wanted. So why didn't He make a world that couldn't conceive of a Holocaust? Why didn't He create a utopia instead of a world where people are free to be evil? I have no answers, and yet I still go to synagogue and pray and I hope my prayers are heard. I still seek answers to those questions. I guess that's what faith is all about. Perhaps someday I will come to a better understanding. At least a workable compromise. And you, Eli Rosen, are welcome to come with my family tonight to seek the same answers if you like, but I can appreciate why you would decline."

"Are you sure you're only twenty-five?"

Mimi chuckled. "Just twenty-five."

"Maybe one day we will sit, and I will tell you of my family and my life in Poland. You are an easy and comfortable person to talk to, Mimi Gold."

"Thank you, Eli. I would be honored."

"I don't know about honored. I'm not all that mysterious."

Mimi smiled. "My mom thinks you are. She thinks you're with the CIA."

"Ha, ha. Please tell your mother that I am definitely not with the CIA."

Mimi bit her bottom lip and looked at him askance. "FBI?"

Eli furrowed his eyebrows. "That's enough talk for today. Happy New Year, Mimi."

❧

"I knew it," Ruth said. "I knew he was a G-man. Baggage tag for Washington? Unexciting government desk job, my giddy aunt!" She leaned forward. "Who do you suppose he's investigating?"

Mimi twisted her lips. "I got an idea. He asks a lot of questions about Vittie."

"Vittie!! Oh, my goodness, he'd better have both barrels loaded taking on one of the most powerful men in the country. Why do you think it's Vittie?"

"I don't know; I just have a feeling. He seems very interested. Unusually so. He's asked me questions about Vittie, about who was at the party and the wedding, and he also asked Nathan questions about him. He even wanted to know about Preston and what he did in Vittie's office."

Ruth smiled. "Imagine that. All this intrigue going on in my building in Albany Park."

CHAPTER THIRTY-TWO

CHICAGO

SEPTEMBER 1965

The Chicago Bears, the Monsters of the Midway, played their home games at Wrigley Field, the home of the Chicago Cubs. It took imagination and creativity to convert a 1914 baseball park into an NFL football stadium for four months of every year. Temporary stands, like those at a high school athletic field, were erected in front of the right field bleachers to seat an additional four thousand fans. Goalposts were set close to the brick wall in left field and on the first base line in front of the baseball visitor's dugout. Padding was installed all along the left field wall ever since 1932, when Bronko Nagurski ran headlong through the end zone and slammed into the brick wall. Though he was wearing his leather helmet, he wobbled back to the bench and told Coach Halas that the last guy gave him "quite a lick."

Preston, Christine, Nathan and Mimi shuffled down the aisle toward their tenth-row box seats on the forty-yard line for the home opener against the Los Angeles Rams. Preston proudly boasted that the seats were fringe benefits he received from being Vittie's "number one administrative assistant." So was the new metallic-blue Bonneville convertible that Preston drove to the game.

"Are you kidding?" Nathan said to Preston. "Who gets fringe benefits like that?"

Preston smiled. "I do."

They settled into their seats, and Christine commented, "I hope the Bears play better than they have so far this year."

"Home field magic," Preston said. "And keep your eyes on number forty. He's a rookie from Kansas named Gale Sayers."

Before the kickoff, when Preston and Nathan left to get hot dogs and drinks, Mimi turned to Christine and said, "So how is married life treating you?"

"Pretty great. I mean, when you live with someone full-time, there's bound to be arguments, but we're doing okay."

"Arguments?"

"Mostly about my job. I've been working crazy hours. I came home late again Friday night, and Preston was furious."

"I kind of understand it. You work a lot of nights, Chrissie. Doesn't your boss have a family to go home to?"

Christine shrugged. "He has three kids, but he and his wife are going through a nasty divorce. He's been kicked out of the house, and he's lonely. I get it. That's probably why he wants me around, but he's starting to get a little too friendly. He tells me what a cushy life he could give some lucky girl when his divorce is final. I laugh. I tell him his wife and kids will get all his money. Then he puts on a sly smile and tells me there's a lot they don't know about. I'm sure he means the cash he's been stashing. Then he offers me a drink."

"Damn, Christine. You can't let that go on."

Christine winced. "He wants me to be his confidant."

"No way!"

"I know. I try to distance myself. I try to keep it all on a joking level. But I think sometimes he's serious, especially when he's had a few."

"He *is* serious. How many clues do you need?"

"What am I supposed to do? He's my boss, and he pays me pretty damn well. I make a lot more than Preston does. I get a lot of overtime pay—time and a half. Besides, he works closely with my dad. Practically every shipment is slated for the military. He and my dad talk almost every day."

"It doesn't matter. You have to get out of there. You don't want your marriage to suffer because of a stupid job or because your dad is doing business with Nicky. You need to find another job. Your dad will understand."

"Meems, don't you say a word! If Preston knew what was going on, he'd go crazy. He's already pissed that I work so many evenings. Meanwhile, where did you get that fabulous vest?"

Mimi smiled and bit her bottom lip. "I don't want to tell you."

"Come on."

She laughed. "I got it at E. J. Korvette for eight dollars. But, Chrissie, that bracelet, it's gorgeous."

She held her wrist out, and her gold bracelet shimmered in the sunlight. "Pres gave me this last week. For no reason. Just 'cause he loves me."

"Wow."

❧

Midway through the third quarter, Preston told Nathan that the same four tickets were available for the Bears/Lions game in two weeks. "I'm supposed to give them away to a contributor," Preston said, "but I'm going to keep them. Do you want to go?"

"Sure I do, but won't it be a problem if you don't give them away?"

Preston smirked. "Absolutely no problem. Fringe benefits."

"Then everything is copacetic at the office?"

"Today it is, but they're all coming in next month for the Columbus Day parade. Vittie, Stanley, the accountant. I'm glad that they're only staying for a few days. Just long enough to give me shit."

"I thought Vittie couldn't come into Chicago this fall because of his demanding legislative agenda," Nathan said. "And that's why he moved up the wedding date."

"Don't play dumb, Nate. You know the answer to that one. I got married five days before LBJ did away with the marital deferment. I told you Vittie doesn't want his son-in-law going off to Vietnam."

At that moment, Rudy Bukich dropped back, threw a screen pass to Gale Sayers, who sidestepped his defender, broke into the open field and ran eighty yards for touchdown. "I told you," Preston yelled above the roar. "I told you to keep your eyes on that guy. He's going to be rookie of the year. Outta sight!"

❧

Eli was standing on the front stoop, leaning his back against the iron banister and reading the newspaper, when Preston pulled up in his convertible. Eli watched as Nathan and Mimi got out of the car, waved goodbye to Preston and Christine, and walked toward the building. "We just saw the Bears beat the Los Angeles Rams," Mimi said. "It was so much fun."

"Beautiful Sunday for a game," Eli responded with a smile, folding his paper. "I see you're traveling in style. Pretty spiffy car."

"It's a brand-new Pontiac Bonneville. Rides like a dream."

"Wasn't that your friend Preston driving the car? The one who was recently married?"

"Yes, it was. He had tickets to the game. On the forty-yard line."

"Doesn't he work for Congressman Zielinski?"

"That's how he got the tickets. Pretty sweet."

"How fortunate. VIP tickets, a beautiful new car—the congressman must be very generous to his staff."

That was more than just a casual observation, thought Mimi. *What is your fascination with Congressman Zielinski, Mr. Newly Arrived Tenant? Or should I say FBI agent? Perhaps my mother's supposition wasn't so off-base.*

"I think Preston and Christine did pretty well at their wedding," Mimi said. "There were several wealthy guests, and I saw a lot of envelopes. We're going upstairs now. Good evening, Eli."

When Nathan and Mimi entered the apartment, Nathan said, "Nosy fellow, isn't he?"

"That money didn't come from the wedding gifts, Nathan."

"I don't know, Meems. That's what Preston says. Earlier today, when we were standing in the hot dog line, I brought it up. I'm sure you saw the gold bracelet on Christine's wrist. He's driving an expensive car. He insisted on buying the refreshments with a pocketful of cash. He's got primo tickets. I asked him what the hell was going on, and he told me it was the wedding money."

Mimi shook her head. "Chrissie told me they spent most of their wedding money furnishing the house."

"Then the money must be coming from his job."

"He's not making that kind of salary as an administrative assistant. Chrissie said she makes a lot more than Preston. She said that they couldn't survive on Preston's salary alone."

"I didn't mean his salary, Meems."

Mimi raised a brow. "Then what?"

Nathan twisted his lips. "Preston told me to forget it, it never happened. But it did, Meems. How do you unring a bell? How do I forget what I believe is a straight line to a disaster?"

"What are you talking about?"

"It's the books and records in the secret room; it's got to be. Remember Preston's words? 'Major shit, the stuff that could send people to jail?' Two weeks ago, Pres and I were at a softball game. I could tell he was upset again. Something happened at work and all he would say was he had a decision to make. 'There's two ways I can play this,' he said. 'Two ways, Nate. That's it.' I asked him what the hell he was talking about, and he told me to forget about it. Now he's spending money like he's Howard Hughes. So, Mimi, what is the obvious conclusion?"

Mimi shrugged. "To me, 'two ways' means he could either walk away or somehow participate in the major shit."

Nathan nodded. "Walk away and keep your mouth shut is certainly one way, probably the ethical and safe way, but Preston's never been a safeway kind of guy. I think if there was money on the table, he'd want to grab some of it."

"Very possible, but Preston doesn't have a business background, so what does he bring to a complicated business operation? What does he offer Vittie?"

"Silence. Let's assume that Preston stumbled onto something scandalous and illegal, something that has been going on for years behind that locked door. Obviously, they don't need Preston's business help, but they do need his silence. It would be dangerous as all hell, but it could be the reason for the sudden splurge of money."

"You mean he's leveraging his father-in-law? Demanding money as a price for his silence? Is that what you're thinking? Is Preston crazy?"

"I don't know what to think. Look, we're just *speculating* here, but what if the ledgers keep track of illegal transactions—bribery, kickbacks, privileges, unusually large campaign contributions. I don't know. He's one of the country's wealthiest congressmen, isn't he? Preston said the books went back twenty years."

Mimi's hand was covering her lips. "Preston discovered his father-in-law has been corrupt for twenty years, and now he's blackmailing him. If that's true, Preston must be out of his mind."

"It doesn't have to be blackmail. What if Vittie learned that Preston got into the back room? Maybe the receptionist saw him. Maybe someone noticed that the accounting records were misplaced. Whatever the reason, let's assume that Vittie found out, confronted Preston and Preston confessed. Maybe Vittie decided to generously ensure his son-in-law's loyalty?"

Mimi scrunched her face. "I've known Vittie for fifteen years. No one would ever accuse him of generosity. He's not generous to anyone, not even his own daughter. My mom, who has very little money, gave me a bigger allowance than Vittie gave Chrissie. Chrissie always complained that her father wouldn't part with a nickel."

"He threw a big wedding."

"That was political; you said so yourself." She shook her head. "Wow. So Vittie's got a scandal going on."

"*Major* scandal. You know what occurs to me?" Nathan said, pointing at the floor. "Your downstairs tenant, Mr. Rosen. He's so damn interested in Vittie and your mom thinks he's CIA. And so do you."

Mimi's jaw dropped. "I said the FBI, but you're right. He has shown exceptional curiosity where Vittie's concerned. Damn, do you think the government's on to him?"

Nathan shrugged. "We don't really know who Rosen is or why he's here."

Mimi smiled and bit her lip. "Are we scripting a television drama?"

CHAPTER THIRTY-THREE

CHICAGO
ALBANY PARK NEIGHBORHOOD
OCTOBER 12, 1965
COLUMBUS DAY

Mimi walked out of the door with a sweater tied over her shoulders and a large pair of fashion sunglasses perched just above her forehead. She looked down at the steps, at Eli sitting with his morning cup of coffee and a cigarette. The *Tribune* lay by his side. Mimi chuckled. "We should have marketed the apartment as a one-bedroom with available sunporch. We could have charged an extra fifty dollars a month."

Eli laughed. "A porch with a southern exposure—isn't it pleasant? Are you headed to the Columbus Day parade?"

She nodded. "It's always a big event in Chicago. The Joint Civic Committee of Italian-Americans work on it all year round. They have over fifty floats. The governor, the mayor and almost every elected official who wants to be seen will be walking down State Street, waving to the crowds. Do you want to come with us?"

Eli smiled. "Thanks, but I'll take a rain check."

"It's not raining, Eli."

He laughed. "You're far too clever for me, Miss Gold."

"I haven't seen you around for the past two weeks. Have you been out of town?"

"I took a short vacation."

Mimi considered whether she should ask him if it was to Washington, D.C., but decided against it.

A horn tooted and Preston pulled up in his convertible, top down. Christine was in the front seat with a green scarf tied over her hair, and Nathan was in the back wearing a Cubs hat.

"Gotta go," Mimi said to Eli. "Last chance?"

"Have a nice time."

❧

"I've seen that man before," Christine said as they pulled away. "The one on your front stoop."

"That's Mr. Rosen. He rents the first-floor apartment," Mimi said. "He's been here since last spring. You've probably seen him around the building."

"No, I think I've seen him out on Kedzie Avenue near my office."

"Seriously, Chrissie? You remember everyone who walks down Kedzie?"

"Very funny. I'm pretty sure I've seen him standing around a few times. He's always nicely dressed, which is more than I can say for some of the people I see on Kedzie. At first, I thought he was going into the book-making parlor behind the Bagel Bakery, but then I saw him just hanging around, standing on the corner. He looked like he was making notes."

"There you go, Meems," Nathan said. "Your mom thinks he's with the FBI. He's snooping on the bookie joint."

"My mom thinks he's with the CIA. *I'm* the one who thinks he's with the FBI."

Preston started laughing. "Ha! The FBI's going to bust Murray's bookie joint."

❧

The group planted themselves with the crowd on the corner of Adams and State, just beyond the reviewing stand. As soon as the Sullivan High School marching band had passed, Christine shouted, "Look, here comes my dad!" She pointed at a flower-covered float with a banner that read HAPPY COLUMBUS DAY—CONGRESSMAN WITOLD ZIELINSKI.

Christine jumped up and down, cupped her mouth and yelled, "Hi, Dad!" He was standing on a pedestal next to a long-haired girl with a crown on her head and a ribbon across her chest. Vittie waved back at Christine and blew her a kiss.

"Who's the girl on the float?" Nathan asked.

"Alicja Purszka," Christine said. "She's also the Pulaski Day queen. I think she's a stuck-up bimbo."

"Sure good-looking, though," Nathan said, and Mimi elbowed him. "Where's Michael Stanley? I thought Vittie doesn't go anywhere without him."

"I told you, he stays out of sight," Preston said. "He's always in the background somewhere. I wouldn't be surprised if he was driving the float."

"Is he in town this week?"

"Oh, yeah. Are you kidding? Driving me crazy. Vittie, Stanley and the accountant. Larry, Moe and Curly. And they have a bunch of meetings set up."

"With whom?"

"They don't clear those with me, Nate. I don't keep Vittie's appointment book. In fact, I've never seen it. I can only tell you that whoever they are, they're heavy hitters. They pull up in limos, and the drivers wait outside on Kimball until the meeting is over. Sometimes there are two or three Lincolns sitting out there."

"What are they talking about?"

Preston smiled and put his finger on his lips. "State secrets, buddy."

"Oh, come on."

"You think I know? They don't let me in the meetings, but sometimes I hear stuff. Sometimes there's loud arguments. Always about money and percentages." Preston reached into his jacket pocket and pulled out an envelope. "Guess what this is?"

"No idea."

"Four tickets to Herman's Hermits!"

"Don't tell me Vittie got you those tickets as fringe benefits."

"Ha. No, I bought them. Do you want to go?"

Nathan grimaced. "I don't know. How much are they?"

"Don't worry about it. My treat."

Nathan slapped him on the back. "Then, yes! Something tells me I'm into something good."

❦

A mob of young girls gathered outside the Arie Crown Theater on Saturday night, waiting to catch a glimpse of Peter Noone and scream. Or faint. As Preston, Christine, Nathan and Mimi bypassed the group on their way into the theater, Preston yelled, "Hey, girls, look at me, I'm Herman," which drew a lot of disgusted looks and a few middle fingers.

The opening act featured a local folk group, and the audience was clearly bored. Nathan leaned over and said, "Is the Washington crowd still at the office?"

"No," Preston answered, "thank God. They left yesterday. I worked till nine or ten every night they were here."

"Did they ever let you in the meetings?"

"Not a chance. Vittie wanted me to guard the door in case some dumbass wandered in. He wanted to make sure no one disturbed his big-deal meetings. So I sat there reading magazines all night."

"Sounds like fun."

"You want to know something? You know the FBI guy, the one who lives in Mimi's building, the one who's going to bust Murray's bookie joint?"

"Yeah?"

"I saw him sitting in a car across the street from our office."

"What do you mean, sitting in a car?"

"You don't understand that? What don't you understand? The FBI dude was sitting in a freaking car all night across the street from Vittie's office."

Mimi leaned over. "Mr. Rosen doesn't own a car."

"Jesus, Mimi, are you that dense? You don't think the FBI can give him a car?"

"Did you walk across the street to talk to him?"

"No. I had to stay in the office. No interruptions, no strangers, no reporters—those were my orders."

"So let me get this straight; you were looking out of the office window, across the street at night and through a car window, and you think you saw Mr. Rosen? I think you're probably mistaken."

"I don't think he's mistaken," Christine said. "I saw Mr. Rosen myself sitting in a car on Kedzie. On Thursday. Two days ago. In the bright sunshine."

"Ooh," Mimi said, with a calculating look in her eyes. "This is getting interesting."

CHAPTER THIRTY-FOUR

CHICAGO

NOVEMBER 1965

The season's first measurable snowfall, four inches of the heavy wet stuff, clung to the branches, bent the small trees and coated Albany Park with a white cream frosting on the late November morning. Aside from creating photogenic scenes on the parkways and the rooftops, the snow managed to snarl traffic, overcrowd the elevated trains and delay Mimi's arrival at work by an hour.

She arrived with her cup of coffee, shook the snow from her coat and sat down at her desk. The morning *Tribune* was waiting for her. The banner headline read, HINT 300,000 GIS FOR VIET.

Her desk phone rang. Nathan was on the line, and he sounded disheartened. "Billy got his orders today," he said. "He's coming home for two weeks and then he's shipping out."

"I'm sorry, Nate. Did he at least get the assignment he wanted?"

"Nope. It'll be infantry. Carrying an M-16 on the ground in Vietnam."

"We'll all pray that he stays safe and his time goes quickly. How does Billy feel about it?"

"He's all excited. He's getting out of boot camp and going overseas. He says he's proud to go with his unit. Says he's gonna kill gooks. Hell, Meems, he's just a dumb kid."

"I'm really sorry, Nate."

"Can I see you tonight?"

"I'll get home about six. Why don't you come by at seven? We'll get a bite to eat."

"How does Chinese sound?"

"Terrific."

Mimi looked down at the copy she was editing. The double-column front-page story carried a sub-headline that read, ENEMY STRONGER THAN EVER, U.S. REPORTS. The story detailed reports that communist forces continued to grow, despite the influx of expanding American ground troops and despite sustained aerial bombing of Vietnamese targets. It reiterated the American command's assessment that there was no clear end in sight.

Mimi knew that the *Tribune,* in line with other major American newspapers, was generally supportive of the administration and its war effort. The media reported daily body counts because that was how the government measured its progress. General Westmoreland had posited that the "crossover point," that point in time when U.S. and South Vietnam troops were killing more men than Hanoi could replace, was "just around the corner."

Mimi scoffed. "I've heard that phrase before," she said aloud. "As the war grows, so does the military budget and so does the money that flows to military contractors. Eisenhower was right on. Why would the military-industrial complex be the least bit interested in a truce?"

☙

Mimi and Nathan exited the subway at the Cermak Avenue station and walked hand in hand along the gayly lit streets of Chicago's Chinatown. Bright yellow, red and green lights reflected off the snow-covered sidewalks. The tiny Min Fong Café was tucked in between two Chinese gift stores on Wentworth Avenue. Bells jingled as they walked in the door. Paper lanterns hung from the ceiling, and murals of the Li River and its hilltopped landscapes colored the walls. Nathan stopped and inhaled deeply. "Love the smell of Chinese food," he said with a smile.

Nathan and Mimi slid into a booth and ordered the five-course dinner special. "I really appreciate you coming out with me tonight, Meems. It's been a tough day. A real downer. My little brother's never been out of the neighborhood. Never even played sports."

"I know. I worry about Billy, too, but he did go through basic training at Fort Dix, and from what you tell me, he's excited to be going overseas with

ELI'S PROMISE

his unit. We're sending a lot of boys over there. Maybe they're turning the corner and there'll be truce talks soon."

"I saw on TV that there'll be over half a million U.S. troops stationed in Vietnam. Half a million, Meems! Can you imagine the supplies and materials needed to support that many GIs?"

"Christine can. She tells me that Nicky is sending out twice as many shipments as he did a year ago. He's doubled his business, maybe tripled. She says it's all military. Semi-trailers going to the East Coast, semis going to the West Coast. Every day. And she's working late every night."

"Preston's pissed. He wants her to quit."

"She's doubled her salary, Nate. With her salary and the cash Preston gets from who knows where, they're going to be the wealthiest two kids in Albany Park."

Nathan grimaced. "It worries me, Meems. What's going down in Vittie's office? Limos pulling up at all hours, secret meetings behind locked doors and Preston guarding the door late into the night like a bouncer? You can bet it's not legislative activity. Something's not right, and Preston's in it up to his neck."

"As much as I hate to admit it, I think you're right."

Nathan stirred the chow mein with his chopsticks. "Nicky's tangled up in this mess with Vittie. Do you think Chrissie is, too?"

"Not a prayer. Chrissie is as innocent as a babe. She has no clue; I guarantee it. She complains to me all the time about the hours she works and crap she puts up with from Nicky. She confides in me. I would know if she was involved in something illegal."

"A shipping company doing business with a congressman?"

"It doesn't have to be illegal. Vittie's the chair of the Armed Services Committee. They're responsible for supporting the troops. Someone has to ship the materials. Shipping companies get contracts."

"With cash delivered in briefcases? C'mon, Meems. What would your friend Mr. Rosen say about that? Preston said he saw him sitting in a car on Kimball. He's not doing that because he's interested in busting a neighborhood bookie parlor. If he's with the FBI, then he's focusing on bigger fish, and Vittie's the biggest fish on Kimball Avenue."

CHAPTER THIRTY-FIVE

CHICAGO

ALBANY PARK NEIGHBORHOOD

DECEMBER 1965

Christmastime in Chicago. Bows and wreaths and thousands of tiny white lights twinkled up and down Michigan Avenue. Red and green lit the sky from the tops of the Tribune Tower and the Palmolive Building. Mayor Daley ceremoniously lit Chicago's official Christmas tree in the Civic Center Plaza. The holiday spirit was alive and well in the Windy City.

Ruth and Sarah were watching the *Andy Williams Christmas Special* Sunday night when Nathan and Mimi walked into the apartment.

"How was your dinner?" Ruth said.

"Fabulous," Mimi said. "We ate at Twin Anchors."

"Ooh, I love that place. Did you have the ribs?" Ruth asked.

"Of course, I did. But wait till you hear the best part. You'll never guess who ate there yesterday. We missed him by one day!"

"Tell me."

"Frank Sinatra."

"Oh, my heart. I heard he was in town."

"He was there last night with Joey Bishop."

"Wouldn't that have been a kick? I wonder if they let ordinary folks come in?"

"Marco said the restaurant was open. Business as usual. Sinatra and

Bishop ate in the back in a closed-off area, but when they left, they walked through the restaurant and out the front door. Can you imagine? Marco said they stopped to shake a few hands, but no autographs."

Just then the buzzer sounded, and Mimi rose to answer the intercom.

"It's ten thirty," Ruth said. "I wonder who that can be? Are you expecting anyone?" Mimi shook her head.

"Mimi? It's Chris. Can I come up? Please?"

Mimi looked at her mother and Nathan and pressed the buzzer. "This cannot be good." Mimi opened the door and waited on the landing. When Christine stepped into the light, a dark bruise on the side of her face became visible.

"Good God, Chrissie. What happened to you?"

"You have no idea. I'm sorry to barge in here, but I really didn't know where else to go." Her body slumped, and she broke into a hard cry. "I could really use a friend, Meems." Mimi put her arms around her and brought her into the apartment.

Nathan grabbed his coat. "Why don't I go and give you guys some privacy? Catch up with you later."

"No, stay," Christine said. "Please."

Mimi went into the kitchen, poured a glass of water and brought it out to the dining room table. "What in the world happened?" Mimi said. "Where were you?"

"At work."

"At ten thirty on Sunday night?"

She nodded, sniffled and took a drink. "Two nights ago, Nicky asked me to work late again. I told him that Preston and I had plans, but he kept pressuring me. He said he had a lot of business this weekend and that he and my dad were counting on me. I told him I would have to talk to Preston. Nicky put his hands on my shoulders and begged me. 'You have to help me. You can't believe the truckloads of materials we have to deal with. I'll pay you triple time if you work Friday night, Saturday and Sunday afternoon.' I told him I'd have to run it by Preston."

"What did Preston say?"

"What do you think? He was furious. Pres and I already had plans for Saturday night, and we were going to shop for a Christmas tree on Sunday. Pres said we didn't need Nicky's money, that this was just Nicky's ploy to get me to spend the weekend with him. I told him that Nicky was going to pay me triple time, and that's almost eight hundred dollars, Mimi. But Preston put his foot down. I called Nicky and told him I couldn't work."

"That was the smart thing."

"Well, it didn't exactly work. Nicky called the house this morning. He begged me to come in. He said he was really, really busy, that he was overwhelmed, that there were twenty-two contracts going out today and he couldn't do it alone. He sounded desperate. I told Pres I would have to go in for a little while. Just for a little while. Pres wasn't happy, but my dad's in town and Pres had to go into the office anyway. So I went in."

"But, Chrissie, your face. What happened?"

"By the time I got to the office, Nicky had been drinking hard. He was loaded. It had been a bad few days for him. He had to give a deposition in his divorce case, and his wife's lawyer gave him a lot of shit. And he wasn't allowed to see his kids over the weekend. His wife accused him of being violent and drunk."

"She's not wrong."

"I know, but today was worse than ever. He was blasted. He kept coming into my office and hanging around. Leaning on the door with a sickly smile on his slobbery face. Then he started coming on to me. How sexy I look and all that. Then he started trying to kiss me. I pushed him away, stood up and walked into the other room. I said, 'You're out of line, Nicky!' It didn't matter. He followed me around and told me how much he cared for me and that he's been planning a life for us."

"Oh my God, Christine, what a creep."

"He grabbed my hand and pulled me into his office, where he opened his safe to show me stacks of cash—hundred-dollar bills all bound up. I don't know how many thousands of dollars he has in there, but, believe me, it's a lot. 'This is what I put away for us,' he said.

"I backed off. 'Let's stop the foolish talk,' I said, 'and get to work on the contracts. I have to get home.' He said, 'I can make you very happy, a lot happier than that bozo you're married to. As soon as my divorce is over, I'm a free man. A free man with plenty of money. Every woman's dream.' He was totally smashed, Mimi, and he scared me."

"Jesus," Mimi said.

"'I don't want to hear any more of this,' I said, 'and I don't want to see your money. Close that safe. Don't you understand you're going through a divorce? What if your wife's lawyer subpoenas me and asks me about all your business dealings, your books and records, receipts and disbursements, about what I see here in the office? I would have to testify that you're holding thousands of dollars in cash in a safe.'"

"True," Mimi said.

"Well, that made him crazy. He took it as a threat. 'You bitch,' he yelled, and he grabbed me by the shoulders and shook me. 'If I ever find out that you squealed on me, I'll rip your heart out.'"

"Holy shit!" Mimi said. "Did you call the cops?"

"I yelled, 'Screw you, Nicky. I quit,' and I ran toward the door, but he got in front of me and blocked me. 'You can't quit on me,' he screamed. 'You can't walk out on me. I confide in you, I tell you my secrets, I pay you triple time and this is how you treat me? You're gonna walk out on me and tell the lawyers that I'm hiding cash in the safe?'

"I shook my head and pushed him back. 'I didn't say I'd do that, Nicky. I said they could subpoena me. But I can't work here anymore. I'm done. This isn't good for either one of us.' I turned around to walk out the door, and the next thing I know he takes a swing at me, clips me on the side of my face and knocks me to the floor. Then he stands over me and starts bawling. 'I'm so sorry,' he says. 'I didn't mean it. You know I love you. Please don't leave me.' I got up, ran out of the office and came straight here. I can't go home, Mimi. I don't know how to handle this. If Preston finds out, he'll go over there and kill him."

"Where is Preston?"

"I think he's home now. They were working today. Nicky wasn't lying about the twenty-two contracts. They're big transports to naval bases. My dad and Stanley came in to work on the details and then they're flying back to D.C."

"Are you going to tell Preston what happened?"

"Look at my face. All the makeup in the world isn't going to hide this bruise. I thought about making up a story, that I slipped at the bus stop, but Pres won't believe it. I'm not a good liar. He'll see right through me."

"Well, you did the right thing today, Chris. I've been telling you for months to quit that job and get away from that creep."

Christine nodded. "I know, but what am I going to do now? How can I go home to Preston? He'll know. He'll go straight to Nicky's and beat the hell out of him."

Nathan shrugged. "Nicky's got it coming. Besides, you quit. What do you care?"

"Nate, my dad's not going to let me quit. He wants me to keep working there."

"You have to stand up to him," Mimi said.

"Easier said than done. But I got a bigger problem: what am I going to do tonight?'

The phone rang and Ruth called out, "Christine, the phone's for you. I think it's Preston."

"Meems," Christine whispered, "tell him I'm not here."

"How can I do that? My mother just yelled out your name. He knows you're here."

"Oh God, what am I going to say?"

Nathan said, "Tell him you're coming right home. I'll go with you."

Christine nodded and took the handset. "Hi, honey, I'm here with Nate and Mimi and . . ." She paused and listened. "No, I don't know why Nicky's been calling the house nonstop." Pause. "He's been saying he's sorry? No, I don't know what that means." Pause. "No, Preston, do not let him come over to the house. I don't want to see him. I don't ever want to see him again." Christine started to cry. "Pres . . . Pres, just listen. I quit my job today. I'm fed up with Nicky and his bullshit and I quit." Pause. "No, don't come over to Mimi's. Really, Pres . . ." She hung up. "He's coming over."

❧

Nathan was standing outside on the stoop when Preston's Bonneville screeched to a stop in front of the building. Preston jumped out and headed for the door, but Nathan stopped him.

"Hang on, Pres. Let me talk to you for a minute."

"What's going on, Nate? Something's wrong. Chrissie's crying. It's that asshole Nicky, isn't it? He's been calling the house all night saying he's sorry. What the fuck did he do? I'll kill that son of a bitch. What did he do, Nate? What happened to Chrissie?"

"Slow down. I want you to take it easy. Chrissie's upstairs and she's upset, but she's okay. Nicky was an asshole today, he went off on Chrissie, but she quit her job and now it's over. It's finished. She's not going back, and she never has to see him again. The last thing we need is for you to get upset and get out of control. She needs our support. Most of all, she needs you to be compassionate and understanding."

"I'm not going to get mad at Chrissie. I love her. I've been begging her to quit that bullshit job for weeks." Preston appeared to calm down, but then he looked in Nathan's eyes. "It's more than that, isn't it, Nate? There's something else, isn't there? It's not just about her quitting her job, or she would have come home. She wouldn't need to stop at Mimi's." He pushed Nathan aside and bounded up the stairs.

Mimi met him at the door and quietly said, "Please be kind to her. She's been through a lot today."

The minute Preston saw the bruise, he flew into a rage. "He did this to you? He hit you?" He spun around and headed for the door. "I'm going to teach that punk a lesson."

Christine ran for him, wrapped her arms around him and held tightly. "Please, please don't go over there. He'll call the police and you'll get arrested. It'll just make it worse. I quit my job today. I'm not going back. Can't we just leave it at that?"

Preston was incensed. His face turned beet-red, his muscles tightened and his breathing rate doubled. He was ready to explode. "The bastard hit a defenseless woman. He hit *my wife,* for God's sake! I'm going over there and teach that prick a lesson he'll never forget."

"Whoa, hold on, Pres," Nathan said as calmly as he could. "Chrissie's right. He's probably at home and drunk, and if you go there and cause a scene, you'll end up in jail."

"*Please* don't go there," Christine said. "Pres, there's something more important. You have to help me talk to my father. He doesn't want me to quit my job. I called him a few minutes ago and told him what happened, and he said he'd straighten it out; he didn't want me to quit. He insisted I return to work on Monday."

"Not happening."

"Pres, it's my job to keep my eye on Nicky and report to my dad every day. Dad promised me it would never happen again, and he wants me to keep working. Pres, I don't want to go back. I'm afraid of Nicky. I think he's crazy. I'm afraid of what he'll do to me. Please help me talk to my dad."

"You're not going back," Preston said, hugging his wife. "I'll talk to Vittie. I'm not going to let you go anywhere near Nicky ever again. If the mighty Vittie Zielinski doesn't like it, he can kiss my ass. I don't give a damn about his crooked business or any of his shady deals, and I'll tell him that to his face. Shit, if he doesn't watch out, I'll blow the whistle on his whole goddamn operation, and he knows it."

"Please, Pres, don't get into a fight with my father. Just help me talk to him."

"I will; we'll call him together. But first I'm calling Nicky. He's been ringing the house every fifteen minutes, and somebody needs to set him straight. I won't go over there, but I'm going to have my say. Someday this guy will pay for what he did, but not tonight. What's his number?"

It was a compromise solution, and Christine accepted it. She gave him the number and grimaced as Preston dialed. What followed was a string of the most vile and threatening language Christine had ever heard from Preston. The message was loud and clear. If Nicky was ever stupid enough to call or contact Christine again, if he even looked at her, Preston would break every bone in his body.

Preston slammed the phone so hard it almost broke. "Okay," he said, "now let's deal with Vittie. Where was he when you talked to him?"

"He was still at the office. If you call, Mike Stanley will pick up. He'll get my father on the phone."

"Stanley knows what happened?"

"He not only knows, he urged me not to quit. He said Nicky's going through an emotional time and he needs me in the office. That we should be understanding."

"Stanley is such an asshole. To hell with both of them."

Christine sighed and watched Preston dial the office. She knew this was not going to go well, and she was right. Vittie was steadfast in his insistence that Christine stay on the job. He would not countenance a resignation. No matter how much Preston kept insisting and trying to reason with him, he flatly refused to consider it.

"She will be at her desk Monday morning, perform her duties as required, report directly to me each afternoon and that's final," Zielinski said. "I will speak to Nicholas. I can assure you that the abuse will stop. You have my word."

Christine sadly shook her head and wept. "I told you. He'll never let me leave," she said. Mimi put an arm around her.

"She's not going back, Vittie," Preston said loudly into the phone. "I'm not going to let her."

"It's not your decision, young man. It's hers. There are too many important people involved. They are all relying on Christine to do her job. Let me speak to her."

Tears were flowing from Christine's eyes, and she mouthed *I can't*.

Preston looked at his wife, he looked at the phone and he exploded. "You're not going to intimidate her, and you're not going to put the pressure on her. You're talking to me, Congressman. Me, Preston Roberts. You're not going to shame or browbeat my wife into going back to that punk. She's finished, and if you cared at all about your daughter, you'd know that. Some father you turned out to be. You care more about your stinkin' defense contractors than your own daughter."

"How dare you!" he bellowed. "I put Christine in that position because I decided it was an excellent opportunity for her. It's vitally important to the defense of our country."

"Who are you kidding, Vittic? You're talking to *me*. I see what you're doing every day. I know each and every one of the millionaires who parade through the office. It's not for the defense of our country, it's for the pockets of the millionaires."

"You better watch yourself, sonny. You have no idea how powerful these people are. They depend on Christine, and she will not disappoint them. Or me. It's a matter of national security, and Christine has been privy to highly classified information. She will not quit her job. I said I would speak to Nicholas, and that should be sufficient."

Preston was enraged. "Well, it's not, Mr. Bigshot. I'm not letting her go back to some guy who punched her in the face, and if you or any of your so-called powerful people bother us anymore, I'm going straight to the *Tribune*. I don't want your damn money; I don't want your fancy cars or your tickets. You can take it all back! Chrissie's not going back to that asshole, and if you give me any more trouble, I'm going to the newspaper and I'll tell them everything I know—and I know plenty."

Preston hung up the phone and put his arms around his sobbing wife. "It'll be okay," he said.

CHAPTER THIRTY-SIX

The *Tribune*'s front page displayed a six-column photo beneath the head-line 1ST INFANTRY BOLSTERS FIGHTING FORCE IN VIETNAM. The photo depicted hundreds of green-clad soldiers disembarking a landing craft in Cam Ranh Bay. Mimi shuddered as she edited a story about Viet Cong guerrillas setting fire to an Esso oil storage tank in Da Nang. Her desk phone rang. It was Christine, and she was frantic.

"Meems, you've got to help me. I can't handle it. I can't deal with it. I'm losing my mind."

"Calm down, Chrissie. What's wrong?"

"Everything. It's Preston. It's my father. I need to talk. Can you meet me?"

"I get off work in half an hour. I'll meet you at home."

Christine was already at the kitchen table when Mimi walked in the house. Her face was red; her jaw was quivering.

"What happened?" Mimi said.

"You know I haven't been back to work in a week, not since Nicky slugged me. Since then, my father's been all over me. He calls the house every night. He tells me that he talked to Nicky and nothing like that will ever happen again. But Preston put his foot down, and he won't let me go back."

"I don't understand your father. Why wouldn't he protect his own daughter?"

"It's all about the contractors, his business associates, the rich men he hangs around with. They want me in the office watching over Nicky and reporting back to them. They say they don't trust Nicky, and who could blame them?"

"Why don't they just stop doing business with Nicky and use some other shipping company?"

Christine hung her head. "Meems, it's not that simple. Nicky knows too much about the operation. They can't afford to cut him out. He's an asshole to me and probably to his wife, but to my father's associates he's essential. Mimi, the large amounts of cash—it all funnels through Nicky."

"What happened today?"

"My father came into town two days ago. He left Washington and a committee meeting just to come in and pressure me. He said he wants to set up a meeting between Nicky and me and he'll be there to make sure everything works out. He wants to meet tomorrow night. I can't do it. Even if I could, Preston won't let me."

"Where is Preston?"

"At the office. He's taking a lot of crap, too, but he loves me so much, he's not letting my father bully me."

"Preston still has a job?"

"He won't lose his job. He knows too much. Everybody knows too much. My father is trying to put a lid on a boiling pot. He's trying to put everything back the way it was a month ago, but too much has happened. Anyway, Preston will not let me meet with Nicky, and he refuses to let me go back to work."

"Chrissie, I feel so bad for you. What can I do?"

"Just be my friend. Everything is so tense at my father's office. There are several men over there right now. Preston says he overheard a lot of shouting."

"Do you want to stay here tonight?"

"Thanks, Meems, but Preston is taking me out to dinner. It's one year from the date he proposed to me. He's such a sweetie. With all this going on, he wants me to know how much he cares about me. I should get home; I'll call you tomorrow."

A telephone call came into Chicago's emergency number at 3:30 a.m. "Fire at 4932 North Karlov." It was redirected to District 2, Battalion 10, Engine Company 124. By the time the first unit arrived, the flames were shooting through the front windows of the redbrick bungalow. Firefighters rapidly opened the pump panels, connected the hoses and pumped heavy streams of water into the house. Additional equipment quickly arrived on the scene. Curious neighbors came to the windows of their homes, and some even stepped out into the cold to watch from their front lawns.

Chicago Police Department patrol cars arrived minutes later. Red and blue emergency lights lit up the area. Neighborhood residents and members of the media continued to gather. When the fire was extinguished and the equipment was being loaded back into the trucks, television reporters who had flocked to the scene showered Battalion Chief Foster with questions. "I won't have too much to tell you," he said. "Everything is preliminary. We'll have more later today."

"Can you give us something?" a TV reporter said. "We go live in an hour."

Foster reluctantly consented. "At three thirty this morning, the Chicago Fire Department responded to a call placed by a neighbor who reported seeing flames through the window of this building at 4932 North Karlov. It was a 'still alarm,' and the response at the time was two engines, two trucks and a battalion chief. When the fire was confirmed, we immediately initiated a working fire response, bringing in an additional truck and an ambulance. Because of the density of this neighborhood and the close proximity of the houses on this street, it was my judgment to initiate a three-eleven alarm. As you can see, we have four engines out here.

"The fire was attacked through the front and side of the structure. We were able to contain it to the east side of the building. My men entered the rear door to check for residents. Two adults were found in the rear bedroom and pronounced dead at the scene. Preliminary assessments required us to contact the Chicago Police Department. I don't have anything more. I'm sure there'll be a statement later today."

"Can you give us the names of the deceased?"

"No, I'm sorry."

"I know who they are," said a woman in a robe and a nylon puff jacket. "They're Preston and Christine Roberts. They just moved into that house a few months ago. Nice kids."

PART III

CHAPTER THIRTY-SEVEN

LUBLIN

LUBLIN, POLAND
MARCH 15, 1941
MONTH 18 OF THE NAZI OCCUPATION

"Eighteen months and Germany's hold on Europe gets stronger every day," Eli said to Esther, who stood behind him in the corner of the basement. Eli navigated the stations on his shortwave radio. "The radio reports that a brick wall has been built around the Warsaw ghetto and has sealed in 350,000 Jews. I also hear warnings about sealed ghettos for Krakow, Lodz and Kovno."

Esther squeezed his shoulders. "They haven't sealed us in here in Lublin. Maybe they don't plan to do so."

"That seems shortsighted, Essie, especially coming from you. From the beginning, you recognized them for what they were and advocated fleeing into the countryside."

"And it was you who pointed out the dangers of such a move. And what about your brother and your father? They'd be arrested and punished if we left. So we'll keep our heads up here in Lublin; we'll endure; we'll wait and we'll pray. Good will always prevail over evil—we must believe that or there is no purpose in the universe."

Eli nodded. "I will continue to operate the brickyard. Business demands are strong, though we are principally filling orders for the German command at a small profit."

"And I'll continue to work at the Lipowa sweatshop until these animals leave."

It was midmorning when Maximilian unexpectedly appeared at the brick-yard and insisted that Eli, Louis and Jakob join him in a meeting. "Big changes are coming to Lublin," he said with an officious air. "But because of my affection for the Rosen family, I want you to be the first to know, and the first to take appropriate precautions. Governor-General Hans Frank has appointed a new leader for the Lublin District. His name is Ernst Zörner, and he assumed command this week. Personally, I think he's a fat slob and ill-mannered—nothing like us—but he will dutifully implement the Reich's policies."

"What about your buddy, Odilo Globočnik? Has he been canned?"

"Oh no, far from it. He will continue to command the Lublin District SS, and now he's been given even greater authority. He's focusing all of his efforts on building and stocking work camps. He's in charge of Jewish labor for the entire Lublin District. Do you remember when I told you about the *Judische reservat,* the Jewish reservation for five hundred Jews in Nisko? Well, that was Odilo's plan, but Governor-General Frank wouldn't fund it, so now that project's been scrapped in favor of smaller work camps widely dispersed throughout central Poland. Globočnik has already set up fifty-one of them in villages throughout the district. There is great pressure to conscript healthy workers for these camps."

"Conscript?"

Maximilian shrugged. "Would you prefer 'collected,' 'rounded up,' 'in-voluntarily appointed'? Odilo insists that everyone do his or her part to support the war effort."

"You mean every Jew?"

"Well, certainly every Jew, but others as well. Look, it's not my policy. I don't approve, but every able-bodied Jew will be assigned to a work camp or factory."

"And those who are not able-bodied?"

Maximilian shrugged. "I'm afraid the administration will look un-kindly on them."

"How does any of this affect us?" Louis asked. "We're all working. We are at the brickyard; my wife is at Lipowa, and so is Esther."

Maximilian raised his eyebrows. "You have a daughter, is that not so? Chava? Able-bodied?"

Louis shot to his feet. "She's only fifteen."

"Ah yes, I know. I have watched her grow up over the past few years and flower into quite a young woman. I saw her just the other day. She is tall and fully grown. A beautiful, healthy girl, if I may say so. Unfortunately, Commandant Zörner's deputy has also seen her. He asks, Why has she not been sent to a work camp? He asked me that directly. He knows I am close to the Rosens."

"For goodness sake," Louis pleaded, "she's just a child. She's too young to sew all day at Lipowa. She's studying. She's a gifted musician."

Maximilian shook his head. "She is not a child in the eyes of the Nazi command. Besides, Lipowa is fully staffed. She is not needed there."

Louis's hands were shaking. "Where is she needed?"

Maximilian raised his chin and looked away. "In a distant camp, I'm afraid."

Louis rushed around the table and hovered over him. "What do you want? Money? How much this time, Maximilian?"

"I'm afraid that money won't solve our problem. She has been noticed by Zörner's deputy."

"Noticed? What does that mean?"

"Unhappily, it means that Chava will be assigned within the next few days."

Eli pounded his fist on the table. "This is unacceptable! You have sworn to protect our family. We have paid you a king's ransom. You cannot allow Chava to be sent away. You must use every bit of the influence that you have cultivated to prevent that from happening."

Maximilian remained calm. "Things change daily, Eli. You know that, and I struggle daily to keep myself in good graces with the authorities and protect my friends. Zörner and Globočnik are intent on implementing Hitler's fundamental plan that Poland is to be depopulated and resettled by Germans. But I suppose I'm not telling you anything you haven't figured out, right?"

Jakob responded angrily, "I don't think we figured that out, Maximilian. You've never said that before. You've always told us that you would protect us, you'd be our buffer and keep us in our homes and working at the brickyard. We've paid you handsomely to make that so."

"I always try to do my best, Jakob. You know that. But some things are out of my control. I came to you today to give you an advance warning about Chava. You should be grateful for that. The ORPO will commence conscripting as many workers as possible to fill Globočnik's camps. You can't put the blame on me; I don't make the rules. I'm only passing along the information. Maybe you can hide her; maybe they won't find her. You'll have to make that decision, but, alas, the ORPO knows how to sniff out Jews."

Louis was trembling. "There must be some other way. There must be something you can do."

Maximilian pulled on his lips and finally said, "All right. For you, Louis, for the Rosen family, I will do this; I will take Chava into my home. I will say she is my housekeeper. In my house, she will be safe. The ORPO will not dare to enter my home. I will do this for you."

"The hell you will," Eli said. "She's not stepping foot into your house and walking around in a nightgown. She's fifteen years old; she's not living in your house, and she's not sleeping in your bed. Period. Besides, I thought Schlossberg's daughter was living with you."

Maximilian scoffed. "She was, but not anymore."

"What happened? Did you get bored with her, Maximilian?"

He shrugged. "It doesn't matter. I will take Chava if Louis wants me to. Otherwise, you may do whatever you deem prudent. There's something more I have to tell you. Zörner plans on designating a specific area for a Lublin ghetto and forcing all Jews to live within its boundaries."

"Warsaw," Jakob said solemnly. "That's what they did in Warsaw. Jewish families live like caged animals behind brick walls. The gates in or out are guarded. It's a prison, nothing less."

"There are no plans for a wall or a fence," Maximilian said. "Not that I know of. But Zörner is an obsequious, fat functionary, and he will do what he is told. The Nazis look at Warsaw and see that it's working well. Very organized. Very efficient."

"Where is this ghetto supposed to be?" Jakob asked.

"Well, that's a good question, and I don't know the full answer, but I've seen drawings. It looks like there will actually be two ghettos in Lublin. On the drawing, there is a ghetto A and a ghetto B. Ghetto A will be the largest and will be located in Old Town."

"Old Town?" Eli said. "That's the poorest, most overcrowded section of the city. It's already unsanitary and full of disease. How is he going to pack forty thousand people into Old Town?"

"I don't think he's concerned about their comfort, Eli."

"What is ghetto B?"

"Ghetto B will be in the area of Grodzka, Kowalska and Rybna Streets."

"That's a very small area, but our house is on Rybna," Eli said.

"Then for the time being you are probably okay. When they finish designating ghetto B, it will be for those engaged in professions: artisans, carpenters, factory owners and those with jobs that can benefit the administration." Then he pointed at Louis. "And *also* those who serve on the *Judenrat*. Jews that were appointed to the *Judenrat* are considered privileged in the eyes of the German command, and they will get to live in ghetto B."

"My house is not in that area," Jakob said.

"Then you will have to move. The SS will seize all vacant houses outside the ghetto. You'll have to find another place to live."

"I've lived in my house for fifty years. It is not vacant!"

Maximilian looked at Jakob, shrugged his shoulders and sighed in complacent resignation. "It will be. I don't know what more to say."

"When will this take effect?"

"Soon. I'm giving you advance warning. If your home is outside the boundaries of ghetto B, you're going to have to find other accommodations."

"Is that it? Is that all your wonderful news today? Can we get back to work?"

"No, it's not, and don't shoot the messenger. I'm doing you a favor by coming here. Remember, Maximilian is your friend. So far, I've kept you in your homes and off the deportation lists. But there is something else. Globočnik wants to open a brickyard in Litzmannstadt."

Eli, Jakob and Louis looked at each other quizzically. "Where is Litzmannstadt?"

"Oh, the Germans have renamed Lodz. It's now called Litzmannstadt."

"Are the seven hundred thousand people who live in Lodz now aware that they live in Litzmannstadt?"

"I would assume. They may not like it, but their city happens to lie within the borders of a new world. Anyway, my superiors want to construct a brickyard just like the one here in Lublin. They say, 'Build us one just like M. Poleski Building and Construction Materials.' I see this as an opportunity for the Rosens. Conceivably, you'll have income from two brickyards."

"No thanks. I know what the Nazis have done with Lodz. They sealed off an area with barbed wire and forced two hundred thousand Jews inside.

The ORPO shot three hundred and fifty people who resisted. I want nothing to do with Lodz or the Nazis."

Maximilian held his palm to his chest in mock sincerity. "I'm only passing along information. The Nazis have moved the Jews out of the Lodz city center and they now boast it's *Judenrein*. There are rumors that Jews in the ghetto will soon be moved elsewhere. They want Litzmannstadt to be a model of German culture, a shining center of the new General Government. I'm sure you can imagine all of the work that will be funneled through the new M. Poleski brickyard."

"Yeah, I can imagine. I'm not doing it."

"I'm afraid you don't have a choice. Those are Zörner's and Globočnik's orders. They're not suggestions. The project is slated for June. Globočnik has delegated it to Zörner, and he will want to meet with you in advance of that time."

As Maximilian was walking out of the building, Louis ran to catch up with him. The conversation lasted only a few minutes. When he returned, Eli said, "What did you do, Louis? Tell me you did not ask him to move Chava into his house."

"Don't lecture me, Eli. I can't send Chava to some faraway labor camp from which she'll never return. You'd do the same thing."

"He preys on young girls. He's a monster. A lecher. You can't let Chava move in with him. Who knows if he's even telling the truth?"

"Leave me alone, Eli. Don't you dare stand in judgment of me. You're not facing this problem."

CHAPTER THIRTY-EIGHT

LUBLIN, POLAND
APRIL 1941
MONTH 19 OF THE NAZI OCCUPATION
"Sylvia is beside herself, Eli," said Esther as she placed the dinner dishes on the table. "Louis announced that he was moving Chava into Maximilian's house for her safety."

"I'm dead set against it, Esther. I told Louis it was a mistake, that Maximilian is a lecherous snake, but my brother is desperate. He's concluded that it's necessary to prevent Chava from being shipped to a distant labor camp. He might be right. But I will have a talk with Maximilian first, and I will make it perfectly clear that he is not to touch her."

Esther shook her head. "I don't have much confidence in Maximilian. I talked to Myrna Schlossberg. You remember that her daughter Sophie, also fifteen years old, was living at Maximilian's?"

Eli nodded. "I asked Maximilian about her. He said she's not there anymore. I assumed she was now back at home."

"No, Eli. Sophie is now living with some Nazi. Myrna went to visit Sophie last week and she was gone. Maximilian told her that Sophie didn't want to live with him anymore, that she had caught the fancy of a German officer and preferred to live with him instead. Maximilian said he was sorry to see her go, but it was Sophie's decision."

"And Myrna doesn't believe that?"

Esther put her hands on her hips. "Eli! I know Sophie Schlossberg.

She'd sooner lie with an alligator than a Nazi. She's a young girl. Myrna said she'd never been with a boy before moving in with Maximilian. Maximilian gave her to that Nazi, probably as a gift in furtherance of his sycophantic relationship."

"Maximilian doesn't give anything away. He sold her."

"You can't let Louis do this. Maximilian'll take advantage of Chava. She's an innocent young girl. You have to stop him, Eli."

Esther and Eli were interrupted by a knock on the door. Jakob stood there with a suitcase. He was shaking like a leaf. "They came an hour ago. Three *mamzer* Nazis. They pushed their way into my house, looked around and said I have until tomorrow morning to move out. 'Take all your Jewish shit, but leave the furniture,' they said. They want a furnished house!"

Esther put her arm around him and brought him into the kitchen. "Please, sit down," she said gently and placed a cup of coffee on the table. "We'll help you, Papa. Don't worry. You can move right into our spare bedroom. Eli and Louis will help you move your things." She pointed her finger and commanded, "Go, Eli. Get Louis, and while you're at it, you can relieve him of his insane idea of putting Chava in Maximilian's home."

Eli picked up the brickyard truck and drove to Louis's house. As he approached the door, he heard screaming and crying from within. Louis answered the door, looked at Eli and said, "Whatever it is, this is not a good time, Eli."

"What's happening here, Louis?"

From the other side of the door, Sylvia's voice boomed. "What's happening, what's happening? I'll tell you what's happening, Eli. My little Chava is now living in a man's house."

Eli shook his head. "Oh, Louis, you can't do that. We have to go and bring her back."

"Listen to him, Louis, he's your older brother. He knows best. Chava shouldn't be in a man's house."

Louis stuck his hand on Eli's chest and started to push him backward. "This is none of your business, Eli. You have no right to interfere with my decision. I am the father, and I will decide what is best for my daughter."

Eli, much stronger than Louis, pulled his hand away. "We'll find a better solution, Louis. Sylvia's right. Chava doesn't belong at Maximilian's."

Tears were rolling down Louis's cheeks. "You don't know, Eli. They came today, the ORPO. They grabbed Chava, told her to take a change of clothes and go to the city center. There would be a truck waiting to take her and others. They were sending her away. I was frantic. I ran to Maximilian. What else could I do? God bless him, he went straight to the ORPO, rescued Chava and brought her back. He waited while she packed a bag, and Chava left to live with him. What could I do?"

Eli gently put his hand on Louis's shoulder. "I will talk to Maximilian and make sure he treats her properly. In the meantime, we need to help Papa move his belongings. They took his house."

☙

Early the next morning, Eli knocked on Maximilian's door. "Do you know what time it is?" Maximilian said, standing barefoot in the doorway.

"Six o'clock. Where's my niece?"

"Sound asleep, I presume, in the guest bedroom. Would you like to see for yourself?"

"Thank you for rescuing her."

Maximilian bowed. "You're welcome. It's nice to hear a 'thank you' from a Rosen once in a while."

"I would like to visit Chava from time to time. Louis and Sylvia would like to visit as well. I'm sure Sylvia would bake you a cake in deep appreciation for your kindness. But if I ever find out that you acted inappropriately with my niece, I will put a permanent end to Maximilian's future romantic endeavors. Get it?"

"Jesus Christ, Eli! What the hell? She's safe and sound in my house. Give me a little credit."

"I have nothing but gratitude for your hospitality. As long as you behave yourself."

CHAPTER THIRTY-NINE

LUBLIN, POLAND
MAY 1941
MONTH 20 OF THE NAZI OCCUPATION

Commandant Zörner decided it was time to talk about building the new brickyard, and he sent for Jakob, Eli and Maximilian. As they walked to Nazi headquarters at City Hall, Maximilian said, "I have come to know Zörner a little better. He is a hateful man, and he has no love for Jews. I think our best approach would be to let me do all the talking."

A three-block perimeter had been established around City Hall. Any civilian who intended to approach the building was stopped, searched and interrogated before entering the perimeter. Maximilian was clearly familiar with the guards and greeted them with a wave and smile. "I am taking these two men to the commandant on urgent Reich business," he said. "You may verify if you wish."

Zörner sat behind a polished desk. A large red-and-white Nazi flag was posted on either side. His gray uniform was neatly pressed but strained at the buttons to cover his corpulent frame. A stone-faced sentry stood at attention to his right. Though his side chairs were empty, he did not invite any of the three to sit. "So these are the Jews who are operating the brickyard?" he said.

"They are indeed, your excellency," Maximilian said. "Under my supervision, they are filling the Reich's every request promptly and efficiently."

"Hmph. Well, our needs here in Lublin are diminishing. The yard will eventually be closed."

"Closed?" Jakob blurted loudly. "The brickyard is *my* business! My family has run that brickyard for three generations. We built Lublin. I am not about to close my brickyard."

The sentry took a step toward Jakob, but Zörner calmly lifted his hand and signaled him to halt. "You best watch your tongue, old man. Your rudeness will instantly terminate your association with any earthly brickyard right here and now. The decision has been made and it is not open to debate. The Lublin brickyard will close when we have no further need for it. A newer and larger brickyard will be built in Litzmannstadt, which is quickly becoming the new center of industry in the General Gouvernment. As you have aptly described, Maximilian, the Reich's needs will be promptly and efficiently served by a brickyard, but it will soon be located in Litzmannstadt."

"As you command, excellency," Maximilian said. "A wise strategy. How may we assist you in realizing that goal?"

He looked at Eli out of the corner of his eye. "Maximilian, I want you to take these two with you to Litzmannstadt. Make a search for land suitable for a brickyard operation and establish the business. You may transfer whatever construction materials and machinery you need from the Lublin yard by motor carrier."

"Very good. We will begin our search immediately, Commandant. As soon as we find a suitable location, we will commence the transfer of materials and machinery."

"The hell we will," snapped Jakob. "How are we supposed to operate our business here without materials?"

Zörner stood. "If you open your mouth to me again, old man, I will shut it forever. You and your son will accompany Maximilian to Litzmannstadt, where you will build and operate a brickyard."

At this point, Eli stepped forward. "Commandant, if I may . . ."

"No, no," Maximilian interrupted. "It would be better if I were the only one to converse with the commandant."

Zörner waved his hand. "What is it, Eli Rosen?"

"The Rosen brickyard has served the Reich's needs since the day the city was occupied. My workers have always responded to your requests. I have never received a single complaint."

"So?"

"Our brickyard is near the rail lines. If we expand our operations just a little here in Lublin, we should have no difficulty filling orders for materials and shipping them by train to wherever they are needed."

Zörner sat back, took a cigarette out of a box, lit it, took a deep draw and contemplated his reply. Finally, he said, "No, that won't work. We need materials, masons, carpenters and bricklayers in Litzmannstadt, where the central command intends to build a model city and the manufacturing center of the country. We would not be well serviced from a yard two hundred kilometers away."

"I have capable foremen," Eli said. "I'm sure I could manage any project from my office in Lublin."

Zörner shook his head. "Discussion closed."

Eli continued. "But, your honor, I have a family here: a wife and a son. The schools and day-care centers have all been closed. My wife is working seven days a week for you in the sewing shops at Lipowa, but she doesn't get home until the end of her shift each night. My father and I watch my son during the day, and I prepare meals for my family each day. If my father and I were gone . . ."

The commandant raised his eyebrows. "We can easily provide for your wife by moving her out of your home and into our shopworkers' barracks permanently. As to arrangements for your son, that is an injudicious request for you to make of an SS officer. Perhaps Maximilian will inform you about the current policies in effect regarding dependent Jewish children. It's not something you would choose. I believe your brother Louis is in a position to care for your son if your wife were to stay in the Lindestrasse barracks full-time. Shall I make those arrangements?"

Eli hung his head. "No, sir. I will go with Maximilian."

Zörner stubbed out his cigarette. "Then it's settled. The Rosens will travel to Litzmannstadt with Maximilian after Mr. Rosen finds suitable management to operate the brickyard here in Lublin?"

"Commandant," Maximilian said, "perhaps you have forgotten that it is *my* brickyard and *my* operation. I will arrange for suitable management."

Zörner scoffed and reached for another cigarette. "Do you take me for a fool, Maximilian? You could no more operate a brickyard than I could pilot a battleship."

"But, your excellency, Brigadeführer Globočnik specifically designated myself as . . ."

"I know what General Globočnik did. And I know what *you* have done.

Or not done. I doubt I would see a speck of construction dust on any piece of your fancy wardrobe, would I?"

Maximilian shrugged. "But managers typically do not . . ."

"Stop! You may continue to strut around Lublin and drink with whomever you will. When I decide when and how you can be useful, I will let you know. In the immediate future, I have decided that you are to accompany the Rosens to Litzmannstadt and begin the establishment of a brickyard."

"Commandant," Eli said, "you might consider leaving my father to operate the Lublin brickyard. No one knows the operation better. A foreman would not have the necessary experience, and the efficiency would suffer, at least in the short run."

Maximilian stepped forward. "And those are exactly my thoughts as well, your excellency. I am particularly . . ."

Zörner waved him off. "The older Rosen may stay. You two will go." He lit his cigarette. "That is all. Good day."

CHAPTER FORTY

LUBLIN, POLAND

MAY 1941

MONTH 20 OF THE NAZI OCCUPATION

Eli was waiting on the front porch when Esther arrived home from her shift. She was tired and weary, not only from the strain of the nine-hour shift and from the thirty-minute walk to and from Lipowa each day but also from the incessant pressure of the overseers. Her gray uniform was worn and frayed, and though she had repaired it multiple times, it was coming apart at the seams.

It had been months since Esther had had a single day away from her sewing station. Not a single day where she did not have to arise before dawn, dress, eat enough food to carry her through an entire day and walk to Lipowa, no matter the weather. Not a single day when she didn't have to bear witness to the disrespect and abuse of the Nazi taskmasters. It had taken a toll on her, physically and mentally, and she had lost considerable weight.

But this evening, Eli sat on the porch waiting for her with a broad smile that caused Esther to chuckle. "What are you doing sitting out here with that silly grin on your face?" she said.

"I thought maybe I'd see a young lady walking by who'd give me a whirl." That was enough to make her laugh. "You're crazy."

He followed her into the house, waited while she said hello to Izaak and hung her coat. Eli still had that Cheshire grin on his face, and she said, "Okay, what's going on?"

"Don't you know what today is?"

"Of course, I do. Nine years with the most wonderful man on earth."

Eli looked a little sheepish, took a deep breath and produced a small black box from his pocket. He held it out and said, "Happy anniversary, honey." Esther's eyes opened wide, her jaw slowly dropped. She did not expect this.

"Did you think I would forget?" Eli said. "Is the bloom off the rose? Do you take your poor husband for granted?"

"Never," she said, with a catch in her throat, "but under the circumstances . . ." She broke into tears and threw her arms around him. "I love you so much."

"And I love you ten times more."

"How in the world did you . . ."

"Never mind. Just open it." She slowly opened the box and took out a silver necklace. Her hands shook, and Eli placed the chain around her neck. "Where . . . ?" she said.

"David Wolff closed his store; it was too dangerous to keep it open. But he still sells a little jewelry from his home."

"It's beautiful."

"And tonight I'm taking you out to dinner. Rabinovitz is saving me a table at his café."

"We can't leave Izaak."

"It's a table for three."

❧

Jewish commerce, or what remained of it, had condensed into the main square in the Jewish ghetto. There were a few restaurants still in business despite the depressed economy and the difficulty of obtaining fresh food. Restaurants, like all Jewish-owned businesses, were required to display a Star of David and the word *Juden* on the front windows.

The Nazis had hung huge German flags and Nazi flags from the roofs and terraces of the taller buildings all throughout the city, and doubly so in the Jewish quarter. Many of the Jewish businesses had been vandalized and had been victim to brazen theft by Nazis, but unlike Warsaw and Lodz, Lublin's Jewish quarter remained open.

Viktor Rabinovitz had set a table for Eli on his outdoor patio. A small bottle of wine and a daisy in a bud vase were sitting on the table when the Rosens arrived. The early evening was warm, and people were out strolling through the square. Living conditions had become tense in the tightly compacted Jewish quarter, and an opportunity to take a walk in the pleasant evening air was a welcome respite, providing they were inside the ghetto by curfew.

Rabinovitz's menu had only three dinner offerings. Viktor recommended the lamb. "It's good tonight, very fresh. We still have our contacts outside the city." He winked. Eli and Esther ordered the lamb, while Izaak opted for a plate of rosol: chicken and pasta in a tasty broth.

In the glow of the setting sun and with a warm breeze from the south, it was a moment to savor, a break from the harsh conditions of the occupation, a reflection of life before the apocalypse, when life was more commodious and decency and respect resided in Lublin. It was a moment to breathe deeply and continue to hope. Eli and Esther held hands beneath the table and smiled. People passed by and nodded a greeting. "What's the occasion?" they would say. "Nine years of marital heaven," Eli would answer.

Viktor picked up the dinner dishes and said, "How about dessert? I have wonderful sernik with early-season strawberries." Izaak made a face. "He doesn't like cheesecake," Esther said, "but Eli and I do. If you have a paczki, it would please Izaak."

While the Rosens were enjoying their dessert, a group of four uniformed soldiers entered the square. People immediately averted their eyes and quickly moved to the perimeter, all of which greatly amused the Nazis. They meandered about the square and soon approached the Rosens' table. One of them, a young blond, no more than a gangly teen with acne on his face and a rifle strapped to his shoulder, reached down to pick the paczki off of Izaak's plate, but his companion said, "Gunther, stop. Are you going to eat off a Jew's plate?" He stopped, made a face and backed away. "Oh, I don't know what I was thinking." Then he noticed Esther's necklace. "Look at what we have here. Silver on that old hag's neck. That's far too nice for a Jewess, don't you think, Hans?" he said. "It should adorn a young fräulein's neck." He held out his hand. "Give it to me."

Izaak jumped up. "You can't have her necklace. It belongs to my mama. It was a present."

The Nazis laughed, but the blond teen did not. "Your German is very poor. Sit down, little boy, before you learn the manners that your father has obviously failed to teach you." Then he turned to Esther. "Now! Give me that necklace."

"No," yelled Izaak, standing up in front of his mother. "You can't have it. It's hers."

The Nazi pulled his arm back to give Izaak a backhand swat across his face, but Eli's powerful hand shot out, caught the man's wrist and twisted it behind his back. "You don't touch my son. Ever. Keep walking."

The blond pulled his arm away and backed up. His jaw was quivering. He looked to his companions for support, but they were teens as well, and everyone was caught in the uncertainty of the moment. Esther started to take her necklace off, but Eli said, "Don't do it, Essie. Izaak is right; it's your necklace. They're not going to do anything, because if they injure any of Zörner's shop workers, they'll have to answer for it."

"Your snotty kid is not a worker," said the blond with a smile, and he took his rifle off of his shoulder. Eli grabbed Izaak and put him behind his back. People who were walking in the square stopped and formed a circle surrounding the table, inching ever closer. The perimeter steadily contracted and the soldiers found themselves in a shrinking bulls-eye.

"Look around," Eli said. "You're not among friends here. Tell me, does the mighty German army now conduct war against defenseless six-year-olds? Is that your specialty?"

The four soldiers twisted their heads from side to side in apprehension of the encircling crowd. "Gunther," the blond's companion said, "forget it." He tugged on his sleeve. "Let it go, Gunther. The Jew isn't worth it, and I don't want to spend my evening making reports on why we had to shoot people. Forget the stupid necklace. It's probably a fake anyway."

Gunther slung his rifle back onto his shoulder and said, "Yeah, you're right; it's a fake. A piece of shit for a shitty Jew." He sneered at the Rosens and spit on their table. As the soldiers turned to leave, the crowd parted to provide a path out of the plaza, and the Nazis quickly retreated.

Eli took a deep breath. He nodded to the people in the square—his people, his Lubliners. They waved back and continued on their evening strolls with smiles on their faces. For just that spot in time, they had made a stand and they felt good about it. Viktor brought out a bottle of Polish whiskey, poured three drinks and sat down at the table. He set a plateful of cookies before Izaak and said, "You are the bravest young man I've ever known."

Izaak shrugged and ate a cookie.

CHAPTER FORTY-ONE

LUBLIN, POLAND
JUNE 1, 1941
MONTH 21 OF THE NAZI OCCUPATION

Maximilian drove into the Rosen brickyard in a dark maroon sedan polished to a mirrored shine. He stepped out wearing a white straw hat, a pastel suit and white spats above his shoes. He was there to inform Eli and Jakob that land had now been specifically set aside and cleared in Litzmannstadt for the establishment of the new brickyard.

"It's going to be a big brickyard," Maximilian said, with his arms wide open, "much larger than this one, but then Litzmannstadt is three times the size of Lublin. It's the largest industrial city in Poland now. There are a hundred new factories. You can't imagine how important the new brickyard will be to the Reich. I'm going to call it "M. Poleski's Litzmannstadt Brickyard and Building Supply Company."

"How very nice for you," Eli said. "But, if you don't mind, right now we're busy trying to fill orders for your buddy, Commandant Zörner. Since he's evicting Jewish families from their homes and forcing them into ghettos A and B, the Nazis want the streets repaved and the confiscated homes remodeled. Orders come in every day. So unless you want to help us fill orders, why don't you just get in your fancy Nazi car, drive to Lodz, set up your Maximilian Company and leave us alone?"

"Have you forgotten Commandant's orders? You are to accompany me, Eli, and your father is to stay. Sadly, Ernst doesn't seem to trust my business acumen. He requires your expertise. And he wants us to leave as quickly as possible. Tomorrow morning."

"Oh, it's *Ernst* now, is it? I seem to recall that you previously described Zörner as a 'fat slob and ill-mannered—nothing like us.'"

"That was then; this is now. Never underestimate my ability to impress the Nazi command. Three nights ago, Ernst and I enjoyed a lovely evening with wine, women and song. My treat, of course. And a lucky thing it is for you, since you're all under my protection."

Jakob stormed into the room and raised his voice. "Protected, am I? Protected? How did you protect me when the ORPO gave me twelve hours to vacate my home? Thankfully, my son has room for me at his home, but I had to pack up everything I could and move into his spare bedroom. I've lived on my own for fifty years, but now I'm my son's permanent houseguest, thanks to Herr Zörner. You did a fine job of protecting me."

"I hope you know that all of that was out of my control," Maximilian said. "I did not design the ghettos. Be thankful that Eli lives in ghetto B and that you have a nice house to move into. Most do not."

"I *had* a nice house. I raised my children there. It belonged to me and it was worth a lot of money. Your filthy Nazis stole it from me."

"They aren't *my* Nazis and it wasn't *my* idea, Jakob. I'm only trying..." But Jakob walked out of the room before Maximilian could finish his sentence. Turning back to Eli, he said, "You Rosens make it so hard to help you. I came over today to tell you that I am going to drive to Litzmannstadt tomorrow and you will go with me."

"No. I changed my mind."

"Eli, you know I can't set up a brickyard by myself. I don't know the first thing about organizing a building supply business. Besides, it's Zörner's orders."

"And if I refuse?"

Maximilian shook his head. "Why would you even pose such a stupid question? You're not about to disobey Commandant Zörner. Besides, you're leading a privileged life in an occupied city. Just go with me. We'll be gone two or three weeks at the most. We'll stay in a nice house."

"A nice house that was confiscated from some Jewish family? You can't get a construction business up and running in three weeks, Maximilian. It'll take much longer, and I really don't want to leave my wife and son. If I have to leave them, I'll be very unhappy, and in my depression I'm bound to do a poor job of running the brickyard. Orders will get mixed up. Deliveries will fail. Deadlines will be missed. Zörner will be extremely unhappy, and you and your royal blood will fall into disfavor."

"You wouldn't do that to me."

"Let me take Esther and Izaak with me."

"You know I can't get Esther released from Lipowa. No one gets released from that camp. We've been going around and around that subject for weeks. Izaak will be fine; he comes here to the office every day with your father, and now your father even lives in your house. Eli, if you foul this up, you're going to put us both in jeopardy. Zörner is an impatient man, and he will take it out on you and everyone else. Besides, my reputation depends on it. You heard him; he thinks I am a foolish dandy strutting around Lublin. You can't let me down."

Eli shut his eyes and shook his head. "Isn't it strange how the world turns? I want something in return."

"What?"

"Esther."

Maximilian sighed. Then an idea came to him. "Is Esther good at paperwork? Can she do office clerical work at the new brickyard?"

"Absolutely. She's brilliant."

"Well, when the brickyard is up and running, I will try to get her reassigned to Litzmannstadt. As long as the brickyard is doing well, Zörner will work with me. What's one less seamstress? Do we have a deal? Will you go with me and not cause trouble?"

Eli nodded.

🙐

Eli's solution did not sit well with Esther. "Litzmannstadt?" she said. "My husband, I love you, but I don't want to move to Lodz. That's like jumping from the kettle into the fire. Two hundred thousand of our people are packed into a squalid little ghetto. The Nazis cage them up like dogs in a kennel. I hear that most of them don't have running water or indoor toilets. It's a *sealed* ghetto, like Warsaw, behind barbed wire with armed guards. They only let people leave to work in the factories and then return at night. They march them out, they march them in. You don't want us to live in that prison. We have a nice house here in Lublin."

"True, but Maximilian says he might be able to get you released from the Lipowa camp. You won't have to work like a slave in the sewing shop anymore. You can work with me at the brickyard. Maybe I can build a home for the three of us on-site at the new brickyard and not in the sealed ghetto. I've discussed it all with Maximilian."

"I don't trust Maximilian."

"I don't either, but in this case he needs me. He can't organize or operate a construction company by himself. He was practically begging me to help him."

"He's begging you today, and tomorrow he will throw his hands up in the air and say it's out of his control. We've seen that act before. Our situation is more secure here in Lublin. I'm able to endure the routine at Lipowa, and your father is now living with us. He'll be happy to help with Izzie. You can go alone."

"But, Essie, I might be away for long periods—weeks, maybe months. Who knows? It's going to take time to get a new brickyard up and running. I don't feel comfortable leaving the two of you. Things are unsettled here, and they get worse every day. Tomorrow some new edict will come down, and I won't be here to protect you."

Esther set her arms on Eli's shoulders. "We'll get through this, honey. You've said so yourself many times. Every time I wanted to give up, you counseled me to be patient, and I've come to believe that you are right. Sooner or later even the roughest seas calm. Floodwaters reach a level and then recede. This madness will pass. The Nazis are going to realize that imposing harsh conditions on the Jewish community is not in their interest, economically or otherwise. At some point, life in Poland will stabilize, the ship will right and things will return to normal. Who knows, maybe Germany's incursions throughout Europe will falter. They failed in the first Great War. There are many reasons for us to adjust, accommodate and wait it out."

Eli looked deeply into Esther's eyes. "How did I get such a wise woman to marry me?"

"I've told you many times, you didn't have a choice. I willed it to be so."

❦

Early the next morning, Maximilian pulled his car up to the curb and waited with the motor running. Eli had packed a small bag of clothes the night before. Esther was preparing to walk to Lipowa, and Eli reached out to kiss his wife goodbye.

"Please be careful," she said. "You know that Maximilian is a snake. He'll make promises he can't keep. Don't let him get you into trouble. You can't trust a thing he says. People leave Lublin and they don't come back. Please promise me, Eli, you'll come back to me."

"I will come back, that's a promise. Don't worry about me; I'll be fine. I'll try to get home in three or four weeks. If you or Izaak need anything, my father and my brother will help you." His eyes filled with tears, and he hugged Esther as tightly as he could. "Take care, my girl. I love you more than life itself."

"You will always be my sunny day."

He lingered in the softness of her kiss as long as he could. Given the uncertainties of their world and the external forces he could not control, he could not be certain when he would hold her again.

CHAPTER FORTY-TWO

FÖHRENWALD

Though it was early in the season, the bitter Bavarian snowstorm was unrelenting. Blasts of winter winds howled down from the Alps and rattled the windowpanes. Upon return from Garmisch and his meeting with Colonel Bivens, Eli discovered that Izaak had come down with a fever and needed immediate medical care. Eli knew he could not take his feverish child out into the elements, and he hoped that he could coax Dr. Weisman into making a house call. Fortunately, Adinah was at the house.

He was in panic mode by the time he reached the clinic. "Please tell Dr. Weisman it's an emergency," he said. "My son, Izaak, is burning up."

The nurse was sympathetic, but she was tasked with serving several patients at once. "I'll get word to him as soon as I can," she said, gesturing to the crowded waiting room. "As you can see, there are a number of emergencies here tonight. This snowstorm has taken its toll on our little community."

Eli paced the floor like a jungle cat. Finally, Dr. Weisman came into the waiting room. "Joel," Eli said quickly, "it's Izaak. He's really sick—a very high fever; his skin is all flushed."

The doctor nodded. "Calm down, my friend. Where is he?"

"At home, in bed. I was afraid to take him out in this storm. I'm really worried, Joel. Really worried. I've never seen him like this."

"Who's with him?"

"Adinah Szapiro."

He nodded. "All right, let me finish up here. I have two more patients, and then we'll go take a look at Izaak."

It was almost midnight when Eli and Dr. Weisman arrived at the house. "He's been asleep the entire time," Adinah said. "I tried to give him a glass of water, but he wouldn't take it. He says it hurts to swallow."

"Has he been coughing?" Dr. Weisman asked. "Wheezing? Trouble breathing?"

"Coughing a little. Mostly he complains that his throat hurts. He was very tired when he came home from school, and he went into his room to rest."

The doctor donned his surgical mask and handed one to Eli, who rejected it with a shake of his head.

"Put it on," the doctor directed. "I don't want both of you coming down with whatever Izaak has." He followed Eli into the back bedroom. "Izaak, Izaak," Dr. Weisman said loudly, trying to wake him up. "Can you sit up, son?"

Izaak's eyelids were heavy, and he could barely raise them above a narrow slit. Eli helped him to a sitting position and watched as the doctor conducted his examination. When he was finished, he patted Izaak on the head, laid him back down on the pillow and motioned for Eli to join him in the other room.

"No minimizing this, Eli, he's a pretty sick boy. His fever is over 102, but his lungs sound clear."

"What is it, Joel? Is it tuberculosis? Does my boy have TB?"

The doctor's lips were pursed, and he shrugged. "It's too soon to tell. His throat is very red, and that may very well be an indication of streptococcus. Strep throat. If it is, I can treat it with penicillin." He reached into his black bag, took out a bottle and poured a few pills into a small envelope. "I'm going to give him an injection and start him on these today. If it's strep, we should see some improvement. The next few days will tell us a lot."

As he prepared to leave, he added, "Aspirin may help keep the fever down. Give him plenty of fluids. Until we know for sure, I want you both to wear the surgical masks when you go into his room."

"I can't thank you enough," Eli said as he clasped the doctor's hand. "You're a true friend to come out in this weather. And a godsend to our camp."

The doctor smiled. "Quite the compliment, coming from you, Eli, a man who has devoted himself to the welfare of our community. I walked three blocks in a little snow; you drove a hundred miles through the storm today."

"We all do what we can."

"How did it go? Will the colonel help us arrest Max?"

"The colonel will do anything to please General Lucius D. Clay, and he assigned Major Donnelly to help me. The plan is for us to visit the nearby camps over the next couple of weeks. We were supposed to go to Landsberg tomorrow. But given Izaak's illness, I'll ask Daniel to step in for me."

"I will stay with Izzie while you go," Adinah said. "Go with the major to Landsberg, and I will care for Izzie."

Dr. Weisman shook his head. "That's not wise, Adinah. You're very kind, but the longer you stay, the more you risk exposure. I don't advise it. I'm sure you know that there are many sick people now in our sanitarium."

She stood tall and defiant. "I have been with him all day. If he is contagious, then I am infected. And so be it. This family needs my help. Can you understand what that means to me? I survived the death camps. Almost everyone I knew or cared about in my life was taken from me. Sent to their deaths. I lived and they did not, and often I ask myself, Why? Why was I chosen to survive when much better people than me were killed? I keep asking God to give me a reason. Why me? And maybe now He answers: 'It is for this, Adinah.' Eli will go tomorrow, and I will stay here with Izaak. I will care for Izaak."

The doctor smiled and nodded. "I will come and check in on him."

"I don't know what to say," Eli whispered. "Thank you, Adinah. I'll make up a bed for you."

Dr. Weisman put on his heavy coat and wrapped his scarf around his neck and chin. He pushed the door against the pressure of the wind, turned and said, "Be careful going out into the community, both of you. You may now be carriers. Until we know for sure, don't get too close to anyone." Then he hesitated and smiled. "The world should only know the fellowship shared among our survivors. They should know how much compassion is rendered without a second thought by the good people in our camps."

CHAPTER FORTY-THREE

FÖHRENWALD DP CAMP
AMERICAN ZONE
DECEMBER 1946

Before leaving for Landsberg with Major Donnelly, Eli stopped by the sanitarium to visit Bernard. Eli was shocked to see how dramatically the disease had taken its toll in such a short time. Bernard had lost weight, his complexion had paled and his breathing was labored. He paused between phrases in order to swallow, clear his throat and moisten his lips. Eli stood patiently by his bedside talking to his good friend through a surgical mask.

"Moshe Pogrund is the director at Camp Landsberg," Bernard whispered. "I know him to be a good man and a strong leader. He is usually counseled by Rabbi Hirsch. I made the introduction for you and Major Donnelly, and I scheduled a two o'clock meeting. Olga told me that her contact at Landsberg was a man named Shael Bruchstein. She and Mr. Bruchstein have acted together in a de facto partnership promoting the sale of Max's visas. Bruchstein would attract interested prospects and then contact Olga. She was the pipeline to Max. Together, Bruchstein and Olga were supposed to split commissions. According to Olga, she and Bruchstein have brokered six visas for residents at Landsberg."

"Were all of the six visas delivered?"

"No, only four. Max is due to deliver the remaining two visas sometime in the next two weeks, and that's when we should arrest him." He reached up and squeezed Eli's wrist. "Eli, listen to me. We can't let this opportunity slip away. Max must be stopped, and his U.S. supplier must be exposed. Be cautious; we don't want any more stool pigeons tipping him off."

"How sure are we of Bruchstein?"

"I don't know him. I suggest we threaten Bruchstein with prosecution, like we did with Olga. Back him into a corner, Eli. Scare the hell out of him. Use Major Donnelly if you have to. He'll cooperate or he'll go to jail." He clasped Eli's hands. "Safe travels, my friend."

Eli made a gesture of kissing the tips of his fingers and touching them to Bernard's forehead. "Take your medicines, listen to the nurses and get back on your feet. We need you."

❧

Eli climbed into the passenger seat of Major Donnelly's jeep and smiled. "Well, this is sure an improvement over the Camp Föhrenwald jalopy. You have a working heater. I'll wager you have working windshield wipers as well."

"I do indeed. Do you really think that Colonel Bivens wouldn't have the latest equipment?" As he drove out of the camp and onto the throughway, he said, "Before we meet with Mr. Pogrund, tell me how you learned that Max was selling visas at the Landsberg camp."

"Our director, Bernard Schwartz, learned about it at a camp committee meeting. It was Bernard who scheduled the meeting with Colonel Bivens, but sadly he took ill, and I became his less-than-qualified understudy."

"What's wrong with Bernard?"

"You may have heard; we have an epidemic in our camp."

"Jesus, TB? He's got TB?"

Eli nodded. "There are at least one hundred fifty patients here. We built a sanitarium."

"There's a sanitarium in Camp Gauting as well. Many believe that the epidemic originated in Dachau."

"We're all praying that Bernard recovers. Our camp doctor is a wonderful man, and he's had some successes."

Changing subjects, the major said, "Do you know the history of the Landsberg camp?"

Eli shook his head.

"It's ugly. Before the war it was a German prison. Hitler himself was locked up there in 1924, and that's where he wrote *Mein Kampf*. He dictated the whole thing to his buddy, Rudolph Hess. Hitler was sentenced to serve five years for treason, but he got out in nine months. He even ordered a new car while he was in prison." Donnelly shook his head. "A gray Mercedes from a dealer in Munich.

"During the war Landsberg was converted to a concentration camp, part of the Kaufering subcamps of the Dachau concentration camp system. That place has a pretty gruesome history."

"They were all pretty gruesome, Major. I was liberated from Buchenwald."

Donnelly smiled. "Patton's boys. Sixth Armored Division, as I recall. Super Sixth, they call them. Let me ask you, how well do you know Moshe Pogrund, the Landsberg camp director?"

"I don't know him at all. Bernard set the meeting."

❧

Moshe Pogrund met them in Landsberg's great dining hall. Rows of long wooden tables filled the cavernous room. A large American flag hung from the center of the peaked ceiling. The entryway was plastered with posters announcing concerts, social gatherings, educational activities and the weekly bulletin from the camp committee. A stack of camp newspapers, the *Yidische Cajtung,* lay on a table. The hall was empty but for two men who sat waiting for Eli and Donnelly.

As Bernard had predicted, Pogrund said, "I have asked Rabbi Hirsch to join us. He is our spiritual leader and my trusted advisor." The rabbi smiled broadly beneath his gray beard. "How is my good friend Bernard?"

"I saw him this morning," Eli answered. "He's holding his own. He's a tough old bird, and the angel of death is going to have a helluva fight on her hands."

"Tell him we wish him all the best," Pogrund said.

"I will, sir. I assume that Bernard told you all about Max, the black-market visa salesman?"

"Bernard's revelations were a shock to us," the rabbi said. "Like other DP camps, we are merely a waiting room, a temporary way station where our residents are reborn, rehabilitated, educated and trained in various occupations before moving on and rejoining the world, wherever they may settle."

"Rabbi is right," Pogrund added. "We are merely a platform, a staging area. Landsberg is not a permanent home. Everyone has his or her name on a list, waiting to emigrate. The fact that some dishonest person can buy his way around the list is an anathema to us. Who's responsible, and how do we prevent such a practice?"

"The man who sells the visas goes by the name of Max. I believe him to be the same man I knew in Lublin whose name was Maximilian Poleski. He was a corrupt man who wormed his way into the Nazis' favor soon after they occupied the city. He used his connections to enrich himself and cheat others. He sold promises."

"What sort of promises?"

"Safety, security, survival. Protection from the harsh Nazi edicts. Sometimes, he delivered; sometimes, he made excuses. He had an office in our brickyard, and on many days there were lines of people waiting to purchase favors. More food, a place to live, mercy for a family member who had violated one of the many Nazi proscriptions."

"He had that kind of power?"

"Sometimes."

"And you believe that this man is now doing business in our camp?"

"According to our source in Föhrenwald, Max has the cooperation of a Landsberg resident that is quietly putting out the word, casting his lines in the water. If he gets a bite, he arranges a meeting with Max's agent, Olga Helstein, a Föhrenwald resident. Sometimes, if Max is in the area, he will meet with the prospect and quote his price. Other times, he will communicate a price through Olga. Nevertheless, Max will always deliver the visa in person. He doesn't trust anyone else to handle his money. We want to be there when Max comes to collect."

"Who is it? Who is Max's contact at Landsberg?"

"I was given the name of Shael Bruchstein."

Pogrund immediately covered his mouth. "Oh no, of all people," he said. "Shael Bruchstein? Can you be certain?"

"That's the name Olga gave us."

Pogrund glanced over at the rabbi and shook his head. "Bruchstein is the last man I'd expect to betray his people. He's such an integral part of our community. An elected member of the committee."

"Maybe that's what makes him such an able facilitator."

Rabbi Hirsch nodded sadly. "Bruchstein is a leader in this camp and in contact with thousands of our residents. They respect him. They honor him for his countless hours of service. He has helped to make Landsberg a vibrant and influential force among all the displaced persons camps. The organization we know as *She'erit haPletah*—the Surviving Remnant—was formed right here and maintains its Central European office here in Landsberg, and Bruchstein is on the board."

"Shael helped bring in people like Jakob Oleski to set up occupational training courses through ORT, the Organization for Rehabilitation and Training, right here in our camp, and Landsberg is ORT's field headquarters," Pogrund added. "Shael stood side by side with David Ben-Gurion when he came to Landsberg last year. Why would a man like that engage in an illegal scheme to circumvent our emigration laws?"

"Frau Helstein was getting twenty-five percent," Eli said. "At six thousand Swiss francs per visa, that's a lot of reasons why."

"Ach, it makes me sick to my stomach," the rabbi said.

"We have to shut him down, but we have to do it discreetly," Pogrund said. "If the residents learn that one of our most respected leaders is involved in a criminal enterprise, it'll bring shame upon all the good work we do."

"We have to do more than stop Bruchstein," Eli said. "Our mission is twofold: first to catch Max in the act, arrest and prosecute him; and second to force him to reveal the identity of his source. He has a well-placed contact in the United States."

"Well, you have our complete cooperation."

"Does Bruchstein live alone?"

Pogrund shook his head. "He lives with a woman. If you want to arrest him, I can take you there."

"No, I prefer it to be in private, not in a crowded neighborhood."

"That's very kind and considerate of you."

Eli scoffed. "I'm afraid it has nothing to do with kindness. If we arrest him in a public place, in plain sight, the news will get to Max and he'll never come back here. I'd like you to lure Bruchstein to the administration office. Tell him that you need to meet with him on urgent committee business."

"He'll want to know what it's about," Rabbi Hirsch said. "What will you tell him?"

Pogrund shook his head. "I don't know; it's not in my nature to be deceitful, but I'll think of something."

CHAPTER FORTY-FOUR

LANDSBERG DP CAMP
AMERICAN ZONE
DECEMBER 1946

Shael Bruchstein arrived at the Landsberg administration office shortly after four o'clock. He shook the snow off his coat, hung it on the rack and greeted Moshe Pogrund and Rabbi Hirsch. Then he turned his attention to the other two men in the room. "I don't think I know these two gentlemen, Moshe."

"This is Eli Rosen, a board member at the Föhrenwald Camp, and Major Donnelly, an adjutant to Colonel Bivens at the U.S. Army garrison in Garmisch."

Bruchstein smiled and shook their hands. "Sounds serious," he said in a nonserious tone. He pulled up a chair to join the four men sitting around a small conference table. "How can I assist? You said it was urgent committee business, Moshe." He smiled at Eli and Donnelly, but the smile was not returned.

"I'll defer to Mr. Rosen," Moshe said.

Eli gestured to Donnelly. "The major is here to arrest you, Mr. Bruchstein."

Bruchstein turned white. He looked from face to face and finally settled on Pogrund. "Is this a joke, Moshe? It's not funny in the least."

"It is not a joke, Shael. I wish it were."

"What am I accused of?"

The major leaned forward, took a breath and said flatly, "Conspiring to commit immigration fraud, conspiring to sell stolen documents, willful violation of the laws of the United States Immigration Service and of the American Occupation Zone, solicitation of others to commit an illegal act and aiding and abetting a United States citizen in fraudulently issuing visas for illegal sale to foreign nationals. That's all I can think of at the moment. I'm sure that the U.S. Attorney will have a much better handle on other included offenses."

Bruchstein sank into his chair. His hands covered his face. "Olga."

Rabbi Hirsch nodded. "How could you, Shael? Why?"

"I knew it was wrong. I didn't do it for myself. I would never have purchased, accepted or used a black-market visa."

"Oh, but you would take a commission," Eli said. "I believe that's equivalent to 'doing it for yourself.'"

"I didn't make a cent. If Max paid Olga, none of it ever came to me. I didn't do it for the money."

"Then why, Shael?" the rabbi pleaded. "I have known you to be such a good man."

"What does it matter? I did it. Six times. I'm guilty." Turning to the major, he said, "Would you permit me to say goodbye to Rachel? We've been together for the past year. She's not very strong, and she depends on me. I'm afraid she's made a bad choice."

The rabbi stood. "What does it matter, you say? It matters to *me*, Shael. You've meant so much to our community, sitting on the boards of ORT and *She'erit HaPletah*. I believed in you. I know you to be a selfless man. I want to know *why*!"

"It might matter, Mr. Bruchstein," Eli said. "Depending on the circumstances, we may ask you to do something."

Bruchstein hung his head. "I'll cooperate in any way I can."

"Tell us how this scheme came to Landsberg and how you became involved."

"It started last June. I was at an ORT conference at Feldafing. Olga Helstein was there as well. She and I have served together on the board for some time. During the day, the conversation got around to immigration quotas, as it usually does at those functions. Why won't the Allied countries open their borders to Jewish refugees? There are only 250,000 of us. The western countries could easily absorb us without even flinching. Why are the quotas so strict for Jewish refugees when they are so generous to others? I mentioned that a friend of mine at Landsberg was desperate to travel to America. His father was dying in a New York hospital, and he would give anything to spend those last days with him. Then Olga said, 'If the man is important to you, I can get him a visa. It'll cost, but I can get it.'"

"Did she mention the name Max or Maximilian?"

"Not at first. She only said she had a source. Six thousand Swiss francs for a genuine U.S. visa."

"And you told her you would make the arrangements?"

"No. I didn't want any part of it. I knew it was wrong, but I felt it wasn't my decision to make. It was Saul's. I told her I would give Saul her contact information, and if he was interested, they could work out the details. I stepped out of it altogether. Six weeks later, a man shows up in Landsberg asking for *me*. Everyone figured it had to do with my work on the board, but it was Max, and he had the visa for Saul. Saul had made the agreement directly with Olga without my knowledge."

"Why did Max ask for you and not Saul?"

Bruchstein shrugged and spread his hands. "Maybe that's who Olga told him to contact; I don't know. I put Saul and Max together, they made the exchange and the next day both of them were gone. A month later, I received a letter from Saul, thanking me profusely for the time he was able to spend with his father before he died. To tell the truth, I felt good about it. I was happy for Saul. It meant so much to him, and I was happy to play my small part. As far as I was concerned, it was a onetime deal."

"But it wasn't, was it?"

"No. Harry Florsheim and his wife came to see me. I don't know whether they heard it from Saul or how they got the information, but they wanted to buy two visas. They had the money."

The rabbi interrupted and turned to Eli and the major. "Harry and Bertha Florsheim were elderly. Harry was an accountant in Berlin and was arrested during Kristallnacht. Bertha was left alone, was taken in a roundup and ultimately ended up at Gross-Rosen. By all rights, they never should have seen each other again. Somehow, after liberation, the Central Tracing Bureau put them together. It was a miracle."

Pogrund picked up the rabbi's narrative. "The concentration camps were hard on all of us, but Bertha never quite recovered. She had vivid nightmares, and not just at night. Her visions haunted her. When she got them, she would shake and moan, and Harry would hug her tightly. No matter where they went, Bertha would cling to Harry like a terrified child."

Bruchstein nodded. "Harry came to me. He said he had made a solemn promise to Bertha to take her to America, far away from Germany, far away from her nightmares. 'That promise is what's keeping her alive, Shael,' he said to me. 'Bertha's eyes still see the horror of her captivity, and I told her that her eyes would soon see America, *Die Goldene Medina,* and when they did, all her past visions would disappear. She lives for that, Shael. You helped Saul, and now I beg you to help Bertha and me. I have the money.'"

"And so you called Max?"

Bruchstein shook his head. "I didn't know how to reach Max. I called Olga. To see them together, Rabbi, it would break your heart. It broke mine. I put them in touch with Olga without a second thought. In two months, they were gone."

Eli leaned forward. "Mr. Bruchstein, this is very important: Did you happen to be present when the money was exchanged for the visas?"

He nodded. "I was always present. Olga would contact me, she'd let me know when Max would be here with the visas, I would notify the buyers and we would all meet with him. But now things have changed."

"What do you mean?"

"Last week, Max called me directly. He has two more visas that were ordered by Aaron and Yetta Davison. He wants to set up the exchange next week."

"Did Olga set it up?"

"Max said he wasn't working with Olga anymore—something about a problem at Föhrenwald. He trusted me and he would only do the exchange through me. He wanted me to make sure the Davisons had their money."

"Did you set a date?"

"Not yet. I have a telephone number for Max in Munich. I'm supposed to call him back after I talk to Aaron."

Eli looked to Major Donnelly. "Are you and your men available next week?"

"I think you know the answer to that. Colonel Bivens was very explicit."

"Tell Aaron to be available next week. Set it up for Wednesday at noon here at the camp," Eli said. "Make sure that no one other than the Davisons know where or when. Tell the Davisons that they must keep the meeting secret or they'll never get their visa."

Bruchstein grimaced. "I hate to deceive Aaron."

"He's breaking the law."

Bruchstein nodded. "May I ask, what is to become of me?"

Eli leaned forward and spoke directly. "First, you go home to Rachel as though nothing has happened. You say nothing about this meeting to her or to anyone else. Contact Aaron Davison and Max and set up the exchange. Let me know when it's confirmed so that Major Donnelly and his military police will be present. If you do this, Mr. Bruchstein, if you help us to arrest Max, you will not be prosecuted. You and Rachel may go on living as before. If you betray us, if you alert Max, you will go to jail for a long time. Do we understand each other?"

Bruchstein stood. "I am truly grateful. I won't let you down."

CHAPTER FORTY-FIVE

ALBANY PARK

CHICAGO

ALBANY PARK NEIGHBORHOOD

DECEMBER 1965

Nathan was sound asleep when the ring of his bedside phone shook him from his slumber. "Hullo," he whispered.

"Nathan, Nathan, get up," Mimi cried.

His throat was dry, and he spoke in a whisper. "What? What's the matter?"

"Get up and turn on the news! Nathan, they're dead, Preston and Chrissie. They died last night. Oh, my God."

"What are you talking about?"

Mimi was hysterical. "Pres and Chrissie. They're gone. They died in a fire. Oh, Nathan, I just can't believe it. Please, can you come over now? Please?"

Eli was standing on the front stoop when Nathan came running up. "Such tragic news," Eli said. "I am so very sorry for you both."

Nathan dashed up the stairs. The apartment door was open, and he could hear Mimi crying. "Meems, what happened?"

"Didn't you see the news?"

He shook his head. "I came right over."

"Here it is," Grandma called from the living room. "NBC is broadcasting from the fire station."

They watched as the battalion chief was interviewed. "The fire was extinguished before it had consumed the rear of the structure. Consequently, the back bedrooms were intact. Firefighters were able to extract the bodies of two adult occupants, who were later identified as Mr. and Mrs. Preston Roberts."

"Do we know how the fire started?"

"Not conclusively. It's still under investigation at this time. I can tell you that we believe it originated in the front hallway, and there are signs that suggest the use of an accelerant. That's really all I have right now."

⁊

The newscast then switched to the outside of an elegant brick home in the Ravenswood Manor section, set one hundred feet back from the parkway. Police were stationed in front of the circular drive.

"This is the home of Congressman Witold Zielinski," the reporter said. "The congressman and Mrs. Zielinski are inside, but, quite understandably, they are not talking to reporters. They were informed by telephone of the tragedy that befell their daughter and her husband, both only twenty-five years old and married barely four months." Photo clips of the wedding were displayed on the screen.

The reporter then tried to interview a plainclothes police lieutenant who was standing in front of the Zielinski home. He shook his head and said, "Out of respect for the congressman, there is very little we will discuss at this time."

"Was it a homicide, Lieutenant?"

The lieutenant gave a nod.

"So," the reporter said, "I take it that the fire was set to cover up a crime?"

"As I said, out of respect for Congressman and Mrs. Zielinski, we will wait for the conclusion of our investigation before releasing any more information to the press. That's all I have to say at this time."

⁊

Mimi and Nathan spent the day trying to process the terrible news. Best friends, practically family, gone in the blink of an eye—it was inconceivable. What kind of monster would do such a thing? How deranged and wicked would a person have to be to commit so evil a crime against such a lovely young couple?

A number of photographs lay on Mimi's coffee table, and she gently arranged them with her index finger. "Chrissie was such a powerful force in my life, and I really don't know how things will ever be the same. There's an empty hole in my heart," Mimi said. "She and I have shared our innermost secrets since we were eight years old. I can't believe she's gone."

Nathan stared at a picture of the four of them taken at the Indiana Dunes State Park. "He was like a brother to me," he said softly. "He always had my back. I remember the time we played Sullivan and some smartass linebacker took a cheap shot at me. Preston came out of nowhere and flattened the guy. He was ready to take on the whole Sullivan team. I know I'll never have another friend like him."

The afternoon news compounded their sadness with the revelation that Preston and Christine had been murdered before the fire was set. The coroner reported that Preston had been shot three times: two superficial wounds and a fatal shot to the temple, execution style. Christine died from a single shot, an oblique wound that severed her carotid artery. Officials speculated that the fire was set to cover up the crime. Theories abounded. Police theorized it was a botched robbery. The house had been torn apart. Drawers lay open. Closets had been rifled through. According to Christine's parents, items of jewelry were missing.

Mimi gripped Nathan's hand tightly. "That was no robbery. You and I both know that the shootings were intended to silence Preston and Chrissie. If Chrissie hadn't quit, if she had returned to work as her father demanded, she'd be alive today."

"Vittie wouldn't kill his daughter, Meems. He loved her."

"I'm not saying that Vittie was the murderer. He would never harm Chrissie. I don't think he cared for Preston, especially after last Sunday's phone call, but he would never have done anything to hurt his daughter."

"Then who? Was it Nicky?"

Mimi shrugged. "I wouldn't put it past him. He's an asshole, he's violent, he's a drunk, but according to Chrissie, he was madly in love with her."

"Remember, he's going through a divorce, and Chrissie knew all about his hidden money. Maybe Nicky's more madly in love with his money than he was with Chrissie. He could have gone over there to threaten Chrissie and make sure she kept quiet. We know he has a hair-trigger temper."

"I suppose that's possible, but why would Preston ever let Nicky into the house in the middle of the night? I don't think we should overlook the corporate executives—Vittie's military contractors, his campaign contributors, his bribers—whatever you want to call them. They're making billions, and they're not about to let two kids get in their way."

Nathan nodded. "Or send them to federal prison for illegal kickbacks. We both heard what Preston said to Vittie last Sunday night. We heard him threaten to go to the *Tribune* and blow the whistle on the 'whole goddamn operation.' And you heard what Chrissie said. 'Everybody knows *too much*.' Meems, there's no doubt in my mind that they were killed to silence them, and it could have been arranged by any one of those billionaires."

Mimi bit her lip. "Should we go to the police? Tell them what we know?"

"Accuse Congressman Witold Zielinski and the country's most powerful businessmen of illegal kickbacks? We have no evidence. No proof of anything. Who's going to believe two twenty-five-year-olds against those people?"

Mimi pointed at the first floor. "I know one person who might."

CHAPTER FORTY-SIX

The top half of Chicago's skyline was swallowed up in a blanket of low, dark clouds, reminding Chicagoans that winter had once again taken up residence. Patches of ice and snow dotted the sidewalk in front of the Ostrowicz Funeral Home, and despite the chilly north winds, the line to pay respects stretched out the door and down Wilson Avenue. The wait time was over an hour.

The mortician had expressed his concern to the Zielinski and Roberts families that he could not do justice to Preston. The head wound had caused too much damage. He recommended a closed casket wake for the married couple, but the congressman rejected the suggestion outright. "Christine's will be opened. You will prepare her properly and I will have my goodbyes," he said.

Nathan, Mimi and Ruth approached Christine's casket together. Mimi stood for a moment, shivered and then slumped into Nathan's arms as though she were a marionette and someone had cut her strings. With his arm around her, Nathan led her to a seat. A few minutes later, Congressman Zielinski came over and sat next to her. The dark circles under his eyes and the slump in his shoulders bore witness to his profound sadness. Mimi had never seen him look so old. A man who carried himself with the bearing of a Roman general had been vanquished by his grief.

"I am so very sorry for you, Uncle Vittie," Mimi said through her tears.

"And I for you," Vittie said. "I have memories, such happy memories of the two of you playing in the yard. Always like sisters. Always two peas in a pod." He took Mimi's hand. "You have been and will always be a second daughter to us, Mimi." They hugged and cried together until the congressman nodded and left to talk to other people.

Mimi and Nathan were talking to Christine's mother when a gaunt man in rimless glasses came over and clasped Nathan's shoulder. He gestured for Nathan to follow him to the hallway.

"My name is Michael Stanley," he said, with curled lips in an unfriendly manner. He did not offer a handshake. "I work for the congressman. I'm his chief of staff. I was Preston's boss."

"I know who you are."

"What do you know about the murders?"

"I don't know anything. What kind of question is that at a wake?"

Stanley lifted his chin and peered down over his nose. "You were his best friend. He confided in you, didn't he? What has he been telling you recently?"

"About what?"

"Don't play cute with me, Mr. Stone. What did Preston Roberts tell you about the reasons Christine was considering leaving her job?"

"Considering? She *quit* her horseshit job, and what either one of them told me is none of your business."

Stanley jabbed a finger onto Nathan's chest. "It is very much my business, Mr. Smart-mouth. What did Preston tell you?"

Nathan smiled and raised his eyebrows. "He told me he didn't like you, that you were an asshole, and I can now confirm that his description was accurate."

"How dare you! Sonny, you don't know who you're dealing with. I want answers."

"Look, I don't have to answer your questions, Mr. Stanley. You're not a cop. This is a wake for my best friend, and you're bothering me. And if you poke that finger at me again, I'll break it off. Go away."

Stanley took a step back. "You're walking a dangerous line here, sonny. You better watch what you say and who you talk to. You can get yourself and your girlfriend in a whole world of trouble. If I was you, I'd keep my mouth shut."

Nathan scoffed and walked away. He waited for Mimi to finish expressing her condolences and they left.

"Did you see that creep who cornered me?" Nathan said. "The guy who thinks he's Joe Friday?"

"It's Mike Stanley."

"I know; he made that clear. No wonder Preston didn't like him. What a jerk. He kept asking me what Preston told us. He threatened me, told me to keep my mouth shut. It makes me think he was right in the middle of the major shit that Preston kept talking about."

"Is there any doubt in your mind, Nate?"

✣

Though the wind had calmed, a large group of mourners stood by the grave sites, shivering in the morning cold. Congressman and Mrs. Zielinski sat with Mrs. Roberts under a canopy. A portable heater had been placed beside them. Mrs. Roberts was bravely fighting to keep her composure. The congressman had his arm around his wife, who sobbed and continually mumbled prayers for their daughter. To his left and slightly behind him stood Michael Stanley.

The roadways of Holy Angels Cemetery were lined with cars and limousines. Well over one hundred people had come to the graveside service. As the priest was offering his final prayers, Mimi glanced to her right and spotted a man standing on the roadway beside a tree.

"That's Mr. Rosen," she whispered to Nathan.

CHAPTER FORTY-SEVEN

CHICAGO
ALBANY PARK NEIGHBORHOOD
JANUARY 1966

Barely four weeks had elapsed since the funerals, but Mimi's pain was still appreciable. After taking a few days off, Mimi had returned to her desk. The *Tribune* valued her work, and she was now an editor in addition to her occasional staff-reporter assignments. Every day when she arrived, the morning paper and several galleys were sitting on her desk. The *Tribune* had been running follow-up stories on the Roberts homicides, focusing on the intense efforts of the Chicago Police Department to solve the crime. The stories usually appeared in a one-column box on the lower right quadrant of the front page. Quotes attributed to Congressman Zielinski or the police investigators urged the public to help find the killers. The congressman offered a generous reward.

Multiple theories about the double murder, one more improbable than the next, were bandied about on TV, on talk radio and in print, particularly in the supermarket tabloids. Preston and Christine were killed by the Russians in an act of revenge against the congressman. They were killed by a jealous lover of one or the other, who was probably engaged in a torrid but deadly affair. They were the most recent victims of a nationwide serial killer who had murdered three Native Americans in Oklahoma the week before. They were killed by a burglar caught in the middle of the act. They were killed because of a gambling debt or a drug transaction or by hippies

tripping on LSD. The police assured the news channels that they were following up every lead, no matter how bizarre.

Time had done little to diminish the sorrow that consumed Mimi's
thoughts. She struggled to maintain her focus. She searched for understanding, an explanation, a reason, but it wasn't there. She unfolded the
morning paper and stared at the front page with blank eyes. The lead story
detailed the previous evening's State of the Union address. The banner
headline read LBJ SEEKS MORE FOR WAR. The president had emphasized
the need for more tax dollars for the ever-mounting costs of supporting the
troops in Vietnam.

"Ever-mounting costs," thought Mimi. Ever-mounting shipments of
military supplies from Nicky's terminals. Ever-mounting baskets of cash in
Nicky's office. Who was divvying up the cash? What CEOs, what government officials, what congressman from Albany Park?

There were other front-page stories. Negotiators for the Transit Workers Union in New York had ended their strike. Former president Eisenhower was recuperating at Fort Gordon Army Hospital, where he had been
admitted for chest pains. Numerous stories covered battles in Vietnam.
But it was the continuing story of Dorothy Kilgallen's death that grabbed
and held Mimi's attention this day, engrossing her thoughts. The fifty-two-
year-old syndicated columnist and television star had been found dead in
her New York townhouse bedroom recently. To all accounts, she had been
in a chipper mood before she retired for the evening, but the medical ex-
aminer attributed her cause of death to alcohol and barbiturates. A suicide.

The night before Kilgallen's death, she had appeared on *What's My
Line?* and was said to be in excellent health and spirits. There was no reason for her to take her life; a suicide was definitely out of the question, her
family said. Conspiracy theorists jumped into the fray and reasoned that
someone, as yet unidentified, snuck into her home and forced her to take
the pills. After all, hadn't she been working on the JFK assassination for
two years, and hadn't she told associates that she was about to break the
case wide open?

As far as Mimi was concerned, it was another woman mysteriously
found dead in her bedroom. Another family shocked and forced to come
to terms with the senseless, sudden loss of a loved one. It was all too much
for Mimi, and she took the rest of the day off.

She didn't want to go home. She didn't want to answer questions from her grandmother about why she left work early, or hear her suggestions on ways to cope with grief. It was at times like this that she would have picked up the phone and called Christine. She could hear the conversation play out in her head. "Chrissie, this has been a real bad day," she would say, and Christine would have immediately come to her. Together they would have taken a walk, shopped for shoes, perused the sale rack at Field's or just met up for a glass of wine. Lord, how she missed her friend.

She walked down Michigan Avenue and took the steps down to the river. She watched an old woman throw corn to the pigeons until the seagulls swooped down and forced her to another location. The weather had been frigid, and the river was starting to form ice floes. The gloom of winter—it mirrored her state of mind. Finally, she raised the courage to do what she had been contemplating for the past two weeks.

She hesitated for a moment outside his door. Did she really want to do this? All of her suppositions could be way off base. She might be making a total fool of herself. Then, as though some outside force picked up her hand and thrust it forward, she rapped on the door. She felt like running away, but she stood her ground. Eli answered and invited her in.

His smile was warm and empathetic. "How are you doing?" he said gently.

"Not so good."

"I understand. It was a terrible, terrible tragedy."

Mimi bit her lip and then blurted, "Eli, they murdered her. They abused her, they beat her, they shamed her and then they murdered her. And I think you know who I'm talking about."

Eli's expression was noncommittal.

Mimi continued. "I know you've been watching them for some time. Preston saw you outside Vittie's office, and Christine saw you outside Nicky's office. You're with some branch of the government. You're investigating some or all of them and that's why you moved to Albany Park in the first place. I'm right, aren't I?"

"Mimi, I have too much respect for you to deny any of what you said, but I can't talk to you about it."

"Someone is responsible for murdering my best friend. Chrissie and Preston were innocent and naïve kids. They stumbled onto something, and it was much bigger than either one of them understood. And you know it, Eli."

Again, he nodded but did not comment.

Mimi stood firm. "I want to help. I want to bring those responsible to justice. I want to do it for Chrissie."

"How do you propose to help?"

"Well, for one thing, I have information. Gobs of information. Chrissie confided in me. We talked on the phone for hours, almost every night. For months, I listened to all of her stories about her job and the shipping business—stories about Nicky, her father, all the wealthy people involved and all the hidden cash. The afternoon that Nicky assaulted her, she came directly to *me*. I was the one who was always there for her. I was present during the conversation she had with her father. I know about the late-night meetings in Vittie's office and the secret room in the back where the ledgers are kept. Eli, I have a very good memory, and I feel like I could be helpful in creating a narrative. I want to help you catch the murderers."

"Why haven't you gone to the police?"

"Nathan says we have no evidence, and we would be accusing the most powerful men in the country. Who would believe us? He says there's not a prosecutor in the city with backbone enough to take on Vittie, and the police would probably file it away somewhere, like the wastebasket."

Eli shrugged. "I can't fault Nathan's logic."

"But you haven't given up. You have a backbone. You're not afraid to chase those people."

After a pause, Eli said, "Mimi, I've been chasing them for twenty years."

"Twenty years? What does that mean?"

"It means it's a long time."

"But now you're closing in, aren't you?"

Eli's expression remained noncommittal.

"Please, Eli, let me help," she pleaded. "I have a lot of information."

Eli pondered the request. "Mimi, this is dangerous business. There have already been two murders."

"And one was my soul sister."

Eli nodded. "Let me think about it. I'll contact you soon."

CHAPTER FORTY-EIGHT

LUBLIN

LUBLIN, POLAND
OCTOBER 1941
MONTH 25 OF THE NAZI OCCUPATION

It was evening when Maximilian motored out of Lodz with Eli by his side, heading for Lublin. It was only the fourth time they were able to return home since Zörner and Globočnik had ordered them to establish a new brickyard in Lodz the previous June. In each case, they were able to return home only under the pretense of needing materials and equipment from the Lublin yard. Visits were short, a few days at most. This visit was planned to last four days before they were scheduled to return.

"How much longer do you think it will be necessary for me to keep traveling back and forth?" asked Eli. "The Lodz brickyard is starting to hold its own. My presence is largely unnecessary, and I'd like to spend the winter in Lublin with my family. You can stay in Lodz and let me go back to managing the Lublin brickyard. I need to give my father a rest. He hasn't been well and he's not getting any younger."

"What about your brother? Why doesn't he assist your father?"

"Louis is a religious man. He studies with the elders. He also serves on the *Judenrat*. Look, the new brickyard is operating well and filling more orders every day. We've done a good job in setting it up and we've hired a capable foreman. We're well staffed. My oversight is not required on a daily basis. You can manage the business all by yourself."

With a quick shake of his head, Maximilian said, "First of all, I don't want to manage the business. I want to *own* the business and have *you* manage it, not some foreman. Besides, I need the freedom to be closer to my German contacts. A great deal can be learned over a glass of wine. That is precisely how we are all surviving this war."

"Maximilian, you don't need me, and I want to be with my family."

Maximilian didn't respond. He stared straight ahead and drove on into the night.

After a moment, Eli said, "I know you heard me. As much as I love your charming company, I want to stay at home and wait out the war with my wife. Sooner or later the war will end, and things will get back to normal."

Without looking at him and in a quiet tone, Maximilian answered, "That's not going to happen, Eli."

"It'll happen if I choose it to happen. If I decide to stay in Lublin, you'll have to return to Lodz without me. Despite all your self-perceived influence, I don't belong to you."

"No, I mean the part about things getting back to normal. It's not going to happen. Not for you. Not for Esther. Certainly not for the Jews, and maybe not for any of us."

"How can you be so sure?"

Maximilian shrugged. "A glass of wine, a snifter of schnapps, late nights, loose lips. Information passes easily in the wee hours. If one stays alert, one learns things. Let me ask you, how do you think Odilo Globočnik got appointed as SS und Polizeiführer of Lublin in 1939?"

"I have no idea."

"He was a Himmler favorite. He still is. They share Hitler's views of racial purity for the Germanic people, both in Germany and in the occupied territories. Himmler appointed Odilo to be the SS Germanic overseer of the Jewish laborers in the ghetto. Do you remember me telling you about the Jewish reservation in Nisko? Five hundred thousand Jews?"

"Yes, but you said the plan was abandoned."

"Correct. Not because of any moral concerns, but because it was too costly. Odilo has remained in Himmler's inner circle and has also found favor with Heydrich and Hitler himself. There may no longer be a Jewish reservation, but Odilo is unquestionably the man in charge of Jewish affairs in Poland. As such he has recently been tasked with Jewish depopulation."

"Depopulation?"

Maximilian nodded. "Removal."

"Where did you hear that?"

"From Globočnik himself, the other night, right before he passed out."

"He told you those things in a drunken state?"

"Drunken does not begin to describe the level of his impairment, but he was still lucid. Sort of."

"So, of the things he told you in this drunken state, how many of them are true and how many are fantasy?"

"I suppose the future will tell us."

"Did he actually say 'Jewish depopulation'?"

Maximilian nodded. "Removal of Jews from all areas of the former Poland. One possibility means evacuation of Jews to the east, perhaps to conquered regions of the Soviet Union, perhaps in Western Siberia; he wasn't sure."

"What is the other possibility?"

Maximilian shrugged.

Eli's voice hardened. "What is the other possibility, Maximilian?"

"At this stage the brigadeführer was starting to mumble. Part of what he said made no sense."

"What did he say?"

"Well, one of the solutions was something about natural attrition—disease, starvation, old age."

"And?"

"Something he referred to as 'bloodless illumination.' I'm sure he meant to say elimination."

"What did he mean by bloodless elimination?"

"He wasn't full of details, but I'm sure we can use our imaginations. Have you seen the ghetto in Lodz? There are over 150,000 Jews crowded behind those barbed wires with more arriving every day."

"Yes, of course I've seen it."

"But have you also seen the Jews being taken out of the ghetto in convoys of trucks? More are leaving than are arriving."

"Are you telling me that those Jews are being eliminated?"

Maximilian shrugged. "The ghetto itself is certainly being depopulated, but what is to become of the deported Jews, I can't say. I'm only speculating. I know that Jews are being taken out of Lodz to the Chelmno camp, thirty miles north. The Germans call it Kulmhof."

"We've been shipping concrete and other materials to Kulmhof."

"Correct. It's a prison camp. The Germans call it a concentration camp. *Konzentrationslager*. They abbreviate it KZ. Similar camps are going up at Belzec, Sobibor and Treblinka, all in the Lublin District. According to Globočnik, Lublin will soon be clear of all Jews. To bring us back to the beginning of this conversation, that is why you cannot stay in Lublin and *wait out the war*. I think it's time for you and all Jews to come to a realization."

"Oh really? And what would that be, Maximilian?"

"Simply that Germany is winning the war. Soon all of Europe will become Germany, one way or another. Half of Poland has already been subsumed and annexed into Germany. Policies will be dictated from Berlin. The edicts we observe, the measures taken against Jews, will *not* be interim or temporary; they will become permanent. We have to open our eyes to that eventuality and plan accordingly. They have made it clear they do not want Jews in their territory."

"So what are we supposed to do? If they want us out, why don't they just let us go? I think all of us would be more than happy to cooperate. Give us our walking papers."

"I don't believe there is a convenient way of doing that. Millions of Jews free to move about Europe runs contrary to the führer's vision. He has preached that Jews are enemies of the state. You have eyes and ears; you see what's happening. In every city, Jews are being forced into enclosed ghettos. They are being encapsulated. Soon the ghettos will be empty. To the Germans, expulsion from Poland doesn't mean freedom. At its most liberal interpretation, it means deportation to some other locations—at the moment, to concentration camps."

"And all of the Jews will be transported out of Lublin to a concentration camp?"

"Lublin, like all of Poland, will become *Judenfrei*."

"What of those who are taken to concentration camps? How long are they expected to live there?"

"The honorable brigadeführer did not get that far before he started snoring. Maybe it hasn't been decided. Maybe Siberia is indeed the answer. Maybe the whole thing is some Gothic fantasy, but I expect there were elements of truth in his drunken blubbery."

"When will all of this come to pass?"

"I can't say. He did tell me that all their plans are still in the discussion stage. Odilo has just returned from Berlin. After tipping a second bottle of the finest Napoleon Brandy my money could buy, Odilo blurted to me that Heydrich is calling for a conference on December ninth, most likely at Wannssee, outside of Berlin. Then he whispered, 'Don't tell anyone. It's top secret.' Odilo is lobbying strongly to have a seat at the Wannssee table and an inside track on resolving the Jewish Question."

"Is he that highly placed?"

"I think so. He has a leg up. He boasts that Chelmno, Sobibor, Belzec, Majdanek and Treblinka are all in his Lublin District. Rail lines are in place. If the conference selects the Lublin District as the center of the solution to the Jewish Question, that would put enormous power in the hands of our dear brigadeführer."

"What the hell is the Jewish Question?"

"Why, simply stated, it's Hitler's dilemma—what to do with all of Europe's Jews?"

"All of them? That's insanity; it's beyond comprehension. There are millions and millions of Jews in Europe."

"Oh, nothing is beyond the comprehension of the SS command. They are quite imaginative. It would be an undertaking, that's for certain, but as Odilo says, no definite plans have been made. So I hope you understand that waiting out the war is a foolish notion."

"What about my family? If we can't wait out the war in Poland, what can you do for us?"

"Ultimately, you will have to flee, but the time is not right. At the moment, Esther is assigned to the workshop, and there is nothing I can do about it. She comes home every night just like Louis's wife does. But I believe that in the near future the Lipowa site is destined to be closed and the workers will be sent somewhere else."

"Then I have to take my family and leave Lublin now. I can't leave the fate of my wife and son to some council's determination on what to do with the Jewish Question."

"Ah, but where would you go, Eli? Where in Europe is there a safe landing for the Rosen family? Austria? Russia? Belgium? France? They are all occupied."

"The Swiss are neutral."

"And every entrance is manned by German guards. Otherwise, there would be ten million Jews in Switzerland."

"Then I will find a place to hide. From what you tell me, they could close Lipowa tomorrow, and I will never see her again. I will take Esther and Izaak and go."

"Listen to me, Eli. Do not take foolish measures. If Esther fails to show up at Lipowa, they will send the ORPO to search for her. Besides, I don't know how far you can get with a wife and a six-year-old boy, but no matter where you go or where you hide, every village or hamlet will have a prefect who is beholden to the Nazis. They would turn in their grandmothers. Take my advice. Wait for a while. There is no urgency to act today. Right now, the air is calm. Everything is still in the discussion stage. And when the time is right, you can trust me. I can and will protect you and your family."

"Is this about the welfare of my family, or is it about maintaining a brickyard for the benefit of Maximilian Poleski and his social status?"

"Well, in this case, one hand washes the other. Don't abandon me. I need you and you need me. In the interim, I will make sure Esther is safe. You have my word."

❧

Despite Maximilian's calamitous revelations, homecoming was sweet. Reunited and in Esther's arms, the frightful images in Eli's mind disappeared. "It's so good to hold you again," he said. "I missed you so badly. How are Izzie and Papa?"

She smiled. "Sleeping. I swear Izzie is growing an inch a day. He's doing well in his studies. He reads almost as well as I do."

"And Papa?"

Esther hesitated. "He's tired. He goes to the brickyard every day with Izzie in tow, but it's hard on him. His arthritis is bothering him. Business is slowing down. There's very little money. We are budgeting as frugally as we can, but we're barely subsisting. You should talk to your father and calm his fears. He's troubled. Also, you should talk to Louis. I see Sylvia every day at Lipowa. We talk at the break and she tells me that Louis is very distressed, but he won't talk to her about it. Maybe he'll talk to you."

"I'll talk to Papa and Louis tomorrow. I'll see what's on my brother's mind. As for money, the Lodz brickyard is doing well, and they pay me a small salary. I brought money with me. And I also brought a bottle of wine. Give me a minute. I'm going to tuck Izzie in and give him a kiss. I'll be right back."

❧

After a few rounds of small talk, Esther said, "When are you going to get around to telling me what's really on your mind?"

"What do you mean?"

"I've known you too long, my sweet. You're holding back. Your thoughts are somewhere else."

Eli nodded. "You do know me too well. I'm worried, Essie. You were right all along. I remember when you said, 'First, they plan to identify us, then collect and concentrate us and then . . .'"

"Eliminate. That's what I said."

Eli nodded. "It's all true. On our way back to Lublin, Maximilian talked about what he heard during his alcohol-laden soirees with the Nazi elite. They are wild stories, believe me, probably ninety percent nonsense, but still . . ."

"What did he say?"

"He tells me that there are discussions under way about resolving the 'Jewish Question.' I asked him what the hell that means, and he told me they're making plans to evacuate all the Jews from Polish cities and transport them to Siberia or into concentration camps."

"That doesn't sound like a wild story to me. It sounds like exactly what they're doing. What else did he say?"

"That the Nazis plan to *depopulate* Poland to make room for an influx of German settlers. They call it *Lebensraum*. Living space for Germans. Maximilian said there are even plans to raze some towns—burn them to the ground—to allow reforestation and farmland for German settlers."

"That's truly madness. Depopulate Poland? There are thirty million people in Poland."

"I know; I said that, too, and he answered, 'There are thirty million sheep.' He said all Jews and nonessential Poles are to be physically removed from Poland and sent east to Russia or to concentration camps being built throughout the Lublin District. And I've seen evidence of that. We've been shipping supplies to Chelmno, Belzec and Sobibor. They are busy building and expanding those concentration camps."

Esther was horrified. She covered her mouth. "This is the work of a madman. We have to get out. I can't let Izzie live in a concentration camp."

"I said the same, but Maximilian correctly pointed out that there are no safe destinations anywhere in Europe. And he warns that if we escape and you don't show up for work at Lipowa, they will send out search teams for us."

"They'd have to find us first."

"Essie, it could all be drunken talk. Blustery nonsense. Maximilian has pleaded with me not to act precipitously. He needs me to help him run the Lodz brickyard. He says he can't do it on his own, and that is the truth. He doesn't have an inkling. He struts around Lodz in fancy clothes, buying drinks for his Nazi buddies, and doesn't pay any mind to the brickyard business. Perhaps all his dire warnings are for selfish purposes, but he promises to protect us from any harm or Nazi reprisals."

"How? Does he have an army? He's just a spineless sycophant. He cuddles up to the Nazi command and believes they care a spit about him. I don't believe a word he says. He's using you to set up a business, and once it's profitable, he'll have no more use for you. Why would he bother to stick his neck out for us?"

"I don't know why, but I do believe him. Why would he confide in me and tell me all about the Nazis' plans if he didn't intend to help us?"

"Quite obviously to scare the hell out of you and persuade you to stay with him and run his business. The more prominent his business, the more prestige points he gets with his Nazi revelers. That sounds like the reasonable explanation to me."

"It's not just prestige points or his reputation. He made production promises to Globočnik, and he can't afford to fail. Globočnik is intolerant. Reprisals would be brutal. Maximilian begs me not to abandon him, and in return he promises to keep us safe and ultimately get us out of Europe. Desperate times are coming, Essie, and he might be the difference between life or death. Maybe he can't or maybe he won't, but so far he's kept us clear of harsh conditions."

"Don't discount yourself, Eli. You're the one who keeps us safe by operating successful brickyards and by being necessary to the Germans."

"And how long will that last? At the moment, Maximilian is keeping me informed about their plans. He says that Reinhard Heydrich called for a top-secret conference on December ninth, which will set policies for Jews. Maximilian says to wait. It will take time to implement; nothing will happen overnight."

"He has been saying that for two years while Germany has trampled through Europe. I'll tell you what can happen overnight, my love. We can be whisked away, thrown on a train and sent to who knows where. Many others have. I have also heard rumors about Lipowa, that it is going to be closed. What happens then?"

Eli leaned over and embraced his wife. "Enough talk of this rotten war. I don't want to think about it anymore tonight. I just came home; I brought a bottle of wine, and I don't want to think of anything other than my sweet Essie." He kissed her warmly. "Let's tell the world to stop, just for the night. Nothing will matter; nothing will happen. There's only you; there's only me. I want your total and adoring attention. I give you mine." He rose, turned off the lights, took her hand and led her into the bedroom.

❧

Dawn had yet to break and the room was dark when Esther rolled over and noticed that Eli was lying on his back, hands clasped behind his head, eyes wide open. "Can't sleep?" she said. "I guess I must be losing my touch."

Eli smiled. "Never. Not in the slightest. That's the one constant in my life."

"What's keeping you awake, my love?"

"I keep thinking about what you said tonight. You're right; you've been right all along. We shouldn't wait for Maximilian; we should get out. I've watched, like a spectator, as the Nazis pecked away at our liberties bit by bit, all the while believing that things would straighten out and return to normal. I guess I've been naïve, lulled to inaction by Maximilian's assurances. He always preaches that he's protecting us, that we have our homes and businesses, that no one has been sent away, but I have watched as my wife was forced into slave labor, as my business was taken from me, as my community was split into two ghettos and as my friends and colleagues have suffered dehumanizing abuses. It's not returning to normal, is it? It's only getting worse by the hour. I've been so blind."

"Do not punish yourself, Eli. You have always done what was best for us."

"Maybe not. The so-called discussions that the Nazis are having, the ones that call for total expulsion of Jews, are frightening to me. Who knows what the Nazis really mean when they say 'bloodless elimination'? Ghettos are being emptied. In Lodz, Jewish families are being sent to Chelmno. In Lublin, there have been transports from ghetto A to Belzec. Essie, we can't stay here. We are lambs being led to the slaughter."

"Where will we go? Where would you take us?"

Eli sat up. "I've been thinking about it. We could try to make it to the Baltic coast. I have money. Maybe we could hire a boat to take us to neutral Sweden. Or maybe you were right weeks ago when you said we should find a place to hide. A small cabin in the country. A home in the woods." He shrugged.

"Whither thou goest, my love. You know I'll support any decision you make."

"Maximilian is correct on one account—we won't get very far on foot. I will have to find a way to use the brickyard truck and drive us as far as possible."

"How will you do that? Won't we get stopped on the road?"

"Not if I can schedule an order to be shipped from the Lublin brickyard to Lodz. We've done that each week. If I can arrange it, I'll have written authority to travel on the roads. But I'll have to make one more trip to Lodz to work it out."

Esther gazed lovingly at Eli, but he could sense she had misgivings.

"Listen, Essie," he said. "I know I've made promises to you in the past that I wasn't able to keep. This time will be different. I will make one last trip, get the authorizations and take us far away from Lublin. I promise."

CHAPTER FORTY-NINE

~

LUBLIN, POLAND
OCTOBER 1941
MONTH 25 OF THE NAZI OCCUPATION
Later that morning, when Eli arrived at the Lublin brickyard, it was clear
to him that the amount of business had lessened considerably. Apparently,
Lodz's gain was Lublin's loss. While Eli was examining the orders, Lucya
Sikorska, the lay business manager of the Saint Peter the Apostle Church,
walked into the office. She had a box in one hand and a paper bag in the
other.

"I brought sweet rolls," she said, laying the bag on a table. From the
other side of the room, Izaak's ears perked up like a puppy, and he came
running.

"Hello, my young friend," Lucya said, squatting down to give him a hug.
"For you, I brought a special treat: a paszki with strawberry filling." Izaak
took the sugar-covered pastry and walked off with a singsong "thank you."

"Is everything all right at the church?" Eli said. "Are you experiencing
any trouble with the work we performed?"

"Oh no," she said, with a shake of her head. "Everything was done so
beautifully, so professionally. Today I am paying a social call because I promised you and Izaak that we would stay in touch, and I mean what I say. Everyone at Saint Peter's is still talking about Louis's masterful restoration. The
statue of the Blessed Virgin has once again become a pilgrimage icon, at least
in our district. Where is Louis?"

"He hasn't come in yet. When he does, I'll tell him you stopped by, and I'll save him a sweet roll."

Lucya held out the box she was carrying. "I also brought something special for Louis. The Women's Club knitted a sweater as a gift in appreciation. I hope it fits."

Eli opened the box and held up a beautiful blue cable knit. "Very nice. I'm sure he'll love it. Do you have time this morning to share a cup of coffee and a sweet roll? Louis might arrive at any minute."

Lucya grinned. "Maybe just one *little* sweet roll."

"You know," Eli said, "Izzie often speaks of the friends he made at the church when his uncle was 'the star.'"

"A star indeed. That was quite a morning." Then Lucya swiveled to face Eli and spoke with concern. "How is your family doing, Eli?"

"As a family, we are solid as a rock. No family has ever been closer."

"That's not what I meant."

Eli exhaled. "I know. What can I say? It's incomprehensible. We're making it from day to day the best we can, and we're waiting for the tide to turn."

Lucya shook her head. "I don't see it turning, Eli. They are steamrolling through Europe, crushing anything in their way. I have never witnessed such abject evil. Cruelty for cruelty's sake alone. I am sorry to confess that I have been wrestling with some very strong emotions that I shouldn't have. My Christianity is being put to the test." She finished her coffee and gestured to Izaak, who sat reading a book and eating his pastry. "I look at Izaak and I wonder what is to become of such a fine young man? These are menacing times, and I feel that we, as Christians, as God-fearing people, are not doing enough. If there is anything I can do to help your family in any way, please do not hesitate to call on me."

"Thank you, Lucya, I apprec—"

"Maybe I'm not making myself clear." She pointed directly at Izaak. "*Anything.* Do you understand what I am saying to you?"

Eli nodded. "Yes, I do."

She picked up her purse, slipped on her coat and said, "I have to get back. Please tell Louis how much we appreciate him. Tell him to come by and say hello. And should the time arise, allow me the privilege of being an instrument of God's charity."

❦

Louis returned to the office in the early afternoon, and he was visibly distraught. Essie was right. Eli handed the sweater to him, and started to tell him about Lucya, but Louis's mind was somewhere else. He waved Eli off and laid the sweater on a table.

"What's wrong, Louis?"

"Chava," he said. His chin was quivering. "I don't know where she is." Then he began to weep and turned away.

"I thought she was staying at Maximilian's house?"

"She was. I was visiting her twice a week since you and Maximilian have been in Lodz. She was living in the house all alone, but I was afraid to bring her home or even to take her out of the house for a walk for fear she would be grabbed by the ORPO and sent away to some camp. Last week when I went to check on her, she wasn't there. I had no way of contacting you or Maximilian. Can you imagine my panic? Eli, my little daughter is gone."

Eli put his arm around his brother's shoulders. "Maximilian didn't mention anything about Chava to me, but he's back now. I'll go over there."

"It doesn't matter. I already went there this morning, and Maximilian told me that he had placed Chava in another man's house. For safekeeping, he said. Safekeeping."

"Whose house?"

"He wouldn't tell me. He said it would be too dangerous for me and for Chava if I went over there. Eli, we have to do something."

"What do you want me to do, Louis? I feared this would happen. I warned you about letting Chava go with Maximilian."

"Don't you dare judge me, Eli. What choice did I have? Don't you remember what Maximilian said? She had been *noticed* by Zörner's deputy. She was going to be sent away. Far away. Maximilian agreed to take her in to protect her. And he did. And I visited. She had her own bedroom. I thought everything was all right. But now she's gone."

Eli sadly shook his head. "I'm sorry to say, she was probably a gift to some Nazi officer. He's done that before. Young girls are a commodity for him. He uses them to serve his ambition."

"Don't say that. Don't you dare say that to me, Eli. She's not a damn commodity. We have to rescue her. Please, Eli. You have to help me."

Eli nodded and hugged his brother. "I'll go to Maximilian. I'll do what I can."

Maximilian stood in the doorway in his usual pose—one hand on the doorknob, one hand on the doorjamb, blocking the entranceway. "I know why you're here, Eli. It's about Chava, isn't it?"

"Where is she?"

He shook his head. "I had no choice in the matter."

"You always have a choice, Maximilian. Sometimes it may profit you less, but it's still a choice. Is she here?"

He shook his head. Eli looked over his shoulder.

"What teenage girl is living with you now?"

"Does it matter? You came to talk about Chava, and she is currently in a good home with a nice young man. I wouldn't send her to an old man or an abusive person. She's with a lieutenant in the Abwehr. He's thirty-six. Never been married. He took a liking to her at one of my parties, and she took a shine to him as well. They get along nicely. If you remember, when you and I were sent to Lodz, Louis begged me to take Chava. He knew she would be left here all alone. She couldn't go out of the house or the Jew Hunters would capture her. She couldn't even leave the house to get food. I had to do something to take care of her. I felt it was the right thing to do. Besides, Horst wanted her, what could I do?"

"She's barely sixteen."

"She's mature for her age. Look, she's being well cared for. The alternative would be a slave labor camp in a distant location. Ask her what she wants. She'll tell you. Ask your brother. He gave her to me."

"My brother didn't *give* her to you; he put her into your care for safekeeping. Now my brother is beside himself. You sold his daughter to a Nazi."

"I didn't get any money."

"I thought it was against the law for a Nazi officer to have a relationship with a Jewish girl."

Maximilian laughed. "Do you think Horst is the only Nazi with a Jewish girl? Who are we kidding? Besides, he's not going to marry her. That would clearly be against the law. Tell Louis she's safe and healthy. She's with a man who treats her well and with whom she's comfortable. And then tell him there's not a damn thing he can do about it. She's with Horst now. Get used to it."

Eli took an aggressive step forward and put a heavy hand on Maximilian's shoulder. "Louis is a religious man and a very protective father. He's a peaceful man, not the least bit belligerent, and not at all given to confronting you. But I am different, and I will not hesitate to wring your neck. You swore to protect her, and you turned her over to some Nazi. Now get her back!"

"All right, all right. Take it easy, Eli. I'll do my best. I'll go talk to Horst. I'll tell him her father wants to see her. Maybe he'll consent to letting them meet."

"I want an answer tomorrow morning, Maximilian. I will see you at the brickyard."

CHAPTER FIFTY

❦

Louis and Eli watched as Maximilian's polished sedan pulled into the brickyard. The back door opened, and Chava stepped out. She had a fur stole wrapped around her neck, covering the open collar of a black jersey dress. The dress was long and form-fitted. She walked slowly to her father in her black pumps and patterned nylons and sheepishly bowed her head. "Hi, Daddy."

"Chavala . . ."

She put a finger to his lips and said, "Don't be mad at Maximilian. I'm okay, really. No one has hurt me. Horst is very sweet."

Louis swallowed hard. "You have makeup on your face, lipstick on your lips. He's dressed you up in nightclub clothes: black nylons, high heels. Look at you, Chava."

She nodded. "Yes, look at me. I'm standing here. Alive, safe, healthy. I'm not sewing in a dark, musty factory like my mother. I haven't been sent off to a labor camp. I'm not scrambling for a meal on the streets of the ghetto. I'm well fed, well dressed and living in a nice home with a German officer. I'm treated with respect and not like a slave."

Louis's voice started to break. "God knows what that man has done with you, Chava."

"Nothing I haven't willingly permitted. In truth, encouraged."

"Oh, my Lord. I don't want you living with him. You're much too young. I insist that you come home."

"That day has passed, Daddy. If I did come home, if I even wanted to come home, what would happen to me? Where would I be sent the very next day?"

Louis, his lips pursed, his face flushed, spun around and pointed at Maximilian. "You did this to her. She's just a child. You promised me you'd safeguard her, and I believed you. You sold her," he screamed. "You turned her into some Nazi's whore!"

Chava wound up and slapped Louis hard across his face. "Don't you ever call me a whore. I am an officer's lady." She turned and walked back to the car. Maximilian shrugged his shoulders and followed her. Louis slumped down into a chair, his face in his hands.

❧

"I feel so bad for Sylvia and Louis," Esther said later that evening. "I've known Chava since she was a child, and I've never thought of her as anything other than a sweet young girl. I've never seen that side of her. I guess that's what the war can do to people. It must have been devastating for Louis to see her dressed like that and declaring herself to be a German officer's lady."

"You wouldn't have recognized her, Essie. She's a casualty of the occupation, but Louis blames himself. He says the whole thing was his fault, he never should have placed Chava in Maximilian's care."

"He did what he thought was best, but I have to admit, I was surprised when he allowed her to move in with Maximilian."

"Maximilian told him that she had been observed by Zörner's office. They wanted to know why such a tall and healthy girl had not been put to work. They said she would be assigned to a work camp at a distant location."

"If they wanted to put her to work, why didn't they send her into Lipowa? Why didn't Maximilian arrange that?"

"Because Lipowa was fully staffed."

"Fully staffed? Who said that?"

"Maximilian."

"Hmph. Well, that explains everything. It's not true. There are always empty sewing stations. Maximilian was the one who *noticed* her, not some deputy."

Eli hung his head. "I should have realized it was a lie. It was probably what he had in mind for Chava all along. I'm sure it wasn't the first time that he supplied a young Jewish girl to a Nazi officer."

"How can we force Maximilian to return Chava to Louis and Sylvia? If she has to be sent to a labor camp, she can work at Lipowa with her mother."

Eli sadly shook his head. "Chava made it clear she wanted no part of that. As she said to Louis, 'That day has passed.'"

CHAPTER FIFTY-ONE

❧

LUBLIN, POLAND
NOVEMBER 1941
MONTH 26 OF THE NAZI OCCUPATION

The home visit flew by too quickly, and before Eli knew it Maximilian was informing him that it was time to return to Lodz. He insisted they return early the next day, but Eli objected. "I can't leave just yet," he said. "I need to stay a few more days. I have to get things in order."

"What does that mean?"

"It means I need a few more days."

"Impossible. I was at the brigadeführer's office yesterday, and Globočnik made it clear that he has urgent plans for shipments of construction materials to his camps. The work at the Lodz yard is going to quadruple. He's drafted new workers, and there are dozens of new orders. You know I can't fill those orders without you."

Eli shook his head. "Everything is too unsettled here. I can't leave my family. The ax could fall tomorrow, and the Lipowa camp could close. I have to protect Esther and Izaak."

"Lipowa won't close tomorrow. Look, I appreciate what you're saying, believe me, but nothing is going to happen tomorrow. I need you at the brickyard. If you don't come back with me, Globočnik will have my ass. He knows that I am barely competent and that I rely on you. He's not stupid. A drunk maybe, but not stupid. He knows that it's Eli Rosen operating the Litzmannstadt brickyard. He brags that he has the finest construction company in the Reich. You can't run out on me. Just give me a few months, and I will use every method at my disposal to get you, Esther and Izzie out of harm's way. Maybe out of Europe altogether."

"To Sweden?"

"Sure, why not? To Sweden. I'll get you there; you just have to help me for a few months while Globočnik is breathing down my throat."

☙

"You believe him?" Esther said.

"I believe he needs me. Globočnik knows that I am the one who's running the brickyard," Eli said.

"I thought they hired a foreman?"

"They did. Avram Horwitz. He was taken from his home in Wrocław and sent to Lodz. He comes from a religious family and he's a very nice guy. We talk at length. But he doesn't have my experience, and Globočnik doesn't trust him to run the yard."

Esther scoffed. "How in the world is Maximilian going to get us all to Sweden?"

"Maybe there is a way. Sweden is neutral in the war, but it does business with Germany. Sweden supplies ball bearings, iron ore and other materials essential to Germany's war effort. We could justify going there on business, maybe to solidify an order or to arrange for shipments. Maximilian could arrange for that order. Once we're there, we're safe. Essie, it might be a lot safer than taking the brickyard truck and driving off into the night. If he can actually arrange for us to go to Sweden, that would solve all our problems."

Esther put her hands on her hips and stood defiantly. "You want to know what I believe? I believe that Maximilian will never help you to escape, let alone me or Izzie. If Globočnik needs you to run the brickyard, then they will never let you go. As you said, the Lodz brickyard is getting busier every day. They'll want to keep you there indefinitely."

"I've considered that and here's my promise to you: if Maximilian doesn't arrange for us to leave in a few months, then we'll go without him. I'll draft orders for materials, forge transit authentications and drive us out of Lublin. We'll get as far as we can."

Esther leaned over and planted a kiss. "I defer to you, my love. I always have."

❧

Maximilian's car horn sounded, and it was time for Eli to say his goodbyes. "Essie, I'll try to arrange another visit in a few weeks. Take care of yourself, Izzie and Papa. I have asked Louis to help out at the brickyard. I'm afraid he's of little business use there, but at least he'll keep an eye on Papa and Izzie during the day. Maximilian says that Lublin is stable for the moment. There are no transports or actions in process. Still, I hate to leave you."

"Don't worry about us. We'll be okay. Come back to me when you can."

"Write to me, Essie. Give the letters to Papa, and he will send them to me with the weekly truckload of materials. Keep your eyes open and let me know what is happening back here."

A tear rolled down Esther's cheek. "I will. Just take care of yourself. Be safe. Maybe in a few months, we'll be together forever."

Eli gently put his hands on Esther's shoulders and spoke quietly but seriously. "Essie, I believe that and I'll do everything to make it happen. But no matter what Maximilian says, no matter what plans we make, things can quickly change for the worse in this chaotic war. Keep your eyes open. If that moment comes, if you sense that Lipowa is going to close, if you witness people being rounded up and transported out of Lublin, if there is a risk that you might not be able to care for Izzie or that you and Izzie are in any danger . . ."

"I know," Esther interrupted. "I'll write to you."

"No, you have to do something more immediate. Listen to me. If things are falling apart and you can no longer be sure of Izzie's safety, I want you to take him to the Church of Saint Peter the Apostle in the Catholic quarter. Do you know where it is?"

Esther nodded.

"Ask for Lucya Sikorska. She will know what to do."

Tears were flowing. Her jaw was quivering. "Eli . . ."

"Say her name to me, Essie."

"Lucya Sikorska."

"That's right. You take Izzie to her. Give him to her. She will take care of him. We can trust her, Esther. She's a good person."

Esther nodded and folded into Eli's arms. "Oh, my sunny day, please come back to me."

"You know I will. I promise."

The car slowly pulled away from the house. "For no good reason that I can think of, I am depending on you, Maximilian. If you don't keep your word, if you don't arrange a plan for us to get out in a couple of months, then I will leave you flat and do it on my own."

"I always keep my word, Eli. I said I would protect your family and I will."

"No, you said more than that. I want us in Sweden by springtime."

"That's a tall order, and I'm not sure I can fill it. We never agreed to springtime. That's just a few months away. It will take more time to make such complex arrangements."

"Don't backtrack on me, Maximilian, or you can turn this car right around and head back to Lublin. I want to see progress. I want to see firm plans in place."

"When the time is right, I will arrange to get you out of Poland, out of Central Europe, perhaps even into Sweden, but you have to be patient. You can depend on me. We have a lot of work to do first at the brickyard. Once you get it running like clockwork, I can cover for you; you won't be missed as much. Then I'll make some excuse for your absence."

"Avram can handle the yard. Just make the arrangements!"

Maximilian shook his head. "Avram does not have your experience. Globočnik will not tolerate a decision to place Avram in charge."

"At some point, Avram will have to take over. I won't be here forever."

"Let's make plans to get you and your family safe before I have to deal with that."

"The sooner, the better."

CHAPTER FIFTY-TWO

LITZMANNSTADT (LODZ)
JANUARY 1942

Eli swung his feet to the edge of the bed and rubbed his eyes as the sun broke through the window shade in his makeshift bedroom: a corner of the office at the Litzmannstadt brickyard. It had been two months since he had left Esther. On the other side of his window, workers were starting to arrive. Their shift began at daybreak and lasted, without a pause, until sundown. "Bring a bag lunch, eat on the fly" was the brickyard catchphrase. Orders for concrete, cement, wooden forms, rebar and bricks were being processed with increased frequency. Other than to military fortifications, the brickyard was urgently shipping materials for construction projects at five concentration camps: Chelmno, Sobibor, Majdanek, Belzec and Treblinka.

Avram Horwitz greeted Eli with a smile and a firm handshake. "I have something for you this morning," he said, holding out an envelope. "It came with the shipment of materials from Lublin. Here's your weekly letter from Esther. I hope everything is well with her."

Eli took the envelope into his office and shut the door. He took his time and read the letter slowly, making the moments spent with Esther's words last as long as possible. He read with longing her opening paragraphs and her chats about how proud she was of Izaak. Then he came to a section that shocked and disturbed him. He put the letter down and said, "I have to get home."

Maximilian strolled in shortly before noon. He smiled as he scanned the activity in the yard. Trucks were entering and leaving the yard in a constant stream. "Say what you want," he observed to Eli, "Germany's economy is as strong as it can be. The führer boasts full employment."

Eli sneered. "Full employment? Is that what he calls slave labor?"

"Not everyone is a conscripted worker. There are lots of opportunities for anyone who wants to work."

"You're an asshole. They are working in a war economy designed to oppress, conquer and kill." He rattled Esther's letter. "I got this letter today. I need to return to Lublin immediately."

"Why?"

"Ten thousand Jews were taken out of ghetto A and shipped off to some camp last week. Did you know that and keep it from me?"

"I knew there were to be transports of unemployed people, but that didn't concern you or Esther. Many of them were homeless, on the streets. Sadly, they are of no use to the Reich, and they are deemed deportable. They did not contribute to the Lublin economy, and the Reich thought there might be work for them at a camp. They were taken to Belzec."

"Deportable? Belzec is a concentration camp. I hear things. People go there and they don't return."

"There are barracks there. Maybe homeless people are better off."

"Every day you sound more like a Nazi. Who's next, Maximilian?"

He answered calmly. "Surely not Esther. She's employed, she's not homeless and she's under my protection. A few weeks ago, the SS registered all Jewish workers, and I'm sure Esther received a stamp mark on her ID card. She's exempt from transport. Besides, she's living in ghetto B, and I'm not aware of any plans to expel any Jews from ghetto B."

"I don't trust the SS and I don't trust you. I haven't seen my wife and son in almost two months. I want to go back."

Maximilian had a pained expression. "Eli, you have no basis to say you don't trust me. I have always had your back, but you can't go right now. Odilo is in town. In fact, he's coming over here this afternoon to view his brickyard and pat himself on the back. It's the best construction yard in Europe. That's what he says. We should be proud. I don't know how long he is staying in Litzmannstadt, but it certainly won't be possible to leave while he's here. I know you miss Esther, but you receive letters from her each week. You know that both Esther and your son are doing fine."

"I would hardly call it 'doing fine.' And letters don't suffice for the time I am missing from my family. I need to be with my wife and son. When are you going to keep your promise?"

"Oh, my good man, I keep it every day. Aren't you safe? Isn't your wife coming home and making dinner for your son and your father every day? Considering the circumstances, your family is privileged, thank you very much."

"Ten thousand people were expelled to a concentration camp. How many more will be taken tomorrow?"

Maximilian shrugged. "I can't say, but your brother may know. The *Judenrat* was tasked with selecting the individuals to be transported. Your brother and his committee picked each and every one of them."

"I'm sure they didn't do it of their own accord. They were responding to the commandant's orders to supply people like they were inventory on a shelf. I'm sure the *Judenrat* had no choice."

Maximilian shrugged. "It's a war, Eli. They are deemed enemies of the state."

"Enemies? Unemployed homeless people? Do they deem them to be a formidable foe? Is this a result of the Wannssee conference in December?"

Maximilian immediately held his hand up and said, "Shh! Be quiet! Don't ever mention that again. I told you it was *top secret*. No one is supposed to know. I don't think that Globočnik even remembers that he said anything about it before he passed out. Besides, it didn't happen on December ninth. It was postponed because on December seventh those fools in Japan dropped bombs on the United States, which declared war on Japan and Germany the very next day."

"The United States is a formidable enemy. It doesn't look so good for the goose-steppers."

"I don't think Hitler is losing any sleep. The conference has been rescheduled for next week."

"Is Globočnik going? Did he get his seat?"

"No, and he's none too happy about it either. That's why he's here in Litzmannstadt instead of Berlin. And he's cranky."

Eli pointed a finger. "Maximilian, listen to me. Steel reinforcement bars, spacers and tons of concrete are scheduled to be shipped tomorrow to Majdanek. We have several trucks going out every day. Majdanek is just a few miles north of Lublin, and the trucks have to pass right through the town. Let me ride out with them, spend a few days with my family and catch a ride back."

"And what do I tell Brigadeführer Globočnik?"

"Tell him I went to oversee construction at the Majdanek camp."

"He doesn't need you to oversee construction. He has superintendents that do that job. In fact, they don't want any outsiders in that camp. What goes on there is private, confidential, top secret. He wants you here. He told me that himself. You'll have to wait until he leaves."

❧

Globočnik came by the brickyard in the midafternoon with two adjutants. He nodded to Maximilian, who energetically pumped his hand. "Herr Brigadeführer, how good to see you. As you can see, we are working at full capacity."

"It had better not be full capacity," he snapped. "We are failing to meet the demand. We are transporting thousands of people"—he paused and looked at Eli—"I mean *workers*. Every day we transport *workers* to labor sites at camps in my Lublin District. In fact, we are far behind where we should be. We need more housing, more workshops and more"—pause again—"*other kinds* of buildings to be constructed at my camps."

"But, your excellency, we are pushing our workers as hard as humanly possible and . . ."

Globočnik waved his hands. "Stop your prattling. There is an easy way to solve this problem. Buy lights."

"Excuse me, sir?"

"Run the brickyard twenty-four seven." He pointed at Eli. "There are two of you to manage this one, single business. If it operated around the clock, there would be no backlog of materials. Go out and buy lights. Fill those orders or, Maximilian, I will have other, less agreeable plans for you." He smirked and waved his arm. "Light it up like daylight. No more excuses and no more discussion on this point."

Globočnik turned and strutted out. Maximilian faced Eli and shrugged.

"This doesn't change a thing," Eli said. "I want to visit my wife, and you're going to keep your promise to get us out of Central Europe."

"I intend to keep that promise. I had no hand in this decision. I don't want to be here any more than you do, but one does not disobey orders that come directly from the mouth of Brigadeführer Globočnik. In time, we'll make that visit to Lublin. In time, I'll get you out of Europe."

Eli shook his head. "*In time* is too indefinite for me."

"Just give me a few months. If the yard is operating around the clock, Globočnik's camps will be fully supplied in a few months, and the pressure will ease. I promise: by April things will be different."

CHAPTER FIFTY-THREE

LITZMANNSTADT (LODZ)
APRIL 1942

April arrived and little had changed. Eli sat on his bed with his stack of weekly letters, which he read and reread so many times he could recite them all by rote. They were his only connection to Esther, but their cumulative effect emphasized the separation and intensified his longing. He missed her and Izaak dearly. He desperately yearned to see her and hold her. To make matters worse, and despite Maximilian's assurances, the tenor of Esther's letters grew darker and conveyed an ever-increasing sense of danger.

Esther's descriptions of life in Lublin detailed how conditions continued to deteriorate. In February, the Nazis imposed and enforced strict curfew regulations upon the remaining Jews in ghetto A. In March, she began to report graphic stories of cruelty and abuse.

She wrote that on the night of March 16, without warning or explanation, ghetto A was surrounded by Ukrainian guards from Trawniki. Families were forced out of their homes and into the street. Many were taken away without explanation. Those who resisted and those who could not travel because they were sick or disabled were shot. The Lublin ghettos were being systematically emptied. Sylvia told her that the Gestapo ordered Louis and the *Judenrat* to identify fifteen hundred people each and every day for "transport to the East." "No one knows what that means, and no explanations are offered," she wrote, "but we all harbor deep misgivings about the consequences."

On March 20, Esther reported that the SS had changed her ID card to *Juden-Ausweis*, which meant that she was a worker and exempt from deportation. The other Lipowa girls had their ID cards changed as well. Though she had experienced no immediate threats, she was worried because Sylvia said that twenty-six thousand Lubliners without a *Juden-Ausweis* ID were snatched off the streets and deported. Sylvia did not know where they were sent, but a young boy said they were sent to Belzec. There was no doubt in Esther's mind that the community was being dismantled. Very few shops were still open in the ghetto, and Jews were prohibited from going into Aryan neighborhoods.

On April 10, Eli received a letter that sent him into a frenzy. It was the last straw.

My dearest Eli.

It breaks my heart to write this letter. The president of the *Judenrat*, Henryk Bekker, was summoned to a meeting with the SS. Later that afternoon he notified all the members of the *Judenrat* that they were ordered to appear with their families at the train station. Bekker knew where they were going and that they would never return. He and his family dressed as though they were going to synagogue and carried no luggage. Louis and Sylvia were among the families and they are gone.

Earlier today, the Nazis commenced a massive roundup operation. I learned that two hundred children from the Jewish orphanage and their teachers were taken out by trucks. The Jewish hospital was cleared of all patients, all doctors and all nurses. They were taken by trucks as well, never to return. The person who told me this said they were driven to the Niemce Forest and they are all feared dead.

I have become so frightened, not for myself but for Izzie. Papa is still exempt and running the Lublin brickyard, and he is still able to deliver these letters to you, but he is not well, and I worry that in a crisis, he cannot protect Izzie. I decided that the moment we spoke about had arrived and I had to do something. I wish I could have consulted with you, but I believe I followed your instructions to the letter. I took him where you told me, and having met her, I am confident it was the right decision. It wasn't easy for him or me, but I know he'll be safe with her. I don't know what the future will hold for any of us, but know that I love you with all my heart and that will never change. You will always be my sunny day. Essie.

Eli shook. Every nerve in his body screamed at him to break out of Lodz, make his way back to Lublin and rescue his family. Like his courageous wife, he had to make a decision. He rapidly filled out a false bill of lading and a requisition form for shipment of forty pallets of bricks. He was heading out to the truck yard when Maximilian stopped him.

"Where are you going, Eli?"

"Get out of my way, Maximilian."

"You can't leave Lodz. Globočnik will punish us both."

"I have to leave. They're clearing out Lublin. They've taken my brother, his family and the entire *Judenrat* and transported them to I don't know where. They are killing children, sick patients, doctors, teachers. Did you know any of this?"

Maximilian's response was sober. "I have heard rumors."

"Are we supplying construction materials for their prisons from which no one returns?"

"It is likely so."

"I have to go back. You can't stop me."

"Esther is safe."

"How do you know?"

"She has a stamped *Juden-Ausweis* ID, and your father has a stamped *Juden-Ausweis* ID. I made sure of that. For the time being, they are exempt."

"How long will the 'time being' last, Maximilian? It can expire on a Zörner whim. I need to protect my wife and child."

"Due to my influence, your family is safe and unharmed. As distasteful as it may seem to you, I'm afraid that we are bound together. I need you; you need me."

"I've been gone too long, and I need to see her. Just let me go for a few days. I'll come back; I promise."

"Two days. Take the truck. I'll cover for you."

"Thank you."

As the sun was setting, Eli walked into the yard and toward the trucks, his phony authorization hidden in his pocket. He did not intend to return. He motioned for Avram, the yard foreman. "Are you going somewhere, my friend?" Avram said.

"I'm going home to Lublin. I need to be with my wife and my son. Things are getting worse by the day."

"I have heard that. There are rumors that Lublin will soon be what the Nazis call *Judenrein*."

"Avram, you're a good man. Between you and me, I don't know what I'm going to find when I get back to Lublin, and I won't know my next move until I get there. You may need to take on more responsibilities here at the brickyard. Maximilian cannot run the operation by himself. He will need you."

"But you . . ."

Eli shook his head. "You'll be on your own."

Avram nodded. "I understand, and I would do the same under the circumstances. You may depend on me. Safe travels, my friend. Good luck to you and your family."

"Goodbye, my friend."

As Eli climbed into the driver's seat, he saw Maximilian watching the two of them from inside the office.

CHAPTER FIFTY-FOUR

❦

It was almost midnight when Eli pulled up to the curb in front of his house. His mind was set. His vision was clear. He was prepared for what he had to do and for the journey they were going to take. He had a truck, he had authorization to be on the road and, God willing, he could make it to the Baltic coast or find a safe haven for his family until the world came to its senses. His only regret was that he hadn't made the decision earlier. He shut off the truck's motor and hurried to the door.

His body ached to hold Esther. He could see her smile; he could feel her arms around him. Together, they would pack whatever they could, pick up Izaak, leave Lublin before dawn and set off for parts unknown. Together, they would weather the storm. Together, they could do anything.

When he opened the door, he stopped dead in his tracks. The interior had been ransacked. Furniture was overturned. Lamps lay broken on the floor. "Essie," he screamed. "Essie, baby, where are you? Please answer me."

A voice, barely audible, called out, "She's not here."

"Papa!" He dashed into the living room to find his father lying on the floor in a corner. There was blood on his shirt and pooled beneath his body. His right leg was twisted to the side. "They came tonight," he said. "The Jew Hunters. They screamed at Esther and ordered her to return to Lipowa, that she had no right to be at home. When she tried to explain that she was allowed to come home at night, they slapped her and called her a liar."

Every muscle in Eli's body tightened. "Oh my God, Papa, what did they do to you?"

"It doesn't matter. I didn't tell them, son. They tried to get it out of me, but I didn't tell them a thing."

Eli lifted him and set him gently on the couch. His right leg was fractured. Eli ran to get a washcloth and some bandages from Esther's medical supplies. "Let me clean the wound, and we'll get you some help," he said.

His father shook his head. "The clinic is shuttered. The doctors and nurses have all been taken away. That was right after they took Louis and his family." He reached up and grabbed a fistful of Eli's shirt. "But I didn't tell them, Eli. They didn't get nothing out of me."

"Tell them what, Papa?"

"The big one, the fat ORPO pig, was yelling, 'Where is the boy?' Esther told him that he was dead, that she had buried him. He said, 'That's bullshit. I know he's alive,' and he slapped her to the floor. Then the other one, the skinny one, said, 'Don't hurt her, Gert. She's not to be injured. Our orders are to take her back to Lindenstrasse.' Then the fat one said, 'Well, no one gave us any orders about the old Jew. He'll tell us.'" Jakob paused and winced in pain. "They beat me with a club, Eli. But I didn't tell them nothing."

"Papa . . ."

"Finally, the skinny one said, 'We gotta go. We have to get her back to the camp. Leave the old man. We'll come get him tomorrow. He's not going anywhere.' The fat one took out his gun, said, 'You're right about that,' and fired a shot at me. It hit me in the side and knocked me backwards. Then they left. But, Eli, they didn't get nothing out of me. I didn't tell them." He strained to sit up, coughed and said, "He's at the church, Eli. Esther took him to the lady at the church, just like you told her to. But they were never going to learn that from me."

"Papa, I'm going to take you back to Lodz. We'll get someone to fix you up."

He started to lift his father, who groaned in pain. Eli's hands were coated in blood. "I've got to get you to the truck. We need to go now."

His father shook his head. "I can't make it, son. It hurts too bad. Find Izaak and take him to safety. They're looking for him."

Eli shook his head. "I have to get you some help. Izzie is safe."

Eli dressed the wound, tried to stop the bleeding the best he could and carried him to the truck. He drove back to Lodz at breakneck speed, all the way exhorting his father to hang on. When they arrived at Lodz and pulled into the lot, the sun had yet to rise and floodlights still illuminated the yard. The workers on the night shift were scurrying about, filling orders. Eli rushed around to the passenger side, gently lifted his father from the seat, turned and walked quickly toward the office, only to realize that he was carrying a lifeless body. He set him on the bed in the office, leaned over and kissed him on the cheek. "They didn't break you, Papa. You didn't tell them anything. You saved Izzie's life, and I'm so proud of you. But I have been proud of you every day of my life. I am so proud to be your son. God rest your blessed soul."

As the day broke, Eli remained seated by his father. Avram came in with a clipboard in his hand and closed his eyes. "Oh, I'm so sorry, Eli. Is that your father?"

Eli nodded. "Tell Maximilian I want to see him. Before he takes another breath, he will answer to me."

A short while later, Maximilian entered but kept his distance. "I hope you don't hold me responsible for Jakob's death. I knew nothing about it."

"You sent them. Don't deny it."

"I do deny it. I sent no one. I learned early this morning that all Lipowa workers were to be permanently confined. There would be no future home privileges. Had you delayed your visit by one day, you would have known as well."

Eli took a step forward. "You're a liar. You've always been a liar. There isn't a speck of truth that comes out of your mouth. They were there, the Jew Hunters, to take Esther into custody and to find Izaak. How would they even know about Izaak?"

Maximilian answered calmly. "The ORPO knows every single Jew in Lublin. Every child, every woman, every man. If you remember, there was a census conducted the first month of occupation."

"Maximilian, you are nothing but a lying opportunist, a slimy snake without a shred of decency. I know you had a hand in all of this. The ORPO acted on your orders. Tell me, why was it necessary to take Esther into custody in the *middle of the night*? If they wanted to keep her at Lipowa, they could have held her at the end of her shift. Why break into my house?"

Maximilian shrugged. "I don't know what their thinking was. Who can reason with the Nazis?"

"Could it be that I was on my way to see her and you suspected that I would take my family and not come back to Lodz?"

"Would my suspicions be well founded, Eli? Despite your promises to me? In fact, I did anticipate that you would be false to me and not return, but that had nothing to do with the independent actions of the ORPO. How would I have the authority to order the ORPO to do anything at all?"

"You might not, but Globočnik would."

"Then you might consider confronting Herr Brigadeführer, but that would be foolhardy. Let's face it, Eli, the Order Police are a wild, unmanageable bunch to whom atrocities come naturally. Esther is immeasurably safer in the barracks of Lipowa than on the streets of Lublin, which will soon be cleared of all Jews. Once again, she is safe because I have protected her."

"I want to see her. I don't trust your ability to protect her. I will strike a bargain with you. I will agree to continue running your brickyard, but I want you to bring Esther here to Lodz."

"Sadly, that's not possible."

"She can work in a shop here in Lodz."

"She is needed at Lipowa, and Commandant Riedel will not release her. We have been over that issue time and again. Besides, you wouldn't want her working in the Lodz shops. Conditions here are severe. The women here work in munitions factories and do heavy physical labor." Maximilian took a step toward the door and stopped. "As I said before, we are bound together, you and I. You will continue to run the brickyard, and Esther will remain safe under my protection."

"I want my father washed, dressed and buried in the Jewish cemetery."

"I will see to it."

CHAPTER FIFTY-FIVE

LUBLIN, POLAND

FEBRUARY 1943

Ten months later, in the midst of a February thaw, Maximilian burst into the office and made a beeline for the file cabinets. Sweat dripped from his brow and his shirt was soaked at the armpits. Gone was the usual cavalier composure. This day, he was frenzied. His breathing was rapid and labored.

"I want a moment alone with Eli Rosen," he brusquely barked to the office personnel, wildly waving them out. When they had left, he closed and locked the door. "Where are the books and records?" he snapped.

Eli shrugged. "If you came around more than once a week, you'd know, Mr. Brickyard Owner."

"Don't fuck with me!" he screamed. "This is serious. Globočnik has demanded a meeting with you and me tomorrow morning. He wants to review the books with us."

"So? Why is that a concern?"

His voice was shaky. "Where are they, Eli? I need to see them."

A smile slowly crept across Eli's face. "Why, Maximilian, I do believe you are worried. Material purchases and bank disbursements—are they going to balance? When the eminent brigadeführer reviews the books, will he see discrepancies? Have you been dipping?"

"Shut up. Where are the books and bank records? They're not in the cabinet."

"No, they're not. They were picked up early this morning."

Maximilian sat down hard. "Son of a bitch, we're in trouble."

"We?"

"You're responsible for running this brickyard. It's your business."

"That's not what the sign says. Everyone knows it's M. Poleski Building and Construction Materials. Are you intending to shift the blame to me, a poor worker under your supervision? Not that I'm surprised, but I just don't think your argument will carry the day. I have no control over the bank account and no authority to withdraw any money. Never have. All payments for materials require your signature. Yours alone. I've never taken a pfennig."

"You have to help me. I've protected your family for years. You owe me."

"You are a pig. Tell that to my father, my brother, my sister-in-law. Remind me how you protected them. Besides, what do you think I can do for you? Can I erase your defalcations? Can I magically change the bank records?"

"You can tell Globočnik that on many occasions we had to buy materials with cash."

"He'll never believe that."

"Listen to me. Don't forsake me. Cover for me, and I will get Esther out of Lipowa. I'll arrange for a material pickup in Sweden. The two of you will go to Sweden. You have my solemn word. You have to help me. I'm in trouble. Globočnik will have my skin."

"I want to leave immediately."

"Tomorrow, I swear it."

❧

Brigadeführer Odilo Globočnik sat behind a polished desk in full uniform. Nazi flags were posted on either side. On the wall behind his desk was a large black-and-white photograph of the führer in his peaked cap, arm stiff in a Hitler salute. Maximilian and Eli were led into the room by an adjutant who stood at attention on Globočnik's right. Eli noticed that the brickyard's accounting books were sitting on the brigadeführer's desk.

Before Globočnik could say a word, Maximilian blurted, "Your excellency, I can explain everything."

The brigadeführer opened his palm and politely gestured for Eli and Maximilian to be seated. "What would you like to explain to me, Maximilian of royal blood? I haven't asked you a single question."

"I mean to say that whatever concerns you may have," he answered nervously, "I'm sure there's a perfectly reasonable explanation."

"Well, let's begin with your reasonable explanation on why there are thirteen thousand marks missing from the brickyard bank account."

Maximilian glanced at Eli, then turned to Globočnik and said, "It's not missing. There are always material deliveries, especially those from small individual vendors, for which we must pay cash. On the spot. They will not invoice us. I must quickly run to the bank for a withdrawal or the man might decide to take his wares to another construction site. These individuals have no sense of loyalty."

"Is that true, Mr. Rosen?"

Eli swallowed. "I'm sure there are occasions when materials are purchased for cash."

"How many such occasions, Mr. Rosen?"

"I can't say."

"Can you tell me, Mr. Rosen, why these cash withdrawals for materials were not noted in the books?"

"No, sir, I can't."

"Aren't you the one responsible for making entries of material purchases in the books?"

"Yes, sir, I am."

"So if Maximilian of royal blood were to rush to the bank in order to withdraw cash to make a purchase before this disloyal delivery truck driver pulled away, wouldn't it be your practice to note the amount paid to that driver and the materials delivered?"

"Yes, sir, it would."

Globočnik nodded. "Well, I will tell you what I think. I think the books probably reflect income and expenses of the brickyard accurately. I don't believe cash was withdrawn to purchase materials, or the transactions would have been noted in these books. I believe the missing cash went into someone's pocket."

Maximilian spun around. "Oh, Eli," he said. "How could you? After all I've done for you and your family. How could you be so greedy and ungrateful?" Then he faced Globočnik. "I am so sorry, your excellency. I trusted him to manage the brickyard honestly. I have known his family for years. I even helped his wife secure placement in the Lipowa shops rather than be subject to deportation to a distant camp. I never expected him to betray me and embezzle money."

Globočnik tapped a pen on the desk. Silence reigned for a few moments. "Herr Poleski, I find it highly improbable that Rosen took the money. He doesn't have access to the bank account."

Maximilian's lips quivered. "Perhaps he requested that I withdraw the money to give to him for materials. Yes, that's it. I seem to remember that happening on many occasions."

Globočnik glanced at Eli. "What do you have to say about that, Mr. Rosen?"

Eli hung his head and did not respond.

"Are you afraid to answer, Mr. Rosen? Are you afraid of reprisals that would affect your wife, Esther? I understand she was sewing uniforms in the Lindenstrasse labor camp and coming home each night—that is, until Mr. Poleski asked me to make other arrangements."

Eli glared at Maximilian. His jaw quivered in rage.

Globočnik continued and stared at Maximilian. "You needn't be afraid to unburden yourself of the truth, Herr Poleski. We already know the truth."

Maximilian leaned forward. "It was all a careless mistake," he said. "From time to time I would borrow the money, clearly intending to pay it back. Most of the time I did, but some of it must have slipped my mind. We were so busy. I will promptly pay the money back. I assure you."

"And how will you do that, Herr Poleski? Will you pay it back from the money you receive from selling forged *Juden-Ausweis* identification cards?"

Maximilian jumped to his feet. "Never did I do such a thing. You have me confused with someone else."

Globočnik motioned to his adjutant, who nodded and left the room. A moment later he reappeared with an elderly man in a striped prison outfit. Maximilian's eyes widened, and he slumped into his chair.

Globočnik rolled his index finger, motioning for the prisoner to speak. "Tell us, Mr. Gottby, what business did you conduct with Maximilian Poleski, he of royal blood?"

The old man gulped and said, "We manufactured and sold IDs to Jews in Lublin and in Lodz."

"Were these fake identification cards a special kind? Were they *Juden-Ausweis* IDs, the kind of cards that show that a Jew is working and therefore exempt from deportation?"

"Yes, sir. That's correct."

"Tell us how the illegal scheme worked, Mr. Gottby."

"Maximilian would make contact with a Jew who wanted a *Juden-Ausweis* ID. He'd bring me the information, and I would manufacture the ID card. Then we split the money."

"He's a liar," Maximilian said indignantly. "Why would you take his word over mine?"

Globočnik grinned. "I do admire your audacity." Then to his adjutant he said, "Take them away." Eli watched as the two of them were led from the room.

"I never took any money, sir," Eli said.

"I know that. You can go. Return to your brickyard."

Eli stood, turned and said, "About Esther, my wife, I'd like to know how she is."

Globočnik tipped his head. "The last I heard, she was alive, but the sewing shop at the Lindenstrasse camp was closed two months ago."

Eli was shocked. "Closed? Where did all the women go?"

Globočnik shrugged. "Some went to Belzec, some to Majdanek, some to the east, to other work camps. Specifically, I don't know about your wife."

Eli returned to the brickyard, his mind in a daze. Maximilian had sworn to protect her, to safeguard her. He obviously knew that the Lipowa camp was closing and concealed it. Even this very day, knowing she was gone, Maximilian falsely promised he would have Esther released from Lipowa and get them all to Sweden. How foolish, Eli thought, to rely on a single word that Maximilian uttered.

Yet if anybody would know what happened to Esther, if anyone would know where she had been sent, it was Maximilian. But he was as good as dead. More than likely shot to death within minutes of leaving Globočnik's office.

CHAPTER FIFTY-SIX

❧

FÖHRENWALD

FÖHRENWALD DP CAMP
AMERICAN ZONE
DECEMBER 1946

Before returning to Föhrenwald, Eli and Major Donnelly met in the Landsberg camp administration office to review the details of the plan to arrest Max the following week. They were joined by Aaron Davison, Shael Bruchstein and Moshe Pogrund. A map of the camp was spread out on a table. Major Donnelly tapped the map with his finger. "My MPs will be placed here and here, behind the administration office and out of sight. I will be here. Mr. Davison, you will stand here outside of the commissary. When Max tenders the visa to you, you will hand over the six thousand Swiss francs to him in full view. We'll have it all on film. Then we'll take him into custody. With any luck and a great deal of persuasion, Max will then give up his source in the United States."

Everyone nodded in agreement.

"Max evaded capture in Föhrenwald," Eli said. "We should have had him, but because one of our residents alerted him to the sting, he didn't show. If Max learns about this operation and doesn't show up next week because one of you tipped him off or failed to keep this operation secret, there will be hell to pay."

"We know," Pogrund said. "No one will say a thing."

Satisfied that everything was in place, Donnelly and Eli left Landsberg for the return drive to Föhrenwald. Eli was anxious to get home. He had only been gone for the day, but he hadn't wanted to leave Izaak at all. He had agreed to go to Landsberg only because of Adinah's kind offer to stay and Dr. Weisman's promise to check in on him. Weisman had said that Izaak was a strong little boy, and he seemed to be holding his own, but Eli was beside himself with worry. He felt helpless and could only pray.

Adinah met him at the door with a cautious smile. "I think he's doing better," she said, crossing her fingers. "Less coughing today since the injection. Dr. Weisman stopped in tonight after his clinic hours and examined him. He said he was pleased with what he saw. 'There is reason for optimism,' he said. He hopes to have the results from the strep test tomorrow or Tuesday, but he wants him to keep taking the medicine."

Eli breathed a sigh of relief. Though nothing was certain, he had seen the dreaded disease quickly consume Bernard without any remission or reason to be optimistic. Adinah's report that Izaak was improving was surely a good sign. He quietly walked into the bedroom to tuck Izzie in and noticed that the rosy-red complexion that had covered his face and chest was almost gone. Izaak did not feel as warm as he had when Eli left early that morning. He returned to the living room to thank Adinah, but she had fallen asleep on the couch.

❧

The aroma of eggs and toast greeted Eli as he opened his eyes. He sat up in bed and listened as Adinah and Izzie carried on a spirited conversation in the other room. When he entered the kitchen, he saw Izaak devouring a plate of scrambled eggs.

"Hi, Papa!"

Eli leaned over to give him a hug and noted that his forehead was cool to the touch. "How are you feeling this morning, my boy?"

"Pretty good. My throat's still sore, but I'm not so tired today."

"That's his second plate of eggs," Adinah said with a smile.

"I can't thank you enough," Eli said, but she waved him off. "It's nothing. You are doing more for me than I am doing for you."

"She taught me some songs, Papa. We've been singing together, except for when my throat hurt."

"Adinah, you've been a godsend. You can say it's nothing, but Izzie and I know better. Is there anything I can do for you?"

"Yes," she said. "You can sit down while I make a breakfast for you."

Eli patted his son on the back and said, "I can't turn that down, can I, Izzie?"
Izaak answered with his mouth full. "No, she's a good cook."

As Adinah stood at the stove frying eggs, Izaak leaned over and whispered, "Papa, can Adinah stay here with us? She lives in a little room in another lady's apartment."

Eli shook his head and returned the whisper. "We don't have an extra bedroom."

Izaak was not about to give up. "Papa, she sleeps on the couch in our front room and she doesn't mind. She told me it was comfortable."

Eli watched as Adinah spooned the eggs from the pan onto a plate. "We'll talk later," he whispered.

Setting the plate before Eli, Adinah said, "How was your trip to Landsberg?"

"I think it went very well, but our business is unfinished. I'm afraid I'll have to return next Wednesday."

"I will stay."

Izaak's eyes brightened. "Can she?"

"I feel like we're imposing on you, Adinah."

"I have no plans. But even if I did, I would cancel them for Izzie."

"That's very kind, but . . ."

She took a step forward and spoke with emotion. "Listen to me. I have nothing. I have nobody. I lost everyone I ever loved. Now I sit alone in my room in yet another camp for Jews thinking only of the unfairness of it all." Tears formed in her eyes. "Why was I given a life to spend in such a way? Why was everything I loved taken from me? I am full of self-pity, and I hate myself for it." She looked at Izaak. "But I have made a friend, someone to care about, a wonderful boy who also cares for me. For the first time since I was taken from Zamość, I have a reason to look forward to the next day."

Eli put his arm around her. "Never again say you have nobody. You have us; we are your family. You can stay with us as long as you wish."

Adinah's lips quivered. She tried to answer but turned her head and left the room.

❧

After breakfast, Eli went to visit Bernard, anxious to report on the progress made at Landsberg. A nurse halted Eli at the sanitarium door and gave him a surgical mask. "He's not doing well today," she said. "There's a lot of fluid in his lungs and he's having protracted coughing spells. It's hard for him to talk. Please don't stay long, and when you leave, throw your mask in the receptacle and thoroughly wash your hands."

Bernard lay on his back with his eyes closed. His breathing was labored. Eli stood beside his bed, and the nurse said, "Bernard, there's someone here to see you."

His eyes slowly opened and a smile came to his lips. With intermittent whispers, he said, "Did you catch him?"

Eli looked from Bernard to the nurse, but Bernard said, "She's okay. You can talk."

"With any luck, we'll have him next Wednesday. The exchange is set inside Landsberg. We'll have the major and the MPs, and we intend to arrest him as soon as he hands over the visa."

"Next Wednesday?" His question was expressed in little more than a whisper.

The sight of his friend in such a state was hard to take, and a knot formed in Eli's throat. "God willing."

Bernard started to wheeze, and it progressed into a violent, racking cough from deep within his chest that lifted his body off the bed. The nurse took Eli by the elbow and led him from the room. "That's enough for today," she said.

*

Izaak was napping when Eli returned. "Is he all right? He doesn't usually take naps."

"I told him to lie down," Adinah said, "he's been a pretty sick boy. I've been giving him his medicine, and I think it's working. I wouldn't make much out of the fact that he takes a little nap."

Eli checked on him and returned to the kitchen, where Adinah had brewed a pot of tea. "He looks good," he said. "He's not warm. I know I've said this before, but I can't thank you enough."

Adinah sat down next to Eli. "Izaak is a fine young man, and we have formed a friendship. Although he's asked me not to tell you, he's been opening up to me."

Eli raised his palm like a stop sign. "Then don't tell me. I don't want you to betray a confidence. If he told you things that he wants kept private, then that's where they should remain."

Adinah had both hands around her steaming cup of tea. She stared straight ahead. "There are times when he feels a need to talk about his feelings, and he brings those to me. I think it is because he does not want to appear weak in your eyes. I listen, and I am accepting of his sadness, his vulnerabilities and his fears."

Eli's jaw dropped. "Does he feel that I am not? Does he feel that he can't talk to me?"

Adinah wagged her finger. "Please do not take this the wrong way. I am not his father. You are a god in his eyes. You represent everything he aspires to be: strength, wisdom, leadership. I am a woman, and I awaken memories of someone warm, gentle and safe. Perhaps in my eyes he sees similar fears, and we relate. One cannot know. There is a matter that sits heavily on his mind, and it is my judgment that you should know, both for your sake and his."

Eli seemed confused.

"It concerns the time your wife left him with the Catholic woman in Lublin. In his mind, you are carrying guilt of abandoning your son, though he doesn't express it quite that way. The matter remains unspoken between the two of you. He says you've never discussed it, but he needs for you to know that he doesn't fault you or your wife. At the time he was taken to the church, he didn't understand what was happening and he was resentful, but now he honors you and your wife for what you did."

Eli swallowed hard. "Esther delivered him to Lucya on my instructions. We felt we had no choice."

"Please understand: he doesn't blame you or his mother. He is far more mature than that. But it's been bottled up inside of him, and I think he's trying to find a way to tell you about it. As necessary as it was to leave him with Lucya, it was traumatic for him."

"I understand."

"Maybe you do; maybe you don't. He describes the day in vivid detail. His mother wrested him from his bed in the middle of the night. She grabbed a pillowcase full of clothes, took him by the hand and ran through the streets to the church. The church was empty, but for a light coming from beneath a closed rectory door. All of this was frightening to Izaak. I can only imagine the effect such an imposing ordeal would have on a seven-year-old.

"The priest quickly ushered Izaak and Esther into his room and closed the door. Then he threw on a coat and left. Minutes later, he returned with Lucya Sikorska, whom Izaak recognized from his uncle's celebration. Izaak doesn't know what was said outside his presence, but ultimately his mother returned and knelt on the floor. She hugged him and told him he would be staying with Lucya. He was told to obey her and follow her instructions without question. Esther couldn't tell him when or if she would come back to pick him up. He remembers crying and begging her not to leave. He remembers his mother crying as well but insisting that it was for the best. Lucya and the priest were holding him tightly when Esther walked away. He remembers screaming for her to come back. That was the last time he saw her."

Eli's heart was heavy as he took it all in. "I have imagined that scene over and over in my mind, and it has haunted me. Indeed, I have asked myself, how does a man leave his son at a time of utmost danger and retain his self-respect? It's only because you tell yourself it must be done in order to save his life. Now I'm at peace with it because Izaak survived and because Esther had the courage to do what had to be done. I know he has fears, but I continue to assure him that no one will ever leave him again."

"But he can't be certain of that, can he?"

Eli slowly shook his head. "No one can."

"Exactly."

Eli nodded. "Thank you for being here for Izzie. He has asked me if you could live here. I don't know how you feel about that, but you may stay for as long as you like."

"He has asked me as well."

Eli took a deep breath. "Adinah, I . . ."

"He doesn't want me to be his mother. He prays that he will be reunited with his mother, though I think he harbors serious doubts. I don't want to replace his mother in his eyes or in yours. Maybe I could just be a placeholder until Esther is found, or until he is older. I know I don't want him to suffer another person leaving him. Perhaps that is *me* talking. Perhaps *I* am the selfish one who fears separation. Perhaps I need him as much as he needs me. I don't know the answer."

"I meant it when I said you could stay with us as long as you like."

Adinah nodded.

Eli smiled. "But that's not the same as *asking* you to stay, is it?"

"No, it's not."

"Then let me be more direct. I can partition off a section of our front room. I can make it very pretty and very private. You don't have to leave. Will you please stay with us?"

Adinah bowed her head. "Thank you."

CHAPTER FIFTY-SEVEN

FÖHRENWALD DP CAMP
AMERICAN ZONE
DECEMBER 1946

Major Donnelly, Eli and three military policemen headed north out of Föhrenwald in the predawn hours, confident that they would terminate the illegal visa sales and arrest the impresario who went by the name of Max. For Eli, there was a more pressing quest—if Max was indeed Maximilian Poleski, then Eli would soon learn the truth about Esther. Maximilian would know.

Eli continued to wonder: How did Maximilian possibly survive? That last day in Globočnik's office played out in his memory. Maximilian's crimes were exposed, and his fate was sealed. He should have been executed on the spot. Maximilian had urged Eli to lie about the missing money on the premise that he would protect Esther and get them all safely to Sweden, yet he had to have known Lipowa was closed and the women had been transported away. Maximilian had to know where Esther was sent. If she was transported to Belzec, sadly, that would have been the end of the road. Half a million Jews were murdered in Belzec's gas chambers.

But Maximilian had sworn to protect her. Maybe there was an opportunity for him to have Esther sent to another workshop, if for no other reason than to continue to use her as a hostage against Eli's threat to leave the brickyard. If that was the case, she could have survived and Maximilian would know where she was. All of these conflicting thoughts went through Eli's mind as he drove west toward Landsberg. In a few hours, he would have the answers.

~

"He told me that noon was a bad time to make the exchange," Bruchstein said to the group. "Max will only do it under cover of darkness, and then only on the road outside of the camp. The plan is for me to have the Davisons' money and meet him at eight p.m. Alone. He doesn't want Aaron Davison or anyone else present. He said he doesn't trust anyone but me. If he sees anyone else, he'll bolt. He's very skittish since the incident at Föhrenwald."

Eli exhaled. "I don't like it. It's a dark wooded area."

"I'm sure he's considered that," Bruchstein said.

The major waved off the concern. "No worries, we've done dark operations before. This is not new to us. We'll be out of sight, and when the time comes, we'll take him into custody. You have my assurance."

Eli pulled the major aside. "When you grab him, before he's taken away, I need a few minutes alone with him. I need to confront him. In private."

"Colonel Bivens told me about the man who betrayed your family. I'll give you the time, but I have to be present. I can't risk you taking out your revenge."

"Please, Major. I need to be *alone* in a room with him. I need to find out about my wife. He might not say anything if you were in the room, but he and I go back a long way. We had a relationship of sorts. I'm hoping a vestige remains. Information about my wife is far more important to me than revenge. It may lead me toward locating her, or it may simply give me closure. Please, just give me a few minutes, and you can have him. You have my word."

~

As it happened, the road to Landsberg wound through a thick pine forest, perfect cover for Donnelly and his men. Light from a gibbous moon gave a soft glow to the snow-covered terrain at the point of exchange. Eli stationed himself behind a clump of evergreens and anxiously awaited the crescendo. Answers to his five-year quest lay in reach.

At precisely 8:00 p.m., a solitary vehicle approached from the east.

Bruchstein took his place by the side of the road, and as the car drew nearer, he waved a flashlight. The car slowed to a halt a short distance in front of Bruchstein. Max left the motor running and walked forward. Twenty paces before reaching Bruchstein, Max suddenly stopped. "Shael, do you have the money?" he called.

"Of course, twelve thousand francs. Did you bring the two visas?"

He gestured back over his shoulder. "They're in the car. Where is the money? I need to see the money first."

Bruchstein held up an open envelope and thumbed through the bills. "It's right here."

Max took a step forward. "Hand it over, and I'll go back and get the visas."

"Max, the Davisons don't want me handing over their money until I check to see that the visas are correct. Go get the visas and let's finish this thing. Just like we did the other times."

Max turned his head from side to side, scanning the forest. "I don't like the way this is going down," he said in a surly tone. "I smell a rat."

Bruchstein chuckled. "Max, you're getting paranoid. Let's make the exchange, get it over with and let me get back into camp. It's cold out here."

Max shook his head. "Nah. This isn't right. I can feel it." He turned and darted back to the car. As he opened the door, he was tackled from the side by an MP. Donnelly and his men quickly surrounded him. One of the MPs searched the car and came out holding two visas. "Aaron Davison and Yetta Davison, just like the man ordered."

Eli came out of the woods and walked slowly toward the group.

With his hands cuffed behind his back, Max said, "Eli Rosen. Son of a bitch. I should have known. You're always around when bad luck happens."

❦

Back at the administration office, Donnelly said, "All right, Eli, you have ten minutes." He left and shut the door behind him.

Maximilian looked around the small office, uttered a snort and said, "You are one ungrateful bastard. After all I did for your family."

"Which members of my family, Maximilian? My father, who was bludgeoned and shot to death by the Jew Hunters that you sent? My brother and his family, who were taken to Belzec with the entire *Judenrat* to be murdered? My sister-in-law, for whom we paid you ten thousand zloty to have released? Or would it be Esther, whom you swore to protect, swore to me even after you knew she had been shipped away? Which ones should I be grateful for, Maximilian?"

"I protected them all for as long as I could. I'm not the one to blame, you know. The SS command made the decision to close the Lipowa camp. What could I do about it?"

"That night when you gave me the keys to the truck, when I went home for my two-day visit, you and Globočnik ordered the ORPO to take Esther and lock her up in Lipowa. You also sent the Jew Hunters to grab my son."

Maximilian shrugged. "My priorities changed. I needed leverage. I knew you were never going to come back to Lodz voluntarily. Talk about breaking promises—you were going to take your wife and son and leave me holding the bag in a brickyard that I couldn't possibly run. Admit it, you were tossing me to the wolves. I had to protect myself. I didn't know your father would be there."

"Where is Esther?"

Maximilian sneered. "Well, maybe she's still sitting at a sewing machine at Lipowa."

Eli's fist shot out and caught him flush on the mouth, knocking him off the chair and onto the floor. Eli reached down, grabbed a fistful of Maximilian's shirt, lifted him to his feet and threw him into a chair.

"Wrong answer, asshole. Where is Esther?"

Maximilian sat back and wiped the blood off his lip. "Where is Esther? Where is Esther? And if I tell you?"

"Then you'll live."

Maximilian smiled and shook his head. "Empty threat, Eli. You're not going to kill me. The MPs are standing outside the door waiting for you to finish." He lowered his voice and said, "Maybe you and I can make a deal? Like old times? I can get you a couple of visas, free passes into the U.S. I can do it, you know; I have influential friends in the States. High up in government. Way high up. So how about it? Can we work something out?"

"Where's Esther?"

Maximilian rubbed his jaw. "Where's Esther today? I couldn't possibly know. When they closed Lipowa, they split up the women. Some were sent to work camps, but most were . . . well, some unfortunately were sent to Majdanek."

Eli's face turned red. "Majdanek! Majdanek was a death camp. Those who were still alive in November 1943 were murdered in *Aktion Erntefest*. Forty thousand Jews in a single day! That's how you protected my wife?"

Maximilian shrugged. "I didn't say Esther was sent to Majdanek. I said most of them were. Some were sent elsewhere. There was a deportation list with names and destinations."

"You bastard. You had to see the list. Where was Esther sent?"

He smiled. "You know, I just can't remember right now. My memory is foggy."

In a flash, Eli hit him again, knocking him back onto the floor. "You dare to smile?"

"Hey," Maximilian shouted. "Hey, help me in here. Help! This man's gone crazy."

Eli shook his head. "My ten minutes isn't up yet."

"This is a waste of your time. Don't you understand? I have connections. I've always had connections. This farce is going nowhere."

"How are you still alive? I saw you being led out of Globočnik's office. You were as good as dead."

"True, but Globočnik sent me back to Zörner for further prosecution in the counterfeit *Ausweis* scheme. There were three others involved. He told Zörner to dispose of me."

"And Zörner was your buddy."

Maximilian nodded. "I had put a lot of money in his pocket, not to mention the few young ladies in his bed."

"You filthy pig. Where's Esther?"

"No matter how many times you hit me, I'm going to tell you the same thing: I don't know."

Major Donnelly opened the door. Eli knew he had gone as far as he could. Maximilian might know about Esther—he probably did—but he wasn't about to give it up. Eli stood over him. "Who is your contact in the U.S.? Who's supplying you with visas?"

"Go fuck yourself. That's the last card I have left in my hand. I'm certainly not giving it to you."

Eli shook his head. "He's all yours, Major."

CHAPTER FIFTY-EIGHT

FÖHRENWALD DP CAMP
AMERICAN ZONE
FEBRUARY 1947

Eli took a seat at the breakfast table. Adinah was at the stove making pancakes for Izaak. Eli laid his winter coat over the empty chair.

"Where are you going today, Papa?"

"I'm headed back to the U.S. Army garrison at Garmisch. Just for the day. Do you remember Maximilian Poleski from Lublin?"

"I think so. He was a tall, skinny guy with a pointy nose. He was always dressed real fancy when he came to the brickyard. Grandpa didn't like him. Neither did Mama. She called him a snake."

Eli nodded. "I'm afraid they were both right. He was a very dishonest man. Do you remember when I went to Landsberg two months ago with Major Donnelly?" Izaak nodded. "We were there to arrest Maximilian."

"What did he do?"

Eli paused for a moment to consider how to answer the question, put his arm around Izaak and said, "A very, very long list of dishonest acts. But today he goes before a judge. He will receive formal charges, and they will set him for a trial before a military tribunal to answer for his crimes."

The sun was shining and the road to Garmisch was clear. As he drove south, thoughts played out in Eli's mind like the pages of a photo album: Lublin, Esther, his father, Louis, Zörner, Globočnik and the endless string of Maximilian betrayals. Now he would finally be brought to justice. Still, Eli felt a deep sense of disappointment. He had longed for the opportunity to confront Maximilian, to learn what had happened to Esther, but when the opportunity arrived, it was wholly unsatisfying. Maximilian showed no remorse and provided no information about Esther. She was right all along. Maximilian had no backbone, no integrity, no morals. Now he would serve his time.

✺

Donnelly met Eli in the reception area. "The hearing shouldn't take too long," he said. "Shael Bruchstein and Olga Helstein are both here, and they're prepared to testify. We have more than enough proof to charge Poleski and set him over for trial."

The two of them walked into the ceremonial courtroom, where Shael and Olga sat waiting. The hearing was scheduled for ten o'clock. At ten thirty, an adjutant came in and asked Major Donnelly to step out. A few minutes later, the major returned and said, "Apparently, there is something going on. The hearing has been postponed until two o'clock. I can show you all to the canteen, but I'm afraid there is nothing much for us to do but wait until this afternoon."

Bottles of Coca-Cola, hot dogs and small talk occupied the recess while the four speculated about the delay. Eli was uncomfortable. "I know this guy," he said. "He's working his witchcraft, looking for an escape door. He said he had connections. If anyone can weasel his way out of a predicament, it's Maximilian. I've seen him do it over and over."

Donnelly shook his head. "Nah, we've got him dead to rights."

Finally, at 1:45 p.m., they were told to return to the courtroom. Precisely at 2:00 p.m., Colonel Bivens entered the room. Alone. "I'm sorry to have inconvenienced you all," he said. "But there will be no hearing today."

Eli sighed. "What is the continued hearing date?"

The colonel solemnly shook his head. "We don't have a continued hearing date. The charges against Mr. Poleski have been dropped."

"What?"

"I'm sorry," he said quietly. "I'm not happy about it myself."

The news took Eli's breath away. "This is unbelievable! How is this happening? You're telling me that the U.S. government is going to willingly permit this man to continue his criminal enterprise?"

He shook his head. "There'll be no further visas, Mr. Rosen. That was a condition of his release."

"Does General Clay know? Has this capitulation been approved by OMGUS in Berlin?"

"General Clay knows," he answered with a sense of resignation. "The orders were approved by his office. That's all I can tell you. The war makes strange bedfellows; I've seen it time and again."

"Why? Why would they do this?"

"I'm sorry, Mr. Rosen, but it's classified. It's one of the many odd arrangements that must be made in the postwar world."

Eli was thunderstruck. He pounded his fist on the table. "This can't be happening. It's wrong and I don't accept it! Who pulled those strings? How does Poleski slither away when we caught him red-handed?"

"I'm not authorized to say anything further, Mr. Rosen. I do offer my apologies for your inconvenience today." The colonel held out a sealed envelope, and he handed it to Eli. "Before he left, Mr. Poleski asked me to give this to you."

"I don't want anything from Poleski."

"I understand. Do with it what you will."

For Eli, the ride back to Föhrenwald was a mixture of sadness, rage and frustration. He had been so sure that if he had the opportunity to talk to Maximilian, he would have learned something helpful in his search for Esther. Maybe just a clue, a course direction. Yet it was all for naught. For all intents and purposes, that door was now closed.

When he entered the house, Adinah was sitting with a giggling Izaak, helping him with his homework. She immediately noticed Eli's deflated expression. "I take it the trip was a disappointment."

"They let him go."

"Oh, no. Why would they do that?"

"Classified, I'm told. Friends in high places, he said." Eli took off his jacket, and Max's envelope fell onto the floor. He picked it up and flung it across the room.

Adinah retrieved the envelope and brought it back. "What is this?"

"The colonel gave it to me. He said it came from Maximilian. I don't want it, and I don't care what it says. If he wrote it, it's a lie."

Adinah tore it open to reveal a small piece of paper with a single printed word: *Ravensbrück.*

Eli read the note and tears filled his eyes.

Izaak picked it up and asked, "What does this mean?"

Adinah looked at Eli, who nodded his approval. "Tell him the truth," Eli said.

Adinah put her arm around Izaak and said quietly, "Ravensbrück is the name of a Nazi concentration camp north of Berlin."

Eli added, "The note implies that when Lipowa was closed, Mama was sent to Ravensbrück. It was a women's camp."

"Was that bad? Was it a sewing camp?"

Adinah shook her head. "The women there did hard work like building rockets, paving roads and working in a textile plant."

"So my mama could have survived. She was a seamstress and a good worker. She could have worked in the textile plant. She could be alive somewhere."

Adinah nodded. "That's right." But Eli said, "Tell him the truth, Adinah."

"It was a very bad camp, Izzie. Many, many women died there. Of the thousands and thousands of women who were sent there, not so many survived."

"But some did, didn't they?"

Adinah nodded. "Some did. We won't give up hope."

CHAPTER FIFTY-NINE

❧

ALBANY PARK

CHICAGO
ALBANY PARK NEIGHBORHOOD
FEBRUARY 1966

The morning *Trib* lay on her desk, and Mimi sipped her coffee. It was a shake-your-head kind of news day. Northwestern University's Committee on Undergraduate Life unanimously rejected a proposal to allow men and women to visit each other in their school living quarters; the wife of the Chicago Bears' coach, George Halas, was found mysteriously dead in the couple's Edgewater Beach apartment; there were anti-American riots in the streets of the Dominican Republic; and state senator McGloon demanded that the March 29 fight between Cassius Clay and Ernie Terrell be canceled, insisting that "the Athletic Commission should call this Muhammed—whatever his name is—in and ask him about his views on being a conscientious objector."

But for Mimi, the story that hit home was on page nine, under the head-line SENATE, HOUSE GROUPS O.K. NEW VIET FUNDS REQUEST. President Johnson, flying back to Washington after an extensive meeting with South Vietnamese leaders in Honolulu, expressed his extreme pleasure with the news that billions of dollars in new war funding had been approved by his legislators. In the House, Congressman Witold Zielinski was proud to lead the Armed Services Committee in unanimous approval of the president's emergency request for immediate disbursement of an additional 275 million dollars. Meanwhile, in the Senate the Armed Services Committee unanimously

approved 4.8 billion dollars, almost all of it earmarked for "aircraft, helicop-
ters, missiles and other military hardware."

"What a banner day for Vittie, Nicky and all the greedy corporate executives," Mimi said aloud. "Maybe they'll throw a big party and decide how
to carve up the kickback pie."

As if on cue, Mimi's phone rang. It was Eli Rosen.

"Mimi, do you have a minute?"

"They're all coming into town for a meeting, aren't they?"

"Why, yes, they are. How did you know?"

"I had 4.8 billion clues."

"A few weeks ago, you offered to help. Is that offer still on the table?"

"You bet it is."

"Well, if you're free this evening, say around five thirty, there are some
people I'd like you to meet."

"Absolutely."

"Why don't you stop by my apartment?"

✌

On her way home, Mimi was so busy thinking about the meeting and trying
to organize her thoughts that she almost missed her bus stop. She had so
much information and so many bottled-up theories that she was anxious to
share. How much did Eli know about Nicky and his closetful of cash? Did
he know the cash was funneled through Bryant Shipping? How much detail
did he know about the tie-ins among Vittie, Nicky, the Defense Department
and the military contractors? Mimi assumed he knew quite a bit, but maybe
not everything.

She was as enthusiastic as she had been for some time. It wasn't just the
intrigue or the opportunity to work with what she suspected was a clan-
destine government unit; it was the chance to play some part in bringing
Chrissie's killers to justice. Payback for her best friend.

When Eli opened his door, Mimi saw four chairs placed around the
coffee table. Two men were standing by the sofa with soft drinks in their
hands. They smiled and nodded to her. Eli made the introductions.

"Gentlemen, this is my upstairs neighbor, Mimi Gold, the woman I've
been telling you about. Mimi, this is Special Agent Cliff Ryan," he said,
gesturing to a middle-aged man in a blue suit and open-collar shirt. The
man took a step forward and extended his hand. "Cliff is with the Chicago

field office of the FBI, focusing on public corruption. Cliff and I have been working this case for a while."

Mimi's attention moved to an older man in a khaki military-style shirt. His trousers were creased, and his shoes were polished to a glossy shine. His gray hair was cut in a crew cut, and he had a lateral scar on his right cheek, but his smile was warm and friendly. He extended his hand. "Frank Mooney."

Eli added, "Lieutenant Colonel Mooney is the U.S. Army liaison to our group. He's with the army's criminal investigation division."

Mimi smiled and wagged a finger at Eli. "My mom had you pegged for CIA from the day she met you. I always thought you were with the FBI. Who's right?"

"It's a domestic matter, Mimi. So if I were one or the other, it wouldn't be the CIA, but neither of you is exactly correct. Technically, I'm with the State Department on loan to the FBI because of my special knowledge of the individuals involved. But, Mimi, everything that we are doing is highly confidential. Can we agree on that? Do we have your solemn word that you will hold everything in the strictest confidence?"

Mimi was struck by the gravity of the question but, at the same time, honored to be brought into the circle. "I understand, and you can count on me to be silent."

Ryan stepped forward. "That means you can't divulge anything that we might discuss to your mother, or your grandmother, or Nathan or . . ."

"I know what confidential means, Special Agent Ryan."

Eli smiled and invited everyone to be seated. Each of the men had a yellow pad and was prepared to take notes.

Eli began. "After Christine and Preston were murdered, Mimi came to me and offered to help. Apparently, she'd come to the conclusion that I was investigating Congressman Zielinski. How she deduced that, I don't know, but Mimi is a very perspicacious young woman. I've been hesitant to accept her offer because she's a civilian, because she has a promising career in journalism and because all this could easily go south if we fail. Long ago I surmised that due to her close friendship with Christine Zielinski and Preston Roberts, she would be privy to information that none of us would have, but I had decided not to involve her. She didn't sign up to put her life or her career in jeopardy."

"I appreciate your concern, Eli, but it's my career and my life, and I want to help catch those murderers," Mimi said.

Eli nodded. "As I was saying, I had decided not to involve Mimi, but recent developments and Mimi's offer have caused me to rethink my position, only if her assistance can be obtained without placing her in jeopardy."

Mimi smiled. Her heart was racing.

Eli continued. "Mimi, no matter how careful we are, joining our group will pose a risk for you on several levels. Given recent developments, however, I'm willing to give you the option."

Mimi spoke up. "Would those recent developments have anything to do with 4.8 billion dollars in government funding for military equipment and the assumption that Vittie's cabal will be splitting up a fortune in kickbacks?"

Colonel Mooney sat up straight, raised his eyebrows and looked at his companions. "Comes right to the point, doesn't she?"

"I told you she was sharp," Eli said.

Special Agent Ryan leaned forward. "You need to think this over, Mimi. The people we're investigating are very powerful and influential, up to the highest level of government. Not only can they ruin a person's career, but we have all seen the steps that one or more of them might take in order to conceal their financial crimes."

The colonel continued. "Just these last few weeks, their influence on the Hill has successfully funneled an additional five billion dollars into their streams of commerce. How much of that funding filters its way down to their personal fortunes is anybody's guess."

Mimi nodded. "I want to help."

"At some future time, your involvement in this investigation will become known. It's inevitable. You are a young woman with your whole life ahead of you. We want you to appreciate the risk, and none of us would think any less of you if you respectfully declined."

Mimi let the message sink in. Maybe she hadn't thought this through. Maybe taking on some of the nation's most powerful men was a bridge too far. What if Eli's plans faltered and resulted in embarrassment for everyone involved? Maybe even a civil liability for defamation of character or false charges? Eli was right: it would crater her career. And what if her involvement were to place her mother or grandmother in danger? Two murders had already been committed. One Albany Park building had been burned to the ground. Powerful men weren't going to go down without a fight.

"We want you to take your time and think it over, Mimi," Ryan said.

Mimi shook her head. "I don't need time. They murdered my best friend, and if I can help put them away, I'm not going to back out."

"Eli told us that you and Christine spoke often and that she shared her private thoughts with you. Did these include details of what transpired at Nicholas Bryant's shipping office?"

Mimi nodded. "Without a doubt, Mr. Ryan. Every day."

Ryan stood. "We're going to leave it there tonight. I want you to go home and think about everything we've said. Tomorrow, if you're still willing, we can begin at noon."

CHAPTER SIXTY

CHICAGO

ALBANY PARK NEIGHBORHOOD

FEBRUARY 1966

"Welcome back, Mimi," Ryan said, without getting up from his seat. On the table lay a deli tray from Kaufman's Bagel Bakery. A pot of coffee sat to the side. "Help yourself," he said.

"Thank you. I'm ready to help in any way I can."

"Are you prepared to have your memory poked and prodded?" Eli asked.

She nodded. "I'm here. No second thoughts. Where do you want me to start?"

"Why don't you begin by giving us a history of your relationship with Christine and the Zielinski family? From the beginning."

"We met at Hibbard Elementary School. We were in the third grade. We became best friends."

"Did you know her father was a U.S. congressman?"

"Everybody knew that, but it didn't matter to a third grader. What I knew was that Chrissie's father was in Washington a lot. He wasn't home all the time like other kids' dads." She paused. "Except my dad."

Ryan leaned forward. "If it isn't too personal, Mimi, can I ask you about your dad? I know you live with your mother and grandmother, but not with your dad."

"My dad died when I was five. He was a soldier, and he was killed in the war."

"I'm sorry," said Colonel Mooney. "What unit, if you know?"

"My dad was with the Sixth Armored Division, the Super Sixth. He landed on Utah Beach on June eighteenth, 1944, and joined up with General Patton's Third Army. He was killed at the Battle of the Bulge."

Eli looked as though he had seen a ghost.

Colonel Mooney walked over and warmly hugged Mimi. "Thank you for sharing. Your father was in one of the finest units the army ever produced. You can be very proud of your dad."

"I've always been proud of my dad. Upstairs in our apartment, we have my dad's medals and the flag that was given to my mom. We have a chair at the head of our dining table that remains empty, like the space in my mother's heart, she would say. We also have my dad's dog tag, which was carried through the rest of the war by his best buddy, Corporal Dennis Reilly."

Eli stared straight ahead. "This is unbelievable," he muttered to himself. "This can't just be a coincidence. This is fated." Tears filled his eyes, and he flicked them away with his fingers. The others looked at him with concern.

"Are you okay?" Colonel Mooney asked.

He nodded and softly said, "There is an extraordinary connection here. I was rescued by the Super Sixth. Corporal Dennis Reilly personally saved *me and my son Izaak*. He lifted me down out of my bed, carried me across the square and helped me find my son. When I was placed onto a medic's stretcher, Corporal Reilly made sure Izaak stayed with me. So many children were separated from their parents at the end of the war, but it was Corporal Reilly who kept us together." Eli stood, cleared his throat and left the room.

"Maybe we should take a short break," Ryan said.

❧

When the group had reconvened, Ryan asked, "Why don't you tell us what you know about Nicholas Bryant and Bryant Shipping Incorporated?"

"I've only met him on a half dozen occasions, generally at social affairs at Congressman Zielinski's home. From what I know, he's a first-class jerk. He thinks he's God's gift to women, always flirting, always making snide, inappropriate remarks. At a political function, he'd come up to a woman he didn't even know and tell her how sexy she looked in her dress and how it turned him on. He made a pass at me two years ago at a dinner party— totally inappropriate—and he put his hand on my knee. I slapped him."

"Did all this inappropriate conduct take place after he and his wife separated?"

"Marital fidelity has never been a serious concern for Nicky. He's been an unabashed philanderer for as long as I can remember. He continually made advances to Chrissie, and it was a constant problem for her, but she wanted to keep her job and she thought she could deflect them. In the end, she couldn't; she quit, and it's probably what got her killed. That and the threats Preston made to her dad and Nicky."

"Is it your opinion that Bryant killed Christine?"

"I don't have enough information to form that opinion, but he'd be my number one suspect."

"Who'd be number two?"

"It could have been any of Vittie's cabal, I guess. They all had motivation to silence Preston and Chrissie. Chrissie's resignation caused quite a disruption, not only for Nicky and his business, but for her dad and the military contractors. There was no one left to keep an eye on Nicky and the cash that was coming in. She knew too much. They didn't want her to quit."

"What about Preston?" Ryan said. "Did he know too much?"

"Maybe. Preston worked in Vittie's congressional office. He saw people come and go, though Vittie never allowed him into the meetings. Right after Christine quit, Preston had a screaming argument with Nicky and Vittie. He threatened to blow the whistle if they wouldn't leave Christine alone. Was it Nicky that killed them both?" She shrugged. "He's a violent man, especially when drunk, and that was every day. He socked Chrissie in the face when she threatened to leave him, even though he professed to love her." Mimi shook her head. "Such a damn shame. She was such a beautiful girl." Mimi stared at Ryan. "What do *you* think? What do the professionals think? Was it Nicky?"

Ryan spread his hands. "Maybe. There are several possible suspects. Bryant is one, but others had reasons to silence Christine and Preston. For the moment, let's focus on Bryant. I'd like you to tell us as much as you can remember about Nicholas Bryant and his shipping company."

Mimi spent the next three hours recounting all of her conversations with Christine that had anything to do with Nicky, Bryant Shipping and the hidden cash. She recalled the day Nicky gave Christine the job. "Actually, Vittie gave her the job. All of Nicky's shipping contracts came from Vittie. Nicky wouldn't have a business at all if it wasn't for Vittie and the military contractors. Military supplies were all he shipped. Chrissie would tell me about the meetings. Businessmen would come in with their briefcases. The meetings were short, and many times the men would leave without their briefcases."

"Did Chrissie's duties involve periodic reports to her father about the cash?"

"Daily, that's what I understand. One evening, when I was visiting the Zielinskis' home, I overheard Vittie telling Chrissie that he suspected Nicky wasn't properly accounting for all the cash. He also wanted accurate details of who came in and who went out. Chrissie also knew that Nicky was keeping money for himself."

Ryan, Mooney and Eli busily took notes and intermittently interrupted Mimi's narrative with follow-up questions. By the end of the afternoon, the men had written several pages in their yellow pads.

As they were putting their notes away for the day, Mimi said, "Why have all these men come to Chicago for a meeting? Why not meet in Washington?"

Ryan shrugged. "I could say it is centrally located, but truthfully Chicago is safer. There are too many eyes in D.C. As a group, they assemble in Chicago once or twice a year. Individuals may come here more often. They meet as a group, but they will each have a private audience with the congressman in his neighborhood congressional office. Tomorrow night, Zielinski; his chief of staff, Michael Stanley; Bryant and representatives of six of the country's largest military contractors are scheduled to attend a dinner at the Palmer House."

Mimi's jaw dropped. "The Palmer House! Those bastards."

"Does that mean something to you?"

"Don't you see the irony? That was the scene of the wedding. Last year Vittie threw this extravagant wedding dinner for Chrissie and Preston, and several wealthy businessmen were in attendance. These wealthy men will now sit with wine in their cups and blood on their hands in the very room where they toasted long life and happiness to Chrissie and Preston less than six months ago. And to think, I stood there, microphone in hand, and thanked these murderers for coming."

"We're not sure who the murderers are," Ryan said, "or the conspirators, but Zielinski did book the dinner at the Palmer House for tomorrow night."

Mimi pursed her lips. "I never thought it was possible for Vittie to have any involvement in Chrissie's death—he loved her so much—but if he can sit and break bread at the scene of her wedding, knowing that one or more of his group killed his daughter, then I guess he's capable of anything."

"He's not the only member of that group who's capable of anything."

Mimi looked hard at Ryan. "Who was it, Agent Ryan? Which one of them did it?"

"I don't think we're there yet."

CHAPTER SIXTY-ONE

CHICAGO
ALBANY PARK NEIGHBORHOOD
FEBRUARY 1966

"Thank you for taking the day off, Mimi," Ryan said when the group reconvened two days later. "The information you've given us is very helpful."

"I'll do anything to bring those killers to justice."

Ryan smiled and nodded. "Of course you would, and I may have a special assignment I'd like to discuss with you."

"Assignment?"

Eli shook his head and held up his hand. "Wait a minute, Cliff. We haven't agreed to proceed with that yet. For the moment, why don't we continue our background discussions? Mimi, we all know that Preston was spending a lot of money last fall. He had that fancy new car, he had VIP tickets to special events and we understand he had a new wardrobe from Marshall Field's. Do you know how he came into all that money?"

"Nathan would know better than I would. Preston talked to him almost every day. Nathan theorizes that Vittie was paying Preston to keep quiet and ensure his loyalty."

"Can you elaborate?"

"It came up at the time of the wedding. Preston said that he sneaked into the secret room at the congressional office. The accountant's room."

"Malcomb Friedman?"

Mimi shook her head. "I wouldn't know his name. He's a pudgy guy with greasy hair and glasses. Preston said he had a locked room at the office. No one was allowed to go in there but Vittie, Stanley and the accountant."

"But Preston went in there?"

"Apparently, they left the door open one day. It was just too tempting, and Preston snooped around. He said he saw ledger books and bank records, and told us it was 'major shit.' That's what he said. 'The kind of shit that could send people to jail.'"

"Did the congressman know that Preston had entered the room?"

"I don't think so, but eventually he must have learned. Preston suspected that the receptionist saw him."

"What did Christine say about the secret room?"

"I never discussed it with Chrissie. In many ways she was so naïve. So clueless." Mimi paused and swallowed hard. "She had the innocence of a child."

"Have you been in the congressional office, Mimi?"

"Oh, many times, but never in the locked room."

Ryan put his yellow pad on the table. "Can you draw a layout of the office and show us where the accountant's room is?"

Mimi took the pen and sketched the office. "Right there."

Ryan sat back. "Ledgers and bank records. That's our smoking gun. It will seal the deal."

The group decided to take a coffee break. During the break, Ryan and Eli walked over to Mimi and said quietly, "Are you doing all right with this? It must raise a lot of uncomfortable memories."

"Of course it does, but I'm doing it for Chrissie."

"You mentioned that you've been in Congressman Zielinski's home," Ryan said. "How many times?"

Mimi shrugged. "More than I can count. Since I was a child."

"When was the last time?"

"November, after the funeral. I went for a few nights. They were holding visitation."

"Have you been there since?"

"No, why?"

"Would you have any reason to go to Congressman Zielinski's house now, say tomorrow or the next day?"

"Is this the special assignment you mentioned?"

"It is, but to be perfectly frank, it could be risky," Eli said.

Mimi locked eyes with Eli "Count me in."

CHAPTER SIXTY-TWO

❧

FÖHRENWALD

FÖHRENWALD DP CAMP
AMERICAN ZONE
FEBRUARY 1947

Föhrenwald's population continued to grow, and despite the initial objections from UNRRA, the camp continued with construction of additional housing. Eli was tasked with supervising, but he didn't mind. His days were filled with meaningful service. As he was about to leave his home for the construction site, Dr. Weisman dropped in.

"How is our little fellow doing today?"

"Much better, Joel. He's eating well; he has a lot more energy; he's back in school."

"The antibiotics worked well. No coughing, wheezing, shortness of breath?"

"I haven't witnessed any of it. How's Bernard doing? I've been so busy I haven't been able to see him for a few days, not since I returned from Garmisch. He'll want to know what happened, and I almost hate to tell him that we failed again. I'm planning to visit him after work today."

Dr. Weisman shook his head. "Bernard's not well, Eli. He grows weaker by the hour. If you have anything to tell him, you should get over there. Now."

❧

The nurse handed a surgical mask and gloves to Eli and whispered, "Don't stay too long. He needs his strength. Every word he says takes a little more out of him. He knows he doesn't have much more time, but he wants to see his friends, especially you."

Bernard was propped up in bed, and his eyes were half-open. His complexion was chalky, his facial muscles had lost much of their tone and his breathing was labored. He spoke in a raw whisper, barely audible. "Hello, my friend. How did it go? When is the trial?"

Eli stared at his friend. Bernard had given so much to his people and now in his last hours, he deserved the truth, and nothing less, but Eli's words caught in his throat. He couldn't tell him the truth.

"Well, we caught him in the act," Eli finally said. "Just like you planned, and I can assure you that his black-market visa scheme has come to an end."

Bernard smiled weakly, a smile of accomplishment. "Tell me what happened in Garmisch? When is the trial?"

Trying his best to hold it together, Eli answered, "There's no need for a trial, Bernard. Max confessed to his crimes. He pleaded guilty. He knew his crime spree had come to an end, so he gave it all up. He even gave up his contact in the United States. They're all going to jail. There will be no more black-market visas through Max or anyone else."

Bernard coughed hard. A spot of blood hit his pillow. "Good work, Eli."

"It was all you, Bernard, from the very beginning. You were the driving force, the man who did what had to be done. Like everything you've ever done for us. You set up the operation and made the contacts with General Clay and Colonel Bivens. You spearheaded the whole thing. I was simply there at the end to mop up."

Bernard suppressed another cough, and his pain was palpable. "Thank you for coming to see me today. You have an important job ahead of you, Eli. You must keep working to rebuild our community. They may not express it often enough, but they depend on you. Our people have been devastated, nearly annihilated, and every single surviving Jew is important."

Eli nodded. "I know. I learned that from you."

"I have treasured your company, Eli. You are a good man. You take care of yourself, your son and that nice young lady. She needs a hand."

"I know. She's a terrific girl."

"And she's very fond of you."

"Bernard, I can't let my mind go there."

He coughed again and wiped blood from his lips. "I understand, and I truly hope you find Esther. I won't be around to know either way, but I'll be looking down on you and wishing you the best."

Eli struggled to hold back his tears. "It has been an honor to know you, Bernard, and I will think of you often. May God be with you." He started to bend over to hug Bernard, but the nurse stopped him.

Bernard smiled and nodded. "Goodbye, my friend," he whispered. "The honor was all mine."

❧

"I lied to him this morning, Adinah," Eli said as the two sat at the table late that night. "I couldn't do it. I couldn't tell him that there would be no trial, that Maximilian had slithered away. It was more important for me to leave Bernard with a smile on his face than it was to tell him the truth. Now I feel guilty that the last words I ever said to my good friend were a lie."

"You did the right thing. They said he died peacefully this evening."

Eli took a sip of tea. His hand was shaking, and he set the cup down. "In his last hours," Eli said, with a catch in his throat, "Bernard thought of you as well. He told me to take care of you. He said, 'Take care of that nice young lady.'" Eli hung his head and turned away to hide his tears. Adinah reached over and put her arm around him.

"It's okay," she said softly. "It's okay to be sad. Lord knows our people have learned that lesson. Bernard was a great leader who was here right when we needed him. I will miss him as well. I remember the first night we met, when he asked me if I knew 'Tumbalalaika.' I am honored that he thought of me in his last hours, but it's not your responsibility to take care of me."

"It's not a matter of responsibility; we care for each other out of love, and it seems to me that you are the one who ministers the most around here. You take care of Izzie, you take care of our home, you make our meals and you do it all with love. You've given our home a woman's touch, and you've filled the role that's been missing from Izzie's life for a long time."

"Thank you. It is all done with love for you both, I assure you. I love that boy with all my heart."

"And he loves you." Eli sat back. "Adinah, I need to say something." He paused and cleared his throat. "Esther could be alive, and Izzie and I pray that we will find her somewhere in Europe. If we do . . ."

"Eli, don't you think I understand that? I've always understood that. I know my place here, and I pray for Esther, too. Her return would mean so much to you and Izzie, and your happiness would be mine as well. But if you feel like my presence here is a betrayal, if I make you uncomfortable, I will understand, and I will go. And I will still love you both."

"No, it's not like that at all. I don't feel a sense of betrayal. Izzie and I are very lucky to have you in our lives. We love you, too. I just thought I should say . . ."

"You don't have to say any more."

"Major Donnelly told me about the Central Tracing Bureau and the work they are doing. They've been collecting information about people missing in the war since 1943. The offices are in Bad Arolsen, where the three occupying zones come together. They have records from the concentration camps. They may have answers. I'm going to go up there."

CHAPTER SIXTY-THREE

FÖHRENWALD DP CAMP
AMERICAN ZONE
FEBRUARY 1947

The memorial service for Bernard Schwartz drew the attendance of the entire camp. His accomplishments were praised, along with his leadership, his guidance and his steadfast integrity. Death had visited this community so many times in the past few years that eulogies had ceased questioning the fairness of it all. It was what it was. The residents simply came to laud the goodness of the man. Föhrenwald was fortunate to have had him for as long as it did.

At the gravesite, after prayers were offered and when the last of the mourners had stepped away, Eli remained. "I have a confession, Bernard," he said to the mound of dirt. "I lied to you, and I'm feeling bad about it. You deserved to know the truth, though perhaps now, in some mystical way, you do. We did not send Maximilian to jail, nor did we expose his pipeline. He got away, just like he did in Föhrenwald, just like he did in Lodz. Just like he always does. I didn't stop him. I failed. I didn't have the courage to tell you that. I wanted you to leave this world in peace.

"I'm headed up to Bad Arolsen today. I've been told that the Central Tracing Bureau has the most recent information about missing people. If anyone would have information about Esther, they would. Pray for me, Bernard."

The offices of the Central Tracing Bureau were staffed with dozens of women—many in white bonnets and Red Cross nurses' smocks. Others were dressed in civilian clothing, as they would be in any London office. One large room was filled with rows of typing stations, and their Olivetti typewriters clicked away. There were rooms of steel shelving filled with boxes of records—boxes with names like BERGEN-BELSEN, DACHAU, AUSCHWITZ-BIRKENAU, CHELMNO, BELZEC, and RAVENSBRÜCK.

There were correspondence rooms where women opened letters from people searching for missing relatives. The letters described the lost loved ones in rich detail and told of their last known location. The women dutifully answered those letters and then retained them in permanently indexed files.

Eli asked for Ann Stewart, the name given to him by Major Donnelly. She was a tall, thin British woman dressed in a white blouse and a fitted dark blue skirt. Her brown hair was pulled back and styled in a low ballerina bun. She had a businesslike way about her.

"Major Donnelly gave me your name," Eli said. "He thought you might be able to help me find my wife, Esther Rosen. I think she was sent to Ravensbrück."

She shook Eli's hand with a strong grip. And then, curiously, she chuckled. "I beg your pardon," she said. "I don't mean to make light of your request or to be disrespectful. It's just that the mention of Wild Bill Donnelly makes me smile."

"Wild Bill?"

"Oh yes. Most definitely so. Wild Bill."

"I guess I don't know that side of him. I worked an operation with him at the Landsberg camp. When I told him about my wife, he suggested that I talk to you."

"I could give you stories about Bill Donnelly that would make your ears burn. He's one of a kind. Where is he now?"

"Garmisch."

Together they walked down the hall toward a records room. She waved her hand at a wall of boxes and said, "That's the children's wall. There are two hundred and fifty boxes of records. Parents seeking missing children. Children found without their parents. We're trying to reconnect two hundred fifty thousand children. In the next room will be the boxes from the Ravensbrück concentration camp. You know, it wasn't originally designed to be a death camp. It was a work camp built exclusively for women. Some worked in textile shops; some, in munitions and rocket-building factories. It was overcrowded, with very little room to sleep, and provisions were paltry. Many were beaten, poisoned or subject to depraved medical experiments. I'm sorry, but that's the sad truth. One hundred and thirty thousand women passed through that camp, and the majority of them were Polish." She looked at Eli, whose lips were tightly clamped. "Really, I'm sorry. I don't mean to ..."

"It's okay. I was at Buchenwald. I know what the camps were like."

She nodded. "I was just trying to say that the conditions were quite bitter, and that most of the women who the Germans recorded as entering Ravensbrück did not survive." She pulled a Ravensbrück box off the shelf and opened it. "Unfortunately, the Germans destroyed some of the records right before the camp was evacuated, as if destroying the documents would destroy the truth." Inside the box was a dark red book labeled TOTEN-BUCH.

"In this book, the Germans listed the names of deceased prisoners, their date of death and the cause of death. Each page lists thirty to forty names. As you can see, most of them say 'cardiac failure,' 'intestinal inflammation' or 'tuberculosis.' Near the end, before the Ravensbrück death march, the Nazis constructed a gas chamber, because Himmler said they weren't killing the prisoners quickly enough. For obvious reasons, the book does not attribute any death to poison gas."

Chills went through Eli's body. He began to think that maybe this was a mistake. Maybe it was better for him to hope that Esther had survived and was living somewhere in Europe than to know that she had died a torturous death at Ravensbrück.

Ann walked Eli into another, smaller room where there were boxes and boxes of alphabetized cards. She pulled out a box and rifled through cards. "We list several women named Rosen as deceased, but none named Esther. There is a Ruth, a Golda, a Fanny, a Vera. But we don't have a deceased record for Esther Rosen. Of course, that doesn't necessarily mean ..."

"Understood." Eli breathed a slight sigh. "If Esther did survive and she is living somewhere ..."

Ann smiled. "Then you get to the heart of what we are trying to do here at Bad Arolsen. On the one hand, for the families of the deceased, we are trying to give closure, but on the other, for the survivors, we are trying to put families together. There are a million displaced persons on the Continent.

People looking for people. Let me take some information from you, and we'll put it into the system."

Eli looked around at the hundreds of workers and thousands of documents and thought, *Into the system, a million people, what's the chance?* Nevertheless, he spent the next few minutes telling Ann everything he thought would be important. Esther was a seamstress. She would have entered the camp with the women when the Lipowa camp was closed. "She was a strong woman, and if anyone could survive, it would be my Esther."

Eli was about to leave when Ann said, "At the end, when the Russians were closing in on Ravensbrück and there was no more time to use the gas chambers, the guards marched twenty-five thousand women into northern Mecklenburg. After a time, the march broke down, and some women escaped. Some found their way into Denmark. We heard recently that one was working in a hospital there."

Eli's heart leapt. "Hospital? My Esther is a nurse. What hospital?"

Ann smiled sympathetically. "I'm sorry. It's not Esther; it's a different woman, but we'll make inquiries of the hospitals in that area. Let's keep our fingers crossed."

CHAPTER SIXTY-FOUR

FÖHRENWALD DP CAMP
AMERICAN ZONE
MAY 1947

By the time warm weather arrived in Bavaria and daylight lingered a little longer, Eli was able to find more time to spend with Izaak, who was once again back on the football field. Or, as he would remind Eli, the *soccer* field. With Adinah on the sidelines, Izzie's cheering section had doubled. The Föhrenwald tuberculosis contagion had slowed considerably, and there had been no new cases reported in the past four weeks.

Eli continued to check on the status of his visa applications, but without a sponsor or a relative in the United States, prospects were limited, and he was constrained to consider other options. There was hope that Jewish immigration into British Mandatory Palestine, blocked by Britain's 1939 White Paper, would soon be opened. Three months ago, Britain had announced its intention to terminate its Palestine mandate and leave the future of the region up to the United Nations. Just last week, the UN had formed a special committee to study the situation, prepare a report and make a recommendation. The newspapers reported a strong possibility that the region would be partitioned into two separate states, one for Arabs and one for a Jewish homeland. People in Föhrenwald regarded the news as a breakthrough, a reason to rejoice, and it was cause for a celebration party at the assembly hall.

The party was well attended, and Adinah, by popular demand, led the residents in song. Eli smiled as they danced and sang, ate and drank, stood by the refreshment table loudly debating politics and breathed the free mountain air. They were reconstructing their community, reestablishing their identity. For people who had lived in a state of dependency for so long, true liberation was on the horizon. There was a palpable joy in the hall that night.

Eli, Adinah and Izaak walked home under a clear mountain sky, ablaze with billions of stars. Izaak and Adinah held hands until Izaak stopped, pointed straight up and stated proudly, "There. Look there—that's the Big Dipper. It points to the North Star, the bright one."

Adinah smiled lovingly. "You know what Jiminy Cricket says . . ."

Izaak squeezed her hand, shut his eyes tight and made a silent wish. He turned to Adinah, who held her finger to her lips. "Don't tell me, or it won't come true."

Later that night, after a very tired Izaak had gone to bed, Adinah and Eli shared a small carafe of wine. In many ways, the establishment of UNSCOP and hope for a divided Palestine was a harbinger of high tide. Would it raise all ships? Would other countries now open their immigration doors to Jewish refugees? The newspapers reported vigorous debates in both chambers of the U.S. Congress.

Adinah took a sip of wine and mused. "If the UN General Assembly approves, would you move to the new state of Israel, Eli? They say it will be a Jewish state."

"The U.S. would be my first choice," Eli answered. "Izzie has been dreaming of the U.S. since the time we were on the run, before we were sent to Buchenwald, but it's so hard to get in there. If we can't get a U.S. visa and Israel becomes a state, I would surely consider it. How about you, Adinah? What would you do?"

The joy slipped from Adinah's face. She looked away.

"What's the matter?" Eli asked.

She shook her head.

"What?" Eli said again.

When she turned around, her eyes were wet. "You just asked me where would I go?"

"Yes, did I say something wrong?"

She shook her head, took her wineglass and walked to the sink. "No. Nothing wrong."

Eli clenched his teeth. He had blundered. "Adinah, wait. Please sit down. I'm sorry. I wasn't thinking. I didn't mean . . ."

"What do I prefer? Where would I go? You and Izzie are all I have. Maybe I am foolish, but I think of you as my family. You said . . ."

He put his arm around her. "You are not foolish. You are family. I told you before, and I meant it, you can stay with us as long as you like. As long as you live. Wherever we go, we'll all go together. I was asking about your preference. I didn't mean to exclude you or to imply that we wouldn't go altogether as a family."

She slowly shook her head. "I know that Esther might come back, that she is Izzie's mother and she is your wife. But I still want to be in your lives no matter where you go. Won't there be room for me? You ask for my preference. It is to be with *my family* wherever you go."

"Wherever *we* go! You are part of our family. When Esther comes back, if Esther comes back, there will always be a place for you, and she will love you as much as we do."

Adinah bowed her head and wiped away a tear.

"My wife has been missing from my life for five years, and I don't kid myself; maybe I will never see her again. But until I know . . . I think about her every day."

Adinah softly covered Eli's hand with hers. "And you should. Has the Central Tracing Bureau found out anything?"

"I've called Ann Stewart each month since my visit, but they've received no response to inquiries they've sent. None of the hospitals reported any knowledge of Esther Rosen. It's a bad sign; I know. But I still hold out hope."

"And I hope, too."

CHAPTER SIXTY-FIVE

ALBANY PARK

CHICAGO

ALBANY PARK NEIGHBORHOOD

FEBRUARY 1966

There was an urgent knock on the apartment door, and a puzzled Ruth Gold rushed to answer it. "Good morning, Mr. Rosen. You're up early," she said.

"I'm sorry to disturb you, Mrs. Gold. Did Mimi leave for work yet?"

"I'm still here, Eli," Mimi called, walking out of the kitchen holding a mug of coffee. "Would you care for a cup?"

"No, thank you. I found something that might be of great interest to you, maybe for a feature article. I wonder if you might have a few minutes to stop by before you leave for work?"

As she suspected, Ryan and Mooney were waiting for her in Eli's apartment. "Feature article?" she said with a grin.

But Eli was serious. "The accountant's room is empty, Mimi. It's been cleaned out. Empty shelves, empty desk, empty cabinets."

"When did that happen?"

"We don't know. Maybe after the murders, maybe more recently, but when we went in last night, there wasn't a single paper, not a single file, nothing in the back room."

"I thought you didn't want to get a warrant."

Eli quickly glanced at his comrades. "Um, we didn't exactly have a warrant."

"According to Preston, the ledgers were there last fall. A lot of them."

"I don't doubt it, but they're not there now," Ryan said. "The room is vacant, and the door isn't even locked."

Colonel Mooney drummed his fingers on the table. "Mimi, are you sure that's where the congressman kept his records?"

"Obviously, *I've* never seen them, but I was present at the wedding when Preston described the room and the ledger books in great detail."

Eli interjected. "I'm sure the records were there, Colonel. Ryan and I have been surveilling the office for months, charting the comings and goings of the conspirators. It would make sense if the books and records were available for their use."

"So now they have all come back into town and the books are somewhere else," Mooney said. "Where are they?"

Eli nodded. "The books will be where the meetings are taking place, and it surely won't be at the congressional office."

Mimi was puzzled. "Mr. Ryan, I appreciate being asked to attend this meeting, but I don't know how much help I can be. I have no idea where they've moved the records or where the men are meeting. Maybe they discussed their plans at the Palmer House dinner."

Ryan shook his head. "They didn't. We were listening."

Eli added, "Mimi, we've decided that the only safe place for Vittie to hold his private meetings would be in his home. In fact, Rupert Grainger was seen entering the house last night. Michael Stanley is staying at the house all this week. The man you describe as the accountant has also been seen entering and leaving the house."

"So the ledger books are in the house?"

Ryan shrugged. "That would be the logical place."

Now Mimi understood why she had been brought into the discussion, and a chill shot through her body. "You want *me* to go into the house and search for the books?"

"Would you have any legitimate reason to enter the Zielinski home without arousing suspicion? We need to know if the records are there, and precisely where they're stored."

Mimi took a breath. "I haven't been there in three months. You're the FBI. Why don't you just go in there and get them?"

Mimi's response drew a smattering of chuckles. "That's an illegal search and seizure, Mimi. Federal law requires the issuance and execution of a search warrant before entering the house. It would be different if we had evidence a crime was in progress, but just to enter to search for records, we'd need a sworn affidavit from an informant. Remember, we'd be asking for authority to raid a sitting congressman's house—a congressman whose daughter was recently murdered. Any slipup and the books will disappear."

Mimi stared straight ahead—a deer in the headlights. "You want *me* to be the informant? You want *me* to swear out the affidavit? *Me?*"

"Can you think of any pretense to visit Mrs. Zielinski?" Eli asked.

Mimi shook her head. "Pretense? No, not offhand. Why Mrs. Zielinski?"

"Well, it would get you into the house without arousing suspicion. If you visited Mrs. Zielinski, found an excuse to walk around and located the ledger books, well, you'd have the basis for an affidavit, and we'd get a warrant. There should be a lot of records. They wouldn't be easy to conceal. Perhaps Vittie has an office in the home."

Mimi nodded. "He does. They call it the library, but it's really Vittie's office, right off the front foyer."

"Perfect."

Mimi swallowed hard. "So you want me to sneak into Vittie's office, dig though his desk and find the ledger books? Vittie's private office? Seriously?"

"Exactly," Mooney said. "That's all."

Mimi smiled. "That's all? Are you kidding me?"

"Well, that's not entirely all," Ryan said, with a slight grimace. "If possible, we'd like you to plant a listening device. If the military contractors are meeting in Vittie's office, and if we could get them on tape, that would be the jackpot."

"Oh my Lord, what am I getting into?" Mimi said, with her hand on her forehead. "What would I have to do?"

"You said he called it the library? Bookshelves with lots of books?"

"Of course."

"Just set the device behind some books on a shelf. Simple as that. If you had a good reason to visit Mrs. Zielinski, maybe to return something that Christine left at your apartment, then a simple in and out would do the trick."

Mimi exhaled. "A simple in and out? Vittie's always in his office. That would be pretty tough to do."

"He has an event tomorrow night at McCormick Place," Eli said. "He's the featured speaker. He won't be home all evening, and Stanley will be with him. We think Mrs. Zielinski will be at home alone. If anyone else is there, abort the plan, have a nice visit and go back home. What do you say? Do you want to give it a try?"

Mimi drew a deep breath. "I must be crazy, but all right, I'll do it. I have a sweater that Chrissie left at my apartment. I'll bring it to Vera and take a look around. If the office is open, I'll plant the device."

Ryan pumped his fist. "Fabulous! I'll set it up and bring the device to you tomorrow afternoon." He left the room to make a phone call. Eli handed a cup of coffee to Mimi and said, "Now who's the spy?"

She laughed. "You're just the person my mom and I always thought you were."

"How were you so sure I was working with the FBI?"

"The very first day, when you were looking for an apartment, you told my mom you were working for the government. Some boring desk job, I think you said. She told me you looked like James Bond. When I came into your apartment, I saw a suitcase with a Washington Dulles baggage tag. Mom keeps an eye on what goes on in our building. She said that you're absent for several days at a time each month. She's also observed businessmen coming in and out of your apartment at odd times. I assume she meant Mr. Ryan and Colonel Rooney."

Eli chuckled. "I like the way you two secretly keep track of me. How do you know I wasn't simply traveling to Washington to visit my family?"

"I guess I don't. Do you have family in Washington?"

"Yes, I do. My wife and I have a home in Chevy Chase, and my son and his wife live in Silver Spring."

"You've never mentioned your family, other than the couple of photographs in your apartment: your father, your wife Esther and your son Izaak."

Eli paused for a moment before he answered. "I brought those particular pictures with me for a reason. I made promises to those people, Mimi. Solemn promises. And each and every time I made one of those promises, it was a sacred oath. I believed that when I gave *my* promise, Eli's promise, it was solid, as good as gold and I would keep it. But I didn't." Mimi watched him pause to reflect, as though he were turning pages in his memory. With discernible sadness, he slowly shook his head from side to side. "I failed to keep those promises to those people, Mimi."

"Failed or prevented?" she said quietly.

"That's very charitable of you. But I've made some bad decisions. Were they otherwise, would it have been any different?" He shrugged. "Who knows? I've come to realize that I can only see the ground in front of my feet. There's no way to know what Providence has in store for me down the road. Nevertheless, one more promise remains, and I intend to keep it." He pointed at the pictures. "I'd like them to be here, at least vicariously, when I do."

Their conversation was interrupted by Ryan, who reentered the room and said, "It's all set. Mimi, you'll visit Mrs. Zielinski tomorrow night. I think you should just pop in, unexpected like. Don't call in advance. We'll have the device ready for you, and we'll give you thorough instructions."

CHAPTER SIXTY-SIX

CHICAGO
ALBANY PARK NEIGHBORHOOD
FEBRUARY 1966

To say that Mimi was nervous would be a gross understatement. This was new territory for her, and she feared she would say or do the wrong thing, arouse suspicion and blow the whole operation. Vera Zielinski had known Mimi since she was a little child. Maybe Mimi's nerves would betray her, and Vera would detect the subterfuge. Moreover, Mimi was not a liar, and she hated the duplicity. Finally, Vera was a good woman who didn't deserve to have her world come crashing down because of her husband's misdeeds.

Earlier in the day, Ryan had given Mimi a listening device the size of a small compact. "Keep it in your purse," he said. "When you get the chance, hide it behind some books on a shelf. Remember, if the circumstances don't allow you to be alone in the office, abort the plan altogether, have a nice visit and go home."

Mimi's phone rang at five thirty. "The coast is clear," Eli said. "The congressman and Stanley have left the property."

A dusting of fresh snow covered Albany Park like powdered sugar. The five short blocks between Mimi's building and the Zielinski home seemed like a long way that evening. As she approached, she saw tire tracks exiting the congressman's driveway. She hesitated, took a deep breath and rang the doorbell. After a moment, the Zielinski housekeeper swung the door open. "Oh hello, Mimi," she said. "It's so nice to see you again. I haven't seen you since . . . well, since that dreadful time. Come on in and I'll tell Mrs. Zielinski you're here."

Mimi waited in the foyer. Her boots were wet, and as she took them off, she glanced to the right. The congressman's office was dark, and the door was wide open. No need to lock it up in your own home, Mimi thought.

"Mimi, darling," Vera said loudly as she bustled into the foyer. "Come in, come in. What brings you out on such a cold night?"

Oh, I'm going to spy on you and plant a bug in your house, Mimi said to herself. She hugged Vera and said, "I was going through my closet, and I found this pretty sweater. It was Chrissie's. I thought you should have it."

The sweater brought tears to Vera's eyes, and she pressed it against her cheek. "I remember seeing Chrissie in this sweater so many times. She loved it. I bought it for her at Lytton's two years ago. Thank you, Mimi. It was so thoughtful of you to bring it to me."

Mimi felt a pang of guilt. *I wasn't thoughtful, Vera, I was deceitful, and you don't deserve it,* she thought. "Chrissie always looked so pretty in that blue sweater," Mimi said. "She was a beautiful girl, inside and out." With that, the two of them gave in to their tears and held each other in a deeply felt embrace. Vera led Mimi into the living room and asked her housekeeper to bring them some tea.

They chatted for a while, with each one recalling what life had been like since the funeral. Days were long and filled with sadness for Vera. Nothing would ever be the same. Chrissie was their only child. They would never have a grandchild. All of Vera's visions of the future had burst like a bubble. Mimi said that not a day went by that she didn't think of Chrissie, and no friend would ever take her place.

Finally, Mimi decided it was time to carry out her mission. She asked to be excused to use the bathroom. "Don't get up," she said to Vera. "I know my way around."

"You should," Vera said, "you've been coming here since you were a little girl. Use the powder room off the foyer."

The door to the office was faintly lit by the foyer light. Mimi ducked into the office, looked around, placed the device on a shelf and breezed out. The whole thing took very little time. She returned to the living room with a bitter taste in her mouth.

ꝯ

"Well, mission accomplished, Eli. I planted the bug behind the books on the third shelf. If there were accounting ledger books, I didn't see them. They certainly weren't on the bookshelves. They weren't on his desk or on the table in the corner. I'm sorry."

"Nothing to be sorry about. You did a great job, Mimi!"

She responded softly. "I did what you asked, but I feel like a shit. I deceived a very nice person. My presence in her home was a lie. I have no illusions; I was there for the purpose of destroying her husband and collaterally, her way of life. Vera's a lovely woman, and she thinks of me as family. She's lost her only child, and now I have betrayed her. She trusted me. I'm a deceitful rat."

"Mimi, you were there to bring murderers and corrupt profiteers to justice. You were doing it for Christine. Witold Zielinski's way of life is a lie. Mrs. Zielinski will understand when the truth comes out. This group of dishonest and unprincipled men betrays society's trust. Christine was murdered because her existence threatened their shameful operation. They are no better than common street criminals, and they deserve no better treatment."

"I know. But Vera didn't do anything wrong, and I'm sure she knows nothing about her husband's criminal activities."

"In time you'll feel better about this. Sooner or later, this was going to happen anyway."

Mimi nodded unconvincingly and went upstairs to her apartment.

ꝯ

Three days later, Mimi received a call and an urgent request to meet at Eli's apartment after work.

"Mimi, we need you to go back to the Zielinskis'. The device has stopped working."

"I was just there three days ago. Please, Eli, I can't do it again. I still feel terrible about the whole thing."

Ryan stepped forward. "The bug worked perfectly for three days. We have hours of prime material. We have six executives on tape, along with Stanley and the congressman. It's dynamite. Then suddenly the bug stopped working."

"Don't you have enough?"

"Enough for the ones on tape, yes, but there are three more contractors who have yet to meet with the congressman. Roland, Johnson and Locker have yet to cut their deals. Mimi, you don't know what a tower you're helping to bring down. It's a bombshell, but we can't let three of the country's most corrupt contractors get away because of a broken device. We have to replace the bug."

Mimi shook her head. "I can't. I was lucky last time. Everything fell into place. No one saw me. I can't use the same excuses again. Am I supposed to find another sweater? Am I supposed to pop in again unannounced? Am I supposed to have a bladder attack again and have to use the powder room in the foyer? It's not going to work, Cliff."

"It has to work," Ryan said. "I want those three. The congressman is going to a community forum at seven tonight at the Albany Park Community Center. Please, Mimi, go over there tonight. You'll think of something. Don't let us down."

CHAPTER SIXTY-SEVEN

❧

FÖHRENWALD

FÖHRENWALD DP CAMP
AMERICAN ZONE
SEPTEMBER 1947
There was great excitement in the Föhrenwald camp on September 27, 1947, for on that day the United Nations Special Committee on Palestine submitted its report and recommendations to the General Assembly. There would be a vote later in the fall. If two-thirds of the members approved, the British mandate would be divided into two states: one for Jews and one for Arabs. Even though the Arab leadership stated it would never accept such a plan, confidence was high that the resolution would pass. The State of Israel would become a reality sometime within the next year. It was almost certain.

To the residents of Föhrenwald and other displaced persons camps, an affirming vote would mean that the door to Israel would open for them. Ships of refugees would no longer be turned around by the British fleet or diverted to Cyprus. It was cause for celebration, and as it had the previous May, the Föhrenwald camp threw a party.

Those who could bake, baked. Those who could decorate, decorated. And those who could make music—well, a klezmer band played joyful dancing music, and Adinah led the hall in a community sing-along. Izaak and Eli were sitting at a table enjoying carrot cake and soft drinks when Adinah came over, held out her hand and said, "Dance with me."

Izaak started to get out of his chair, but Adinah said, "Hold on, Izzie. This time I mean the old man."

"Old?" Eli said with mock indignation. "Who's old?"

"You, if you don't get up and dance with me."

Izaak looked at Eli, smiled and nodded. "You better do what she says."

"It's just a dance, Eli."

Eli rose, took Adinah's hand and walked onto the dance floor. "You know, I haven't danced with anyone in—"

She put her finger on his lips. "Shh. Dance with me."

❧

Later that night, after Adinah finished telling Izaak a bedtime story, after she had kissed him good night and tucked him in, she walked out to the kitchen. "It's your turn," she said to Eli. "And, fair warning, he might tease you about your dancing."

"I had a lot of fun at the party tonight, Papa. Do you suppose we'll get to go to Israel next year?"

Eli shrugged. "It's a good possibility. If we don't get a visa to America, I would surely take us to Israel."

"Would Adinah come, too?"

"I think she probably would."

Izaak smiled broadly. "That's good. I like her a lot."

"I know you do. I like her, too."

"And I still love Mama."

Eli nodded. "Of course you do. And you always will."

❧

Izaak's words were sitting on Eli's mind when he returned to the kitchen. "Something wrong?" Adinah asked.

Eli shook his head. "No. Not really." He tipped his head toward Izaak's room. "It's a little complicated for him."

"I think I understand. It's a little complicated for me, too."

Eli sighed. "I know."

"Am I overstepping my bounds here? Would you tell me if I was?"

"You're not. The love that you've given to Izaak means so much to him. You can see it in his eyes, in the joy of his expressions. As far as Izzie is concerned, love is not a finite quantity. He knows his mama may never return—no one knows what tomorrow will bring—but in his mind, he has love for you both. Life has to go on. He spent two years with Lucya, and he loved her, too."

"You never told me how the two of you reconnected."

Eli nodded and took a sip of wine. "In 1943, word came down from Berlin: all the Jewish labor camps were to be closed and Europe, then totally controlled by Germany, was to be cleansed of Jews. They kept the brickyard going because it was essential. Globočnik needed me. I didn't know the extent of his crimes at the time. I knew he was a contemptible monster, but I didn't know how diabolical he truly was. He was responsible for constructing the poison gas facilities at Sobibor, Majdanek and Treblinka. His building materials helped kill a million and a half Jews. But for all I knew, we were shipping materials to build barracks and utility buildings."

Eli took a breath and shook his head. "Globočnik committed suicide, you know? He bit a cyanide capsule when the Allies were questioning him after the war. Architect of the gas chambers. A quick death was too good for him."

"How did you and Izzie find each other again?"

"In 1943, Globočnik was reassigned from Lodz to Trieste in German-occupied Italy. A new SS officer was sent to oversee the Lodz brickyard, but he didn't know what he was doing. Toward the end of the year, I had him sign a document that allowed me to travel throughout the General Gouvernment for the ostensible purpose of checking on deliveries to his installations. I told him I would be gone for a few weeks. The credentials were solid.

"I drove to the church to find Lucya. By that time, in early 1944, almost all the Jews in Poland were imprisoned in concentration camps or were being hunted down or were dead. When I arrived, a nun told me that Lucya was no longer affiliated with the church, that she had moved away and that no one knew where she had gone. I was struck with panic. How would I ever find my son? I could only hope that the church officials were lying to me to protect Lucya and Izaak.

"One night I waited until the church was empty, and I knocked on the rectory door. Father Jaworski answered. 'You were told that Lucya is no longer here. We don't know where she went,' he said, but I could tell he was lying. I pleaded with him. 'You're a man of God,' I said. 'Don't stand there and lie to me. Tell me the truth. Where is my son?' He shook his head. 'I can't tell you where she went; she made me promise. She took the boy with her. He's safe. Let them be.'

"'I am forever grateful for what she did,' I said, 'but a father has the right and responsibility to make decisions for his son.'

"'You're making a mistake,' he said.

"'Maybe I am, but I have the *right* to make a mistake. I'm his father.'

"He looked at me with his gentle, aged eyes. 'Yes, I believe you do. She's keeping him in a basement of a home near Białystok.'

"He gave me the address and I drove up there. As I entered Białystok, I could see rows of Nazi soldiers. I was stopped twice by patrols, but my authorization held. I waited until nightfall and visited Lucya. She urged me to go away. 'Turn around,' she said. 'Izaak is safe. Don't be a fool. Leave him here.'

"I hesitated. Maybe she was right. She had kept him safe for all these months. I said I wanted to see him, but she thought it was a bad idea. 'He's adjusting to his separation,' she said. 'It's been hard on him.' I nodded and left.

"All that night I argued with myself. Maybe it was me who couldn't handle the separation. Anyway, the next day I changed my mind. I went back to the house.

"Lucya remained insistent. 'Białystok is overrun. Remaining Jews are all being ferreted out of their hiding places. They're shooting them, Eli— shooting them in the streets. If you move Izaak, it's likely he'll be discovered. Your very presence here is a danger to him. You must go.'

"I shook my head. I was determined to keep my son with me. I reasoned that he was safer with me than hiding from the Jew Hunters in a basement. In retrospect, it would have been wiser to leave him with Lucya. I've made my share of mistakes. I took him from her that night, and we drove out of Białystok.

"For the next ten months, Izzie and I wandered the countryside. I picked up odd jobs helping farmers in rural areas in exchange for food and a few nights in a barn, all the time moving closer and closer toward the Baltic coast. It was February 1945; the reports of Allied advances were promising, and I was convinced we would make it. Then one night, a farmer denounced us to the local prefect. We were arrested, thrown into a truck with other Jews and taken to a concentration camp. It was a time when thousands of prisoners were being marched from distant camps to camps deep into Germany, and Buchenwald was a principal destination.

"The camp was terribly overcrowded, and provisions were inadequate. As far as the Germans were concerned, we were all expected to die. I cursed myself for my arrogance, for believing that I could protect Izzie better than Lucya. Then a miracle happened. We were rescued by the Americans in April 1945. Truth be told, I couldn't have lasted much longer, but the U.S. Army liberated the camp and saved our lives. That's my story. We were lucky."

CHAPTER SIXTY-EIGHT

FÖHRENWALD DP CAMP
AMERICAN ZONE
OCTOBER 1947

Eli was supervising the renovation of an apartment building when a worker tapped him on the shoulder. "There's a call for you in the administration building."

As he walked toward the building, Eli wondered about the call. He hoped it was good news. Maybe it concerned his visas to the U.S. Maybe it was Major Donnelly telling him that they had reconsidered indicting Maximilian Poleski and that Eli would be needed as a witness. It was neither.

"Eli, this is Ann Stewart. From Central Tracing Bureau." Eli's heart leapt, but only momentarily. "I'm afraid I have sad news. I wish it were otherwise. I hate making this call, but I didn't feel right about sending a letter."

Eli was stunned. He stood speechless.

"Eli? Are you there?"

"I'm here. Did she die at Ravensbrück?"

"No, not at Ravensbrück. We went through Ravensbrück records. Although they're not complete, there are records from 1943, and we found no mention of Esther Rosen in any of the records: intake, transfer, *totenbuch*. We determined that she never entered the camp."

"But, Ann . . ."

"Then we decided to check the Lublin records, especially those for the Lipowa labor camp, which the Nazis called Lindenstrasse. Beginning in

1942 and continuing to November 1943, Lipowa workers were routinely transported or marched to Majdanek. There is no record of sending those women to Ravensbrück."

Eli interrupted again. "But Esther would have been a special exception. She was being protected by a Nazi collaborator. She could have been sent to Ravensbrück irrespective of the other Lipowa workers."

"She would have been noted on the intake records, and her name is not there."

"You don't understand. She was under the protection of a man who had contacts with Commandant Zörner and Brigadeführer Globočnik. He was connected to the highest levels of the Nazi command. He could have arranged for Esther to be sent anywhere. He gave me a note that said Ravensbrück. Why would he do that if it wasn't so? I'm pretty sure . . ."

"Eli, Eli . . . she didn't make it. I'm so sorry, Eli, but Esther did not survive. I reviewed the Majdanek records for the women transported in 1942, specifically those transfers from Lublin and Lipowa. I found her name on a deportation list for October 1942. That transport went to the Majdanek camp. Those women . . . it was a killing center, Eli. They all perished. I'm so sorry."

Eli stared at the telephone, at the black handset that had delivered the news. It had been five years since he had seen Esther, five years since he had held her or heard her voice, yet for him she was alive until this very moment.

"Eli, are you still there?"

His response was soft and slow. "What do I tell my son?"

"I wish I had an answer for you."

Eli exhaled. "Thank you, Ann. I appreciate the work you did and that you made a personal call."

"You take care, Eli."

Adinah was hanging sheets on the line when she spotted Eli walking home. His gait was slow, his shoulders slumped, his eyes were red. Adinah dropped her laundry and ran to him. "Eli?"

It took effort, but he finally said, "She's dead, Adinah. They murdered my Esther."

"Oh, Eli," Adinah cried. She put her arms around him and walked him into the house.

"I have to tell Izaak," he said.

"Do you?"

"He needs to know the truth. I've always been honest with him."

"Please, Eli, tell him only that she didn't survive. Spare him the details. Don't let his mind form a picture of his mother in that way. He has beautiful memories. Don't let that gruesome image creep into his mind. Not now. Not at this young age."

Eli nodded and walked back to Izaak's room. A few minutes later, Izaak burst out of his room, running to Adinah, arms wide open, tears flowing. He sat on her lap while she cradled him and rocked him back and forth.

CHAPTER SIXTY-NINE

~

ALBANY PARK

Mimi braved the bitter winds and headed off on the five-block walk to Congressman Zielinski's Albany Park residence. Once again, she was on a mission to plant a listening device and delude a woman who had shown her nothing but kindness since she was a child. She had strained to conjure up another pretext a mere three days after she had popped in unexpectedly with Christine's sweater. She finally decided that returning a book was the best solution. Mimi and Christine had often exchanged books. That might also provide a reason to enter Vittie's office. She could put the book onto the bookshelf and, in the process, hide the device.

She settled on Bel Kaufman's *Up the Down Staircase*, which topped the bestseller lists the previous summer and was a fun read for the two of them. She remembered when Christine brought the book over and urged her to read it. They had chuckled about the tribulations of the dedicated first-year high school teacher and her students who couldn't care less. She remembered the night they sat around and cast the principal characters with Von Steuben teachers and classmates, laughing until their sides hurt.

As she approached the driveway, she noticed a white Commonwealth Edison truck parked in front of the neighbor's house. *Pretty cold night for emergency service,* she thought. *Pretty cold night for lying to a lovely, unsuspecting woman. Pretty cold night for anything.*

"Mimi! It's great to see you again, but what brought you out on this nasty night?" Vera said, taking Mimi's coat. Mimi glanced to the right and noticed that the light was on in Vittie's office.

"I don't mean to trouble you, Vera, but I forgot to bring this with me when I came by earlier in the week. Do you remember how much Chrissie loved *Up the Down Staircase*?"

"Oh Lord, yes. She urged me to read it, but I didn't get the same enjoyment out of it that you two did."

"This book belonged to her. It has her name written on the inside cover. I thought you should have it. It might bring back happy memories."

"How thoughtful. Would you like some tea to warm you up on this bitter evening?"

"That would be very nice; thank you." As Vera left for the kitchen, Mimi slipped into the office. A cabinet door was ajar, and Mimi could see that there were several green-bound ledger books stacked inside. "Well, lookie here," she said to herself, "and now to get the replacement device onto the shelf." She opened her purse, and a voice behind her said, "What in the hell are you doing in here?"

She spun around to see Michael Stanley, arms folded across his chest, peering down at her through his wire-framed glasses. A hawk on a branch.

"It's not your concern," Mimi said, quickly clasping her purse.

"Oh, that's where you're wrong. If you're in this office, it's my concern. If you're in this house, it's my concern. What are you doing in here? What are you looking for?"

"I don't have to answer to you. I don't work for you. I'm a guest in this house." She turned to walk out the door, but Stanley stepped in front of her. "Let me by."

"What are you doing in my office?"

"Since when is it *your* office?" she said boldly, clutching her purse.

Stanley's face broke into a satanic grin. "Are you looking for this?" He held up the first listening device and waved it in front of Mimi's face. "I found this little thing sitting on the shelf yesterday. Imagine that."

"It's got nothing to do with me. Now let me go."

Stanley stared. "What are you holding on to so dearly? What's in your bag? Hand it over." He reached for the purse with one hand and grabbed Mimi's wrist with the other.

"Let me go! It's none of your damn business."

Stanley snatched the purse out of her hands, opened it and pulled out the new listening device. "You little bitch. Another one. Who put you up to this? Was it Thorsen? Was it Nicholas Bryant? Which one of those greedy assholes put you up to this?"

"Leave me alone. Let go of me."

He squeezed her arms and shook her. "Don't play with me, young lady. You don't know who the hell you're dealing with."

"You're wrong. I know exactly who I'm dealing with. You're the man that everyone hates." Mimi lunged for the door, but Stanley held her wrist and flung her backward.

"Let me go! Help!" she shouted. "Help!"

Stanley laughed loudly. "I'm afraid there's no cavalry in sight, and you've stuck your little nose where it doesn't belong. Who told you to plant those listening devices? It was Bryant, wasn't it? That snively little bastard. Always complaining. Always drunk. Never enough money for his salacious appetite or his greedy wife. Was it him? Or was it *your* idea? Maybe that's it. Maybe Mimi Gold covets a front-page exclusive? Too bad no one will ever read that story."

"Listen, I'm working with the FBI, so you better let me go."

He laughed again, a loud, mocking laugh. "The FBI? Mimi Gold, special agent? Ha, ha! It seems to me that Mr. Hoover is going to lose one of his top agents. You made a fatal mistake today, little lady agent."

"Are you going to kill me like you murdered Christine and Preston and then burn the house down?"

Stanley smiled. "This house? Goodness, no. I built this house and everything in it. Vittie was a clueless freshman congressman from a know-nothing immigrant district when I met him. Probably still is. I showed him how to manage this district. I opened his eyes to the opportunities available to a creative congressman. Do you think that wealth and power come easily? I worked hard to build this house. It's a monument to me. I certainly wouldn't burn it down. But you, little lady, have become a threat to my monument. You know too much."

"Is that why you killed Chrissie and Preston? Did they know too much? Were they threats to your monument?"

"Well, on that account you're mistaken. I didn't kill anyone. Not that I'm sorry that the whiny little bitch and her boorish husband were silenced. It was well done, but not by me."

"Listen, Stanley, the FBI knows I'm here. You'd be smart to give yourself up right now."

Stanley laughed heartily. "Oh my God, the FBI again. I don't see them, Mimi, where are they?"

Mimi stood tall. "They know those ledger books are in here, and when they seize them, all of you will end up in jail."

Stanley slowly shook his head from side to side. "They'll never find the books, and sadly they'll never find you either."

Suddenly Vera appeared in the doorway holding a cup of tea. "What's going on in here?" she demanded. "I heard shouting."

"Help me, Vera," Mimi cried. "He's threatening to kill me. Call the police. Hurry."

Vera dropped the cup. "What are you doing, Michael? Are you crazy? Let her go."

"I'm afraid not, Vera. Things have reached a critical stage in my professional career. And, I'm afraid, that of your husband's as well. As his trusted chief of staff, you know I am charged with the responsibility of protecting him and you. Now I want you to turn around, go upstairs and close your door. Do you understand me?"

"Michael. She's just a sweet girl, a friend of Christine's."

"Turn around, Vera. Go upstairs. Now!"

Vera sighed, turned and walked out of the room.

Stanley pulled Mimi over to the desk, opened a drawer, extracted a silver pistol and stuck it in his belt. "Now it's time to dispose of this inconvenient problem. We're going to take a ride."

"I'm not going anywhere."

Stanley shrugged. "Dead or alive, you're going."

"Freeze, Stanley," Cliff Ryan said, entering the room, followed by Eli, Vera and two other agents. "Hands up where I can see them."

Mimi pulled her arm from Stanley's grip and stepped to the side. "Thank God! Where did you come from?"

Ryan smiled. "We were in the truck outside, listening and recording. Mrs. Zielinski let us in." Vera raised her eyebrows and nodded.

"You heard everything that was going on?" Mimi said.

Ryan nodded. "Every bit."

"And you stood by and let him threaten to kill me? He could have shot me. Or I could have had a heart attack."

"We wanted to get as much as we could."

Stanley looked at Eli. "Well, if it isn't Eli Rosen, I'll be damned. I should have figured you were behind this somehow. You've been plaguing me for thirty years."

"End of the road, Maximilian. Your scheming days are over."

"It's Michael Stanley, if you please. He's a much more successful man and I'm quite fond of him."

"All your schemes, all your lies—it's all over. I've been waiting for this day for a long time. You're finished."

Stanley had a confident smile on his face as he was being cuffed and led away. "Maybe yes and maybe no." He looked at Ryan. "I know where the grapes of wrath are buried, Special Agent. Ring me up when you want to make a deal."

CHAPTER SEVENTY

✎

Mimi watched Stanley's interrogation from behind the one-way mirror. In the room, Stanley sat on one side of a long metal table facing Eli and Cliff Ryan. Kenneth Berman, First Assistant U.S. Attorney for the Northern District of Illinois, stood to the side. Several of the green ledger books lay open on the table. Stanley was drumming his fingers on the table and shrugging off questions as they were being posed. Ryan would fire questions at him, pound the table and point their fingers in his face, but Stanley remained indifferent and smugly shook his head. Finally, he said, "When you're prepared to make me a reasonable offer, I'll answer all your questions. In fact, I'll give you what you need to bring the house down."

Eli slammed his fist. "Not this time, Poleski. No end runs this time. There'll be no white knight riding in to cut you loose. Congressman Zielinski will be arrested, as will all of the crooked military contractors. We have hours of tape, more than enough to keep all of you behind bars for the rest of your lives."

Stanley scoffed and shook his head. "Don't take me for a fool. Zielinski hasn't been arrested or he'd be in this room listening to your threats instead of me. You have nothing. No evidence to take down Zielinski or anyone else."

"Well, we certainly have you, Stanley," Ryan said. "Caught red-handed, and it's all on tape. 'They'll never find the ledger books or you either,' wasn't that what you said? And then there's the hours of meetings on tape. You have a very recognizable voice."

Stanley wasn't fazed. "Oh, I was present at all those meetings, but when you listen to your tapes, what do you hear? We were very careful about what we said and how we said it. The possibility of eavesdropping was always on our minds. Do you think a jury will convict someone of agreeing to contribute forty-five thousand dollars to the March of Dimes? Is that evidence of corruption, or is it a selfless act of civic charity? You heard conversations of donations to worthy causes. Did you ever hear the word 'payoff'? Did you hear the word 'kickback'? No? I didn't think so. You heard us speak of military contracts and the necessity for weapons and war materials desperately needed by our troops valiantly fighting the communists in Vietnam. A congressman is supposed to do his background research before recommending large military expenditures. Holding meetings with contractors is hardly a crime. That's the business of a congressman."

"The ledger books are no longer locked away. We have reviewed them, and to quote Preston Roberts, they contain major shit. You're all going down."

Stanley smiled. "You won't see my name or Zielinski's name in the ledger books. Do you really understand the entries on those pages? I doubt very much that a simpleton like Preston could or that you could either. The accountant was very skillful . . . no, maybe we should say obtuse. Unclear. He used codes and entries that only he would understand. And I'm sure that he can explain each entry in a way that is consistent with sound accounting practices and legitimate purchase orders. Face it: you need my help. You have six businessmen on tape. How many more are out there that aren't on your tapes? What evidence do you think you'll need to bring down a powerful twenty-year congressman? And, of course, there is the matter of the unfortunate deaths of Christine and Preston Roberts. Imagine what I could do for your career, Assistant U.S. Attorney Berman."

"You're facing the electric chair for murdering those two kids," Eli said. "We saw you with the gun in Zielinski's office."

Stanley let out a short chuckle. "I've never fired a gun in my life. I doubt the pistol was even loaded." He looked at Ryan. "Was it?"

Ryan shook his head. "It doesn't matter. You threatened a woman with a gun. And you can be held equally responsible for the Robertses' murders as a coconspirator, even if you didn't pull the trigger."

Stanley sat back and glanced at Berman. "Conspiracies are so hard to prove, aren't they? The when and how, what was said and the steps in furtherance—all beyond a reasonable doubt. Not a slam dunk for you, is it, Mr. U.S. Attorney?"

Eli stood and leaned over the table. "Who killed those kids?"

Stanley held up his index finger. "Sounds like there's room for a deal. I can give you the murderer. I can give you the military contractors who aren't on your tapes. I can decipher the ledgers and tell you exactly what each of them agreed to do and where the money went. Once again, Eli, you need the services of Maximilian Poleski, he of royal blood. As I have always told you, we are bound together."

"I needed you once, and all your promises meant nothing. You betrayed me without a second thought."

"Times were different. I had my own skin to protect."

Eli lunged forward, grabbed Maximilian by the throat. Through clenched teeth he snarled, "You were supposed to protect Esther! She was executed at Majdanek, you son of a bitch. And you even lied when you wrote Ravensbrück on the note."

Ryan stepped forward, took Eli's hand away and held him back from Stanley.

Stanley coughed and rubbed his throat. "It was an excusable error."

With his lips drawn in a contemptuous sneer, Eli said, "I'd sooner see every one of those corrupt contractors go free before I'd agree to lessen your jail sentence by one single day."

"Ah, but it isn't your call, is it, Eli?" He turned to Berman. "I can give you the murderer, the other contractors, the source of every payment and be your star witness at trial. Do we talk?"

Berman nodded. "If what you say is true, if you can provide corroborative testimony and the information you've just described, we can discuss recommending a reduced sentence in exchange for your cooperation."

From behind the mirror, tears rolled down Mimi's cheeks.

"I want it in writing before I say a word," Stanley said, popping his finger on the table.

"It'll have to be cleared by my chief."

"You can't let him do this," Mimi pleaded. "He's as guilty, or more so, than all the others put together. I don't believe that he didn't commit the murders. I saw the evil in his eyes when he held that gun on me."

Eli placed his hands on her shoulders. "Mimi, I feel the same as you. There isn't a man alive who wants Maximilian Poleski punished more than I do. In fact, no punishment would be severe enough for me. But Berman is right. If Poleski's testimony puts all of the corrupt contractors behind bars, takes down Zielinski and brings the murderers to justice, then we need to make the deal."

Mimi's jaw was shaking. "I need to know who killed Chrissie and Preston. Please, Eli, before we go any further with this man, make him tell us about the murders."

"There'll be no deal without that information. No deal without his testimony in the murder trial."

❧

Two days later, a written Plea and Cooperation Agreement was drafted by the U.S. Attorney's Office and brought to the interrogation room for Stanley's signature. Berman turned on the tape recorder and pointed to the multipage proffer that lay on the table.

"Mr. Michael Stanley, also known as Maximilian Poleski," Berman said, "so we are clear this morning, do you understand and accept the importance of complete honesty and full disclosure?"

Stanley looked at Eli and Ryan and nodded.

"Please respond verbally."

"I do."

"Do you also understand that even though the government will recommend a reduced sentence, we cannot guarantee it? Ultimately, it will be up to the judge."

"Yeah, yeah, I get it."

"Keep in mind, Mr. Stanley, if any of the information you provide is untruthful or if you fail to fully cooperate and respond to any request, the agreement will be voided, and you will be prosecuted."

"I understand; I understand. Let's get on with it."

"When did you first meet Congressman Witold Zielinski?"

"It was in September or October 1945. The Allies were preparing to start the trials at Nuremburg. I had a lot of information on Hans Frank, and I agreed to be a witness in his trial in exchange for a visa to the U.S. Vittie was in Europe on a joint congressional study about reconstituting Poland. We met in Munich and hit it off. I was amazed at how smooth and easy it was for me to get a visa, and I mentioned that to Vittie. You wouldn't believe how incredibly valuable a U.S. visa was in those days. Vittie shrugged and told me that visas were under his jurisdiction. It didn't take much imagination to see there was a way to make some real money. So I pitched the plan to Vittie. We'd run it like I did with the *Juden Ausweis* cards; I would find customers, and he'd get the visas. Simple as that."

"Talk to us about December seventeenth," Berman said.

Stanley nodded. "That was the day of the fire. Things had spun out of control in Chicago. Nicky was getting buried in his divorce case and he was drinking heavily. He kept coming to us demanding more and more money, but we couldn't steer any more shipments his way. The little shit was making a damn fortune and stuffing all the cash in his office safe to hide from his wife."

"And Christine saw the money?"

He nodded. "Sure, Christine saw the money. Hell, Christine knew all about the money. She was reporting the amounts to her father every day. She knew that money was coming in from contractors left and right. Nicky was the pivot man. All the money was funneled through Nicky. No one was foolish enough to drop money on the congressman."

"Christine kept track of bribes?"

Stanley shrugged. "She probably didn't know they were bribes. She was kind of naïve. She thought it was all shipping fees."

"What happened on the seventeenth?"

"Well, you have to go back a week or two earlier. That's when Nicky went over the edge. We knew the situation was bad. Christine had been complaining to her father about Nicky's behavior, but we didn't know how bad it was. Vittie tried to put a lid on Nicky, but Nicky was a time bomb. Then on December tenth, Nicky hauled off and punched Christine in the face, and she marched out the door.

"She called her father that night all weepy and whiny and said she wasn't going back. Vittie blew up at Nicky, but he couldn't allow Christine to quit. She was our eyes and ears. Vittie pleaded with her and promised that he would straighten everything out, but Christine wouldn't budge. No matter what, she wasn't going back. Then Preston butted in and started threatening to go to the newspapers." Stanley made a face and shook his head. "I told Vittie he never should have hired Preston to begin with. We didn't need him; he didn't do a damn thing except piss people off.

"Well, it all came to a head on December seventeenth. Christine wouldn't return to her job, and Preston was mouthing off, so Vittie and I decided to set things straight. We talked to Nicky. We told him he'd never get another shipping contract unless he behaved. And he agreed. He said he'd treat her respectfully and leave her alone to do her job. 'A perfect gentleman,' he said.

"Vittie and I were satisfied. Then we had to convince Christine to go back to work. He called her and he was firm, but she was adamant. 'Under no circumstances,' she said. It shocked the hell out of Vittie; his daughter had never defied him before. She said she didn't trust Nicky and didn't want to talk about it anymore. Vittie got angry, said some things, and Christine hung up on him. It was late in the evening, and Vittie turned to me and said, 'That impudent little bitch. After everything I've done for her and her husband. They'll not turn their backs on me. I'm going to go over there and lay down the law.'"

From behind the mirror, Mimi's hand shot up to her mouth. "Oh my God," she whispered. "Vittie killed his own daughter."

"Vittie didn't go to the house to hurt anyone," Stanley said. "He loved his daughter. He only wanted to be firm, to tell her that he needed her to go back to work. He was exercising his parental rights and demanding obedience from his daughter. What's wrong with that? But he was worried about Preston. Preston was a big guy with a hot temper, and Vittie was worried that he might get physical. So he did something stupid. He had a silver pistol—you saw it the other night. He took it to scare Preston in case Preston got out of line."

Stanley took a sip of water. "The way I understand it, things got out of hand. There was a lot of screaming and crying. Vittie was insisting, Christine was resisting and finally Preston asked him to leave. He told Vittie to get out. Vittie said something about no young punk was going to tell him what to do. Preston tried to push Vittie out of the house, and Vittie pulled the gun. They wrestled and the gun went off. It was an accident. The bullet hit Christine in the neck. She immediately fell to the floor. It had severed an artery. There was no hope for her. Preston was kneeling over her, crying and screaming, 'What did you do?' Vittie panicked. He shot Preston.

"He called me, told me what happened and said we have to hide the bodies or something. I came up with the idea of burning the house down and destroying all the evidence." Stanley shrugged. "I thought it was a good plan; it should have worked. I didn't expect the fire department to get there that fast. They doused the fire before it got to the back of the house." Stanley spread his hands. "That's the whole story. It was never meant to happen. But it did, and by then it was too late."

EPILOGUE

Five copies of the Sunday *Tribune* lay on the coffee table in the Gold apartment. The forty-eight-point headline read: ZIELINSKI, THIRTEEN OTHERS INDICTED. The sub-headline read: CONGRESSMAN CHARGED WITH DOUBLE MURDER. Beneath the headlines was the following byline: "Exclusive to the *Tribune,* Miriam Gold, Staff Reporter."

"Pulitzer stuff," Nathan said. "Your series will run all week in the *Trib* and be syndicated nationally. I always knew you'd be a famous writer!"

"Cut it out," she said.

Ruth picked up the paper and shook her head. "I still can't believe that Vittie killed his daughter."

"According to Stanley, it was an accident," Mimi said. "Vittie loved Chrissie; I know he did."

"Damn shame," Ruth said. "At least they'll all stand trial for what they did."

Mimi's lips were quivering. "It won't bring her back, Mom."

Ruth put her arm around Mimi. "But they'll all get what's coming to them."

"All but Maximilian," Eli said. "He never gets what's coming to him. He gave the prosecutors all the evidence they'll need to convict Vittie and the crooked contractors. He detailed twenty years of criminal conduct, and for that he gets a sweet deal."

"Just like he did in Germany," Mimi said.

Eli nodded. "In exchange for his cooperation and testimony at the defendants' trials, he'll get a substantial reduction in sentence. I suppose there's a possibility that he'll die in prison, but I'd never bet against Maximilian. That snake has a way of reappearing."

"Attorney Berman said there will be significant jail time. I think the world is rid of Maximilian Poleski. Eli, you kept your final promise. After all those years, you brought him to justice."

Grandma came out of the kitchen with a plate of baked goods. "Enough talk about those nasty criminals. I baked a cake and some cookies to celebrate Mimi's exclusive series. Our star reporter."

"What do you have there?" Eli said with a smile. "Is that what I think it is?"

Grandma nodded. "Babka."

Eli raised his eyebrows. "With raspberries?"

"And a little whiskey."

Eli and Mimi locked eyes. "A *bisselah*?" she said.

"Aye," Eli said, and they each took a pinch off the bottom of the cake.

❧

During coffee and cake, Mimi said to Eli, "So I suppose you'll be giving up your apartment now and returning to Washington?"

"I'm afraid so, but not without some regret. During the last year, I've really come to enjoy living here in Albany Park, and especially in your building. You, your mother and your grandmother are special people to me, but I have to get back. Washington's been my home since 1949."

"We'll miss you. *I'll* miss you, Eli. I'll miss our talks. I'll miss your wisdom. You've been a good friend and a comfort to me."

"Oh, you'll not be rid of me so easily. I'll have to return from time to time for the trials. And later this spring, you, your mother and your grandmother will come to Washington as our guests."

"We will?"

"You most certainly will; I insist. The director would like to thank you personally and present you with official recognition for your exceptional service. I wouldn't be surprised if the ceremony took place at the White House."

"Oh, my God, Mom, did you hear that? We're going to the White House! I don't know what to say."

Eli smiled. "Then say you'll come to Washington and accept your award. And while you're there, you'll honor me by having dinner at my home."

"I would be delighted. I'd love to meet your family." She paused. "When I first saw your photographs and learned you were from Poland, I suspected the worst. Eventually, you told me that you and your son were rescued by my father's unit, the Super Sixth. Then I heard you tell Stanley that Esther died at Majdanek."

Eli nodded. "She did. I lost a lot of family in the war. I wish you could have met them—Esther, my father, my brother, my niece, my sister-in-law—all beautiful people, but they didn't survive the slaughter."

"I'm so sorry. But Izaak survived. Will I get to meet the little boy in the picture?"

Eli smiled. "Yes, you will, but he's not so little anymore. I will make sure that Izaak; his wife, Sarah; and my eight-year-old granddaughter, Esther, will all be there. Little Essie is Grandpa's favorite, the apple of my eye."

"And your wife . . . ?"

"Adinah. I've been telling her all about you for months, and she'd love to meet you and your mother. She's a very good cook, and we'll have quite an occasion. She makes a mean babka, too, but I have to admit: your grandmother's is the gold standard. Anyway, you'll come to Washington and meet my family. I'm sure you'll love them all."

"I can't wait." She leaned forward and whispered, "Do you think I can get you and Adinah to come back to Albany Park if it was a very special occasion?"

"Would this have something to do with Mr. Nathan Stone?"

Mimi blushed and nodded.

"Did he . . ."

"Not yet." She winked. "But if I may borrow a lovely expression that I once heard in a story from a mysterious but wonderful man, 'I have my eyes on him, Eli Rosen, and I will it to be so.'"

Eli smiled. "Then to borrow the words of a courageous and brilliant reporter, 'Count me in.'"

ACKNOWLEDGMENTS

Eli's Promise is a work of historical fiction. I have endeavored to accurately portray the historical settings in which the plot unfolds and the characters appear, however, the plot and the principal characters portrayed are products of my imagination and do not refer to any actual person, living or dead. Eli and his family, Mimi and her family, Maximilian Poleski and Congressman Zielinski are all fictional. The story is presented in three locations over three time periods: Lublin, Poland, during the war, Föhrenwald in the mid-1940s and the Albany Park section of Chicago in 1965.

Prior to the Nazi occupation, Lublin was the seat of Jewish learning, the center of Jewish education. The Yeshiva Chachmei, School of the Wise Men, was an immediate target of the Nazis. It was ransacked, the books and literary materials were burned, and the building became the headquarters of the dreaded German Order Police. Lublin's Jewish citizens were forced to wear armbands, and they were separated and confined within two ghettos. They were systematically transported from the ghettos to labor camps, and ultimately to their deaths. As one of the story's main characters, Esther Rosen, prophesized, "They will identify us, they will collect and concentrate us and then they will eliminate us." Ultimately, all but two hundred of Lublin's forty thousand Jews were murdered.

On the whole, the Nazi officers portrayed in the story were real, though their interactions with the principal characters were imaginary and merely representational. Odilo Globočnik was in fact a Nazi general who was placed in charge of Jewish resettlement and depopulation in the Lublin

District. Many scholars believe that it was Globočnik who conceived of the extermination camps and mass murder by poison gas. He was instrumental in construction of the Belzec extermination camp, the first such camp in occupied Poland, and he oversaw the construction and operation of Sobibor, Majdanek and Treblinka. He committed suicide in May 1945 by swallowing a cyanide capsule during Allied interrogation. Hermann Dolp and Horst Riedel were in fact the Nazi officers in charge of the Lipowa Street labor camp, later renamed Lindenstrasse. Ernst Zörner was appointed governor of the Lublin District by Hans Frank, as related in the story.

The portion of the story taking place in the postwar displaced persons camps is fictional, though the settings are authentic. The Föhrenwald and Landsberg Displaced Persons Camps were real and I have endeavored to accurately portray life and events as they occurred, including the tuberculosis epidemic. General Lucius D. Clay was the acting American military governor and chief administrator of occupied Germany, though his involvement with any of the elements of the plot is fictional. Colonel Bivens and Major Donnelly were fictional characters. Similarly, Bernard Schwartz, Adinah Szapiro, Frau Helstein and the other Föhrenwald and Landsberg characters are imaginary. What is not imaginary and is clearly documented in the narrative, is the imposition of restrictive immigration quotas by Allied countries and the reluctance to relax them for Jewish refugees. It was a dark time in our history. As President Truman's envoy observed, "The civilized world owes it to this handful of survivors to provide them with a home where they can again settle down and begin to live as human beings." But the immigration quotas were not increased until years later, and not without fierce opposition.

The history of Albany Park and its development is accurate, and the neighborhood is lovely, just as described. In the postwar years, Albany Park became a destination for Jewish and European immigrants. Even today, it is a widely diverse community. That said, Witold Zielinski is an invented character and is not meant to be representational of any elected official in any way. Quite the contrary, Albany Park has been well served by its congressional representatives for many years without scandal.

Eli's Promise is at its heart a story about corruption and war profiteering. It was my intention to draw a line of commonality from 1939 through 1966 during which profiteering could and did occur. False *Juden-Ausweis* cards were marketed to desperate Jewish victims in the Polish ghettos during the Nazi occupation. Black market sales of various products were prevalent in the displaced persons camps in postwar Germany. American courts have provided a forum for prosecution of false U.S. immigration documents for years. The years 1965 to 1966 were a period of major expansion of men and materials for the Vietnam War, opening opportunities for unscrupulous war profiteers. Court records evidence numerous prosecutions of corrupt defense contractors and government officials for fraud and bribery in connection with military contracts.

I have received wonderful help and encouragement during the research and writing of this book. I have had access to a wealth of information and material from several institutions, and I am grateful for the assistance of their staffs. The Berlin Jewish Museum, the German Historical Museum, The Illinois Holocaust Museum and Educational Center, and in particular, Yad Vashem, whose archives hold precious personal histories of Lublin's survivors. Personal memoirs, diaries and video interviews helped to provide a backdrop to the Lublin chapters.

Once again, thanks to my supportive group at St. Martin's Press: my editor, George Witte; assistant editor, Kevin Reilly; my publicist, Sarah Schoof; and vice-president of marketing, Brant Janeway. I am deeply appreciative of the thorough and insightful copyediting of Angela Gibson. Thanks to my energetic and upbeat literary agent, Mark Gottlieb.

My heartfelt thanks to my cadre of readers and their invaluable advice: Cindy Pogrund, David Pogrund, Linda Waldman, Richard Templer, Richard Reeder and Benjamin Balson. And, as always, my deepest gratitude to my patient and tireless wife, Monica, who reads each and every page as they come out of the printer. She has read and edited the story a thousand times and has always stayed positive and encouraging. I'm a fortunate man.

1. Although it is easy to condemn one's actions when we have the benefit of hindsight, are you critical of Eli's decision to keep his family in Lublin when Esther urged them to leave? Are you critical of any of his other decisions?

2. How was it possible for a scurrilous profiteer like Maximilian to gain the trust and dependency of his community, and especially that of a man like Eli Rosen?

3. Is there one particular character with whom you feel a kinship? Why?

4. The Allies established camps for displaced persons in postwar Germany and assumed responsibility for their residents. How did the Allies succeed in this, and how did they fail?

5. President Eisenhower observed that "We annually spend on military security more than the net income of all United States corporations." Then, he famously quoted, "In the councils of government, we must guard against the acquisition of unwarranted influence, whether sought or unsought, by the military-industrial complex." In your judgment, did that expression and the influence of military contractors warrant closer observation in the 1960s? Does it today?

6. Sometimes we don't know how much courage we possess until we are called upon. Which characters displayed surprising courage and in what way? Which characters disappointed you?

ST. MARTIN'S GRIFFIN

7. Conflicting emotions beset the characters throughout the story. Discuss how Eli and Izaak handled their relationship with Adinah.

8. Water seeks its own level. In every era, Maximilian was able to forge alliances with equally despicable but powerful characters. Discuss those relationships and whether they profited him in the end. Was justice served where he was concerned?

MONICA J. BALSON

RONALD H. BALSON is an attorney, professor, and writer. His novel *The Girl from Berlin* won the National Jewish Book Award and was the Illinois Reading Council's adult fiction selection for the Illinois Reads program. He is also the author of *Karolina's Twins, The Trust, Saving Sophie,* and the international bestseller *Once We Were Brothers*. He lives in Chicago.

TURN THE PAGE FOR A SNEAK PEEK AT
RONALD H. BALSON'S NEW NOVEL

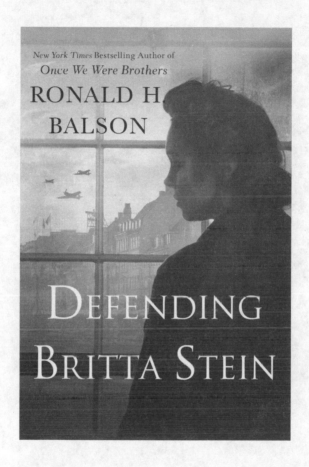

Available Summer 2021

CHAPTER THREE

―――∞∞∞――――

CATHERINE LOCKHART'S FOUR-ROOM, storefront law office is on Clark Street a couple of miles north of Chicago's Loop. She has what is commonly referred to as a neighborhood practice—wills, trusts, real estate transactions, criminal defense, personal litigation matters—all in sharp contrast to the high-profile, institutional clients she served when she worked for Walter Jenkins.

At precisely three o'clock, a young woman with curly black hair, large expressive brown eyes and a bounce in her step opens the door to Catherine's office. She holds it open for her companion, an elderly woman in a wool suit with fashionably styled white hair and perfect posture.

"You must be Ms. Fisher and Mrs. Stein," the receptionist says. "My name is Gladys Valenzuela. I am Catherine's assistant. It is nice to meet you both. Catherine is expecting you. Please follow me back to the conference room."

Catherine enters the conference room moments later with a brown file folder, which she lays upon the table. Emma extends her hand. "I'm Emma Fisher and this is my grandmother, Britta Stein."

Catherine warmly takes their hands. "It's a pleasure to meet you both." She gestures to her file folder. "I asked Gladys to run down to the courthouse and pick up a copy of the lawsuit that was filed against you today,

Mrs. Stein. As you no doubt recall, Mr. Sparks threatened to file it first thing this morning."

Britta sits erectly in her chair. She does not seem at all nervous. She nods her understanding. "I haven't seen the lawsuit yet," she says matter-of-factly. "I bet it's a doozy."

Catherine lifts her eyebrows. "Yes, I'm afraid it is a doozy, Mrs. Stein. It alleges that on six separate occasions you trespassed upon Mr. Henryks's property for the purpose of defacing his building by painting scathing insults concerning Mr. Henryks, harming him in his good name, his business, his health and his reputation."

"Hmph," Britta interjects. "Reputation indeed."

"Bubbe, hush," Emma says. "Let Ms. Lockhart finish."

"On each of the six occasions, the complaint alleges that you intentionally wrote false and defamatory declarations on the outside walls of his restaurant. Further, that your illegal and tortious conduct followed the announcement that Mr. Henryks was to be honored by the Danish-American Association."

"Honor?" Britta says. "He deserves no such thing." Britta dismissively brushes away the accusations as though they do not affect her. "Who are they anyway, this make-believe association? As far as I am concerned this Danish-American nonsense is just an excuse for young men to congregate for the sole purpose of drinking beer. For them to bestow an honor upon a traitor only means that the members of the association have been hoodwinked. I'm sure it must be the younger ones; they wouldn't know any better. They probably want an occasion to honor a popular personality and have it shown on TV, as if that would bring them some credibility. Silliness, is all . . ."

Catherine taps her finger on the lawsuit. "Let's focus on the complaint-at-law, shall we, Mrs. Stein? Are the allegations correct? Did you intentionally paint those words on the side of Henryks's building?"

"Yes, I painted those words on the side of his building. And of course it was intentional. I don't see how one could possibly paint those words unintentionally. But, Ms. Lockhart, the words were not false nor were they defamatory. The words were and are true."

"Why, Mrs. Stein? Why did you go over there and paint those words at all?"

Britta lifts her chin. "I am a Danish lady; I can't abide the charade. He is no hero. He is nothing but a liar and a coward. Worse, he's a traitor."

Catherine turns the pages of the lawsuit to the page listing the painted statements, which she reads one at a time. "Liar. Informer. Traitor. Nazi collaborator. Nazi agent. Betrayer. Is the list correct? Did you write all of those?"

"He is a liar and a traitor and all those things and more, and I'm not the least bit sorry that the truth is there for all to see."

Catherine sits down. "Mrs. Stein, this lawsuit is not to be taken lightly. It charges you with 'defamation per se.'"

Britta shrugs. She is impassive, as though they were talking about someone else.

"Defamation per se means that the words you have used accuse Mr. Henryks of criminal conduct, crimes of moral turpitude and of coalescence with the Nazi Party. As such, the words themselves are innately harmful." She lays her pen down. "And actionable in a court of law, with serious consequences."

"What about the First Amendment?" Britta says. "My freedom of speech."

"Freedom of speech is not absolute, Mrs. Stein. You are not free to use words that wrongfully defame another person." Catherine extracts another document from her folder and places it on the table. "This is an order of protection; a temporary injunction which was entered this morning against you by Judge Obadiah Wilson. It strictly prohibits you from coming within fifty yards of The Melancholy Dane or Ole Henryks's residence on Lake Shore Drive."

"Nobody notified me of any court hearing," Britta says defiantly. "How could a judge enter an order against me if I wasn't even there? What about due process?"

Catherine rolls her eyes. "It's a temporary injunction. The order was entered ex parte, in your absence, because it was presented as an emergency to prevent you from committing further unlawful conduct. The language of the order recites that a video of you spray-painting on Mr. Henryks's building was shown to the court."

Britta looks at the order, sets it down and scoffs. "Fifty yards! Does that mean I can't take a taxi down Clark Street or Bryn Mawr? I guess if my taxi driver decides to drive along Lake Shore Drive, the both of us are going to jail, right? Does Ole Henryks now own the streets? Such nonsense. I will go where I choose. It's a free country."

"Bubbe!" Emma pleads. "Listen to Ms. Lockhart. You can be jailed for willfully violating an injunction."

"She's right, Mrs. Stein. I wouldn't test Judge Wilson's mettle. You can be sure that Mr. Henryks will immediately call the police if he sees you anywhere near his establishment or his condominium building. A willful violation of an order of protection could subject you to fines or even punitive incarceration. And I know Judge Wilson. He's not one to fool with."

"Listen to your lawyer, Bubbe. Don't go anywhere near The Melancholy Dane or Henryks's apartment. You don't need to paint any more signs; you're bound to have accomplished what you set out to do. The whole world knows what you think about Mr. Henryks."

Britta leans forward and raises her index finger. "It's *Hendricksen*, not Henryks. He even lies about his name. I wrote the truth." Turning to Catherine, she says, "You called the order temporary. Does that mean it expires? There are additional statements I have in mind."

Emma's head flops forward. "Bubbe, Bubbe. No! No more painting!"

Catherine slowly shakes her head. "Definitely no more painting. Believe me, you've done enough. More than enough. The order is temporary because you weren't there. Judge Wilson scheduled a hearing for all sides next Thursday to consider whether the injunction should be extended, and I'm fairly certain it will."

"You'll go with her to the hearing, right?" Emma says. "I mean, she needs to take a lawyer with her, doesn't she?"

Catherine holds up her palm. It's a stop sign. "She does, but Emma, we're getting ahead of ourselves. I told Walter I would agree to *meet* with the two of you and we would talk. There is a lot to consider before deciding how a lawyer can defend a case like this. Or whether I am the right person to defend your grandmother. I don't have a handle on this. Mrs. Stein, you must have expected that there would be serious consequences when you painted all those harmful statements."

Britta clamps her lips. She inhales deeply through her nose. Finally, she says, "Consequences? You mean the kind of consequences where

people learn the truth about an evil person? Those kind of consequences?" Tears fill her eyes. "I pray for those consequences, Ms. Lockhart."

Emma gently lays her hand on her grandmother's arm. "I think that
Ms. Lockhart is referring to the criminal charges and the five-million-
dollar lawsuit against you, Bubbe. What is my grandmother going to do
about these charges, Ms. Lockhart?"

"I don't think she has much of a choice. She'll pay the fine and she's
going to have to defend herself in the civil case in some way. Ole Henryks and Sterling Sparks are not going to disappear. They want vindi-
cation. Henryks wants his reputation repaired. He wants his pound of
flesh and he's hired the right lawyer to pursue it. Sparks is an aggressive
publicity hound. That's why they call him Six-o'clock. I think you can
look forward to months of contentious hearings and depositions. Sparks
would like nothing better than to play out this drama in front of a jury
and the evening news. He'll call numerous witnesses who will all say they
heard about or read about the statements which caused them to question Mr. Henryks's character. Henryks will claim that his reputation has
been irrevocably damaged. I'm sure that Henryks's doctor will testify that
Henryks has suffered and continues to suffer extreme and pervasive
mental and physical trauma. It will be a bitter battle. A nightmare for
you, Mrs. Stein."

"Bubbe, what she's saying is that the lawsuit will be very stressful for
you and, no doubt, very expensive."

Britta stares straight ahead. "I can handle the stress," she mutters. "I've
been through worse." She opens the clasp on her leather purse and takes
out her checkbook. "I don't have a lot of money. I can give you three hundred dollars to get started."

Catherine shuts her eyes. When she opens them, she is smiling. It is
a warm smile that one would show to a child who has acted in a simple
but unrealistic manner. Catherine gently reaches over and closes Britta's
checkbook. "I appreciate your offer, Mrs. Stein, truly I do, but money
is only a secondary consideration. As Emma correctly pointed out, the
most important thing for you to consider is your health. You are ninety-
two years old. I've seen much younger people lose their balance in such a
contentious proceeding. Mr. Sparks's attacks can and will be very cruel."

"What are you suggesting, Ms. Lockhart?" Emma says. "You said she has no choice but to defend herself."

Catherine reaches out and pats Britta's hand. "Look, Mrs. Stein, the lawsuit is really not about the money. They know you don't have five million dollars. There may be another way to resolve this; a nonmonetary way. Mr. Henryks may be amenable to a consent decree. If you agree to publicly apologize, admit that your accusations were in error, and agree never to insult him again, maybe he would drop the suit. Or agree to a judgment of a small amount, perhaps one hundred dollars."

Britta's jaw begins to quaver. Her eyes widen. "Error? But there was no error, Ms. Lockhart. Why should I apologize to Hendricksen for writing the truth? I'm sorry, but there's no way I'm ever going to do that. I grew up in Denmark during the war. I was there. I know what ordinary people did, and I know what Hendricksen and his family did. Ordinary people were the heroes, and the Hendricksens were not. Quite the contrary. They were no better than the Nazis; maybe worse, because they helped the Nazis. Ole Hendricksen can file his lawsuit, and he will soon learn what a true Dane will do in times of adversity. A true Dane will stand her ground and fight."

Emma squeezes her grandmother's hand. "I know there were terrible tragedies that happened to the Danish people and to our family, Bubbe. Nothing can reverse that. I respect your resolve, but I don't want to see you get sick. Henryks is not worth it. You should listen to Ms. Lockhart and let her try to settle the case."

Britta's jaw is set. "Emma, the truth is always worth it. I'm not going to quit and I'm not going to apologize. I'm sorry if that means you won't take my case, Ms. Lockhart."

Catherine is moved. Rarely do her clients show such dedication, and there is something about Britta's steadfastness that appeals to Catherine. "I think I understand you, Mrs. Stein, and I'll take your case. But you have to help me here. How do I make a defense for you?"

"Isn't truth a defense to a lawsuit for defamation? Aren't I allowed to speak or write the truth no matter how hurtful it may be?"

Catherine nods and answers softly, "In theory, yes, you are, Mrs. Stein. Truth is an absolute defense to a suit for defamation."

Britta gives a sharp nod of finality. "Then we will prevail."